D1231875

THE
LOVER

Also by Rebecca Sacks

City of a Thousand Gates

THE
LOVER

A Novel

R E B E C C A   S A C K S

HARPER

An Imprint of HarperCollins*Publishers*

THE LOVER. Copyright © 2023 by Rebecca Sacks. All rights reserved. Printed in the United States of America. No part of this book may be used or reproduced in any manner whatsoever without written permission except in the case of brief quotations embodied in critical articles and reviews. For information, address HarperCollins Publishers, 195 Broadway, New York, NY 10007.

HarperCollins books may be purchased for educational, business, or sales promotional use. For information, please email the Special Markets Department at SPsales@harpercollins.com.

FIRST EDITION

Library of Congress Cataloging-in-Publication Data has been applied for.

ISBN 978-0-06-328423-4

23 24 25 26 27 LBC 5 4 3 2 1

This book is for the one who lit my house on fire.

THE
LOVER

One

It was a small box.

Each time I take a break from marking exams, I go tidy a bit more in the guest bedroom we're turning into a nursery. I was on my hands and knees cleaning the last of the junk out from under the daybed—soon to be replaced with a crib from my in-laws—when I saw it. A small box in the dusty dark.

My first reaction was to pretend I had not seen it, which is an odd way to respond to a box under a couch. But that's what I did. I stood up and puttered off to the closet, suddenly determined to sort through the various sweaters that my husband and I have accumulated over the years. Some we'll store; others we'll donate.

Winter mornings in Tel Aviv have a pervasive chilliness. I wear fuzzy socks with sticky soles that prevent me from sliding around our condo too haphazardly. Funny how none of the buildings here have much insulation. It's as if winter were a surprise each year, as if next year might really be one endless spring. Call it Israeli optimism. "But you're Canadian!" people exclaim when I complain about the cold. My husband and I laugh about this: how people seem to think I can grow a fur pelt.

I'd thought I was going through the sweaters in the closet—I mean, I was. I was going through them, beginning to make piles of "yes," "no," and "maybe," but somehow I found myself on my hands and knees again, squinting at the box under the daybed. The box was like a sizable sewing kit—pale wood, metal latch. I strained for it. But no matter how hard I tried, my fingers barely grazed the latch. Out of my reach with this belly.

In my tummy, baby shifted. His hearing is starting to develop, and I'm gassy all the time. Technically, we're keeping the gender a surprise— "You mean the sex, not the gender," my sister would correct me—but in my heart I know it's a boy. My mother-in-law thinks so too, because, she says, a mother looks beautiful when carrying a boy; it's a girl that steals all the beauty from you. Baby boy kicks when I laugh and wiggles when I shower. According to his due date, he'll be a Taurus—a creature of comfort, at home in the world.

Instead of leaving well enough alone, I took a broom from the hallway closet and used it to pull the box closer to me. It came out clotted with dust and what looked like dog hair, although we don't have a dog. As soon as it was in my hands I knew what it was. Who it was from.

Eyal—the soldier I loved so long ago. His name came to me across the years. Eyal. Like it was yesterday that I touched him, that I sat in his parents' car as we drove him to war, that I wrote him letters, that we dreamt of each other sleeping. Like it was still happening and not nearly a decade ago.

In Hebrew they call such a person *ha-ex ha-mitologi*: "the mythological ex." The one who changes you forever.

Now, here I am, tracing the box's latch with my middle finger. *Don't open it*, I caution myself. *There is so much to look forward to, don't subject yourself to the past—that sirens' call of longing.* What do I miss most about Eyal?

I think it is how deeply I let myself feel. My husband and I love each other—desire each other, care for each other—but in that love there is an element of calculation. We assessed our needs and priorities; we found they aligned. With Eyal, it was hopelessly improbable. Nothing about us made sense. We fell in love against the odds, and never before or since have I been in love so completely. We only get to do it once. That seems to be the rule: we only get to do it once, before we direct such hopeless devotion onto our children.

"*Yalla*," I say. I say it aloud, that popular Arabic exhortative. *Let's go.*

For once, I listen to myself: I shove the unopened box back under the daybed. *Yalla*, time to mark some exams.

My home office is in a small anteroom accessible through the master bedroom. It recalls to me the successively interior chambers of a temple or tomb. Or do I mean womb?

I won't return to campus after the winter break. It's easier to take a long maternity leave than to duck out halfway through the spring semester. Is that why I am putting off this final round of marking? Am I scared of how it will feel when I am no longer a professor? Just a mother. Am I scared that I'll be relieved? Sometimes I worry I enjoy housework more than I'm supposed to. "Being a mother is the most important job in the world," my husband said, kissing my belly. He's not wrong. Also, he's not right.

As I mark the sight translation section of the exams—my students always struggle when it comes to the more narrative portions of the Talmud—my left hand rubs steady circles around my belly. Left hand rubs, right hand works. He's quiet now, my little nester. I wonder if he'll be different once he's born—fussier than he's been inside me; I wonder if I'll be different too. Will old versions of myself be severed along with the umbilical cord?

Our baby will grow up in a warm, lively chaos that I never had. Some years, his birthday will fall during the week of Passover, a holiday he'll celebrate at a long table, unruly with cousins and spilled grape juice. From kindergarten on, he'll learn the stories of Jewish peoplehood: delivered from Egypt to Israel, delivered from Europe to Israel. And he'll learn my story. How I came to Israel from Canada for a few months, how I never left. Will I tell him I stayed for love? The story would be neater had it been my husband who convinced me to stay, whose love bound me to this land. Maybe I'll lie. All stories have their own internal logic, and this logic sometimes presents itself as a lie: a promised land found empty of inhabitants, waiting for us. Maybe we'll tell our son that we fell in love and I could not bear to leave, as if it were the promise of the very baby I'm carrying that pulled us together inevitably. That's the kind of story you tell your children.

I know what's in the box in the dark under the daybed in the nursery. Of course I know what's in the box. I don't have to open it to know.

I never think about Eyal these days. I'm married and expectant. Why would I think of him? I don't think about Eyal. Well, okay, maybe I think about him a little. But only recently. And only a little! Not often. Or at least not terribly often.

The memories sneak up on me. Recently, I noticed a student wearing one of Eyal's expressions while she wrote her translation exam. Her squinted focus, the tip of her tongue peeking out of her mouth—it all recalled to me his almost panicked expression the first time he entered me, staring at a spot on my forehead, the tip of his tongue peeking out in concentration. Of course she had no idea, this young undergraduate student translating late antiquity text into English. She was the same age Eyal had been when we started.

My students are not from Israel. The Americans and Canadians are Jewish, here with funding from various Zionist institutions. We have an instant understanding. "I'm originally from Montreal," I tell them. "I

came here for a semester of graduate school, fell in love, and never left."
This makes them smile. It's a familiar story for Jews from their communities: falling in love with the country, falling in love with an Israeli. That
I am now pregnant only perfects the narrative.

Slightly outside of this familiarity are the gentile students from Europe who come as part of their doctorate programs. Sometimes they
come to class with a keffiyeh worn like a pashmina, I suppose to remind
us that Palestinians exist. Some of my best students are the Evangelical
Christians from South Korea; their passion for Talmud is unmatched.

Watching Eyal's features flash across the face of that young girl, I
wished I could have excused myself from the classroom, taken a moment
to step outside and breathe, taken a moment to collect myself—but as I
said I was proctoring the exam, so I sat in a classroom with fluorescent
lighting, listening to the soft scratch of pencils on blue booklets.

So there you have it. I suppose I have been thinking of him recently.
Ever since I got pregnant, if I'm being entirely honest with myself. When
I first knew that I was pregnant—that we were pregnant—I was three
weeks late for my monthly. We'd had our hopes dashed before. We were
feeling cautious. But this time felt different. I hadn't taken the home
test, but I knew it was different. How did I know? I was home alone. I
don't mind. I like the little ship of our home, rising above the sea. I like
waiting for my husband here. I was home alone, standing in front of our
full-length mirror, hands on my belly, trying to sense the indiscernible
life growing there. We were weeks away from a heartbeat. *Where are you?*
I thought toward my belly. And his name came to me. *Eyal, where are
you?* Isn't that odd? As if we would name our baby after one of my ex-
boyfriends. I hadn't thought of him in years, and now I was saying his
name, "Eyal, where are you?" I said it aloud.

Since then, I've thought of him on and off. Now that my life in Israel
is blossoming, am I recalling the roots? How it began, who I was when
I arrived, and who I have become. Is that what I was thinking of as I
watched my student's tongue dart across her upper lip? For all I know,

I missed rampant cheating on that exam, distracted as I was. No, they wouldn't cheat, would they? It was, after all, a fair exam: several short passages to translate and parse, none of which were surprises. I will be interested to see how they manage the verb tenses in the section where Moses ascends Mount Sinai to find God, Master of the Universe, tying crowns for the Hebrew letters. "Turn around," the Holy One says. Moses turns around to find the future behind his back: he is transported thousands of years past his own death, to a rabbinic house of study where he witnesses his own legacy. The future is behind us, not in front of us. (Students will get bonus points if they note that the root of the temporal word "after" in Hebrew also yields the somatic word "buttocks.")

It is an image that has instructed my whole life: we walk backward into the future we cannot see, eyes on the past.

After marking a few more blue booklets, I pad to the kitchen to make a carafe of coffee. Oh, the indignities of decaf! My husband is drinking the stuff in solidarity, at least at home.

As I wait for the water to boil, I habitually inspect the fridge and freezer. Why do I always imagine there will be some surprise waiting there? Our fridge is filled with leftovers, and our freezer is filled with limes. This is one of the more charming elements of Israeli life: the country grows its own produce, so we all eat by the seasons. In March there are fresh fuzzy almonds to sprinkle with salt. The figs arrive in June. The summer months are for prickly pears: *tsabar*, they are called here. Once, I ate one off a cactus. You want limes? There's about two weeks each September when you can find them, overflowing in plastic tubs at every grocery store. Then they are gone. I love limes. I prefer them to lemons whenever possible. So each September, I buy as many as I can, slicing them to preserve, juice, and freeze. One year, we went on vacation in September and I missed the limes. Tragedy!

When the coffee is ready, I drink it from a mug while standing. Decaf or not, it sends me to the bathroom almost immediately after a few sips. I spent my first three months of pregnancy feeling clogged, sometimes going days without a poop, but recently, I can't make it to the washroom fast enough. On the toilet, I make mental lists of my obligations for the day. Correct my students' exams. Run another load of laundry. Go through those darn sweaters. Confirm with Talia that she and her husband will come for Shabbat.

Wipe, flush.

Muted midmorning light seeps in the bathroom windows from behind heavy clouds. There is a soft, sleepy quality in the air. From the bathroom sink, I can see the curve of the shoreline. I still get a quiet, joyful thrill when I catch sight of the glittering buildings of Tel Aviv rising out from the Mediterranean. *Jews built this*, I think. It never stops feeling a little miraculous.

In the nursery, the box is waiting like an invasive thought.

Telling a story is a sacred act. The world was created in words. Let there be light. A people is bound together in narrative—survival and redemption. And what of my story? How do I string together the thousand invisible decisions that shaped my life and led me here, here to where I am washing my hands in a condo over the sea, pregnant and remembering a boy from long ago who paced my room, who pulled me in for desperate kisses.

God, I can still feel him. I am thirty-five years old, married and pregnant, but I can still feel him. As if all the years and changes, my marriage, my mortgage, my career—all of that was just a coda to the summer that Eyal and I were in love, and he was at war.

Two

We held hands in the car all the way to the train station. We gripped and regripped each other's fingers, traced inner wrists, ran circles over finger pads. We sat in the back. Eyal in the middle, me on one side, and his older sister on the other. His parents sat up front, father driving. Kids and adults, like we were going to an amusement park.

In his uniform, Eyal's body always seemed a little foreign—obscured under all that army green and accented by his assault rifle, which he secured with his left hand, his right hand in mine. The army radio station played a saccharine pop song. We drove past the trees of his neighborhood—leafy and pale. Commuters pooled toward Tel Aviv. Students in backpacks waited at bus stops.

He looked out the window, and I looked at him. The gold of his buzzed hair, his fairy-tale apple-pink cheeks.

Today, Eyal was invading Gaza. To get there, he would take the public train.

"Your phone charger, you have it?" his father asked a bit too loudly, looking at us in the rearview mirror. He was taller than everyone in the family by at least half a foot, and his bald head grazed the roof of the compact car.

"He has it," his mother interjected, a tiny woman who wore silver bracelets with dangling charms. She sat with her dog on her lap—an ancient, bug-eyed pug. Nearly blind and a little gassy.

"You have your charger?" Eyal's father asked again, ignoring his wife.

I couldn't remember the last time I was in a car with my own family. The rare times that the four of us were alone—my parents, my sister, and I—one got the feeling we were uneasy, like characters in a play searching for their lines.

"We should get him one of those wireless chargers," his sister said. Koral. ("Like the jewelry," she'd told me on the day I met her, and held up a bracelet of squiggly orange beads. A thoroughly modern Israeli name, not from Hebrew at all. "Coral," I attempted to repeat, but said it too much like the word in English, mashing the "r" and emphasizing the wrong syllable. Koral had laughed in delight to hear her name sound so wrong.) She and her mom used the same relentlessly blond hair coloring kit, which lived under the sink in one of the family bathrooms. Their roots came in a soft brown not so different from mine. Neither parent responded to Koral's comment about the wireless charger.

Eyal freed his hand to squeeze my knee. "I have my charger," he said, rolling his eyes. He loved communicating to me like this—expressing exasperation with his parents through a look, a gesture. The way he rolled his eyes, indulgent and a little theatrical, you could tell he wasn't really annoyed. Each time he did, I was reminded that he was not yet twenty. So young.

This is war, I thought. *War is happening.* It didn't feel real. I couldn't make it feel real. I was in the car with Eyal and his family, but I was also already in a story I was telling about being in the car with Eyal and his family—a Facebook post I would write about dropping off my boyfriend at the train that would take him to the front. *We held hands in the car*, I'd write.

It didn't feel real, but it was real. For over a week now, rockets from Gaza had been sending us to bomb shelters. He was going to war, but also war was here, in this car. War was in my Hebrew class. War was in the library. War was everywhere.

The night before, we had lain in his twin bed. All around us were remnants of his boyhood. An ad for Goldstar beer hung framed and crooked; he'd had it since before he could order it legally. Notebooks and binders from high school were stacked on a high shelf. Science green, English blue, math red. Recent additions: the army-issued rifle under his bed, the seventy-five-liter backpack he brought back and forth to the army after weekends home, lace-up boots by the door, shined and neatly together.

We lay concentrically.

I hugged him from behind, my pelvis cupping his bum, the soles of his feet resting on my foot bridges. The back of his neck was scratchy, always scratchy, always recently buzzed.

What was my line? This was a question that came to me often, though I had never done any theater. What was the line of a soldier's girlfriend the night before the invasion? If I said, *Don't go*, that might be too cruel, too painful. Instead, I said, "I will be here." He gripped my hands to his stomach but did not reply. I pressed my face into his back.

He sat up swiftly then. He was lean and strong, like a jungle cat in his movements, recalling to me that poem of Rilke's about the pacing caged panther: *It seems to him there are a thousand bars; and behind the bars, no world.*

Inaudibly, I whispered, "Don't go." Words lost in a breath.

He went to his desk—the desk where he had studied for all his high school exams—and hunched over his stapler. He stapled something again and again. For a weird, horrible second, I thought he was stapling his own hand, but when I propped myself up on my elbow, I saw he was stapling a piece of paper. Then he was writing intently.

I could hear his parents in the kitchen, talking over the television. The dog, whose toenails were hardly ever clipped, clacked down the hallway, barking and farting at whatever shadows haunted its failing vision. In her bedroom, which shared a wall with Eyal's, his sister was watching a reality TV show on her laptop. "I thought we had a connection," a woman was saying, in English, through tears.

Eyal returned to sit at the edge of the bed, handed me a folded piece of paper stapled all the way around.

"What's this?" I asked, knowing. We were in the practice of writing each other letters, but this one was different. I knew this one was different. I was only to open it if . . . No. Something began to spill over in my throat. "Eyal, no."

He kissed my forehead. "Don't open it unless," he said.

"No," I breathed. I couldn't let him say it. I couldn't let this be any more real. I pulled him toward me. No more words. I bit his bottom lip. Not violently, but enough to make him kiss me back hard.

In the car on the way to the train station, my hands moved along his kneecap, his thighs, the little muscle tucked into his shinbone like an oyster. I wanted to touch all of him. His muscles had the taut density I associate with being overworked and understretched. Up front, his father was talking to his mother about Koral as if she wasn't there. "I told her to apply to more internships," he said. Eyal's older sister had served at a desk job in the army, and was now studying business management at a distance-learning university. She was younger than I, younger than my younger sister.

For a long time after, I was ashamed of the age difference between me and Eyal. I was twenty-seven, and he was nineteen. Didn't that make me a little predatory? But now that I'm well into my thirties, we both seem impossibly young to me.

"I know, I know," Eyal's mother said. "Applying to three isn't enough."

"*Ima*," Koral said, elongating the syllables into a whine, "I'm right here!"

We could have all been going to the mall.

I pressed my nose into Eyal's shoulder, remembering how the night before I had been seized with something like a terrible hunger for him af-ter he'd given me the letter, the letter I would only read if . . . if. I needed him inside me without foreplay or escalation—right away. I had kissed him so forcefully that our teeth clinked.

We had breathed into each other, entwined in his bed. Already, I was trained not to make too much noise. The apartment was not huge. Koral's room was on one side, and his parents' room was across the hall. At first, I had been horrified by this arrangement. It seemed too perverse to have sex with his parents close by—so perverse, in fact, that it turned me on a bit, even as it repulsed me. What was I doing in a teenager's bedroom within his parents' earshot? But they never remarked. Everyone they knew had full-grown children living at home, so maybe everyone they knew had heard their kids having sex at some point. After a while, their presence had lost its charge until I hardly thought of it at all. Anything can come to feel normal.

We kept our clothes on, just pushed fabric to the side. He was sitting up in bed, and I was wrapped around him. He kissed my mouth, my eye-lids. His mouth was soft, his cheeks were just shaved. I wanted him closer, closer and closer. We were ready for each other. He gripped the back of my hair as I took him. With him inside me, I felt grief rising up—don't go, don't go—so I pressed my hips into him harder until he whispered, "Allie, I'm close." He didn't like climaxing before me, but this time it was what I wanted. "Come inside me," I whispered. "Stay with me."

In the car, he squeezed my hand. I used my phone to take a photo of our fingers entwined, resting atop the military green of his uniform. I liked how the photo came out. My hand looked small in his. Meanwhile, Eyal's father continued to quiz him. What time was his train? *Eight.* How would he get to the base? *Bus.* Which line? *Why?* Never mind, how long between the bus and the train? *Fifteen minutes.* It's not enough time. *It's enough.* He squeezed my hand again.

After months of dating, I'd become accustomed to this kind of exchange between him and his father—testily reviewing the logistics of whatever public transportation Eyal would take to get to wherever the army told him to go. True, he'd never been called into Gaza before, but his life—our life—was set to the rhythm of continual mini-deployments. Two weeks in East Jerusalem, guarding Jews from the Palestinians who wanted their homes back; then home for a long weekend, his mother doing eight loads of laundry as he and I tried to fit a week's worth of activities into a few days; then back to another base for two weeks, supporting infantry units as they raided Palestinian birthday parties and arrested teenagers at protests; then home again. Each time, he took public trains and buses.

As long as I had known him he was going away into zones of combat. So why did this feel different? In part it was the word: "invade." A verb so much more active than its static counterpart, "occupy." In part, it was the increased risk. Gaza radiated with the specter of Palestinian autonomy—a fenced-in region by the sea that Israel did not have full control over. And in part, I think, it was that the boundaries between combatant and civilian life had begun to blur that summer as rockets were shot from Gaza toward us in Tel Aviv.

I touched his fingertips with my fingertips. His chin rested on the top of my head.

At the train station there wasn't much time. We didn't have a parking spot, just pulled over to where the taxis dropped people off. Eyal's father put on the hazards, and we all got out of the car.

His mother and Koral hugged Eyal first, each putting an arm around his shoulder. Two blond women. I was holding the pug. Heavier than you might imagine, its breathing labored in my arms.

A man was arguing with a driver about the proposed fare to the harbor.

Eyal's sister had stepped back, and his mother was whispering loudly into her son's neck, "I will pray for you. I will pray." Her nails were painted bright orange. I couldn't see Eyal's face.

All around, soldiers were saying goodbye. Boys and girls with guns and grenade launchers. The beep of the metal detector was like a metronome as they all went in to board their trains.

The pug squirmed in my arms. Her name was Charlotte. It seemed to be a trend among middle-class Israelis—giving their dogs the most Anglo-sounding names possible. Susan, Sawyer, Charlotte. When Eyal and I took Charlotte for walks she always sought out smaller dogs, not so much to play with but to tower over. That was this hefty pug's pleasure: drooling on smaller, yappier dogs until their owners pulled them away.

Koral took Charlotte back from me. "Give her a kiss," she told Eyal.

He leaned over to kiss the pug. "Good girl," he said softly. "Such a good dog." He was a child when his parents brought Charlotte home. They grew up together. Now her eyes were cloudy with age.

His father was next. Shaking his son's hand heartily, then pulling him in for a slap on the back. Such a tall man. Toward me he was neither warm nor unkind. I think he was a little confused why a full-grown woman was dating his young son. Even after I was almost fluent in Hebrew, he continued to speak to me in English, nearly yelling, as if that helped me understand him better.

I was the last to say goodbye. I'd worn a white cotton dress, simple and pretty. I had chosen the outfit with care, because this is how Eyal would remember me. He wrapped an arm around my shoulders, and I gripped his waist. He kissed my forehead. His mother cried as she filmed. My hair was long, lighter than his. I was older than him, but I was shorter and slight. My hip bones pressed against him when he held me close. And oh God, his body. The young strength of his body. Restricted as we were by each other's languages, we said so much with our bodies.

He pressed his forehead to mine. "I'll come back," he whispered. His eyes were closed.

In my peripheral vision, I could see bystanders taking photos of us. We were an image: the departing soldier embracing his girl, her hair in a long braid. War and its counterpart, its justification even.

"I'll come back to you," he said again.

I was horrified to find I had to suppress laughter. I bit the inside of my cheek to stop it. What was wrong with me?

It was only as he stepped away from me that I felt my body pitch and shift, some center lost when he was not physically close. "Don't go," I said. The night before as he had come inside me, I had rocked back and forth over him, feeling us inside each other, feeling myself through him feeling me. "Don't go," I had whispered then and I whispered now, but he was stepping away from me, and as he did I could feel part of my own self pulling away with him. Did it feel the same for him? He was in me and then he was gone.

So no, it wasn't laughter that had wanted to bubble up in me but panic, terror as Eyal hoisted on his enormous duffel-backpack and walked toward the train station gates.

"No," I said. His mother grabbed my arm to pull me back, although I wasn't aware I'd been going after him. The dog began barking, panicked and staccato, almost an echo: *Don't go, don't go.* Eyal looked back, but he did not reply. Then, he was gone.

We were quiet as we got back into the car. The family would drop me off at the university campus, not far from their home, so I could go to my morning classes. After, I would return to my own apartment in southern Tel Aviv—back to a tiny kitchen with no oven, just a rickety old hot plate, yes, but also, back to the high ceilings of my peaceful room, the romantically mismatched tiles of my floor. My flatmate and I each had our own bedroom. Talia, her name was. A soft-spoken Israeli musician who made what she called *music for the displaced*—electronic beats haunted by the worlds her grandparents left behind to come to Israel.

The letter Eyal had written me—not to be opened unless (unless, unless)—was in my wallet. Waiting there like a bomb under the seat of a bus. Compulsively, that is, without my own consent, I began to try and imagine what it said.

Allison, my love, if you are reading this, it means that I am not coming home.

Stop it, I begged myself.

Allie, my love, these past few months have been the happiest of my life.

Stop doing this.

A, thank you for loving me. Thank you for giving me——

Please, no——

a place in your world.

I covered my mouth with my hand so that I would not cry out.

Eyal's father gripped the steering wheel. His sister was hunched into her phone, her face obscured by sunglasses. His mother was already praying, reading from the book of Psalms——prayers said to arouse divine mercy. These are the words that reach God directly. Our ancients imagined an angel who grasps these prayers as they rise up to heaven and weaves the words into a crown for God. I'd never heard Eyal's mom pray before. She was a beach-loving woman who wore metallic eyeshadow and shirts that revealed her freckled shoulders. Usually, she was playful, girlish even——singing along to ABBA songs while she hung Eyal's uniforms to dry. But now she was praying. The verses dipped and rustled through the car. Without pausing in her prayers, she reached behind her. For a second, I thought she had dropped something, but no——her daughter, without looking up from her phone, took her mother's hand. They stayed like that the rest of the car ride, the mother reaching back, the daughter reaching forward. I'd never touched my own mother with such casual, sustained intimacy.

Growing up, my family had always felt——is this the right word?—— faded. The ties between us felt fragile, washed too many times. In high school, we all ate dinner at different times. My parents both spoke of their grandmothers' soups and roasts, but never made them for me or my sister. We seemed to live on chicken breast, hummus, and baby carrots. Food that made me feel somehow alone and smothered at the same time. Always, it felt that some nourishment was lacking, some communication between generations that had stopped with me. Or stopped before me. Watching Eyal's sister hold her mother's hand, I thought about how, in some families, there is an unbroken line back to the ancestors—generations, tending to one another. I wanted that. I still want that.

Instead, my inheritance was keeping secrets about my body. I didn't learn how to wash myself properly until university, after seeing other girls on my floor with loofahs in their shower kits. I called my sister. "Did you know we're supposed to use cloths in the shower? To wash, I mean."

"No," she said, "are you sure?" Two years younger, Erica was still at home then.

I told her yes, we were supposed to use a cloth to clean our bodies, including our legs.

"But the water just runs down our legs, doesn't it?"

"No, we're supposed to wash."

Most sisters I know fought when they were young and grew closer as they became adults, but for us it was the reverse. As kids, Erica and I parented one another. I got my period first, of course, and learned about pads from other girls at school. I never told my mother about my period, and she never asked. Erica and I bought pads with our allowance. Later, we tried to figure out tampons—a disaster until we found the slim-fit teen kind with plastic applicators. Together, we made light of our mother's weird food issues (how many times "I'm hungry" was met with "Have a cucumber," we could not say) and our father's beleaguered resentment of our mother earning more money in real estate than he did teaching math at the university—a resentment he never expressed in words but only in the way he did the dishes; he banged those pots and pans together with such force that once a neighbor knocked on our door. ("Is everyone okay?" For years, Erica and I retold that story in the whispered dark of our room: "No, it's not okay," we giggled in secret, "our parents are insane.") More than once, we asked Mom why she married Dad. We wanted a love story. "He was nice to me," Mom said, smoothing out her work slacks. "Nobody had ever been that nice to me." We were openly bored by that answer. Privately, I think we were both frightened. Was that all that waited for us?

As children, our favorite pretend game had been playing orphans. It was the most glamorous fate we could imagine. We would tie scarves around our heads and pull dresses down to expose our shoulders. We luxuriated in the tragedy that marked us. This is how we spent those gloriously unscheduled hours between school ending and our parents coming home: in our small urban patch of a backyard, pretending that we were surviving in the woods beyond the reach of any adult. At least once, I scared my sister. "I miss them," I said. I was clutching the kerchief at my neck. It was summer, but we were pretending it was cold; we had to scrounge enough kindling from the imaginary woods, otherwise we would freeze to death. That's what I'd told Erica. "I miss them," I said, "but we must be brave." Erica started crying. Sniffling and gasping under the pile of dress-up shawls I had made her wear. "I miss them too," she said, her nose running. "I miss Mom." I was excited and afraid; the game had never felt this real before. I held her then, hushing and shushing as she wept into my arms.

Until I moved away for university, we slept in the same room: twin beds separated by a single dresser. My clothes in the top two drawers, hers in the bottom. If our parents were downstairs fighting about money, we both slept in my bed. When I was spanked—more often, it was I who was spanked, burden of the oldest—then we slept in Erica's bed.

I think the drifting really began when I went away. "Please don't leave me alone with them," she'd whispered into my neck. I didn't have to go—I could have stayed for a second year of cégep, then gone to McGill. A typical path. But instead I followed my ambitions to Toronto, which is, I suppose, how Mom got Erica. Our mother had always felt bad for herself, I know, to have two pretty daughters who abruptly stopped talking when she entered the room. "I guess I'm just a horrible mother, then" was her favorite rejoinder in a fight, and I'd say, "No, no," all panicked, but once Erica said, "Yeah, I guess you are."

During my first year in Toronto, I called Erica less than I meant to, and eventually, she called me less than I expected.

She came out as bisexual at the end of my second year. She told me at the same time as our parents. All of us were seated on the couch while she paced in front of us. "I have something to tell you," she said. She'd cut her hair short and was wearing oversized clothing. I thought she'd say she was pregnant. I was surprised by the loneliness that welled up in me when she said she was queer. I'd had no idea. Afterward, she hugged Mom, who rubbed her back with small circles, and that's when I knew: I knew that Erica had told our mother first. We hadn't learned at the same time. Mom knew first.

So much I felt I'd lost, watching Erica comforted by our mother: the fantasy that Erica and I might mother each other, yes, but also, I think, the fantasy that one day my mother would love me the way I deserved.

In my third year, I decided to apply to grad school in the States.

Eyal's father turned the radio off. Perhaps it was my old fear of exclusion that made me worry that the family saw me as an interloper in their vulnerable moment.

What would I do if this were a normal day? Or, normal for me and Eyal—if instead of going to Gaza he was going to the West Bank for two weeks of surveillance around Israeli settlements? The answer: I would send him cute photos. I would make him feel remembered, loved.

Charlotte the pug was sleeping on the seat next to me, breathing nasally. I coaxed her into looking at the lens of my cell phone, holding up her chin gently with one hand. SHE MISSES YOU, I captioned the photo that I sent to Eyal.

He wrote back almost immediately. I'M ON MY TRAIN. He sent a photo of his boots in the frame with at least three other pairs of boots, red or black—soldiers, all of them, headed south. My phone dinged an alert when he texted; his father looked in the rearview mirror to ask, "That's Eyal?" Then, without waiting for a response, "He's on his train?"

"Yes," I said, relieved to remember that of course I was not an interloper. I was the girlfriend—part of the threads connecting our soldier to his home. "He made his train."

On my phone, I uploaded the photo of our fingers entwined for a Facebook post. *We held hands in the car all the way to the train station*, I typed into the status update box. *Now, you are going to the Gaza border and I am remembering how good my hand feels in yours.* Who would see this post and like it? First, my new friends from Israel. Then Eyal, who would leave a heart in the comments, as would his mom and sister. Once it was morning in Canada, my mom would surely leave a well-intentioned comment that missed the point of my post entirely: *Be careful over there.* Erica might not respond at all. In the years since I'd left home—moving to New York for grad school after Toronto—she had gotten harder for me to predict.

All the while, Eyal's mother kept praying, one hand reaching back for her daughter, the other keeping her prayer book steady.

Three

My first memory of Eyal is a rifle pressed into my knee.

We met on the bus. It was spring then, a warm and sensual season. I was on a research errand—fetching a book from another university's library. He was on his way to a memorial ceremony. His commander always chose him to go to this type of thing, he told me later, because he had such a classic Ashkenazi look, with his fair European features.

He had noticed me at the bus stop: a girl with a green ribbon in her hair waiting for a bus, hand shading her eyes against the Tel Aviv sun, paying no particular attention to the interchangeable soldiers who drooped in the meager shade of every bus stop in the country. In the story that we came to tell about this day, it was important that I did not see him— that he was the one who saw me. It suited his role in the army: A combat soldier in an intelligence unit. A watcher.

He watches the girl—or is she older than him? Hard to tell, with that girlish hair ribbon—peering down the highway. He is exhausted and bored. Before the army, he didn't know you could be both simultaneously, but that's his life now. Bored and exhausted, he sees a girl like a cartoon character. It's the green bow in her hair that gets him. So sweet, so out of place. That's exactly what he wishes to be: out of place, out of here. Not part of the scenery but a person moving through it. An American, or something like that. She waves down her bus when she sees it. The bus stops. The doors open. She steps on. Nice legs. He is waiting for a different line. Too bad. There she goes.

That's where it should have ended. But in a moment we came to mythologize—after the courtship and the uncertainty and the long drives in his car working up the courage to kiss, after hours napping in sunlight by a river in the park, after days slipping away in the dark heaven of my bed as he lay on top of me to lick my eyelids—he lurches forward. "Wait," he calls out to the driver, making his voice deep, making it, he hopes, irresistible. The bus doors open again. He will be late for the memorial ceremony. He does not, strictly speaking, know where this bus is going. The driver is an older man with a long pinkie fingernail. "Nu?" he says, looking down at Eyal. Now or never. Eyal nods and gets on.

He stands at the front of the bus, which is moving again. He sways in place as he scans for the girl with the green ribbon. There—sitting by a filthy bus window. There she is—reading.

In those days, I always left the aisle seat free. I had a fantasy that someone would sit next to me. Someone would find me. A man. A lover. Someone who would change the course of my life by sweeping me up into his.

By the time I met Eyal, it was almost time for me to leave Israel. I'd only come for a semester—that had been the plan. A semester of coursework and writing my dissertation. The circumstances weren't ideal for dating; I'd gone on two first dates, both with men my own age. The first was with a guy who'd gotten my number while we both waited to order drinks at a crowded bar. He was short, the same height as me, but I liked how forward he was about asking for my number. We met up for ice cream in central Tel Aviv, taking our cups and little plastic spoons to Yitzhak Rabin Square, named for the prime minister who was assassinated there in 1995. They say that even in his dying, Rabin still could not believe it was a Jew who killed him. My date worked in marketing, he said, but before that he had worked "in the prime minister's office." "Oh," I'd said, "like PR?" I was bored. None of this was sexy. "No," he said, "*in the prime minister's office*," and his voice was laden with meaning. "You know what it means?" I told him I didn't, and he explained that it meant working in intelligence. A euphemism, I said. "Yes," he said, "but everyone knows and now so do you." I felt an electric current run through me. But then he started explaining his current job—online marketing, search engine something, viral tweets—and I lost interest again.

The other date had been with a law student who asked me out by the library copy machine. He was tall and gaunt, a bit scruffy. Bolshevik chic. We met for cheap coffee at a university cafe. "Do you eat corpses?" he'd asked me, which was his way of telling me he was a vegan. The date only went downhill from there.

"Where are you?" I whispered to my ceiling at night. Where was my intense and irresistible lover? Each time I took the bus, I moved over to the window seat in case he—whoever he was—finally came.

Now, here was this boy, perhaps a teenager, working up the courage to take the seat.

"Why *did* you sit next to me?" I asked him. We were lying on a blanket in a park just north of Tel Aviv. In one month, the invasion would be called, but we didn't know that yet. Huge trees reached over us and toward the river that runs through the park and into the sea.

Like all lovers, Eyal and I took a heady joy in sifting through the initial stages of our romance the way you pan for gold. "How could I not?" he said. He held my hands up to the sunlight. Our fingers entwined, our legs entwined. Somehow, throughout the day, our blanket kept slipping, closer and closer to the riverbank, almost as if time itself was pulling us in, pulling us closer. "How could I not sit next to you?" he repeated.

But even after he followed me onto the bus, I know he had second thoughts. Because isn't it better to leave the fantasy intact? Let the girl in the green bow remain perfect, which is to say, unknown.

When he sits down next to me, his rifle presses up against my knee. "I had never been so close to a gun before," I told him, picking up the story. I'd had no way to tell if the safety was on. It would be months before he sat with me and showed me the safety on his rifle, months before we fell asleep with his rifle and combat boots under my bed. "Mostly, I was annoyed," I said, bringing our hands toward me to kiss his fingers. "Your gun was in the way!" He pressed his nose flat into my neck.

What I didn't tell him—not that day in the park, nor any other time we rehearsed this origin story—was how I had watched him too. In the myth, he is the one who acts: he follows me onto the bus, he sees me, he sits next to me, and he is the first to speak. We needed him to be bold in our telling so that my age did not overpower him. We needed his desire to be the primary actor. But when I felt his rifle pressing into my knee, I looked up at him. I saw how his head fell back on the seat, his eyes closed with something beyond exhaustion. I wanted to know what that something was. Every Israeli I met had stories about the army. These were the experiences that had shaped them. I would never be in the army, but now I was close.

His buzzed hair was a golden wash, his eyebrows were strong, his jaw defined, his cheeks flushed. His frame was powerful, lean—broad shoulders and a thin torso—and gave off a harsh musky note from, I would eventually learn, an Armani body spray sold in his dad's pharmacy. My first impression, one that would be echoed each time I watched him undress, was that this body was new to him. Short months before, he must have been a scrawny high school boy. Now he was something else. A new-hewn man, his freshly bloomed muscles still tender and swollen. His buzz cut made him look like a child. Not yet twenty, I guessed. Correctly, it would turn out. Taking him in for that first time, I felt like some lecherous old man wandering the Classical wing of a great museum, ogling the bleached, marble youths who throw discus and wrestle with the pythons that will kill them.

But in the story we told each other, I do not look up from my book. "I could feel you looking at me," I told him as we spun our love story that day in the park.

"I thought you were my age," he said. The blanket was slipping again, down the park's grassy embankment, down toward the river. In a class on comparative Semitic grammar, I had learned the literary Arabic word for "day," specifically day measured from dawn to dusk, is almost indistinguishable from the word for "river," to the extent that their plural forms are identical: "*anhur*" means both "days" and "rivers." Our afternoon was trickling away into early evening, a chill creeping into the air, but we didn't want to get up yet and go back to our respective homes. We had to finish telling the story.

"My heart stopped when you grabbed my book," I said.

It is an impulsive gesture for a stranger to make—grabbing the book, a notebook actually, out of my hands. For less than a second, fear glints in me, but then he is laughing as he flips through the pages. "What is this?" he asks.

My notebook is filled with etymologies, references to articles about the degeneration of one letter or another in the various iterations of Hebrew over the centuries. I'm in Israel as a graduate student, attempting to write a dissertation on nexuses of longing in the Talmud—a slippery collection of documents that reflects the Jewish struggle to salvage a religion, or really, reinvent it, after the loss of the Great Temple in Jerusalem.

I struggle to answer him in Modern Hebrew. "I study the sages," I say, "and their stories." In those days, I had to be careful when I spoke Hebrew to Israelis. So often, I was tempted to use the syntax and vocabulary of archaic Hebrews—rabbinic or biblical. Once, Eyal called me from a stranger's phone at some desolate southern gas station. "Baby," he crooned over the phone, the word filling my chest; I could live in those two syllables, ba-by. *Where are you?* I wanted to ask. So I said, "*Ayeka?*" He laughed so hard he had to hang up. Now that I know the difference, it's hard to explain in English, but I had said, essentially, *Where art thou?*

It's how God calls to Adam in the garden, when the man and his woman are hiding their nakedness, newly ashamed.

On the day we meet, his face droops a bit when I tell him I study rabbinics. "Oh," he says, "the Talmud?" Like most Israelis, he had studied foundational Jewish texts in his public high school right along with math and science. When I lived in New York, my studies had been exotic, at least to a stranger on the bus. Here, it was all mundane.

Desperate to keep his interest, I scramble. "I study poetry," I say. "Beauty. Metaphor."

"Metaphor-ah," he repeats, adding that charming extra syllable.

In the park, he was kissing my ear. "Metaphor-ah," he whispered. I could feel a chill rising out of the earth below our blanket. I rolled to face him. We kissed, softly, but the softness belied an urgency. We could feel it swelling. We both enjoyed this dynamic: building intensity that we tried to restrain. Tentative opening of our mouths, baby kisses on each other's lips, when what I really wanted was to suck on his tongue with everything I had. We were in public. On the trail a few meters away, a father was teaching his young daughter to ride a bike. Probably, he had a wife my age, this man calling after a girl with a huge helmet and a pink bike. And here I was with a boy so many years younger than me. I pressed myself close to him so that nobody could see when he slipped his hands down the front of my jeans and rubbed me. The chaotic danger of it all— the nearby pedestrians, the families packing up picnics—heightened the need, and after only a few minutes I could feel it happen. The spasms came at diminished intervals. I was almost scared when I whispered that I was going to come, and he kissed me hard so that the small sounds that escaped me were swallowed into his mouth.

His name was an abstraction. From a root that originally referred to a ram, "*eyal*" came to mean "strength" or "might." It appears once in the Bible—in Psalms, in fact: *I am become as a man that has no strength.*

All this I looked up in my historical Hebrew lexicons and dictionaries. That was perhaps my favorite part of graduate work: wading into the history of words. How beautifully convoluted those histories always became! Roots tangled with other roots.

I do sometimes regret my vocation. When I consider my tiny contribution to our savings account, when I end up embroiled in the pointless little disputes endemic to the more obscure academic disciplines, when I find that I am (right now, for example) dragging my heels on marking a towering stack of exam papers—then yes, I do ask myself why I didn't find a more typical job. But oh, to spend months inside the history of a word, teasing out its changes over time and embellishing those changes into meaning. Sometimes my husband will speak to me while I am deep inside an ancient etymology and I won't hear a word he says. During those engrossed hours, I believe I might be happy.

"Where you from?" Eyal asked me on the bus. Such a typically Israeli syntax. *Where you from?*

He asked in English, but I wanted to answer in Hebrew. It was good to practice the spoken form. "*Avarti la-aretz mi-New York*," I said in Hebrew, cautiously picking my way through the words to explain I had moved to Israel from New York but was from Canada. "*Aval ani mi-Canada.*"

"Canada," he repeated, his face blooming into an unexpected tenderness.

I had never really spoken to a soldier in uniform. Although all day, every day I saw soldiers around. They were a kind of living scenery—in their uniforms, toting around their weapons, taking buses from one base to another, crammed into commuter trains going north, going south. On lunch breaks from the central Tel Aviv base, they ate ice creams with their olive-color pants slung low. Rarely was one of these soldiers older than twenty-three. What I actually knew of life inside the army was semi-mythological—remembered by people who were out of the army. The adult men I met spoke of it wistfully. Before I met Eyal, Talia and I had gone to pick up a table we'd bought from a stranger online. The seller was a man of about thirty in a yellow T-shirt cut into a tank top, some kind of insignia over his heart. "Golani *sheli*," Talia said as he unscrewed the table legs so it could fit in the car Talia had borrowed for us. It's a combat unit, Talia told me later—the one her brother and a bunch of her cousins had served in. It would be a long time living in Israel before I could recognize certain shorthand. Golani, for example, referring to a front-line infantry unit that, historically, non-European Jews were funneled into. On that day, Talia and the man selling his table spoke in a secret code.

Now, I asked the soldier on the bus, "Is it hard, in the army?" It was a flirtatious question, giving him a chance to sound tough.

Eyal gripped his neck with his left hand—a gesture of frustration that would become familiar to me. "On the body it is tough, yes," he said, with so much more sincerity than I had expected. "But also on the *nefesh*." He touched my arm not entirely gently, a boundary crossed. I liked it. "You know what is *nefesh*?"

I knew the word's tangled history. In Modern Hebrew, "*nefesh*" means "soul." In biblical Hebrew, "*nefesh*" refers to a living thing and, in more archaic usages, can mean "breath." The evolution of this word is a favorite among Semitic philologists. The story of "*nefesh*" begins with the ancient languages of Akkadian and Hittite, long-dead relatives of Hebrew, where there is a cognate that means "throat." (Here is a history of meaning not premised on difference but on association: over time, "throat" became "breath," issued from the throat, and "breath" became the "soul," i.e., the divine breath of God trapped inside these bodies.) But how could I say all of that to him? I answered simply. "Yes," I said. "I know *nefesh*."

The bus continued its route north away from the city center, stopping periodically to let out passengers. Often, the driver needed to be prompted to open the back doors of the bus. "*Nahag!*" passengers shouted. *Driver!*

Eyal fiddled with the strap of his rifle. "How old are you?"

I was twenty-seven. At Tel Aviv University, twenty-seven put me on the younger side for a graduate student. Because of the typical timeline of a few years' military service followed by a year or two to decompress, the majority of Israeli PhD students I met were already in their thirties. But no matter how you looked at it, I was too old to date Eyal. "I am twenty-seven," I said.

"No," he said.

I nodded, flattered and disappointed. Surely, there was not much else to say.

"How old am I?" he asked, still not looking at me. "Guess."

"You are nineteen," I said. And I knew I had guessed right, because he closed his eyes, let his head fall back against the headrest, deciding—I knew this too—whether or not he would give up on this flirtation. I wonder what doubts filled him before we smoothed down the moment into a mythology that told us our love was inevitable.

I didn't want him to give up. I wanted him to keep wanting me. "You know," I said, "in Hebrew I feel younger." I was speaking Hebrew in the plodding way I had of attempting the spoken language in those years. "Because I have so much to learn."

He turned to me hopefully. His eyes were a gray-green, stormy sea eyes.

I went on. "I'm still in *kita gimmel*," I exclaimed. Third grade. I'd told him I was in third grade, which was true—it's how the school ranked our proficiency.

He laughed then. "*Kita gimmel*," he said. "*Gadol.*" (I knew this slang: Literally "big"—in effect, *That's rich*, or *That's amusing*.)

And so we continued. We were so shy. We hardly looked at each other's face. We spoke about the weather, looking at our own hands. I pressed my lips together; he pressed his ear into his shoulder. But for a moment, Eyal did look at me, took in my face, and I could feel the question coming before he asked it. I knew what he was about to ask me. Outside the window, I watched an old Toyota speed past the bus.

Eyal asked the question I knew was coming. "You Jewish?"

All the months I'd lived in Israel, and I hadn't learned how to answer this question. So much depended on who was asking. Before I came to Israel, I had thought of myself as Jewish. Mostly because I was no other religion. But as soon as I got off the plane in Tel Aviv, I found myself questioned, not by the border patrol—they were satisfied with my paperwork and, surely, my whiteness—but by the cabdriver who drove me to the apartment I'd blindly arranged by searching Facebook for a rented room.

"Where you from?" the cabdriver asked. Then guessed, "London?" His accent was heavy, but at the time, I could not tell if it was clogged with Hebrew or Arabic. Nor did I recognize the pennants of the soccer team hanging from his rearview mirror—a team I would come to recognize as having notoriously nationalistic and anti-Arab fans, its base formed by Jews who had emigrated from the Arab world to Israel only to be subjugated to the racism of European Ashkenazi Jews. But on that day, all I knew was that his coloring was olive, what I want to call Mediterranean, and I did not know what language accented his English.

"I'm from Canada," I said, which was true, even if I'd most recently lived in New York. Canada always seemed like a more neutral answer to me.

"Vacation?"

"Study." This was a less than entirely accurate answer. I was in Israel through the summer semester at the university, then back to New York—something closer to a semester abroad. *I should probably clarify*, I thought. But I didn't. "I'm here to study," I repeated.

Then, for the first of countless times, "You Jewish?" He was looking back over his shoulder as he drove.

I was too shocked to do anything but nod.

He was watching the road again but looking at me in the rearview. "Both parents? Jewish?"

"My father is Jewish," I said.

"Ah, but not your *ima*."

"What?" I said, understanding the question but still in shock. I'd never been asked such a thing by a stranger before. In my graduate program in New York, the visibly Jewish scholars of the Talmud had an understanding that excluded me, but it was never made explicit.

"Your mother, she is not Jew?" he pushed on.

"No."

"So you are not Jewish!" he was joyful, triumphant even as he announced this to me.

This is how I learned I had come to the land of Jewish mothers. If my mother were Jewish and my father were not, then I'd be a Jew by any standard, and it would be my inheritance to squander. But a Jewish father does not a Jew make. My father's great-grandparents fled Lithuania before World War I. By the 1970s, their great-grandchildren were getting nose jobs and marrying gentiles. I know some Jews bemoan assimilation, but to my father's parents, I think it was a relief to see their children become Canadian—become white. Now, they must have thought, you'll finally be safe.

But in Israel, a mixed marriage had the opposite effect. My Jewish mother was missing. The way Israelis responded, you'd think I had no mother at all.

I didn't tell my mother about the constant refrain, "You Jewish? You Jewish?" I didn't want her to get into one of her self-pitying states. *I guess I'm just a horrible mother, then.*

The first time we all Skyped as a family, I'd been in Israel for about a month. "I love it," I said to their blurry faces on my laptop screen. "Everyone is warm, and life feels"—I hesitated while I found the right words—"new and purposeful." I'd arrived in the spring, just in time for Passover. I'd stay through the summer. Then I'd leave. That was the plan, even if summer already seemed too close at hand.

On the screen, my family was silent. So much that I wondered if my computer had frozen. In the background, I could see our dimly lit living room, the unused piano, the framed prints of bridges. Beige carpeting, wall to wall. How lonely I had been growing up in that house. Always, I feel the need to fill the space with chatter until someone else speaks. "A professor at the university invited me to Passover seder," I said. "It was joyful!" This was true. I'd barely met the man before he insisted that his wife would never forgive him if he let me spend Passover alone. At an elegant house in a North Tel Aviv suburb, this professor of Maimonides presided over a table of his well-educated Ashkenazi clan. (Their grandparents hailed from Germany and Hungary.) The children all had skits prepared about slavery and liberation, falling on the floor in giggling heaps when it was time for the Egyptian firstborns to die. This professor was my father's age but already a grandfather—they marry so young here, even the secular ones. Rather vulnerably, I told my family, "I liked the feeling of being part of Jewish life." Pause.

My dad, who had never been to Israel, said, "Well, just let us know if you need anything." He meant money, which made my mom and sister glance at him then at each other, and I knew they'd talk about it later.

After high school, Erica did not follow me to U of Toronto, nor to the less prestigious university where our father taught. Instead, she went to McGill, lived at home, and after, moved not far away to the Plateau, where she commuted to work on a bike she kept locked on her balcony. As she and Mom got closer, what could I do? I turned to Dad. Is that why I became an academic? Following him? Good heavens, I hope not. Once, when I was home for Christmas break during my master's degree—Erica was still an undergrad then—my father and I were having a chummy exchange on the challenges of academic publishing during a family dinner. Mom leaned into Erica, saying, "I guess you're too intellectual for us, right, Erica?" Erica returned her nudge. Whatever we'd had growing up was lost.

On the Skype call, I thanked my dad for the offer. "I'll let you know if there's an emergency," I said.

"What?" he asked. "I think you froze." He was raising his voice, as if that would make it pass through the internet more effectively. "Allie? Can you hear me?"

"Stop shouting," I heard Erica say to him.

"I said, 'I'll let you know if there's an emergency,'" I repeated.

"Ah, very good," he said, still with his voice raised.

"Jonathan," my mother chastised, "you're yelling."

I had a memory of my father leading a brief seder for just the four of us when Erica and I were in grade school. "This year we are slaves," he said, holding up a plate of matzah, "next year may we be free in Jerusalem." Pause. "Or at least Westmount," he added, referring to a particularly affluent neighborhood. Whenever we did Jewish ritual, we made jokes like this. *Back in the shtetl, back in the old country, back during the pogroms.* Not quite sure how to act Jewish without it being a kind of performance.

"Did you do a seder?" I asked.

"Not this year," Mom said, sighing a little. "We always mean to, but since you two have grown up . . ." She trailed off. I wondered if I had hurt her feelings. Made her feel she wasn't Jewish enough. Was she Jewish enough? Was I?

"Next year in Tel Aviv," Dad offered.

"Better than the shtetl," I countered.

"Will you go to Palestine?" Erica asked suddenly. It was the first question she'd asked me during this call.

"You mean, to the West Bank?" I asked, trying not to say anything that would make her and Mom talk about me later. When she nodded, I continued. "Hmm," I said, thinking it through, "I'd have to check if it violates the terms of my grants." I was beholden to various American and Canadian governmental travel advisories regarding areas controlled by the Palestinian authority.

"Now, Erica," Mom said, indulgently. Her earrings were big round pearls. "We don't all have your brave spirit." Some special look passed between them. But why wasn't I the brave one? I was the one who had left. I was the one across the world!

"Play it safe," my dad advised.

"Never a bad policy," I replied gamely, but in my heart I felt a well of bitterness.

The airport cabdriver was the first to ask about my mother, but since that day I'd been told countless times by Israelis that I was not a Jew. On buses, in classrooms, when they came to fix my toilet. Always, a kind of glee motivated their pronouncement that no, without a Jewish mother I was not a Jew. Where did it come from? Their joy in this moment? I think it was this: nothing made them feel more Jewish than informing me that I was not.

On the bus, I answered Eyal the way I was accustomed to answering. "My father is Jewish," I said. I braced myself for him to explain the concept of matrilineal descent.

"Not your mother," he clarified.

"No," I said. My muscles were tensed, waiting.

"Do you feel Jewish?" he asked.

Nobody had ever asked me this before. My whole body relaxed. "I'm trying to figure it out."

"Your eyes are amazing," he said, then looked away.

In my chest, my heart was blooming.

He was telling me about basic training, something about a tent, when the elderly lady interrupted. "When we get inside, it's filled with gas," he was saying, his face contorted hilariously in a way I found a little disturbing. "We are in the gas, crying."

"It sounds scary," I offered.

"No, no," he said, gripping my arm again. "Not scary. Funny, it was funny."

I was shocked by the strength of his grip—the urgency of it—and how bereft I felt when he suddenly let go and stood up. For a painful instant, I thought we'd reached his stop, but no: he'd spotted an elderly lady attempting to lug her shopping basket up the bus stairs.

"*Khayal, Khayal!*" she called out to him, beckoning with her free hand. *Soldier, soldier!* I would come to see that when he was in uniform, Eyal was a kind of public property. Not just in helping old ladies, but in entertaining the nostalgia of middle-aged men or the grief of women his mother's age.

"*Shniyah,*" he said to me, then, catching himself, "One second."

He looked tall and capable as he pulled her cart, overflowing with the leafy tops of root vegetables, up the bus stairs. "*Todah lakha,*" she said, with a nasal formality. "*Todah, khayal.*" *Thank you, soldier.*

He sat back down, his smile a little sheepish. He touched my arm again. "What were we saying?"

We never mentioned this part of the story, but it was I who asked Eyal out. After half an hour spent cobbling together a conversation, we were approaching the interchange where I would transfer buses. My time was running out, and I—what did I want, really? Maybe just for him to keep looking at me with hunger and wonder. "Let's get ice cream," I said, not sure of the drinking age in Israel. "Next time you are in Tel Aviv."

"Yes," he said. He was fumbling to get his phone out. "Yes, good idea." He dropped his phone at his feet, and a man's voice a few rows behind us yelled, "*Leyat, leyat, yeled.*" *Slowly, slowly, boy.* I realized that the entire bus must have been listening to our courtship—rooting for the teenage soldier, laughing at the foreign woman, so easily won over by a kid with a rifle. For the sake of Eyal's dignity, and my own, I pretended not to have registered what the man said.

We were careful, he and I, to maintain a sense of balance. It would have been so easy for me to overpower him in certain circumstances: a woman in lipstick, speaking a language in which she has two degrees, pulling her lover in closer during sex with thighs made strong from years of running. Although perhaps he wouldn't have minded that; perhaps he liked imagining that I was experienced enough to mentor him into the world of sex or love; perhaps he would have found it exciting had I over-powered him, had he felt that he was drowning in me, losing himself in me. I'll never know.

Four

Eyal's mother was still praying as we drove north toward the university. Whispered rustle of her supplications. *Lama, Adonai, ta'amod b'rakhok? Why, Lord, do you stand so far away?*

I wished I could hold her. She'd welcomed me in right from the start. I was so nervous the first time I came over with Eyal. She squealed when she opened the door, hugged me before I could even give her the gaudy yellow flowers I'd brought. "You have family in Israel?" she asked almost right away.

"No," I said, "just me." I was dreading questions about my age, but they never came.

"*Ezeh yofi*," she exclaimed, smiling at Eyal and then at me. "It is so good you are here," she said, wrestling with the vowels in English. "Israel is the safe place for the Jews, so you should stay forever."

"*Ima-a-a*," he moaned miserably. *Mom-m-m.*

"What's the problem? It's not true?" she said to him in Hebrew. Then to me in English, "You should stay here all your life."

Now, she was whispering and rocking in her seat. "Deliver me, O God, for the waters have reached *nafesh*." The voweling of this word is a little unexpected: "*nafesh*" instead of "*nefesh*." Some versions of the Bible translate the word as "soul"; others translate as "neck." Perhaps our souls live in our necks. *Deliver me, O God, for the waters have reached my divine breath.* I thought of Eyal, his hand on my arm: *You know what is nefesh?*

"*Ken, hu b'derekh la-gvul,*" Koral said into her phone, presumably leaving a voice memo to her boyfriend. *Yes, he's on his way to the border.*

I scratched Charlotte's neck—rolls of skin, prickly with her short pug fur.

As children, Erica and I raced each night to be the one to brush our mother's hair. Her eyes closed as the wood-handled brush ran along her scalp. We did not have a dog. Instead, we brushed our mother. "That feels good," she would say, her voice dreamy. We were fascinated by this sentence, something exciting and almost repulsive in the way she said it. "That feels so good." The wide brush made oily waves in her blond hair.

These are the only times I remember touching our mother. Was it possible that Erica still brushed her hair? No, right? Wouldn't that be too weird? But how would I know? Erica lived a ten-minute drive from our parents, although I assumed she took the bus or biked. Their life had a whole rhythm without me. I felt excluded, but also I felt relieved.

Eyal's father stopped the car at a red light near the spot where, when I was commuting to campus from my own apartment, the bus let me off. "You can drop me here," I said.

He didn't turn around. "Okay, bye-bye," he cried out, a little too loudly.

But the women turned their attention to me. Koral reached over the pug to give me an almost-hug. "*Nihyeh b'kesher,*" she said: *We'll be in touch.* She looked glamorous in her huge sunglasses, her blond hair and linen shirt. Eyal's mother paused her fevered prayers to twist herself around and face me. She was a pretty, petite woman, but today her face looked worn and crumpled. "Pray for him," she said, her thin hand reaching toward me. "We need to pray for him." She said it in English so I would be sure to understand. I nodded.

"*Yalla*, it's green," the father said, gesturing with his chin toward the stoplight. I hustled out of the car so they could pull away.

The university gates weren't gates in the grand sense. Just a security check manned by guards who asked if you were carrying a weapon. Young Jewish Israelis with handguns and walkie-talkies, aged between me and Eyal—twenty-three, twenty-four, twenty-five. They had finished their army service in combat units, taken their trips to Nepal, Patagonia, Amsterdam. Now, they worked security. With me, they were generally unconcerned. Most days they pushed their colorful sunglasses down low on their noses to half-heartedly check my face against my student ID, saying my name with attempted American accents, "Allison! What's up?" Everyone was so friendly to me.

I'd remarked on this during the second of the two unsuccessful dates I went on before I met Eyal—the one with the vegan law student. I was squinting into direct sunlight, shading my eyes so I could see him. He was one of those men whose approach to flirtatious banter becomes increasingly hostile as a date wears on. After he asked me if I ate corpses, and I said, "Yes, I take it you do not," keeping my face pleasant and neutral (you never know what a man will react badly to), I tried to infuse the conversation with a bit more goodwill. I'm always doing this: I think I can salvage anything. I'm often wrong. "It's lovely how everyone in Israel is so welcoming!" I said. This was the kind of observation that my Hebrew teacher loved to hear from me. How the campus security guards made sure I was comfortable, the bus drivers encouraged me as I sounded out Hebrew place-names, and strangers all over, when they heard my uncertain Hebrew, told me how good it was that I had come to Israel, how proud of myself I should be.

My date and I were drinking cappuccinos from paper cups.

"Do you understand that your experience isn't universal?" he said. Because of his shaved head, it was hard to tell where his forehead ended. "Like, being an Ashkenazi Jew in Israel is like being white in America. You do understand that, right?" Then he talked about how the architects of Zionism—Ashkenazi Jews from Europe, like my father's family—were obsessed with creating a European country when Israel was founded in 1948. Any immigrants who threatened this vision were essentially erased:

Jews from Yemen and Morocco had their babies confiscated by the state; Jews from Ethiopia were sterilized without their consent; Jews who emigrated from all over the Arab world were forced to live in crowded, slum-like conditions in so-called development towns and even in contested parts of East Jerusalem. "Like cannon fodder, you understand?" His pale bald head was sweating in the sun.

Some of this I had learned from my roommate, Talia, who was Moroccan on her dad's side and Yemenite on her mom's. Sitting on our patio, drinking milky coffee she had made for us, Talia told me about her parents growing up in East Jerusalem and South Tel Aviv respectively—places their parents, her grandparents, had been forced to live by the state. "Ashkenazim don't like when we use this word," she said, "but ghettos, basically." I'll admit I did feel myself prickle at the word "ghetto," remembering the whispered references to Jewish ghettos all over Europe. But what's interesting, Talia went on, is that her parents grew up around the sounds of Mizrachi Jewish life: grandmothers speaking various colloquial Arabics, men singing liturgical piyyut on Shabbat, and all the time, cassettes circulating of all the suppressed "Arab-style" music that was never played on the radio. "But I did not grow up in this soundscape," she said. Her parents made it to university—got out, some would say. "More education, more privilege, yes, but also more Ashkenazi, less roots, you know?" She dunked a cylindrical cookie, her favorite, into her coffee. "That's what I'm looking for in my music."

It was easy to forget, I suppose, that my experience of Israel might unfold in the shadow of other, less visible experiences. Although apparently there were lots of leftist men eager to remind me. "Not everyone is treated like us," the vegan was saying. "Not everyone is the right kind of Jew." He put "right" in air quotes.

I could have told him that I was in fact the "wrong" kind of Jew, lacking a Jewish mother. But the truth was, I liked how he saw me in that moment: as if I really belonged here.

We didn't text each other again.

The day Eyal took the train toward Gaza, the university guards seemed graver than usual as they checked my backpack for a weapon.

Once through, I melded into a group of what turned out to be English-speaking students headed to class. From the way they talked about a guest speaker—"He was an advisor to Moshe Dayan, it's crazy"—I guessed they were in the university's counterterrorism program.

One college-age boy said to another, "Do you think they'll green-light the Gaza invasion?" He was chewing gum.

"Dude, we should just bomb the shit out of them," the other said, in a way that made me sure he was American.

The words startled me more than any slur could. *Bomb the shit out of them.* As if it were all a game, as if my beloved weren't going there now, while these boys chewed gum in Tel Aviv.

Overhead, a seagull was calling out.

Early on in dating Eyal, his mother had sat down between me and Eyal on the couch to show me something on her phone. "Look at this," she said, holding her screen up to me. It was a video of Israeli soldiers kicking a soccer ball around with children. "Do they show you this? In Canada?"

"*Ima-a-a,*" Eyal groaned in good humor.

She shushed him. The children, she went on to explain to me, were Arabs. And people say the Israeli army is racist!

You can play soccer with Palestinians and still be racist, I thought about saying, but didn't as I looked for a stamp on the video—something that would indicate which news site it was from. But no, I realized after a moment, it was on her camera roll. One of the soldiers laughed. *"Yalla, achi!"* he called out. I knew the voice. "Wait, is this Eyal?" I took the phone from her.

"This is what I'm telling you!" she exclaimed.

On the couch next to me, Eyal was rolling his eyes. In the video, he was tapping a soccer ball with the inside of his foot. There he was, with two other soldiers in army boots, ballistic helmets, kneepads for getting low to take a shot, assault rifles by their sides, kicking a soccer ball with three young kids—no more than ten—in jeans and T-shirts. "Arabs!" his mom said, tapping the phone with a pink fingernail. "And Israel is racist? Arabs!"

Even at the time I understood that this was rhetorical. My status as an outsider—a Canadian and a wrong-half Jew—made me valuable for his mother to convince. But all I really cared about was that in the video, Eyal was awkwardly kicking the soccer ball in a slightly stooped motion I found familiar. His body in the world was already so familiar. A Palestinian boy yelled, "Goal!"

As I entered the university library out of the harsh sun and into the air-conditioning, I texted Eyal: I MISS YOU. What else to say? But I wanted to say more. I took a quick selfie, not particularly flattering—I looked a little bleary-eyed—but it was sincere, so I sent it.

He did not answer, which meant perhaps that he was sleeping already.

Or not sleeping.

∽ ∾

There are no seats on the train, so Eyal stands, crammed against a few infantry soldiers. Civilians with backpacks and rumpled dress shirts scroll through their phones or, if they are old, read the paper. Men and women with reading glasses, taking up all the seats as the train passes through the southern core of Tel Aviv.

A text alert dings on his phone. I MISS YOU, Allison has written, along with a selfie. Where is she? In the library maybe? Her eyes look sad, but she is still so beautiful. An open face.

He rubs his thumb over the image of her lips on his screen. He thinks but does not reply, *I miss you too.*

He closes his phone as more texts from her come through. Much as he wants to read them all now, he'll save them for later, same as all the handwritten notes she gives him. It's comforting to think of all her words accumulating—unopened, waiting for him.

He wishes he knew more poetry. When he looks for poems in Hebrew, he Googles "beautiful poetry" and gets mostly inspiration quotes—nothing that gives language to all his unnameable feelings. Well, maybe it's better that way.

The train begins to clear as commuters get off on the last stops in Tel Aviv. Then south. Lod, Yavne, Ashdod. At each station in the south, more soldiers get on. Warriors, logistics girls. Everyone on the phone with their commander or their mom; everyone headed south.

In the south, there's more patriotism, more open support for the army. On a platform, Bnei Akiva scouts hold up signs that read THANK YOU, SOLDIERS, FOR GUARDING OVER US. Girls in long skirts wave books of psalms.

He looks around for someone he knows, but the train is so packed it's hard to see beyond the two infantry guys standing next to him in the crowded aisle. One of them is on the phone with his ima. "But, Ima, I can't go to the doctor's appointment." He speaks Hebrew with a slight French accent, one of the newer immigrants from Paris maybe. This is confirmed when he switches to French. Allie would understand it all, but Eyal's high school French only lets him understand a few words. *Because something-something in Gaza, Mama!* A few people on the train laugh. He can't go to the doctor, lady, because he'll be in fucking Gaza. He wonders if Allison would find that funny or just sad.

In the unit group chat, his commander has sent coordinates to the location of the base where they're assembling. Commander Avishi will give more details in person. It's going to be a mess, Eyal is sure of it. His stomach is going crazy. Maybe he had too much coffee. His stomach and his heart are pounding, making it hard, he's finding, to focus on any one thought.

He's seen images of Gaza from other wars. Filth and chaos. Anxious-looking soldiers trying to effectively scan a maze of apartment buildings. Ima is probably praying. He remembers being a kid and her holding him close, running with him, pressing him to her. How old was he? Maybe six? Kita aleph. She was running with him across a street. He doesn't remember the explosion. Later, she showed him a photo of the exploded bus. Body parts in the street. The Arabs did it. Maybe that was the year they got the dog.

The train chimes as it pulls into the Ashkelon station. Why is his stomach being so crazy? If Charlotte gets too many treats, she'll fart so loud she can wake herself up from a nap.

When two Arabs board the train, everyone notices. He feels it. Two teenagers. *Shabab*, they would say. Slim guys in tacky, overembellished jeans that sit low on their hips. In high school, he used to have these super-indulgent fantasies about saving a girl in his class from a terrorist, sometimes by fighting the Arab off and sometimes by sacrificing himself. He's had similar fantasies of saving a unitmate—an act that would finally close the distance he feels between himself and the other guys.

Allie was devastated when he got the order to come down to the border, but Eyal was secretly relieved. Part of him had worried that everyone would be called down except him. When Avishi has to send someone away—to a ceremony or medic training—it's always Eyal he chooses. Why? Why is he the soldier that can be spared? Is he less reliable than the others? More annoying? Even as he asks himself, he doesn't want to know the answer.

One of the Arabs whispers to the other. The train announces the next stop, Eyal's stop.

He pushes down the swell of an unnamed feeling mounting in him.

You have to be careful. To feel too much was dangerous. He knows that. Whatever he feels—dread, fear, annoyance, excitement, hope—he has learned to regard it as an object he can place back on a high shelf.

ာ ာ

At my graduate student locker in the library, I took down the books I needed (postmodern literary theory, late antiquity rabbinic commentaries) and settled into my designated library cubicle. I was lucky—mine was by a window. Granted, it looked out onto an unswept concrete roof, but in the distance I sometimes caught a glimmer of the Mediterranean over the high palm trees. I would stay here making notes until it was time for class.

I checked my phone one more time—nothing new from Eyal— before putting it away.

The danger, I read, *is to try and repair longing with belonging.* I was reading Svetlana Boym's treatment of the various forms of nostalgia—a book way beyond the boundaries of my discipline. Back in New York, my research had been characterized by a fairly traditional mode of philology, that dusty history and science of language. However, in recent months I had begun edging into something closer to poetics. It was with some trepidation that my mentors—dedicated to ancient languages, systematic in their grammatical studies on historical linguistics—watched me tend toward theorists who seemed more concerned with meaning than evidence. Once, a professor had called my mind "agile," and I had gone home crying, because I understood he meant "agile" as opposed to the more favorable "rigorous."

I had entered the discipline of philology for the purest reason: philologos. *Lover of words.* And I really did love words. We all—all of us, the students and professors—shared this obsession. I love the field I have tried to call my own, because it allows me to pursue a belief that words have lives. I was taught that if you study a word closely enough—if you make note of its appearances (in the Bible, for example) and, conversely, the places it does not appear even if you might expect it; if you look at its changes over time; if you pursue its cognates, not just in all the historical modes of Hebrew but also in the other languages nearby on the Semitic language tree—if you do all of this, you may begin to reach down into the roots of the word, and, in that dark and secret dirt, you may find the roots of an idea.

Take, for example, Tsion. Or, if you like, Zion. In the narrative books of the Bible, "Zion" refers to a particular geographic region of Jerusalem—the section where King David built his residence. However, in later books of the Bible such as the prophets, "Zion" shifts from a concrete referent to something more metonymic as it comes to refer to the entire city of Jerusalem. The way, for example, "Hollywood" might refer to an area of Los Angeles or, more abstractly, the movie industry generally. This is interesting to the rabbis. (Really, everything is interesting to the rabbis. I can't imagine anyone before or since having read the Hebrew Bible as attentively as these men did in the first centuries of the Common Era.) They note that "Zion" might echo the word "*zayon*," which refers to a dry and ruined place. Therefore, the reasoning goes, "Zion" becomes a shorthand for Jerusalem only in the later books of the Bible that emerge during exile. Only when the city is lost and smashed, only when its fields are salted and its people in bondage—only then is Jerusalem called "Zion." *By the rivers of Babylon, there* (not *here*, where I am in my heart, but *there*, where I am in the flesh, in this strange land) *we sat down, yea we wept, when we remembered Zion.*

We can witness how the word "Zion" grew beyond its original referent and into a shape that contained Jewish longing, Jewish nostalgia. It is a dry word—dry enough to absorb centuries of weeping. By contrast, the word "Zionism" seems to hold so little longing, replacing it, Boym might say, with belonging.

The spoken reason I'd come to Israel was to spend a few months sharpening my Modern Hebrew skills and TA-ing a class on modes of rabbinic storytelling. I have never quite gotten over the Talmud's approach to narrative—circling stories upon stories, answering one question then shifting to another, or answering one question while secretly posing another. They begin talking about purity but end up addressing intention; they establish parameters for baking bread with neighbors, all while tacitly questioning the social contract.

But the unspoken reasons for my coming to Israel were, like all truths, more complicated and less clear. Surely, I came to Israel to find a new version of myself. Almost as soon as I landed, Israelis made me feel that I was doing something important and special just by being here. Neither I nor my sister had been on Birthright—a free trip to Israel for anyone who has so much as a Jewish grandparent. Or, not exactly free: You submit yourself to light indoctrination in exchange for your plane ticket. Still, not a bad deal. But I did not go. If you asked her today, Erica would say that she boycotted for political reasons, but I don't think that's true. I think her politics emerged later. I think she avoided Birthright for the same reason I did: because we found real Jews intimidating. They all went to the same summer camps and talked openly about their anxiety medication. Whatever made them a people, Erica and I didn't have it. But now I was finding an alternative to being a Canadian Jew: being an Israeli. I didn't need to know about the religious day schools of Montreal to be absorbed into an Israeli family. I simply needed to live here.

Here, I found vibrance. Sitting at the tables of friends I'd only just met. Their mothers telling me I was pretty, their fathers grilling chicken hearts for me to eat. Warmth. I had never before experienced such warmth as I did in Israel. The boundaries between Jews—between us— were not rigid. Even today, after all these years living here, I am struck by this difference when I go back to Canada to visit my parents. How cold it is there. Not just the weather, but the heart. In Israel, everything runs on shared history and personal connections. You find a bank teller you like? Get her cell-phone number. When the bank messes up your account and freezes your funds because the government has mistakenly indicated you did not pay your social security contribution because a clerk accidentally inverted two numbers of your national identification number on a form—these kinds of bureaucratic mix-ups are inevitable, especially for a new immigrant—that phone number will come in handy. Don't worry: that same clerk will be texting you ten years later to help her nephew get into the elite combat intelligence unit that your husband was in. In Hebrew, it's called "*protectsiah*"—this web of connections and, some might say, of privilege, spun between some Jews, to the exclusion of others.

But what I'm describing, really, is a culture. In Israel, I have found a culture. It may be problematic, but it's mine. In Canada, I did not have a culture. My parents' ancestors gave up so much to become white. When I imagine them, all of them, they are on ships from the Old World, lightening their loads by throwing my inheritance overboard. Gone, Yiddish. Gone, Gaelic. Gone, embroidered tunics. Gone, hair covering. Gone, folk magic. Gone, songs their mothers taught them. All of it, sinking to the bottom of the Atlantic Ocean. This is lighter, they say to each other, isn't it? Now they are in jeans. Now they are Canadian, saving up to buy single-family properties and put their parents in nursing homes. This is progress. Those were customs. Now we are white. "Did our ancestors financially benefit from the slave trade?" Erica once asked my parents while they were watching a documentary about the American Civil War.

My father sputtered. "Good lord, I would hope not."

When my father married a gentile, his parents did not hold a funeral for him as some religious, anti-assimilation Jews would do. No, they paid for the wedding to happen in a church. They celebrated. If you are a fair European Jew, this is one way to stay safe: hide so well that not even you can see yourself.

Is that what tugged at me as soon as I got here? The promise that I, at last, might have a culture?

∽ ∾

After getting off the train, Eyal waits to board the bus that will take him to base. In front of him, two combat engineers are talking about the prime minister. "Will he send us in?" one asks. For sure, the other says, he's got balls.

The bus drives along a highway, past broken fields of summer-dry crops. He presses his forehead to the window. On the army radio station, a woman is talking about the number of reservists called up. Next to Eyal, a round-faced girl is leaving a voice memo for her commander. "The bus is ten minutes away from base," she fudges. Her voice is nasal and clipped.

Someone says loudly, "Look, Gaza City."

Eyal squints out the window. Past the crops and the churned red dirt, he can see the tips of white buildings close to the Mediterranean Sea. There it is.

He presses his phone against the blurry bus window to take a photo, not that it will show up as anything. He wishes he could show Saba, but his grandfather is dead almost a year now, his memory for a blessing. He lived to see Eyal complete basic training. That was something. That had mattered. One of the last meals they all had together was a Shabbat dinner just after Eyal had been released from basic. Ima had made something vaguely Asian: sweet-sticky sauce from a supermarket bottle. But there was normal challah bread, which Saba placed a napkin over when he made the blessings for wine, holding up the wineglass and everyone at the table—ceremoniously—standing too. They never did this unless Saba came over for dinner. They had not done it since he died.

It was a special meal. All his childhood, he'd heard about Saba in the early days of the country. Evading the British, fighting the Arabs. Stories Eyal knew by heart like a private mythology. His own father was less of a storyteller, offering mostly images when it came to describing his service—feet dangling out of a chopper over Ramallah. Now it was Eyal's turn. His grandpa sat at the head of the table. Eyal sat on one side and his father sat on the other.

When they stood to bless the wine, Eyal did not have a kippa on. All the other men had them—produced from a box kept somewhere with the free ones handed out at weddings and bnei mitzvah. But not Eyal. "Go get a kippa!" Ima urged, almost whining, embarrassed in front of her father, who created a sense of occasion just by being there.

Eyal gestured in a way that said, *Stop it, no way.* He didn't want to be a little boy running around where his mama said. He'd completed basic. He'd lost weight and gotten no sleep. He'd learned to crawl with a weapon, to shoot it, to withstand hunger and exhaustion. He was not a child.

"Nu, Eyal," Aba started.

"No need," Saba said, silencing the table. He held the glass of wine in one hand. The other hand he raised up. Eyal understood. He lowered the crown of his head so that his grandpa, who was shrinking every year, every month, toward death, could cover his head. His kippa was his grandfather's hand. And they stood like that—two men, two fighters—one shielding the other from the presence of God while Aba looked on with so much pride. "Blessed are you, king of the universe," Saba intoned in his rich and archaic tenor. He was born in Jerusalem, as was his own grandfather, and that man's grandfather before him. All of Eyal's other grandparents had come from Eastern Europe, casting off different versions of Yiddish when they arrived to begin again in Hebrew. But Saba was different. "Did you grow up speaking Arabic?" Eyal asked him when he was young, maybe in kindergarten.

Saba had been more annoyed than Eyal expected. "Why would you ask that?" His voice rose a little. "Why would you ask me that?" he repeated. Then: "We're Jews." As if Jews couldn't speak Arabic. He was leaning forward in his chair.

Eyal faltered. "I was just curious," he said, regretting he had asked.

Saba settled back down in his leather living room chair. "Well, my mother spoke a little," he conceded. "Just enough to do her shopping."

Eyal didn't ask about Arabic again.

∽ ∾

After an hour in the library, the sun was high enough in the sky that it cast a long, hot band across my library desk. I packed up my computer and headed to the building next door for my first class of the day: Modern Hebrew, my favorite because it was the easiest. The instructors were not, strictly speaking, affiliated with the university. My teacher was a middle-aged woman who half-heartedly wrote vocabulary words on the board as she spoke to us (in Hebrew, to be fair) about her neighborhood, her grandchildren, her late husband. She wore patterned scarves and had the kind of thick body I think of as maternal, although my own mother is more athletic than I am.

Her name was Smadar, a biblical word for "blossoming." The syllables sounded heavy to my ear. Smadar. Fleshy dogwood petals drooping with rain.

There were about twenty other students in my class. Some graduate students, some undergrads on semesters abroad, and some were recent Jewish immigrants learning Hebrew for their new lives.

Smadar came over to my desk as soon as I sat down. "*Hu b'aza?*" she asked, her voice at once probing and tender—such a distinctly Israeli set of inflections. *Is he in Gaza?* An acute intimacy passed through us. One woman to another.

"*Ken, b'derekh,*" I said. *Yes, he's on his way.* I made eye contact, and then I looked away. It was impossible to know how I felt, when more than anything I was so aware of her looking at me.

She reached a hand over my hand. The other students in the classroom made a big show of flipping through their textbooks as they pretended not to listen. Her hand was soft and her nails unpainted. She had been delighted when she found out about my soldier. She knew because of the slang I used without realizing it was distinctly army slang—turns of phrase I had heard from Eyal. Some of it she didn't understand, because as soldiers age out of service their slang enters the mainstream and new slang develops. "They're in *karnaf*," I had said once, referring to two people ignoring each other. She had laughed. "What are you trying to say?" she asked me, because that word means "rhinoceros." I told her that I knew, but I meant the word in the sense of, like, *I see you, but I don't see you.* She had cocked her head then, looked at me with a sharpened interest. "Do you have a boyfriend in the army?" she asked. I couldn't suppress my smile when I nodded. I liked the idea that I had revealed it without realizing it; that even on the level of language, I was changing.

Now, there was a special understanding between us. Her late husband had served in every Israeli war through Sinai. Smadar squeezed my hand. "*Yihyeh beseder*," she said to me, only to me. *It will be okay.*

❦ ❦

Everyone is gathered around Avishi at some picnic tables on base. All around, different units are in tight little scrums getting briefed by commanders. "We'll get word about mobilizing to the border soon," Avishi says. "Until then, stay in readiness."

Eyal's arms are crossed, and he nods. Sounds like more waiting.

"So, more waiting?" someone asks.

Avishi shrugs. "For now."

Eyal was the last one to make it to base. This happens a lot, since he's the only one in his unit from Ramat Aviv Gimel. When they first introduced themselves last year, in a circle just like this, Avishi had whistled when Eyal said where he was from. "Do you have a pool?" Avishi asked, sounding kind of young even though he was at least twenty-two. Eyal thought it was a joke; he laughed. Everyone looked at him, waiting for an answer. They thought he was rich. He told them no, he didn't have a pool. Even now, a year later, he knows he has a slight film of glamour because of where he lives, and the misconception that his family is loaded.

Off on the base's firing ranges, he can hear the percussion of live fire drills. Beyond that, the echoes of mortars being shot into Gaza.

When old men talk about the army, they talk about brotherhood. For all the suffering that comes with being a combat soldier—as opposed to those spoiled jobnik desk soldiers—it's worth it for the sense of brotherhood. He has heard it his whole life: how putting your life in someone's hands, and holding his in yours, creates a bond like no other. But he has never quite felt the closeness he hoped he'd find in the army.

Now and then he'll feel surges of it, sure. When they suffer together on a long surveillance mission, for example, silent for days, shitting into plastic bags lining their combat helmets. There are moments where he can feel them all bonded in shared experiences. But always, when they come back to base, there is that distance again. Are they holding back from him? Or is he resisting them? He's not one of those bullied soldiers, that's for sure. He's not some tragic reject who ends up shooting himself on guard duty, thank you. Still, he stands apart. He's closest with his commander, Avishi. In more vulnerable moments, he tells himself that this is only because Avishi pities him.

He misses Allison already. *Please*, he thinks, *let me see her again.*

◦◦ ◦◦

After class, I checked my phone to find a single text from Eyal: I AM SO FAR AWAY.

Five

Eyal and I had begun in the season of memorials. By summer, he was invading Gaza. But we began in the spring, a time for national holidays of remembrance.

We would never have met had his commander not sent him to that Holocaust memorial ceremony. That same week, the university held Holocaust memorials on campus. Old women with fragile, shaking hands addressed the students. They spoke of the death marches in Poland; how they walked with bloody feet through dark forests; how the bodies were piled like wood logs with nobody left to recite the mourners' kaddish, the prayer that nobody can say for herself. "It happened once and it can happen again," a woman with a Viennese accent said. "That is why we have Israel." After, we stood for the national anthem. In my journal from the time, I taped a graphic torn from the memorial program: a frayed yellow Judenstern patch morphing into the angular blue star of the Israeli flag.

It's not that I was unaware of how these images were being used. I understood the manipulative quality of the narrative—a straight line from the gas chambers to the creation of the Jewish state. I understood, and yet, I liked how the ceremony made me feel: the swell of grief and pride, the sense of belonging. My college boyfriend—a mean-spirited boy about whom my only fond memory is a particularly lovely freckle on his left inner thigh—once said to me, "Don't you get tired of being so much smarter than everyone?" His was a bitter, rhetorical question not meant to be answered. But the answer is yes. Yes, I do get tired of it. I get so very tired of outthinking myself. So yes, I was aware of the dangers of an ironclad national narrative, but I wanted to suspend my understanding and just let myself feel.

In Hebrew class, Smadar told us about memorial decorum. "There will be sirens," she said. First for the Holocaust remembrance, then a week later, for fallen Israeli soldiers. The custom, she explained, was to stop and stand out of respect. Cars pull over on the highways, buses too. Everyone stands for the duration of the siren. "But if it's a rocket siren then go to the bomb shelter," she added jovially.

I was alarmed. "How will we know the difference?"

"The rocket siren goes up and down," she said, in English so we'd be sure to understand. "For the memorial it's just one note." Then she imitated the memorial siren—a flat note held for a long interval.

Another student—a Russian woman in her late twenties, early thirties maybe, who had immigrated to Israel—piped up. "The rocket siren is more like this," she said, and then imitated the falling and rising sound of a siren. Later that year, when the fighters of Gaza began to shoot rockets into Israel, I would find that her impression was very good. She had captured the eerie quality of those arpeggios.

The day after I met Eyal on the bus, I wrote a Facebook post about the visibility of soldiers in Israel. This was something I did about once a month—writing out an anecdote into a few paragraphs, posting it along with a photo: the time I got on the wrong bus and ended up at a late antiquity Jewish graveyard in the ancient port of Jaffa (photo of the headstones facing the sea); how I bought a used office chair off the Israeli equivalent of Craigslist from a man whose divorce was finalized that day, so he threw in a free desk lamp (photo of me and the man, flashing peace signs); and, in this case, my initial shock at watching teenage soldiers commute around the city with firearms, and how that shock was softening into familiarity (photo of the Judenstern patch morphing into Israeli flag).

I wrote how the soldiers were so ubiquitous they became invisible—the more I saw them, the less I noticed them. I noted how the country celebrated its boys with a predatory reverence; I refrained from referencing the theories of the French thinker Georges Bataille, who himself noted that the victims of human sacrifice were venerated before being offered up.

Instead, I described an ad that had begun to circulate that spring. In it, a troop of young men, scruffy and good-spirited, march through the chic streets of Tel Aviv, much to the shock of the cosmopolitan cafe-goers who look up from their cappuccinos in surprise. The rugged young men are out of place. They carry stretchers and contact radios. *What are they doing in Tel Aviv?* the viewer is supposed to ask. This is clearly a unit's initiation march—dozens of kilometers as a final team-building exercise. They usually do this in the rural north or desolate desert. Why in Tel Aviv? The answer comes when the boys climb up the stairs of an urban apartment and knock on a door that is answered by a lone boy in a leg cast. Contextually—I explained in my post, proud of the ways I was learning to read the place where I was living—you understand that he was hurt in some kind of training exercise, thus was unable to participate in the final march, at the end of which he would have received his unit beret. So they have brought the march to him. The soldiers draw into a circle; they are singing; the music of the ad is building; their assault rifles bounce against their thighs as they move together around the boy with his leg in a cast, the living room barely big enough to contain them. "We are with you," the ad says. The ad is for a cell-phone carrier. The only woman in the room is the mother standing off to the side who cries as she watches the young men dance.

Talia rolled her eyes when the ad came on. "You see that?" she said, jutting her delicate chin toward the screen. "Women are the national womb." As long as I've known her—even today—Talia has struck me as someone who is a little trapped. She sees racism and misogyny around her, but this knowledge has never given her more options.

In my Facebook post, I mentioned Eyal, although I did not call him by name. *On a bus, I met a soldier—he seemed at once very young and very old. I asked him if it was hard in the army. "Hard on the soul," he said, but I could tell by the way he said it that he was proud.*

The post was especially well received by Jewish girls I knew from undergrad. I LOVE HOW YOU SEE THE COUNTRY! one commented. YOU NOTICE EVERYTHING! These girls and I were beginning to share a set of references, a private language. Another commented teasingly: SO WAS THIS SOLDIER CUTE? MAYBE YOU'LL FINALLY GET YOUR BIRTHRIGHT ROMANCE? WINK!

I responded with a laughing emoji. I DOUBT HE'LL TEXT ME, I wrote, even as I hoped he would.

I noticed that Erica liked the post but didn't leave a comment.

I thought about Eyal's words. *Hard on the soul.* That's what he'd said of the army. *Hard on the soul.* I wanted to know more. I wanted to get closer.

On jogs in Tel Aviv, I let myself imagine that anyone who saw me running—young, fit, determined—thought I was a soldier in training. There were girl warriors in the IDF. They were a minority, although disproportionately represented in the army Instagram account, which loved to post pretty girls with enormous weapons, smiling in the desert sun. The strategy was obvious: these attractive teenagers were being used to soften, even eroticize, the image of the IDF to outsiders. Still, I saw them and wondered who I might have been had I come here earlier. Fresh-faced and capable, tough and sweet, as I protected the borders of my country and braided my unitmates' hair.

"Do you think about staying longer?" Talia asked one evening.

We were on our small balcony. She was rolling a cigarette; I was hanging my laundry to dry. "I think about it all the time," I said truthfully. "It feels like I'm just starting, and it's almost time to leave."

"So stay," she said, lighting her cigarette. "That way, I won't have to find another roommate." She laughed.

"Don't tempt me," I said.

For two days after giving Eyal my number, I checked my phone nervously, disappointed each time I didn't see a text from the soldier. Snap out of it, I scolded myself. I was acting like a teenager, like someone his age.

You're only here for a few months, I reminded myself. Just a few months. It was absurd to get caught up in any of this. So why was I reviewing postings for last-minute grants and inquiring about the process of getting an Israel-based professor on my dissertation committee?

∾ ∾

After Eyal got her number on the bus, he waited two stops so he wouldn't look like he was following her, then got off at some random highway interchange. He stood on the sidewalk, not noticing as people brushed up against him, and stared at his phone, unbelieving. He had saved her as ALLISON CANADA. He was not where he was supposed to be. He would be late for the ceremony. It didn't matter. He'd get shit for it, but it didn't matter. He had her number.

He didn't text her that first day. Too nervous, yes, but also he wanted to savor all the possibility. He'd gotten the number of this beautiful woman—for she was a woman—and even if this was as far as it went, even if he texted and she didn't respond, maybe that was enough. Just the possibility was enough. Just remembering life had possibilities.

He spent the rest of the day drafting and erasing dozens of texts to her. Somehow, he made it to the Holocaust ceremony, where a survivor in a wheelchair told elementary school students about the ovens and death marches. He stood where he was supposed to stand, saluted when he was supposed to salute, then got on the bus back to his base, all the while obsessing over variations on the same unsent message. *Hi, it's me.*

The base he returned to felt drab and depressing in ways it had not before. Or, in ways he hadn't previously let himself notice. The camo netting, the crooked doors, the scuffed metal trailers, the blocky script on the buildings. Every brutal detail told him that he could not outthink this place. The army owned him. He thought about her tongue between her teeth. Her eyebrows furrowing to listen to him when he talked about basic training. He felt that, briefly, he had been a whole person. A unique person.

That night he went to bed in a damp-smelling bunk thinking about her. He still hadn't texted. What to say? He didn't know what to say.

When he did finally write his first text to Allison, it was a group effort. Everyone was hanging out in a spot with old couches behind the base trailers. They'd just gotten back from arresting someone—some Arab who kept trying to bring his sheep to water on settlement lands. The man was crying when they handcuffed him. "This is the water of my father," the Arab had attempted in Hebrew. Nobody responded to this. The settlers who called it in looked on approvingly.

Now, Eyal sat on a broken sofa next to Avishi. A few other guys were on old plastic chairs and benches made from plywood, all snacking on chips that a South African synagogue had sent to the base as a care package. There was camo netting draped all around and a unit's insignia—not his—painted lopsided on the back of a trailer. What was supposed to be a snake had a head that was way too big. This was his whole world. Mud green and piss yellow. Then there's this girl. Pink tongue and minty hair ribbons.

"Okay, focus," said Avishi, their lanky commander, smoking with his long legs stretched out in front of him. "We are going to text Allison."

"Focus, bro," someone said, and slapped Eyal on the shoulder.

It was a little foreign for Eyal, being inside the jovial camaraderie. Not his usual place in a group. But now, thanks to Allison, here he was at the center. It was nice. Not that any of the guys had a clue about how to text her.

They argued as Eyal stared at her name in his phone. "Tell her you've killed Arabs," someone said.

"Bro, shut up," came the reply.

"What, American Jews love that."

"He said she's Canadian."

"Quiet," Avishi cut in, so everyone was. Then, nodding in Eyal's direction, "How old is she?"

"She's older," Eyal said cagily. He fiddled with his phone as he spoke, texting Gil, the only friend from high school who'd ever had luck with girls. HOW DO I START WITH THE CANADIENNE? he wrote.

"What? Like, twenty?" Avishi asked. He was twenty-two.

Eyal felt suddenly ashamed. This was too far out of the norm. She was so much older than him. Eight years ago, she was his age and he was eleven. Eight years was a lot of time. A lot of time to have fucked other guys. "Twenty-three," he lied, which got a few appreciative whistles.

"Wow-wow, an older woman!"

He got a text back from Gil: JUST SAY, HEY, IT'S EYAL FROM THE BUS. I'VE BEEN THINKING ABOUT YOU.

"Nu," Eyal said, "what do you think of this?" He read the text that Gil suggested.

"Nice," Avishi nodded, his mouth downturned in approval. "That's nice."

༄ ༄

On the third day, he texted me. The message came through from an un-known number: HI IT'S EYAL. Then, FROM THE BUS. Then, I'VE BEEN THINKING OF YOU. By then he was already back at the army for another ten days of rotation—this time, he was on a base in the West Bank. (This was the routine that the Gaza invasion would eventually disrupt.)

Embarrassed that I'd been hoping for his text, I waited an hour to respond: HI! I HOPE YOU'RE HAVING AN EASY WEEK. I deliberated over which emoji to include. I ended up going with a strawberry.

ལྕ ལྕ

When he got her reply sixty-seven minutes later, he kissed his phone screen. She'd sent a strawberry emoji. Adorable!

ལྕ ལྕ

From then on, we texted every single day.

BOKER TOV, he wrote the next morning at 8:00 a.m. WHAT ARE YOU READING?

At the time, I was working on a lecture I'd been invited to give con-cerning rabbinic commentary on the book of Ruth. She is the Bible's most famous convert: "Your people will be my people," Ruth tells her grieving mother-in-law. Although that translation is impossibly clunky next to Hebrew, which says all that in four perfect syllables: *amekh ami*. It is perhaps my favorite feature of Semitic languages—that you can form certain sentences without a verb; the Hebrew literally reads, "your people my people." The verb "to be" is implied.

However, none of this struck me as a particularly romantic response to give the young soldier texting me, so I told him I was reading the *Odyssey*. DO YOU KNOW THE STORY? I asked.

NO, he wrote back. PLEASE TELL IT TO ME. PLEASE, PLEASE TELL IT TO ME.

So I did. Book by book. The longest text messages I will ever send.

Odysseus fought in a war, a terrible, pointless war. The journey home is not far. But years and years after the war ends, he is still traveling. Coming home, it turns out, is not that simple. There are obstacles—in the world and in his heart. He is slurping down oysters with island goddesses; he is peeping on a teenage princess doing her laundry; he is wrist-deep in blood, fighting back the hungry ghost of his dead mother. And meanwhile, his son is wading around the kiddie pool of the Mediterranean; his wife is weeping, always weeping, until Athena shows up and, mercifully, puts her back to sleep.

I've always had a soft spot for the Hellenic world, which is more relevant than many would imagine to the study of late antiquity Jewish texts. The Jews always had one eye on the Greeks. What is the reclined, storytelling holiday of Passover if not a symposium? But this was an application of classics that I had never imagined: flirting with a soldier.

TELL ME MORE ABOUT ODYSSEUS, he texted back. PLEASE, MORE.

That first week, Eyal sent more photos than typed messages. Photos of the base's stray cat who subsisted entirely on the hot dogs none of the soldiers wanted to eat. Photos of the sunset over a Palestinian village. Photos of blood on a cement floor (combat medic practice, he said). Photos that pretended to be of his boots, but which were really photos of his assault rifle.

We had not yet gone on a date, but already we were beginning to reach toward each other throughout the day. When I noticed a vibrant piece of graffiti or overheard an amusing turn of phrase, it was Eyal I thought first to tell. He sent me photos of sunrises and wildflowers. I punctuated my texts with the strawberry emoji.

You need to tell him, I reminded myself. *You need to tell him that you're leaving at the end of the summer.* Was I a bad person for wanting him to like me? *I'll tell him*, I reasoned. *I'll tell him when we meet in person.*

One week after I met Eyal on the bus, I went to an outdoor memorial ceremony for Israel's war dead. Violin music played through loudspeakers as the crowd watched slides of smiling men in uniform, young mothers holding their babies, children on bikes. These were the dead. Some fell in combat, others in terror attacks. Their images were projected on a suburban building. In the crowd, teenage soldiers held hands with other teenage soldiers while photographs of dead teenage soldiers flashed on the wall. Name, birth date, death date. All his age. All so young.

I texted Eyal, I'M AT A MEMORIAL CEREMONY AND THINKING OF YOU.

He replied, YOU SEE DEAD SOLDIERS AND THINK OF ME?

Fuck. That's it, I told myself. It was over. Before it began, it was over. *You see dead soldiers and think of me?* Was he right? Was I rendering him into a symbol? I was too embarrassed to respond to his text.

A few minutes later, he wrote again: I THINK OF YOU WHEN I EAT STRAW-BERRIES.

I made another Facebook post, this one about the weeks of memorial. *Israel's memorial holidays are punctuated by sirens made to sound distinct from air-raid sirens*, I wrote, as if I'd ever heard an air-raid siren. *These long, sustained notes are issued from speakers in every corner of every city.* I wrote about hearing the Holocaust siren on campus, standing in place with my books; I wrote about watching from my window with Talia as the cars on our busy boulevard pulled over and the drivers got out for the memorial siren. *You stop and stand and find out how long a minute can last.*

The accompanying image I used was from a news site: a highway filled with still cars, their drivers getting out to stand for the memorial siren.

My father sent me an email in response to my post—he never got Facebook; Mom must have showed it to him. He was restrained as ever: *Your descriptions are very salient.* It was a sweet email. Or at least, a courteous one. So why did it leave me feeling somehow rejected? What did I want him to say that he couldn't say? *I'm proud of you.* Or maybe *I'm sorry.* As if my writing the right words would crack open his heart like a spell and make him love me the way I'd always hoped for.

My whole childhood, I only saw him cry when watching documentaries about the world wars, not even when his own father died.

Before my flight from Montreal to Israel my parents had thrown me a farewell dinner. We'd reserved a big table at one of the Plateau's interchangeable farm-to-table bistros. By this point in my life, I hadn't lived in Montreal in years; still, the atmosphere was lively with aunts, cousins, and a few high school friends who had stayed in our city. Erica brought her new love interest—Cee. They met through friends, Erica said, which I assumed meant online. My father and I had been carefully primed on Cee's nonbinary pronouns in an email from Erica. *Cee uses they/them pronouns*, the email said. *For example: Cee is a social worker. They are capable and compassionate. I care for them.* I didn't know why my mom wasn't on that email. Not true: I did know. Erica and Mom had already talked about this; maybe had even written the email together.

My father and I practiced beforehand. This was years before the university would mandate gender-sensitivity training for all employees. "Cee seems nice," he said. "Erica says that they . . . has, no, they *have* family in Costa Rica."

Then I tried, "As long as they are nice to Erica, I am okay with them."

We spoke slowly and deliberately, scared of what we might reveal of ourselves should we mess up.

At dinner, we'd all been struck by how stunning Cee was: closely shaved dark hair and a bone structure I wanted to call avian, perfectly disrupted by a ring through their septum like a bull. Next to them, Erica looked plain. For a moment, I felt a fierce tenderness for my sister. She had always been the little one. Throughout our childhood, her hand was small in mine as we walked home from school each afternoon. In winter, the street plows left great drifts that we always walked over instead of around. Sometimes the snow held, and sometimes we fell through—me up to my chin, Erica disappearing completely. "Hurry!" I'd cry out, pulling her up from the drift with wooly mittens. "Hurry!" she'd echo back, as we ran the last few blocks home in swishing snow pants. We had a private rule that we had to be home before the sunset, which in the coldest months was no later than 4:30 p.m.

Erica and Cee held hands throughout dinner, offering observations on gender and polyamory. I ordered the lamb chops and, as the wine was poured, answered questions about how long I'd be in Israel (five months unless I decided to stay longer, haha) and if I was nervous (mostly excited).

"*L'chayim*," my father said, standing with a glass of the house red. "To Allison, who continues to toil toward her PhD." I'd always found him distant, but he did, I had to admit, always create a sense of occasion—presenting birthday and Chanukah presents with gravity and flourish. Only once did I attend a lecture of his on theoretical math. Sitting in the back of his classroom, I'd been shocked to hear his passion when discussing the secret narratives of the numbered world. "Next year in Israel," he said, recycling one of the few jokes we had premised on Jewishness.

"Or in Palestine," Cee chimed in. The way they said the words, I could tell it was meant to be lighthearted. Perhaps they were used to existing in circles where "Palestine" was not an unspoken word.

My parents, whose only true politics was being agreeable, smiled awkwardly.

I frowned at Erica, who whispered something to Cee.

I flew out the next day.

Without telling my family, I applied for additional funding; I inquired with the professor I was TA-ing for if he might consider sitting on my dissertation committee. None of that meant that I would stay on beyond the summer. It was just exploratory, I told myself. Nothing more than that.

Homages to fallen soldiers continued to dominate Israeli TV and every social media feed I had. One clip kept showing up: a girlfriend, gorgeous in her distress, struggling through a eulogy at her boyfriend's funeral. All around her were men and women in uniform. She looked slight in her oversized black T-shirt—one of his, I realized as I watched her at the podium, her hands covering her face, barely able to speak. She let out a small moan. "My beloved, my life," she said. She spoke not to us but to the boyfriend who had died on a raid. A stone smashed in his face. "You said you would guard yourself—"

I had heard this a lot in Hebrew. "Guard yourself" is the literal translation; another option is "Take care of yourself," but the word "guard" conveys more of the Hebrew associations, which can mean to *protect* (as in a city) or even *uphold* (as in a commandment). *He keeps Kosher; he defends Jerusalem.* Both use the same Hebrew verb and both give the sense of a divine act. *We are guarding over you* was a caption I saw not infrequently when soldiers posted photos of themselves at one border or another, smiling up at the camera with their weapons in the frame.

"You said you would guard yourself, but where . . ." Here, her weeping overtook her and she slumped over the podium. A woman wailed out from the audience. A girl in uniform moved to help her, but a man gestured no. The grieving girl gasped out, "But where are you now? Oh, my beloved, my life, my life."

Her grief was enormous. Total. It was impossible to look away. Watching the clip, I cried with her. I was aware that there was something distracting in it, if that's the right word, "distracting"—that her grief, which was true, obscured other truths and erased other questions. What are the dynamics of power? What structures, bigger than any one person, are driving this violence? What is the history? Where is the money? Who is erased? I was aware of all this, and yet I felt the tug of her beautifully contorted face. What would it feel like to let those questions dissipate?

My sister often spoke in terms of "making and holding space": for feelings, for marginalized voices, for whatever. But now I found myself losing space. Turns out, it feels good.

When the soldier on the bus eventually became my boyfriend, I learned how exhausting the constant worry is. He was always on missions. WE'RE GOING OUT TONIGHT, he would text me, and I knew it meant he was on a mission. To make an arrest, to do surveillance, who knows. He did not take his phone. Then my world narrowed to a single point: Where are you? My love, where are you? Friends had to repeat themselves when they spoke to me. I could not absorb the words. I was always checking my phone. Even in class. Checking to see if he was back. The more I checked, the more anxious I became. I would have dreams that he was texting me, that my phone was chiming, but I couldn't open his texts. He was there, but I couldn't reach him, and I would wake up to text notifications that made my heart clench until I realized they were not from him. My palms tingled—a nervous response I'd never experienced before.

All that was to come. But not before our first date.

Six

Our first real date was an unlikely one: we went to the modern art museum in Tel Aviv. It was my idea. He had been there once, he said, in high school, and I knew he was stopping himself short of telling me it was on a class trip.

He picked me up in his parents' car. As we drove to the museum, I looked straight ahead, but from the corner of my eye I could see him turning to look at me every few seconds, as if checking that I was truly there. How I dreaded telling him that I would leave Israel at summer's end. Still, it wasn't fair not to tell him, was it? *I'll do it at the museum*, I promised myself.

At the museum I paid the student price; he was admitted for free when he showed an ID card confirming he was an active-duty soldier.

We began in the permanent collection, walking through oil paintings of haystacks and seated portraits. Nothing held our interest until we came to the twentieth century. We stopped in front of a grotesque Max Ernst pencil drawing of an eye in some kind of mechanical cocoon. I wanted to make a joke about surveillance but couldn't think of how to frame it. We were both self-conscious. I could feel it. How close was too close to stand next to each other? The molecules between our hands buzzed.

He was a little hoarse when he asked, "What do you think of Israel?"

Neither of us looked away from the terrible eye.

I needed to tell him now. This was my opening. I could say that I like it so much I want to stay past the summer. As I hesitated, two little boys ran through the gallery, their mother on the phone coming after them. "*Nu*," she said, "the mistake was yours, and now I should fix it?"

We laughed as she disappeared. "Everyone here seems tough," I said. "Israelis, I mean—you all seem tough." When I glanced at him we made eye contact, then looked away. "The other day, I saw a kid negotiating for an ice cream like a politician." I was setting Eyal up to say something like, *We have no choice but to be tough.* Israeli men loved saying things like that to foreign women.

But he sounded concerned as he touched my arm—at last! Touching me!—to say, "We seem tough to you?"

"Yes," I said. "Is it all an act? The toughness?"

We had started walking again, slowly. He sped up past a Munch litho-graph of a woman's nude torso. I wasn't sure if he would answer at all, but as we exited the permanent collection toward the special exhibit he said, "It's an act, but also it's real." Later, he would use this wording again to explain the harshness of his basic training drill instructor.

"I understand," I said. "Maybe the act becomes real."

"Yes, it's just like that," he said, relief in his voice as he touched my arm again. "The act becomes real." His sincerity disarmed me.

The special video art exhibition was in a new addition to the museum—a freestanding building of conceptual, asymmetrical architecture that looked, Eyal and I agreed, like a toy rhinoceros.

We entered a room of screens and projections. Films looped. Some black and white, some color. "Whoa," he said.

We stood in front of a video piece by Douglas Gordon: a grand piano in flames on a verdant moor, somewhere between Scotland and England. We watched as the piano burned. Its frame began to collapse under itself, and still it burned. In the background, highland grasses shifted in the wind. At times, other gallery-goers walked behind the screen, their outlines visible. The piano kept burning. We stood with our hands at our sides. Almost touching—we were almost touching.

"It reminds me of something," Eyal said at last, his voice soft.

I waited, knowing he would continue. On the screen, flames whipped around the piano.

"When I was in high school, we went on a class trip to the Golan Heights," he said. "You know what it is?"

"Yes," I whispered. I knew it was a place in northern Israel, seized from Syria during the war of 1967.

"We went there by bus," he said. He fell asleep on the long ride north, woke up with his forehead on the cold glass. It was winter. The Golan was lush and wild, trembling green in the moody gray of winter storms.

I could see it. I was there with him in a landscape that looked more like the Scottish Highlands than anything I'd expect from Israel. "It sounds beautiful," I said.

"It is beautiful," he echoed. "But it is wounded. The land is wounded." He said the bus stopped by a big field. It was raining lightly; everyone had their sweatshirt hoods up. They stood by a fence of barbed wire that cordoned off a field of land mines. DANGER! the bright yellow signs exclaimed, punctuated with a skull. He and Gil took a selfie together, squinting against the rain. Then everyone got back on the bus. "We drove by—how do you say '*churbot*'?" he turned to me.

"Ruins," I said. It was the same root as the word used to speak of the great destroyed temple of Jerusalem.

He nodded. "Ruins," he repeated. "We drove by the ruins of homes." Stones strewn on the ground, as if they had been bombed.

I wondered if those were depopulated Syrian villages, but I didn't want to interrupt Eyal's story to ask.

"I wondered who had lived in those ruins," Eyal said. He raised his hand to ask his teacher, who stood at the front of the bus, narrating about the liberation of the Golan from Syria. He'd liked that teacher well enough—an easygoing dad type who didn't give a lot of homework. Yes, his teacher said, pointing to Eyal: A question? "Who lived here?" Eyal asked. "Who lived here before us?"

"Nobody," his teacher said. "Nobody lived here."

"What did you think of that?" I asked. A nervous agitation tickled the backs of my knees. What if he said something racist? Or the opposite? What if he had some kind of ethical crisis right here in the art museum? What if he didn't want to be a soldier anymore? What if he needed me to help him and I didn't know how?

But he was assured when he answered. "It's like we said before," he said. "It was an act, but also it was real." The piano's keys were on fire. "I guess a country is just a story." By instinct, this beautiful teenager— barely out of high school—had summarized an entire academic movement related to narrative and nationalism.

I felt a surge of desire. Not to be touched by him, but to be inside him. To feel him as he felt, to watch him in pleasure. I touched his arm gently. He looked at me, startled. "What would you think," I asked, "if you had seen this in the Golan Heights?" I gestured toward the video. "If you had seen a burning piano on that class trip. What would you have thought?"

He answered like a soldier. "I'd search the area for a nearby person or his trace," he said.

I pushed: "And if you found none? No trace?"

He hesitated. "I would think it was God." He said it as if admitting it.

There was so much I wanted to tell Eyal, but our shared languages were too limited. I knew, for example, that like the Golan Heights, the landscape of the burning piano was crisscrossed with invisible boundaries. Somewhere in all that greenness between Scotland and England were the ruins of Hadrian's Wall—named for the same Roman emperor who crushed the last great Jewish revolt. Two thousand years ago, that wall marked the limits of the Roman Empire. Beyond it lay wild, unconquered lands. The wall defined culture as words define a story. Even the word "define" comes from the act of establishing a boundary—this is true in English and Hebrew alike.

But none of this seemed worth articulating into the imperfect understanding between us, as we stood in front of that projection with our hands almost touching. So instead I said, "I would think it was God too." Rather than frustrated by my limitations, I felt relieved. Whatever brilliance had burdened me all my life—whatever sharpness of mind had pushed past lovers away, made them feel diminished or made them want to diminish me—in Hebrew I was free of it. Before moving to Israel, I had been nervous about learning to actively speak Modern Hebrew, as opposed to reading and translating archaic Hebrews as a scholar. But I was finding that I liked myself better in Hebrew, a language in which I had so much less to say.

Some night before he went to war, Eyal and I watched a romantic movie—a silly one about high school students engaging in some kind of bet or dating contract that starts with mutual annoyance and ends with love. In English, I think I would have commented on the movie as a reaction to the anxieties of loving within capitalism. The hope the movie offered—the comfort and therefore the pleasure—was that even romantic structures premised on ownership can offer true intimacy. This is the kind of comment I would have offered to my mean-spirited college boyfriend, the one with the beautiful freckle. He in turn would have accused me of wanting to feel smarter than the very movie I had chosen, and by extension, smarter than everyone else, by which he meant smarter than him. But in Hebrew, I didn't have the words for "transactional" or "anxieties" or even "intimacy." I could only comment that the lead actress was pretty.

We left the museum. Eyal drove me back to my place. I lived on a wide boulevard, an imitation of Berlin built by refugees who could not call that place home anymore. My building was elegant Bauhaus from afar;

close up, you saw it was a crumbling facade with exposed PVC pipes, all covered in bat shit.

Without the art exhibit to distract us, we were silent. I watched his hands on the steering wheel. I kept reminding myself he was only nineteen. He looked young in his jeans and T-shirt. Younger than he had in uniform. But something about his grip on the steering wheel, the proprietary way his knees spread when he drove the car (his parents' car, I reminded myself) made him seem like a man.

"When do you go back to the army?" I asked.

A helpless look seized his face for a moment. "Tomorrow," he said. "I go tomorrow."

"For two weeks?"

"Probably, yes," he said. "That is the rhythm."

I liked how he pronounced the word "rhythm," giving it more bump and roll. A heaviness had entered the car. I could feel him thinking about the army, about the bus he would take to the West Bank, where he waited around for someone to tell him what to do.

"What do you want to do after?" I asked. "After the army, I mean."

He hesitated. "I want to study," he said, "bioethic-ah." Always with that extra syllable.

"Bioethics," I repeated. "I don't know anything about that."

"Nobody does," he said. "Not yet." A shy smile. "That is what makes it so interesting." He did not have the word "unregulated" in English, and I did not have it in Hebrew.

While he was talking, we drove past my apartment. It was my fault. I saw it coming up on the right but didn't want him to stop talking. "That was my apartment," I said, only after we passed it.

He nodded and drove down to the end of the boulevard, then circled back up.

We drove once again toward my building.

"You got me in trouble," he said. His tone was not serious.

"Oh?" I asked, hope creeping into my voice.

"Yes, because of the *Odyssey-ah*." He told me that he had been enthralled by my retelling of the *Odyssey*. To have time alone to read my texts, he hid in empty storage closets; he broke into an officer's room to charge his phone when it started to die. He couldn't put down his phone, he said, so engrossed was he in my retelling of the Sirens' call.

For my part, I had arrived late for class more than once because I'd lost track of time—texting him long and elaborate messages about Odysseus's wanderings. What I loved was to imagine Eyal reading what I'd written. Like he was Odysseus himself, so far away, reading the story that Penelope was weaving.

We drove past my apartment a second time.

"Sorry," he said, glancing over to gauge my reaction, relieved, I'm sure, to see that I was unconcerned, leaning back in the seat and turned toward him.

You're leaving, I reminded myself. *You have to tell him you're leaving at the end of the summer.* "I'm trying to stay longer," I blurted out.

"What?" he asked. "In the car?"

"No, I mean, I'm only supposed to stay in Israel for a few months," I said, looking at the car speedometer rather than at him.

"And then you go back to Canada?"

"To New York, to finish my degree," I said. "But I think maybe I can finish it here. I mean, I think I want to."

He was silent. This was it: he was going to slip away from me. I knew it. I knew it, and there was nothing I could do. Why did this hurt so much? I looked out the passenger-side window, afraid I would cry. Hands in my lap. He still hadn't said anything.

Slowly, he reached for my hand.

I inhaled.

Our fingers interlaced.

"I hope you will do what makes you happy," he said, as I turned to him.

I could not believe he still wanted to be close to me. *If nothing else happens*, I thought. *If it's only this, it will have been enough.* Neither of us moved our fingers—any rubbing would have been too obscene. But my hand was in his. I could feel the calluses all along his palm. We were silent then. Silent and terrified by what we might do.

We kept looping, no longer pretending we were looking for my apartment at all. We drove around the block again and again, circling. We wanted to get lost, I think, more and more lost, but were afraid to start and unsure if we'd even get the chance.

Eventually, he parked his car, freeing his hand from mine. I felt momentarily bereft, then embarrassed at my own reaction. "Do you want to come in?" I asked. "I have something for you." It was true, I had a gift for him. How pathetic that seemed—as if I were luring a child with candy from the cracked window of an unmarked van.

"Yes," he said, breathless.

We hesitated at the threshold of my apartment building. We were shy. It was another muggy Tel Aviv evening; the light had faded but the heat had not. Our skin shimmered with sweat. Down the boulevard, a pack of men were jogging shirtless. Girls laughed with ice cream. Sex was everywhere, even in the fragrant leaves of the shrub that grew wild next to my front door.

He picked a small leaf off the shrub. He could not look me in the eye. I liked the way his collarless cotton shirt opened onto his hairless chest. I liked how strong it made him look, the swell of the muscles converging on his sternum. I wanted him to suggest we go inside.

I leaned against the whitewashed wall. I kept my voice soft when I asked, "How do you call this tree?" I didn't know how to say "shrub" in Hebrew.

He smiled a little. He was charmed by my attempts at Hebrew. Already he had begged me to repeat certain Hebrew words, especially ones with the "r" sound. We had not yet kissed, but I could tell that he wanted to kiss me, to suck those flat "r"s right off my tongue. Yet here we were, each of us waiting on the other.

He was about to say something when the front door opened and my roommate, Talia, came floating out—all spry and delicate, her curly hair long down her back. Talia's music was on the verge of becoming a little fa-mous in Tel Aviv—part of what Israeli newspapers were calling a Mizrahi cultural revival. In Hebrew class, I had learned that well into the 1980s, Is-raeli radio would not play "low" Mizrahi music on the air; it disrupted the Zionist fantasy of a European Israel. But now, our teacher Smadar told us, Mizrahi-style music was ubiquitous. That's progress. When I asked Talia about this, she said it was more complex than what was played on the radio: "It's a question of cutting off music from its source, turning it into a—how do you say—like, a symbol. A token! Yes, a token." Years later, in a Hebrew interview with *Haaretz*, Israel's sole liberal newspaper, she would elaborate: "I am trying to recover my own roots, but at times, I fear I'll only make my displacement more acute," she was quoted as saying. "My parents made sacrifices so I could get an Ashkenazi education, but sometimes I won-der, if we'd grown up in a development town, would I know more Arabic? Would I be more connected to my lost homelands?" These last words—"lost homelands"—became the headline of the article, which elaborated on a sad irony: the Arabic music Talia sampled on her tracks might have been her rightful cultural inheritance, but she accessed the samples not through her own family, but through an ethnomusicology archive at the university.

All this was to come. Now, Talia was heading out for the night, for it was nearly night—the day having slipped away. "Hey," she said to me in English, smiling dreamily. Even then, I could sense that her mind was always somewhere else. "You guys coming in?"

Eyal responded in Hebrew. "I was just leaving," he said, his voice a little hoarse. He touched my shoulder. "I'll call," he said, in English. Then he was off, walking quickly to the car he'd parked nearby. His parents' car.

The present I had gotten Eyal—the one waiting for him in my room, unclaimed—was a translation of the *Odyssey* into Hebrew. Inscribing the book, I had wanted to paraphrase a line I'm partial to—*All strangers are a gift from Zeus*—but I chickened out, worried it was too romantic, or too polytheistic. I was sensing that even Israelis who claimed to be completely secular had an ingrained religious sensibility. Instead, my dedication echoed the first lines of the epic itself. *To Eyal*, I wrote, *he of many ways*.

As he disappeared around the corner, Talia asked, "This is the soldier?" I had told her about him.

"Yes," I said.

"Cute."

I cringed a little. I was always trying to make him feel powerful.

In those days, I harbored a secret fantasy that a man would find me and take my life away from me. Not kill me, not exactly, but relieve me of the burden of self-determination, which I was finding too hard to bear. Isn't that who I was waiting for when, in riding the bus, I moved over to the window seat? Someone to give my life direction. How exhausting to figure out who to be in the world and how. Where should I live? Was it a mistake to enter academia? What was important to me? (Talmud and male attention, apparently.) I didn't know much about myself. I wanted someone to find me and tell me who I was. *Please*, I begged each night before I met Eyal, *please come find me*.

Talia went out and I went in. I put down my bag and lay on my bed. Why did I miss him? This boy I barely knew? Why did my room, which had never held him, feel empty without him? His copy of the *Odyssey* waited on my desk.

My phone dinged.

Eyal: DID YOU SAY YOU HAVE A PRESENT FOR ME?

My breath quickened. YES, I replied.

I'M COMING BACK.

Eyal sat on my bed, holding his new copy of the *Odyssey*. He traced over my inscription with his finger. *To Eyal, he of many ways.* "What does it mean?"

he asked. I think he found the inscription in my hand more thrilling than the book itself.

"It means that you have many parts to you," I said, improvising. "You are not just one thing."

"That I am not just a soldier," he said, with what struck me as inordinate relief. He opened the book and began to read.

I watched him. He was so young. He was so young and so eager to learn. While he was away, he'd texted me endless questions about the *Odyssey*. What happened to Odysseus at Troy? Why is he always lying? Why does Penelope sleep so much? Why do the suitors have to die? All he wanted was for his world to grow. It was wrong, wasn't it? For me to want him?

I sat next to him on the bed. "The style of Hebrew is very old," he said, looking up at me, and I think he would have said more but something about my gaze silenced him.

For a second that lasted my whole life, we held eye contact.

"I need to tell you something," I said, unsure of what I was about to tell him. Maybe, *I'm too old for you.* Or *You're too young.* Or maybe just *I'm sorry,* and he could fill in the rest.

"Okay," he said. I could see he was bracing himself for rejection.

"I want to kiss you, but I'm scared," I said. I do not know where the words came from. My heart? My throat? My soul?

He was stunned. And then he was moving toward me. His hand behind my head, his fingers in my hair with a delightful trace of fierceness, but his mouth was soft on mine. We kissed gently—so gently that it was all lips and breath. He was touching me with his breath. I did not defile the moment with tongue.

That night, he stayed. At first, his father kept calling. Eyal texted him, but he kept calling. "One second," he said to me, getting up from our kissing. "Hello," he said into his phone. I could hear his father exclaiming in Hebrew. "I'll be back tomorrow," Eyal said. His father yelled some more. "I'll be back in time," he said. Then he hung up and put his ringer on silent.

It was a remarkably chaste night. We lay fully clothed on my bed while he memorized my rib cage, his hands pressing over my shirt, seeking out the borders of my body. I wanted to become known to him this way: from the outside in, then from the inside out, wanted more and more, but also, I was afraid. I was afraid that I would feel too much and regret it when, inevitably, he disappeared the next day and I never heard from him again.

For his part, Eyal did not touch me anywhere but my ribs, my hair, my neck, my mouth; he didn't try to take off my clothes or lead my hand into his pants. Later he told me, in English I think he'd practiced beforehand, "I didn't want you to worry that I would take advantage." During the night, I sometimes touched his shoulders or the prickle of his buzz cut, but often I lay still with my eyes closed as he used his body to obsess over mine.

When we heard Talia come in the front door, we shushed each other, giggling like children.

Without the plotline of penetration or even orgasms, we continued for hours in a slow touching that in retrospect reminds me, somehow, of swimming and its movements syncopated with breath. We tried out different kinds of kissing: small soft bites, more lip, then more tongue.

Night slipped away—slowly, slowly, but not slowly enough. Soft blue light began to fill the room with the sounds of morning, a rumbling bus, the complaints of birds. When the alarm he had set went off, he sat up. "*Zehu*," he said flatly. "That's it." It was time for him to go back to the army. He took his wallet, his keys, and the *Odyssey*. That was all he had.

I walked him to his car. The parking attendant eyed us greedily as we kissed. I wondered how old I looked.

You're leaving, and he's young, I cautioned myself as I waved to his car pulling away. *Don't take this too seriously. Don't expect anything.*

My ribs were sore.

Seven

Was it a dream?

That was my first thought upon waking later that same day. Had I dreamt that night with the soldier? When I checked my phone, I saw he hadn't texted. *Don't get attached*, I warned myself. *Don't expect him to text you. It was a onetime thing. He's nineteen. Nineteen! A literal teenager. He belongs to the army.*

After walking Eyal to his car, I had hurried home in the chilly gray morning. Why did it make me so sad to imagine I'd never see him again? I set an alarm and retreated into sleep. Now I was waking up a second time into daylight that was almost harsh. The buses were running. The coffee shops were open. But still no texts from Eyal. The caustic musk of his drugstore cologne lingered in my bed. Instead of getting up, I went back to sleep, hiding from a feeling I was afraid to name.

When I woke for the third time it was late morning. Why does every day feel lost by 10:00 a.m.? Still, no text from Eyal, but no time to dwell: I had missed my Modern Hebrew class and would have to rush to make it on time to meet with the professor who had hired me as a summer TA. Perhaps we'd also discuss the possibility of me extending my time in Israel? *Don't get too hopeful. Don't get attached.* The words were like a drumbeat as I hurried to dress and get to the bus stop.

I was on the northbound bus to the university when I got a text alert from Eyal. I expected something noncommittal—maybe *Hey, thanks for a fun night.*

Eyal: WAS IT A DREAM?

I gasped. The bus was filled with shoppers and students. Nobody noticed.

IF IT WAS A DREAM, WE DREAMT IT TOGETHER, I replied. It felt good to match his ardor.

Eyal: ON THE WAY BACK TO BASE I REMEMBERED EACH OF YOUR RIBS AND EACH OF YOUR SIGHS.

Never before had anyone sent me such unguarded romantic messages.

He was still typing: I WILL BE ON BASE FOR TWO WEEKS. PLEASE LET ME SEE YOU WHEN I COME BACK.

And so just like that, and right from the very start, it was a love story. He made it a love story.

He never told me what happened between him and his father when he returned home that first morning, having lain in my bed all night, ignoring his phone. He left as the sun was rising, so must have gotten home before 7:00 a.m. Was his father already making coffee in the kitchen when Eyal quietly opened the front door? Was there anger in a strained whisper? Or did the men have an understanding? A new mutual respect premised on manhood, which is to say, access to my body? I didn't know. I did know that he now belonged to the army for another two weeks.

How would I wait that long to see him? Two weeks! After my meeting with the professor—a spry, excitable scholar of rabbinics who, after he reviewed the course syllabus with me, expressed a genuine interest in my work ("There are ways to stay here," he said sagely, and he would know, since he emigrated from the States)—I sat on the concrete steps of a campus building and I texted Eyal endless questions. WHAT DO YOU

DO WHEN YOU'RE AWAY? WHERE ARE YOU NOW? ARE YOU SAFE? ARE YOU HUNGRY? ARE YOU TIRED?

He responded with a laughing emoji. I MISS YOU, he wrote.

YOU DIDN'T ANSWER ANY OF MY QUESTIONS! I responded. Then conceded, I MISS YOU TOO.

Another laughing emoji. THIS WEEK IT'S SURVEILLANCE NEAR HEBRON. MAYBE A MISSION. (A mission? What was a mission? Like this was some kind of spy movie? What the fuck?) I AM TIRED AND I AM HUNGRY. BUT WHEN I REMEMBER YOUR BED, I AM HAPPY.

Later that night, long after I had gone to bed, he texted again. I saw it in the morning: I WANT YOU TO KNOW THAT YOU ARE ALWAYS WITH ME. THAT YOU WILL STAY EVEN IF YOU GO.

It was hardest that first time. The days crawling by while he was away.

In the biblical poetry of exile, songs of the Babylonian captivity in the sixth century BCE, time itself seems to collapse under the weight of Jewish longing for Jerusalem. *When the Lord restores us to Zion*, the psalmist sings, *we were as dreamers. Then will our mouths be filled with laughter.* The verb tenses are an intoxicating, discordant mess. A conditional present (*restores us*) blurs with the past (*we were as dreamers*), which ultimately blooms into the future (*will our mouths be filled*).

I felt these verses more acutely than I ever had before. I dreamt of Eyal's hands pressing into the places where my bones met skin. Clavicles, ribs, hips, kneecap, foot bridge. I woke alone.

His job was to hide and watch. His unit was famous for how they could disappear into the landscape. Watching and waiting, waiting and watching, then . . .

He's everywhere, I told myself. It was an oddly comforting thought—imagining myself as the object of his surveillance. *There he is, disguised as that rock. No, now he's in the tree. He's clinging to the side of the bus, invisibly, watching me.*

After a while, you figure out that soldiers are weapons who don't know how to operate themselves. They do what they're told. But I didn't understand that yet.

Somehow, I made it through those first two weeks. We made plans to see each other as soon as he got back to Tel Aviv. He dropped his bag off with his parents, showered, then came to me.

I waited at the threshold of my apartment building. Somehow terrified he wouldn't come. But he did, bounding up toward me to squeeze my waist.

His body was a revelation. "It's you," I whispered. Touching the base of his neck, his ear lobe, his lips, the small of his back. "It's you."

He closed his eyes, experiencing a pleasure so profound it looked like grief. Every moment of intimacy was shadowed by the threat of my departure. This was our second date. He came inside.

It was the middle of the day. My room was filled with sunlight as we undressed each other. We could not stop. We took off our shirts first, pressing skin to skin. It wasn't enough. Nothing was enough. We were naked in bed. We had the slender bodies of children. I led his hand to feel my wetness, how I was blooming for him. He gasped to feel me, almost as if he were in pain, pressing his forehead to mine. I had a condom I'd gotten from Talia. "Please," I whispered, kneeling on the bed.

He nodded.

We rolled the condom on together.

If I'd had fantasies about him being some devastatingly experienced lover, they slipped away almost immediately. I could tell he was nervous as soon as he entered me. He concentrated on my forehead as he moved tentatively inside me, pressing his hands into the mattress, beaching himself. He was trying, I think, not to express too much, trying not to betray that my body was a miracle he had never imagined. Also, trying not to come too soon.

At the time, I couldn't bear the thought that I was his first. How predatory that seemed! But in the years since, so much pretense has fallen away. I have learned more about myself than I ever wanted to know, and still I do not hate myself. So yes, I deflowered the boy.

Afterward, he was sheepish with his head on my chest. "I know you didn't come," he said.

"It's okay," I started to say, but already he was kneeling in front of me, ready to use his mouth. My thighs pressed against his ears.

Over time, I would come to understand that more than his own pleasure, he was invested in mine. His exuberance made my body feel new. He could spend hours using his fingers and mouth and cock to create sensation deep inside me. I had never given this much attention to my insides, tending to rely on rubbing myself for pleasure. Together, we opened me.

Now, he settled on using two fingers to massage a secret spot inside me.

"When you press there, it feels like I have to pee!" I exclaimed.

He laughed, lifting his tongue off my clit. "So pee!" he said gleefully. His mouth was glistening. I do not know how many times I climaxed that night, but by dawn I was weeping from exhaustion.

He crawled up to lie next to me, his nose in my neck. *I love you*, I thought, knowing I couldn't say it. How weird would that be? We'd known each other for barely a month. Plus, what if people his age didn't even use the phrase anymore? Maybe they only pantomimed *I love you* by making a heart shape with their hands. If I said it, he might laugh. He might leave. He might not say anything. *Don't say it*, I warned myself.

He turned to me. "I love you," he said.

I covered my face with my hands.

"I love you," he said again simply.

He was the bravest person I have ever known.

More than anyone else I'd ever been with, he wanted to know me: Why I loved the *Odyssey*. (Its narrative shapes.) My first memory of crying. (Bee-sting.) What drew my attention in the postcard of an old master's oil painting I kept tacked above my desk? (Trace of brushstroke.)

And he wanted to be known by me. He played me the music he had listened to during basic training. The one margin of freedom, he explained (not in those words), was the song they chose to wake up to at 3:00 a.m. for crawling through the desert. Together, the guys in his bunk had agreed on a dance hall track that I found mindless to the point of terror. Enormous electronic beats were suspended then came crashing down as a warped female voice sang the same words over and over again. *We changed, we changed, we changed.* Eyal and I lay on my bed listening to this song, somber as if it were church music.

As summer began, we continued to pattern our lives by the rhythm imposed on him by the army. We rarely talked about the looming deadline: by September I would be gone, unless by some miracle I got the grant I applied for to stay a full year.

I still hadn't told anyone in my family that I might extend my time in Israel. Instead, I messaged Erica about Eyal. SOOOOO I'VE BEEN SPENDING TIME WITH THE SOLDIER . . . I wrote to her and only to her—trying to recapture some of the closeness we'd had all those years ago, I suppose.

And it worked! Or at least, it seemed to work. THE ONE YOU MET ON THE BUS??? she responded a few hours later.

YESSS, I wrote, right away.

WAIT, HOW OLD IS HE?

I hesitated. Would she find it pathetic that he was so much younger? Younger than her, my younger sister, by at least five years. HE'S TWENTY, I lied. He was nineteen.

She started and stopped typing a few times. Finally she wrote, SCANDALOUS ;). The wink made me feel better.

RIGHT?? I fell back on my bed, warm and happy.

She was typing again. MAYBE YOU'LL BE ABLE TO EDUCATE HIM, she wrote.

I didn't know what she meant. Like, tutor him? Wait did she mean teach him about sex? No, right? Ew, what? I didn't know what to reply, so I wrote, OH?

YEAH, YOU KNOW ABOUT THE OCCUPATION, she wrote. ABOUT PALESTINE.

I suddenly had the image of Erica sitting on Cee's lap, while Cee told her what to type. OH YEAH MAYBE, I wrote.

ARE YOU KEEPING IT A SECRET FROM MOM AND DAD? she asked.

NAW, YOU CAN TELL THEM, I wrote, embarrassed at how lonely I felt. SAY HI TO CEE FOR ME.

Even when Eyal was away, there was a deeper kind of away: going on what he called "missions." A mission might be an arrest. Not an arrest as I thought of them. For Eyal, an arrest meant surveillance, tactical gear, a ground unit banging on a door at night, women hurrying to cover their hair, Jeep headlights, young men without shoes up against a wall. ("Do you read them their rights in Arabic or Hebrew?" I asked. I was curious because these were not citizens of Israel he was arresting. "Their what?" he asked blankly.)

All the words meant something different here. When Eyal went on a mission, he called that place "the field." When I first heard him referring to the field, I imagined a specific area. For example, contested lands or Palestinian-controlled areas. But I was wrong. "The field" was anywhere Eyal went as a soldier. If Eyal and I spent a day on a kibbutz—indeed, in the kibbutz fields—we were not in "the field." But if Eyal went to that same kibbutz in order to secure it from some threat that the intelligence machine had sensed, then he was in "the field." The residents of the kibbutz couldn't say they were in the field; they were at home. "The field" is defined by intention, I concluded while on the phone with Eyal, sounding like a rabbi of the Talmud as I reasoned my way through this term. "Yes," Eyal said, "by who intends to kill you."

Missions were the worst because he was not permitted to take his phone. This happened periodically in the months before he was deployed to Gaza. It was part of the routine. Also, it was unbearable. On those days, I felt that my whole body was one raw, pulpy nerve. Please be safe, I said to him. Please let him be safe, I said to God.

My parents didn't understand. Couldn't, really. "Oh my," my mother said on video calls when I told her that Eyal was on a mission. "Oh my."

I wanted more. More closeness, more support, more understanding. I got it from Eyal's mother. When Eyal was away, we were joined in the frantic hum of our concern. *Have you heard from him?* I'd ask his mother, and she'd say, *No, lovely one, we haven't heard yet.* We assured each other that we'd give updates. We compared notes on how long he had been away this time, how long the time before. In those exchanges, I felt like her daughter, or maybe her sister. Bonded in concern for our soldier.

And so it would go, until my phone chimed and, thank God, oh my God, thank God, it was a text from him. A blurry selfie in the semi-dark of whatever truck was taking them back to base: HEADED BACK, WILL CALL AFTER I SLEEP, LOVE YOU.

Each time he was released from his base, we spent the weekend entwined. We held hands when we went grocery shopping with his mom. We held hands on the boulevards of Tel Aviv, tickling the inside of each other's palm, letting desire build until we got back to my apartment or his room, where we could touch and kiss. We watched movies lying on top of each other, legs twisted, faces smooshed. Or, if he was tired, his head on my lap as I scratched his scalp. He was a mighty sleeping cat. A unicorn in a medieval tapestry, subdued in the maiden's treacherous lap.

At his family gatherings we sat side by side on couches, my legs swung over his. He had a habit of gently running his thumb over my inner wrist, an unintentionally possessive act that thrilled me more than any explicit one could. "*Yafim*," his mother would say, taking photos of us. *Beauties.* After, when she sent me the photos she would always edit in cartoon hearts.

"Why doesn't your *ima* hate me?" I asked Eyal again and again. "Isn't it weird to her?" Weird that her son was dating someone nearly a decade older.

"She wants me to be happy," he answered each time, never looking away from what he was doing. On his phone or watching a movie or carefully and clumsily braiding my hair for no reason other than we wanted to see if he could do it.

It was true that his mother's biggest concern seemed to be not my age but that I would be indoctrinated by liberals at the university. Fueled by intense patriotism, she went through the country's past prime ministers, telling me who was good and who was "giving too much to the Arabs." She was very serious when she said, "The Arabs, they want to erase us."

I almost giggled in discomfort. It all sounded so extreme—to assume the Palestinians hated us simply for existing, instead of having legitimate grievances. But I could not bring myself to speak up and say, *I'm not sure I agree with you.* That seemed too uncomfortable, too scary. Instead, I nodded without replying. Over time, hearing these kind of utterances against "the Arabs" bothered me less and less, until eventually, I stopped noticing them at all.

Anyway, it wasn't always war she was telling me about. In early June, she explained to me the holiday of Shavuot. "We eat dairy on this holiday," she said, cutting me a slice of cheesecake. We were at a suburb in the home of Eyal's cousins. Someone was playing hand drums. Eyal was gamely chasing children who squealed with a panicked joy while the adults picked over the dessert table, avoiding the little ones weaving around their legs.

I nodded, accepting the perfect white slice onto my plate. Over the stereo, someone was playing an Israeli oldie—a sweet, folksy song: *Hee kol kakh yafah, zeh tzobet balev shelkha. She's so beautiful, it pinches your heart.*

Across the room, Eyal looked at me as he lifted a toddler above his head. He winked. He'd put the group, Kaveret, on a playlist of Israeli music for me.

I sang along to the chorus of the song as Eyal's mom served a slice of cheesecake to her sister. The two women turned to me, excited. "How do you know this song?" Eyal's mom asked. "Wow, wow, wow."

"You're really Israeli now," Eyal's aunt said. *"Ezeh yofi." How beautiful.* You could tell they were sisters: two petite women in slim-cut jeans and resort-feeling shirts that left their shoulders exposed.

Eyal's mom wrapped her free arm around me, the other hand holding the cutting knife. "We made her Israeli," she said. Our shoulders were pressed together.

Nothing had ever felt this good. Nothing in my whole life had ever felt as good as being welcomed not just into a family but into a people. How could I go? I couldn't go. *Please*, I whispered in my heart, *please let me stay.* This is praying.

When Eyal went back to the army after his brief weekends home, it never got easy to say goodbye, even if it was just for two weeks. These goodbyes were practice—I'm sure we both felt this—for the long and painful one that would happen at summer's end if my funding did not come through.

Often, I'd stay over with him at his parents' the night before he went back to the army. Then in the morning, his dad would drop me off at the university on the way to bringing Eyal to the train or bus. On those days, Eyal sat in the front with his father, I in the back.

One night, before he went back to Hebron, we walked to a playground near his apartment complex. By now it was summer. The invasion was coming, but we didn't know it. The sun set late, inflamed as it sank west toward the sea. We sat on swings with our feet dragging in the dirt. "Will you work on your thesis-ah this week?" he asked, tacking on the extra syllable I loved.

At the time, I was working on a chapter of my dissertation about rabbinic metaphors for loss. I wanted to share what I did with Eyal, so I tried. "Yes, I'm writing about metaphor," I said. Then added, "Meta-phor-ah." We smiled at each other. I could feel the understanding be-tween us, pulsing and warm.

"Tell me about metaphor-ah," he said softly. His feet dragged against the ground as he leaned toward me on his swing.

"When a feeling is too big, we don't trust language." I spoke hes-itantly, avoiding the ready-at-hand wording of the academy—"anxiety over the limitations of language, tension between a word's sonic and se-mantic qualities." I tried to speak plainly: "Loss, for example. Language can't always carry the weight of loss."

He nodded but I felt I was failing him. We leaned toward each other on our respective swings. The sun was disappearing quickly, huge and red on the horizon. "Like the sun," I exclaimed. I was improvising. "During the day, we can't look at the sun directly," I said.

"It is too much to see," he said.

"Yes!" I was encouraged. "It is too much to see, but we can see it reflected."

"Reflected?"

"In a pool of water, for instance," I said. "We could see the sun's image in a tide pool."

He was looking at his feet.

I struggled to keep up the momentum. "Metaphor is like that pool of water," I offered. "Figurative language that helps us see what is beyond our comprehension." Too abstract. Surely, I'd lost him now. I kicked my legs in agitation. I'd lost him.

"Like love," he said finally.

I stilled. "What?"

"You said words can't hold a whole feeling," he said. "Like when I tell you I love you, it doesn't feel like enough." He touched the back of his neck, speaking almost to himself. "The words don't feel like enough. But if I told you that you were the sun, maybe it would feel closer." The last sliver of sun disappeared. "Closer to the truth."

"Yes, exactly like that," I whispered.

He stood up from his swing and stood behind me. He kissed the top of my head, then pushed my back softly to give my swing momentum. He spoke to me between pushes: "I hope that no matter what"—push, flying, return—"no matter where you go"—push, flying, return—"you will continue with your dreams."

I watched my feet soar over the empty playground, haloed in the light of a single streetlamp.

We lay in his twin bed. Tonight, he was the big spoon. "You are so far along in your studies," he said. "I'm scared that I'll never get a chance to start."

"To start studying bioethics?" I clarified.

"I don't even know what faculty to apply to," he said. "Biology? Philosophy? Law?"

"Let's write to professors and ask," I said.

"You can't just write to professors," he said, squeezing me from behind. "Can you?"

"Sure, I do it all the time," I said. "Let's break it down in steps." I told him step one would probably be looking online for academics in Israel who are writing or teaching in the field of bioethics.

"Wait hold on," he said. He untangled our limbs and reached for his phone. "I'm going to write it down." His face was lit by the screen. "Step one is to find people writing about bioethics."

"Right," I said, propping myself up on one elbow to face him. "Then step two is to email them."

"What will I say?"

"We can write it together," I said in Hebrew. I switched to English. "Basically, say that you're a soldier who is interested in their field, and would like advice about how to approach your studies after the army."

This was so easy for me, I could do it in my sleep. But Eyal was focused and intense as he typed into his phone.

"Wait, slow down," he said. He must have been translating. He'd become functionally fluent so quickly thanks to a young, pliable brain. "A soldier who is interested in their field," he echoed. "Do you think it's the same word in Hebrew?" he asked in Hebrew. "The field," he said in English, "and *the field*?" He switched back to Hebrew, using the word for the nebulous zone of combat.

"Whoa, I have no idea."

"We'll look it up later," he said. "Let's keep going."

I continued, "Would they have time to answer questions over the phone or, if they prefer, email?"

"And they'll answer?"

"At least one will," I said. "Honestly, they'll be flattered that someone so young and promising is interested in their work."

"Really?"

"Really."

He put down his phone. The room was dark again. "It's magic," he said.

"What's magic?" I asked. It seemed simple enough, what I'd done.

"It's magic how you make it all feel possible."

We had not talked about what would happen if I did not get the grant: if I had to leave Israel at the end of the summer. But we both knew what would happen. It would be goodbye.

In my sleep, weeks later, he would tell me that I said aloud, "But what *is* magic?" Magic is words whose power does not require understanding or even belief—religion's unregulated cousin.

There are those who say that all words are magic, every sentence a spell. *I live in Israel*, I said in my heart at night, *I am Israeli*, trying to harness the secret power of the words.

Eight

It all came down to a single email. There it was, nestled between promotional spam from beauty shops and the Democratic Party—an email from the university with the subject line *Grant Application Results*. I hesitated. That seemed like an ominous subject line. Surely, if I'd won the grant, the subject line would be more enthusiastic.

I opened the email. *We heard from many qualified applicants*, it began. What's more insulting than someone softening the blow of a rejection? Blah blah blah, *the committee made some tough decisions*, blah blah blah, *your application was selected*. Wait, what? *Congratulations. You have been awarded the full amount.* What! I read the paragraph again.

"Talia," I yelled. I jumped up and ran to her room. "I got it!" I yelled from her doorway.

She looked up. She was sitting on her bed, working from her laptop with huge headphones holding down her wild, curly hair. "What?"

"I got the money."

"You're staying?" she took her headphones off excitedly.

"I'm staying! Wait, I can keep my room, right?"

She laughed. "Of course." She hopped off her bed and hugged me.

Then, maybe embarrassed, she took a step back, so I lunged forward and hugged her. "You've told Eyal?" she asked as we pulled apart.

"I'll tell him tomorrow," I said. "He's back from the army tomorrow."

I wanted to do it in person. I fantasized about how I'd reveal that I'd gotten the funding to stay in Israel a year. Maybe a reversal? I'd make him think that I had bad news: *So, I heard from the grant committee and I have bad news*, I'd say glumly, not meeting his eye, his heart would fall, and then I'd say, *You're not getting rid of me anytime soon*, and he'd look up with wild joy, understanding that I was staying.

The next day, he called me as his train got into Tel Aviv.

"I have something to tell you," I told him.

"I'm coming over," he said.

I met him outside my apartment, as he was parking. I got into the car. He turned off the engine. We kissed. Without the air-conditioning on, we started sweating almost immediately. I began. "So, I heard from the grant committee . . ." I said, trying not to betray too much emotion.

"Okay," he whispered. He was looking at my hands, which were in his hands, and my plan to trick him into happiness seemed all at once too cruel. Let us suffer as little as possible in the time we have.

"I'm staying," I said. "At the end of the summer, I'm staying for a year."

He brought the crown of his head into my chest wordlessly.

Our sweat left outlines of our bodies in the seats, but we stayed like that for just another minute.

That afternoon, he went to visit with his paternal grandparents while I attended to logistics: emailing my parents and professors, requesting some additional university paperwork.

Had he been happy? When I told him? I replayed the scene in the car.

He returned in the evening to pick me up for Shabbat dinner at his parents'. We were quiet on the drive north. Twice, he glanced at me without saying anything. Weren't we supposed to be happy?

At last, he spoke. "You're staying for you, right?" Concern in his voice.

"What are you asking me?" I asked. The window was open and the evening air warm.

"I mean, it's okay for your career-ah? That you are staying?" he said. He glanced at me. "I don't want you to make a sacrifice."

I nodded. "It's okay for my career," I said. A heaviness descended in the car. I had a new fear: that my staying scared him, that he'd only let himself fall in love with me because I was leaving. Wasn't that so like me? To take a game too far? Was that what this was? A game? Had I made it too real? "Does it feel okay to you?" I asked. "That I'm staying?"

He took my hand forcefully. "Are you kidding?" he said. He gripped my hand, bringing it to his mouth to kiss as he drove. "Are you kidding? I am so happy it is illegal."

I laughed.

"Arrest me!" he yelled out the open window. "Arrest me!"

As always, Eyal returned to the army for another two weeks. He was still stationed in the city of Hebron. This is my life now, I thought: a soldier's girlfriend. How could I know that the rockets were coming? That everything would change so quickly?

I wrote another Facebook update, this one with the dual purpose of informing friends who didn't know about Eyal and my decision to stay longer in Israel.

My boyfriend is stationed in Hebron. It's a dangerous place, I wrote although I'd never been there myself. *He's caught between the Palestinians who want their homes back and the Israeli settlers who want to live on holy land.* I went on to expound poetically on the biblical mentions of Hebron—how the patriarch Abraham bought land for a burial cave that still exists today, enshrined by an Ottoman-era worship complex. *It is split*, I wrote: *One entrance for Jews, one for Palestinians.* Like the lineage of Abraham himself. Two lines diverging: Sarah and Hagar.

I likened these diverging lines to the diverging impulses in myself: to leave Israel at the end of the summer as planned, to stay and see who I might become here. *Would I stay, and continue to meet a new version of myself in this new and ancient language? In this new and ancient land? Or would I go?* So much depended on the funding, I explained, trying to build a little suspense before I described the email waiting for me in my inbox:

It all came down to a single email, I wrote. Of course, I continued, my parents were nervous. (This was true: "Are you sure about this?" my mother had asked me when I told her. My father echoed her concern: "Will this affect your PhD timeline?") But I assured them that the university seemed enthusiastic. I wasn't losing anything—just gaining. *More time, more learning, more love. I'm staying.*

Writing these posts, I felt just a little bit like Odysseus. He is a man who tells his own story. Much of what we call the *Odyssey* is framed as a tale he is telling in the court of kindly King Alkinoös. "The gods spin destruction," Alkinoös says, "so that the bards will have a story worth telling."

Not long after the post went up, Erica FaceTimed me, a rare event. I answered with enthusiasm: "Hey!" I assumed she was going to congratulate me on my big news.

"Hey," she said. Her face was friendly, but there was something measured in her voice, something that indicated whatever she said next, she'd practiced saying. She looked to be on her balcony, midmorning in Montreal, evening in Tel Aviv.

I waited for her to say congratulations.

"I saw your post about Hebron," she said. Brown eyes, dark eyebrows like our father. She looked so much more Jewish than I.

"Nice," I said, unsure where this was going.

"Yeah," she hesitated. "I guess, I, well, did you know that there's a street there that's only for Jews?"

"What?"

"I'm not trying to criticize or attack you or Eyal!" she said hurriedly. "But it feels, well, it feels important to acknowledge what's happening there."

"I mean, how do you know what's happening there?" I asked. Any warmth I'd felt was draining away.

"I'll send you an article," she said, with a forced peppiness. "Hang on."

On my Facebook page, a message popped up from Erica, linking me to an article.

"You want me to look at this now?" I asked flatly.

She nodded. "Just take a look!" Her voice was this weird high octave.

The article's headline was about freedom of movement and segregation in Hebron. The opening photo was of an Orthodox Jewish woman—easily identifiable because she covered her hair in a way that left her neck and ears free—yelling or maybe even throwing something at a Muslim woman, equally identifiable because her own hair covering veiled her ears and neck. None of this was what I pictured the fleeting times I had imagined Eyal in Hebron. A sense of hiding and waiting. A sense of outmaneuvering combatants, everyone with face painted and weapons in dark corners. But what the article portrayed seemed—What was the word? Civilian, almost.

"Are you getting all this from Cee?" I asked. I had an image of this counterculture gender revolutionary whispering anti-imperialist slogans into my little sister's ear.

Now it was Erica's turn to act surprised. "Getting what?"

"Is she giving you these articles?"

A hardness passed over my sister. "They," she said. "Cee uses 'they' and 'them' pronouns."

Oops. Now I list "she/her" in my email signature, but ten years ago it was all new to me. I should have just apologized, but I guess I was looking for a fight. "But Cee is a she, right?" I asked.

"No," Erica said. "Please do not say that." Clear and forceful. "When you refer to my partner, you will use 'they' and 'them' pronouns." It was the first time I'd ever heard her refer to Cee as a partner.

"Okay, calm down," I said.

"I am calm," Erica said decisively. "Respecting someone's gender is not a big ask."

"But like, *they* were born a woman, right?" I emphasized my use of the correct pronoun.

"Assigned female at birth, yes," Erica said.

"It seems so complicated," I said.

"Allie, someone's genitals aren't the truth about that person," she said. "You're smart enough to understand that." Then, because she's kind, probably too kind, Erica softened. "You'll get there," she said. "Just keep practicing."

"Okay," I acquiesced. I think she might be a better person than I am. "I'll do better."

In Hebrew class, I asked Smadar if there was such a thing as "nonbinary" in Modern Hebrew. "What are you asking me?" she said, genuinely confused.

I explained to Smadar about "them" and "they," peppering my response with English. What would come to be called the Nonbinary Hebrew Project didn't exist yet, but from my studies of the Talmud, I knew of a variety of historical Jewish sources that acknowledge people who, today, might refer to themselves as trans and intersex. "You know, there is a tradition about Mordechai and Esther," I began to say. It's a bit notorious: the rabbis of the Talmud imagine that the biblical hero Mordechai breastfed his niece Esther.

But Smadar cut me off. "In Hebrew everything is feminine or masculine," she said to the whole class. "Even in plural." She shrugged. "Sorry!"

For less than a second, I experienced language as performance—a kind of play that we were, all of us, putting on. In this play, you were supposed to call a person by their genitals. Like any piece of theater, it required we suspend our disbelief and buy into the artifice that what we call a thing is somehow linked to its essence, like God speaking the world into existence. How brilliant I found Cee in that fast-disappearing moment, and how frightening. So much was destabilized just by their existence, which reminded us of how much power we have beyond the systems that hold us. My last thought, as the moment closed and I reentered the stage, was that I could never live like Cee.

And then the moment was over, and what I cared about most was that I maintain the warmth I enjoyed with Smadar, who had been so delighted to hear that I was staying. I knew so few things about myself, but I knew that: I wanted Smadar to like me.

"I understand," I said.

Smadar had already moved on to the business of the day: encouraging everyone in class to sign up for something called "Conversation Club."

"It's very nice," she said, passing around a sign-up sheet.

I put down my name.

"You will be matched in a *zug*, a pair," she continued, "and speak English half the time and Hebrew the other." This is the best way to learn, she said. She winked at me. "Just ask Allison," she added.

All of the elements were organizing themselves into a new narrative, although I had no way of knowing that yet. Eyal in the army, the conversation partner I had yet to meet, a girl named Aisha waiting to enter stage right, Erica sulking in the orchestra pit. Everyone waiting on the cue we did not know was coming—the cry of the rocket siren, so soon in our future.

I have a clear memory of the last weekend Eyal and I spent together before the rockets began. The moment before everything changed. Eyal said he wanted to take me to a special spot on the beach. A quiet spot.

In his parents' kitchen, we made sandwiches from white bread and an off-brand Israeli hazelnut spread with a lingering chemical note that I found oddly pleasant. It was morning, but already it was hot. "It will be crowded," his mom warned us between loads of laundry. She always looked chic, even just to do chores around the apartment. Loose, flowing pants and layered pendants on thin gold chains.

"I know a spot," he said. "A quieter spot."

We were standing close. He made sandwiches, and I cut an apple into segments. My hip came up to his thigh, and sometimes, probably without registering what he was doing, he would kiss the top of my head.

"You two are so cute," his mom said. She had been overjoyed to hear about my grant, repeating what she'd said the first time we'd met about Israel being a safe place for Jews.

Koral walked into the kitchen. "It will be crowded," she said. She was a replica of the mother. Not a miniature, because she was in fact less delicate, sturdier. From a distance, they could have been sisters, one tinier than the other. The two women were aligned on their thinking in almost everything, and yet—or maybe, therefore—they were often bickering.

"I told them," her mom said. "So crowded."

"And I said I know a place," Eyal repeated, looking at me and rolling his eyes.

But Eyal's mom was busy noticing that Koral—in a white sundress and platform espadrille sandals—was dressed to go out. "Oh, you're going out?" she said, her voice sweet. She adjusted the spaghetti straps of Koral's dress. "You're done working on your presentation?"

Koral fussed with her hair in agitation. "*Ima!*" she said, her voice plaintive and whiny. "I'll work on it after."

"After what?"

"I'm meeting friends for a coffee."

"Wouldn't it be easier to finish the presentation first?"

Just leave, I thought to myself. She can't stop you. But Koral stayed fixed. "It's not fair," she said, her voice soft now. That the phrase she used—*zeh lo fair*—is a little childish made it all the more painful. "I can't get even a little break." She covered her face with her hands. Her exasperation was painful. I was meant to be cutting up more fruits, but mostly I was following the exchange.

Eyal was now folding towels into a beach bag—not so much actively ignoring the tension but, I think, immune to it. It passed over him and his father, whatever it was that bound the two women together. "Do we have the *matkot*?" he asked nobody in particular, referring to the paddle-and-ball game so popular on Israeli beaches. Nobody answered him so he answered himself. "Maybe in the hall closet," he said, wandering away.

Now it was the three of us in the kitchen.

The mother approached Koral. "*Beseder, beseder*," she crooned, gently removing her daughter's hands from her face. "I'm sorry, I worry, but you're right, *zeh lo fair*."

Theirs was such a claustrophobic, obsessive love, this mother and daughter. Foreign to me. It disgusted me, and I envied them.

In a year or two, Koral would become engaged to her boyfriend, an affable man with a boyish smile. Both his parents had immigrated to Israel from Iran as children. In the army, he'd done something related to computer intelligence, and now he had a demanding and promising job at a start-up. When he was at the apartment, his presence was muted—agreeing with Koral as she whispered frantically about her mother. "*Beseder*, my love," he'd say to her, one hand rubbing her lower back, the other scrolling through his phone. I was older than them both.

"Are you ready?" Eyal asked me. He had a bag with the towels and, if he'd found it, the paddle game.

"I'm ready," I said.

"Have fun!" his mom called out when we left.

Koral was back in her room.

We didn't have a picnic basket, so we put the food in a plastic bag, which, of course, we forgot in the car when he parked it alongside a few others on a dirt patch overlooking the sea. We were in northern Tel Aviv, not far from teeming beaches, but he was right in that we could have been in a far more remote spot. There was no true path leading down to the water, so we sidestepped carefully down the gritty embankment. Handfuls of toilet paper were caught on scrub brush.

When we reached the beach, it wasn't sand but craggly sheets of rock reaching out over the water. It was hot, but the sea was restless. The rocks under our feet were porous and sharp.

The only other people in sight were two older couples sitting in a small natural pool. By "older," I mean they were my age. The men were hairy, the women full-figured in supportive bikinis. I was supposed to be like them—in stable pre-marriage relationships, sitting in a pool of stagnant water. But here I was, holding hands with a beautiful boy as we approached the ledge. They had been talking among themselves, laughing, but now they were silent as Eyal and I eased ourselves to sit in the place where the rock dropped off into deep water.

The waves came hard, and before I could get into the sea, they pushed me onto my back. I fell the way you fall in water, in slow, foreseeable but inevitable motions. The older couples remained untouched in their tide pool. Eyal helped me back to the edge of the rocks—"*At beseder?* You're okay?" I sat again on the ledge, my legs in the water that seemed to have no bottom. So unlike the other beaches in Tel Aviv, with their soft sand and gradual increases in depth. I told Eyal I was *beseder*. He nodded. Together we pushed off into deep water.

Nobody describes the sea. Its hugeness is not a quality so much as a referent. We could not see anything below us. It is possible that creatures on those hidden sands looked up at our legs, cast in green like the night vision images Eyal sometimes sent to me without explanation. Four wisps of flesh, kicking, kicking, kicking.

We gripped on to each other's hands as long as we could until we were torn apart. Eyal laughed, a desperate and hysterical sound that frightened me. The waters swelled like a muscle. His head seemed so small, bobbing away from me.

Do you know what it would mean for the sea to swallow you? It would mean nothing. That is why it is the sea.

Nine

Morning is pitching toward noon, and I've barely made a dent in the stack of blue exam booklets. Instead, I'm slipping into nostalgia. Lost in thoughts of Eyal and those dreamy months before the invasion, as if the past itself were leaking out from that box in the baby's room. Pale pinewood. Almost like a coffin, except for that imitation brass latch. I wonder if Koral bought it especially for its purpose.

I do not want to open the box. What is there to be gained from letting myself be pulled into the past?

I stand slowly from my desk, my joints sore from sitting. In my lower back, there is a tightness that has not let up since I hit week fifteen.

Through the closed windows, I hear the wind and cars. Someone is speaking into a cell phone on the street below. But the world seems very far away. Very, very far away. In the kitchen, I pour myself a glass of water, which I drink and refill and drink again. Our kitchen has plants hanging in the windows—philodendron with leaves like cartoon hearts. On the fridge are magnets printed with photos from weddings, our own and those of our friends. Our faces are sweaty with happy exhaustion from all that dancing. One of those magnets holds up an ultrasound of our baby, his head like a waxing moon. We've never made it this far before. Our OBGYN says he's healthy (*Baruch hashem*, my mother-in-law would add after in a superstitious gesture to the divine—*Thank God*). *I love you*, I think, each time I touch the shadowy image. It is the simplest sentence ever to come to me—utterly uncontested. *I love you.* Whatever you cost me, I love you. The hours away from my work, the deadlines I'll miss while tending to your colic or constipation, the nights I'll beg for sleep as you scream, the mornings I'll spend kissing every feature on your perfect face instead of marking exams—I want it more than I've ever wanted anything for myself.

In a way, Eyal gave me this life, didn't he? I am not sure I would have been brave enough (foolish enough?) to extend my short semester stay into a full year—which became two years, which became, well, forever—had Eyal's hand not been held out to me, like a stepping-stone across a river. When we imagined a future where we were both at the university, he for his first degree and me as a researcher, I think we really believed it. The more we fell in love, the less the age difference seemed to matter. Is that delusion? I don't know. They marry so young in Israel. Not only the religious. They marry young, and everyone brings a check as a wedding present to help them cover the cost of the wedding. Tradition.

This semester I'm teaching a course on freedom and restraint in the "rabbinic tradition," meaning, the rearticulation of Judaism following the destruction of the Temple in 70 CE (or AD, as my Evangelical students insist on saying). The heart of religious life had been ripped out, the sanctuaries destroyed and looted. The pillaging is famously depicted in the Arch of Titus—gleeful Roman foot soldiers carrying away the lamp wrought for God. Gone was the inner sanctum, that holy of holies where, once a year on Yom Kippur, the high priest entered to speak to God. There was no one else on earth who could enter this room—a room that no longer exists. When the high priest went in, he wore a rope around his ankle so that if he died in the presence of the divine, he could be dragged out. "What do you pray for?" the high priest asked one Yom Kippur, standing before the divine name that nobody may say. The Holy One answered: I PRAY MY MERCY OUTWEIGH MY JUDGMENT.

Once Jerusalem was lost, where could we go to talk to God? What room could hold all our devotion? The answer was radiant and unforeseeable: in the text. Sanctify no new ground, but inscribe our stories in your heart. In this schema, study is as sacred as prayer. My course focuses on instances in the Talmud when the rabbis seem to be calling their own project into question. How far should they let themselves depart from the religion of Temple Judaism in order to save it? I teach my students to read in search of anxiety. (Academics love anxiety.)

I suspect it is their relationship to loss that draws me to our sages. These were men who knew the power of negative space. The city is ruined, the Temple is smashed, the people are scattered. In that absence, your longing may flourish into a new song, one that lives inside your heart. Call that place Zion—the place we love from afar. My lover is mine, and I am my lover's, but only at a great distance.

There is a theory of attraction that states desire and intimacy are at odds, because desire is premised on distance and intimacy on proximity.

I AM THINKING ABOUT YOU, Eyal might text. Then, almost immediately, correct himself: NO, I AM TOUCHING YOU. I'M THERE.

YOU'RE HERE, I echoed back. I FEEL YOU.

But more than texting, we wrote love letters. Actual, physical letters. Not ones to post in the mail—he often changed bases, and anyway there was the military censor to worry about. Instead, we spent the weeks he was away writing letters that we exchanged when he came home for those brief weekends of sleep, laundry, family time, and furtive sex. Each time he left to go back to base—or, eventually, to Gaza—he did so with a small stack of letters from me.

When I wrote to him, I imagined him hiding in some barracks storeroom or crawling into an out-of-commission tank—stealing away, seeking out a moment for himself amid the random chaos of the army.

Each letter made note of the hour: *It's 1:17am and I love you.*

It is 7:03pm. The cats have begun to scream through their coupling.

Inscribing time, inscribing me in time.

Each night, our baby wakes me up at 4:00 a.m. with his kicking. Our OBGYN—an American man in a kippa who made *aliyah* from Maryland—says this means that once baby is born, 4:00 a.m. will most likely be the "witching hour"—that is, when baby is awake and fussy.

In a sense, this baby could have been Eyal's. I mean, not really. I was on the pill when we were together. But in a larger, more abstract sense—there is another version of my life, and in that version I am carrying Eyal's baby. Kick, kick.

I know what's in the pine box. It is our love letters, calling out to me from under the daybed.

This was not a done thing, the writing of letters. Certainly, no soldier expected it of a girlfriend or boyfriend. But in a way, it was an Israeli who had given us the idea. Early in our romance, Eyal told me about a letter he had found stashed in a hidden compartment of some ancient grenade launcher. "What, like they have pockets?" I asked. He didn't bother to answer this question. He said it was a love letter, written to a girl by a soldier who was not sure if he would come home. It was dated from the time of the last war they had up north.

I asked Eyal if the soldier had survived. He said he didn't know, but he had to assume the guy was dead because why else would he leave his letter in there? I asked him to read me the letter, but he said he didn't have it. He remembered a single full sentence to translate into English for me. *And if I do not make it through this night, know I loved you.*

I wanted, very badly, to read the whole letter; it seemed precious, more precious than anything anyone had ever written to me, but he let another soldier keep it, or so he told me. I'm not sure I believe that. I suspect he kept the letter a secret from the others in his unit. I imagine him reading the dead soldier's letter during downtime at some muddy combat drill or while waiting his turn at the firing ranges. All around him, there is the pantomime of war, but here, on this torn piece of notebook paper, is a life, just as pointless and indistinguishable as all the others. Here is a document of all the doomed longing that we, each of us, walk around with every day—that we will die with. Too precious to share with anyone, even me. He must have kept the letter for himself.

Soon after, we began writing our own letters.

The light that pours across my desk is clean. White light, reflecting off the white buildings of our neighborhood. Old North Tel Aviv has a quiet, insistent romance. The streets are wide, lined with trees, cafes, and bookshops. In the air, I smell jasmine and oranges wherever I go. A Mediterranean Europe created by exiles, drawn from memory, the way that centuries before, the synagogues of Europe were decorated with paintings of a misremembered Jerusalem.

Poets and philosophers walk these streets. Every other week, I see perhaps the greatest living translator of Hebrew into English taking lunch with his editor at a round table cafe. Both men live in Jerusalem; I do not know why they choose to meet here, except that there seems to be a spiritual pipeline between Jewish Jerusalem and this particular corridor of Tel Aviv. Yehuda Amichai famously called inland Jerusalem "a port city on the shore of eternity," which I think makes the Old North a port on the shores of Jerusalem.

Our building has an interior courtyard. Half our windows look onto the ocean, while the other half open to the lush sanctum of a gated garden. Neighborhood cats snooze under the wide leaves of the flowering plumeria tree. Always, there is a breeze.

In a moment when my mind is not racing—that's all I've ever wanted, isn't it? To calm this mind—I hear the piano. This happens now and then. One of our neighbors will be playing piano. I can never figure out which of our neighbors it is. What a challenge it must be to keep a piano in our humid city. How often they must need to tune it. From experience I know it will go all day like this—the piano player repeating variations on the same wistful, forlorn chords that slip between major and minor progressions, sweet and sad. I lean against the kitchen sink, listening as the piano tells the one story that is every story: we are small, we are scared, we are brave. We love, we hurt, we fall apart, we change, we let go, we go on. We become unrecognizable. We stay more or less the same—small and scared. It goes forever. Stay as long as you can.

Perhaps this is the song from the burning piano we saw at the museum. If he found it in the fields, he'd have thought it was God. Our hands were almost touching. Almost touching. Each atom in the air between us was electric. God, everything mattered so much.

When you teach narrative long enough, you learn to note that beginnings contain their endings. Most stories are told twice: the first time in such a way that it necessitates the second, fuller telling, which is the book itself. So too in a relationship. If you pay attention you can see it all unfolding right from the first day—the dynamic that makes love possible is probably the one that will destroy it—you understand and you go forward anyway. Or, better to say you walk backward until you find you are kneeling on the cold floor of your baby's room, reaching under the daybed for a box that holds what's left of once-love.

I groan a little as I reach for the box under the bed. It won't be there.

It will be gone—whisked back into the past. But it's not gone. My fingertips graze the wood. The box is closer than it was before; I pull it out without the broom.

The piano player is still playing the same simple, devastating refrain.

Baby kicks, startling me. Kick, kick. Little fist at the door. "You're awake?" I ask, rubbing my belly as I sit up. Maybe he wants to read the letters too. Or maybe he's warning me not to.

I touch the latch. What am I doing? The love letters are waiting for me. Not the ones Eyal wrote me—those are tucked in one journal or another—but the ones I wrote him. Love letters that have made their way back to me. Scraps of all my devotion.

When I open the box, the flood of memory is unbearable. Pages of letters, papery and faded. Dried flowers I pressed between pages. All the letters I wrote to him. I catch glimpses of sentences as I shuffle through the pages: *need you*, *miss you*, *he was praying*, *without you*, *someone else*. Here is his name in my slightly blocky Hebrew.

I sort through the letters I have not seen in almost a decade. Koral brought them in this pine box on the day she returned my things to me. It's true that I tried my best to forget about them, but it's also true that I've moved twice since then—it is as if this box slipped itself into a suitcase, determined to follow me.

The pages are soft. Some have been creased and uncreased many times—in and out of one of his uniform pockets, maybe.

It's afternoon, I wrote on an index card cut into the shape of a child's valentine heart, *and the sun is warm and sleepy-making in my room*. The crease at the center of the heart is worn to softness; he must have opened this one often. *I am thinking about how when we are together—when I am alone with you—the room we are in becomes sacred. This room has been sacred with us in it.*

I switched between English and Hebrew—writing simpler sentences in Hebrew and more complex ones in English.

Usually, my handwriting is borderline illegible, but when I wrote to Eyal in English, I wrote in a large, clear print. Like almost every Israeli I've ever met, he couldn't read cursive.

When I wrote in Hebrew, the words were a little oversized and shaky at first, although this improved in time.

So many times I wrote, *I'm not sure if I'll let you read this.* I remember how often I really did hesitate! It was difficult to give him writing in which I knew I appeared in less than the best light: too jealous (*I wonder if there are a lot of girls on your base . . .*), too desperate, too obsessive (*I feel you everywhere*). Or maybe just trying too hard to turn him on (*I said your name as I touched myself*). But in the end, I always gave him the letter. Why? Well, it felt good to do it; I remember that. It felt good to imagine that the letters belonged to him—that even if I wanted to, I had no right to keep them. This was a way of saying: *Parts of me belong to you.*

Who is this girl who offers herself so fully? It is I, but also, she is gone. I can't quite remember being her.

Written on French stationery of the palest lavender: *I found a shell on the beach. When I held it up to my ear, it sang your name.*

By the date at the top of the page, I know he wasn't in Gaza yet when I wrote this letter.

It's nearly 6pm and my toes are in the sand and I just read a poem I love. Reread, actually. I am crying. Salty water drying on my shoulders. (I swam!) Salty water in my hair. Salty tears falling in the book of poetry.

I wish I could remember which poem made me cry.

There is a persistent delicacy in my letter-writing voice. So different from the *I* who wrote—writes—essays, Facebook posts, or even emails. I noted what flowers were in bloom. I pressed their petals between the pages. Here they are, all these years later. Pressed flowers, fluttering down onto the bedspread—translucent and nearly colorless. When I try to pick one up, it crumbles.

Leafing through these pages—so many pages!—of writing to Eyal, I find I was often mired in our shared history. *Do you remember the park? Do you remember the old woman on the bus? Do you? Do you remember?*

My correspondence with Eyal was not entirely one-sided. He wrote me love notes, brief and urgent. Less of a production than what I wrote him, his missives were written on sheets of graph paper, folded into squares and creased with desert dirt.

He wrote to me almost exclusively in English, a choice he explained early on: *I don't express myself much in my own language, but in your language I can say this: I feel that I already know you.*

I know I shouldn't do it, but of course I am already getting up to find the journal that houses his letters to me—the overstuffed, faux leather one I used that year. Like the box, the journal is bursting with ephemera: leafy twigs from olive trees, programs from academic conferences, photos of soldiers ripped out from magazines. And here, tucked in the back, here they are, his letters to me. All these years I've moved around with this journal and never cracked it open.

Barefoot through the apartment, I take the journal and the box of letters with me and go back to bed. I never nap. I pride myself in discipline, but I am getting back into the soft, unmade haven of bed. The covers are cool and clean.

I spread the papers out before me in bed like a child surveying her Halloween candy. Indulgences. Old letters, old journals—all the detritus of love. I'll read through it all. Just this once. I'll read through it all and immerse myself completely. Then I'll throw it all away.

In a longer note he'd written a month or so before the invasion, when he was on duty in the West Bank, he tried to explain the struggle of having a self in the army. *I do not own my time nor my body*, he wrote in his slightly formal high school English. *The army owns me. I want to know who I am, who I really am. I took your advice and emailed a professor in bioethics about how to get "into the field."* He put this part in quotes.

When we looked it up, we had found that only in English can "the field" refer to both an academic discipline and a nebulous zone of combat. In Hebrew, they were two different words.

I hope the professor will write back. (He did, I recall, advising Eyal to pursue an undergraduate degree in biology.) *Thank you for believing in me. Thank you for believing I am more than I seem right now.*

Note from Eyal on a Post-it bearing some other unit's insignia, dated early summer, less than two months before he went into Gaza. *Know that on this date, someone loved you.*

My favorite notes have a simple urgency: *I want to smell you. So bad.*

Letter from Eyal on another piece of graph paper: *Do you remember the weekend we stayed trapped in bed? The strawberry ice cream? The bus headlights flashing in your room?*

Before he went down to the Gazan border, our biggest challenge had been time. That's what we wanted: more time. More and more time. There was so much life he wanted to catch up on during these brief stays home. We planned restaurant meals, trips to the beach, concerts, hiking. Yet often, after a meal with his parents and a movie with his sister, we fell asleep together on the couch, and that was it—the next day he went back to the army.

But one weekend he said we were going to do it all. He'd stay with me the whole time. So on a Thursday night we lay in my bed, planning out the next day. His boots were by the door, and his rifle was under my bed.

"Okay, what time should we get up?" I asked him. We lay perpendicular, his head on my belly.

"Eight," he said sleepily. It was past midnight.

"Maybe eight thirty?" My hands ran along the prickles of his scalp.

"Eight fifteen," he said, and then in one quick movement he was standing up, pulling on boxers. There was an explosive power to his movements that reminded me of the acceleration drills my high school soccer coach had put us through.

Sitting at my desk, he used a gel pen to write up a schedule on a piece of printer paper. He wrote in military time.

08:15: Up, make healthy breakfast. An ambitious start, but the next day we slept past ten and when we woke we were already making love, softly moaning into each other's mouths. I climaxed first, with his fingers inside me. Only then did he enter me, cupping my body from behind. We faced the same direction. Big spoon, little spoon. Moving together. He came that way, clutching me close, his face in my hair. "Don't forget to pee," he reminded me, sinking back into the pillows. He had learned about UTIs in his medic training course. When I came back from the bathroom, he was asleep, and his sleeping pulled me in.

09:00: Finish eating, shower. But it was nearly noon by the time we got out of bed for the second time. Bashful at our lack of self-control. We ate handfuls of a sugary breakfast cereal—*puff* something, or was it *pop* something—that I'd bought from a Russian-owned convenience store where everything was imported and overpriced.

10:00: Walk to beach. In the shower, his lean and powerful body was delightful. He had very little body hair. Perhaps he would get more as he got older, I didn't know. But the warm water bounced off his skin, and when I pressed up against him it was as if our bodies were communicating without our minds. We kissed with wet mouths. I maintained eye contact as I dropped to my knees. When I took him in my mouth, his hands were in my hair and he said my name.

I do not know what happened to the piece of paper that Eyal scribbled our doomed schedule on. It is not in the box and not in any journal I've leafed through. Thrown out, most likely. No matter. The gel pen ink would have faded by now anyway. It disappears with the years.

The schedule had us arriving at the beach by 10:30 a.m., but it was well into the afternoon and we still hadn't left the apartment. By this time, according to the schedule, we were meant to be getting lunch at a new and popular Tel Aviv spot that—this was novel for Israel—served breakfast 'round the clock like an American diner. All day we had lingered in each other's bodies, and now we were rushing to salvage the hours. Eyal brought a plate of cut-up fruit to my room. I was tying the strings on a bikini I'd only recently felt confident enough to wear. At that age, you never understand how beautiful you are. Looking back, I see how perfect my body was—thin but supple. Touchable, Eyal had told me. "Oh no," he said, watching me from the doorway, holding a plate of melon and citrus. "Oh no," he said again, putting the plate down on a chair midstride, not stopping, moving toward me with a momentum that made my stomach rise. "Oh no." His face in my neck, my delight as he pushed us down to the bed. "Oh no." He was hard for me, for me. We never made it to the beach.

We lay in bed eating strawberry ice cream from the carton, the schedule abandoned. The ice cream was Häagen-Dazs, despite the ready availability of superior Israeli ice cream from the parlors all over my block. Eyal had picked it out—I think he found it exotic.

"There's something I'd like to try," he said, tugging an earlobe nervously. "I hope you won't think I'm gross."

My bedroom was ground level on a main boulevard. At night, when the buses were still running, their headlights filled my room and I could hear the station announcements in my dreams—"The next station is . . ." A sentence that, in Hebrew, is dominated by "a" vowels. *Ha-takhana ha-bah . . .*

I used my spoon to scrape off a delicate spiral of pink ice cream. "Tell me," I said, eating it and tasting nothing. I was nervous too. I knew it was about sex. Sex and ice cream. Would he ask to put ice cream inside me? Was that a thing? Could I get a UTI that way? Would I say yes anyway?

But Eyal said, "I want to kiss you when you have ice cream in your mouth." He traced a circle over my knee, afraid to make eye contact. It tickled lightly.

Don't laugh, I cautioned myself, *don't laugh. You'll hurt his feelings. You'll dash this intimacy. You'll seem like a worn-out old slut.*

I picked up his hand and kissed the inside of his wrist. Outside my window, a bus went by, its headlights casting mad shadows all over the room. *The next station is . . .* I waited for it to pass to say, "Yes." I kissed up the inside of his arm. "Yes," I whispered again. His neck. "Yes." His eyelids. "Yes, yes, yes."

Note written on a piece of scrap printer paper: *I remember your strawberry tongue. Sometimes remembering makes me sad.*

On the reverse side is a blurry topographical map printed on a black-and-white printer with low ink. On it are markings I will never decipher and all the secret names the army gives the places it watches.

Here is a secret: Eyal was the better writer. It's true, because he wrote not toward a desired effect but in an attempt to convey the truth in his heart. He was not trying to come off a certain way in his writing. Not strong, not powerful, not sensitive, not wise. No, he was using words to explain something to himself. That's what makes him so good.

Regarding his mother and sister, inseparable and constantly bickering:

They are trapped inside each other. When Ima sees Koral she really sees herself, and when Koral tries to imagine herself all she can see is Ima. It is not like this for me and Aba. Not even close.

Regarding the field of bioethics and what drew him to it:

I remember a scientist from Haifa on TV explaining about the work in his lab. A Russian Jew pushing his glasses up on his nose. If we can manipulate the genetics of an unborn baby, should we? Could blue eyes be a luxury item? These questions seem little, but they cast huge shadows. That's what he said: huge shadows. Questions like, What is life? Do we need God?

The questions remind me of metaphor-ah. How you explained it to me. Do you remember? You pointed to the sun, you said, "It's too much to see." To look at it hurts. To see the sun we watch its reflection in tide pools. "Metaphor is a reflection," you said. You were speaking so beautifully. I had never heard anyone speak so beautifully. My heart was throwing up. Anyway, what I am saying is bioethicah is metaphors: little questions as reflections for the questions that are too big to ask.

Regarding his grandfather, his *saba*:

He gave up so much to help build this country. Even parts of himself he gave up. Foods he didn't eat anymore, words he stopped saying. Whatever he was, he let go to become Israeli.

Rereading now, it strikes me that I don't quite recognize the person behind Eyal's letters. The ambition I recognize. He always seemed like someone driven and focused beyond his years, which is perhaps why we both truly believed that when the impediment of the army was done, he and I could start our lives together. But what I didn't hear at the time was his questioning. He is thinking about the stories we tell ourselves. What makes us a family? What makes us a people? Here, I see the seeds for despair and even, possibly, resistance.

What else did I not see at the time? It is as if I am scrutinizing a self-portrait by someone I know well—finding an imperfect overlap between my seeing and the painter's seeing of himself. The author behind Eyal's letters is not a stranger, and yet he is not, precisely, the person I had imagined I was writing to all those years ago.

And surely, the reverse must be true. Surely, his letters are addressed to someone who is not precisely me, but rather the version of me he created to love me. Was there a brief disappointment each time he came home? Did the person he imagined—the person he wrote to, the person who wrote to him—become further and further from the person he found waiting? It is as if there were four of us in the relationship. Both of us competing with an imagined counterpart.

Some might say it doesn't sound terribly romantic—to engage in acts of mutual distortion. But I suspect that acts of mutual distortion might simply *be* what we call romance. And I wonder, what happens to those imagined counterparts? The person I was in his eyes, the one he was in mine—what happens to them? When romance is over, that is, when we are done with our distortions, do they disappear? The girl with the green bow in her hair, the one he followed onto the bus that first day—where is she now? I think she must live outside of me, made true by the fantasies that Eyal wove for her each time he read my letters.

I didn't tell Eyal this, but I often thought about the doomed soldier and the forgotten letter he tucked away into the grenade launcher before he died. *And if I do not make it through this night, know I loved you.* Sometimes

I caught myself thinking that the dead man was the other version of my lover, and all along it was to him, not to Eyal, that I'd been writing—someone already lost, someone waiting, someone who didn't exist except as someone I have written.

Does this mean—I hate asking myself this question—that I erased Eyal? That I needed him to play a role? That I never saw him as a whole person? I'd rather not think about it.

On uncharacteristically delicate blue paper, Eyal recounted the day we spent in the park, slipping toward the river, mythologizing our first meeting. *I am nostalgic for these things even as they are happening.*

I've spent my adult life writing sentences, and I've never written one as true as that.

The letter goes on: *When I remember that day, the park is empty. Nobody is there, not even us.*

Ten

What changed everything was the air-raid sirens, like an alarm cutting through a dream.

Eyal was on a mission in Hebron—in "the field" without his phone—the first time I heard a rocket siren, trilling up and down my spine.

I was home at my desk. I froze. *Go outside? No, stay inside. Oh my God.* I felt my sphincter spasm, and I understood for the first time in my life how people can shit themselves out of fear, although thankfully I did not.

Talia appeared in my doorway, sleepy eyes in an oversized sweatshirt. "*Bo'i*, Allie," she said, a note of apology in her voice. *Come.*

Together, we left the apartment and entered the hallway. "Our building is old," she said. "We don't have a bomb shelter." We stood by the bikes locked under the stairs.

"Is this safe?" I asked. My stomach was seizing. The siren was still going. Our upstairs neighbor—our landlady, actually—came down the stairs with her two middle school–aged girls. As a landlady, she was a difficult woman who sometimes showed up at our door without warning to peek in and comment on how dirty the apartment was.

"*Bo'u, bo'u*," Talia called up to them as they, all three of them, clopped down the stairs in flip-flops.

They reached the landing, panting as the siren stopped.

Quiet.

Our landlady huddled with her girls in the back of the stairwell. Away from any windows, I realized. That's why we were here.

The boom was so percussive I thought it meant a nearby building had been hit. Talia and our landlady looked at each other. The thought that came to me: *They really do hate us.* As if I hadn't quite believed Eyal's mom all the times she said it.

Twice more: *boom, boom.* Car alarms started going off.

One of the middle school girls was recording a video of her face as she responded to the booms.

"Three," Talia said, and the landlady nodded. "Three booms." Later, I learned that the boom is the sound of the antimissile defense system intercepting a Hamas rocket.

I texted Eyal: SIRENS.

"Uh-oh," Talia said to me as we returned to our apartment, "maybe you regret that you will stay?"

"Of course not," I exclaimed, sliding off my shoes in our vestibule. Fear was still prickling across my skin.

"No? I shouldn't look for a new roommate?" She was joking, but there was a sad note in her voice. I almost want to call it embarrassment.

"Don't you dare!" I protested, playing along a little.

Talia smiled then. "It's nice for me to hear. That you want to be in this crazy place." She locked the apartment door behind us.

It was later that night, just as I was getting into bed, that Eyal responded to my text about the sirens.

FUCK I WAS IN THE FIELD, he wrote. WHERE DID YOU GO?

I told him Talia took me to a safe place in our building.

YOU HAVE A BOMB SHELTER?

I replied that no, we didn't, but that apparently the Israeli army was good at shooting down missiles with other missiles. TELL THEM I SAY THANKS, I texted, hoping I sounded plucky. Hoping I sounded Israeli.

I WISH I COULD BE THERE, he wrote. I'LL BE HOME IN A FEW DAYS IF THEY LET ME OFF BASE.

Odd that now, he was the one worrying about me. As if I were on a mission, as if I were in "the field," which in a way I was as the divisions between war and home blurred.

Smadar seemed almost amused when she addressed our Hebrew class. "Hamas is sending us presents from Gaza," she said. "When you hear the siren, you go either to a shelter"—she had taught us the Hebrew word for "bomb shelter"—"or, minimum, to a hallway." She adjusted the floral shawl she wore against the summer air-conditioning.

The new immigrant from Russia raised her hand. "Stay out of the washroom," she added. "So much glass." How effortlessly glamorous she seemed—nonchalant in her business casual pencil skirt as she gave helpful tips for missile strikes.

"Don't be scared. We have the *kippat barzel*," Smadar said, referring to the antimissile defense system.

We went back to our lesson on reciprocal verbs.

When the rocket siren interrupted class, everyone froze. "*Yalla*," Smadar said gently. We stood, a little awkwardly, and shuffled into the basement bomb shelter. *Boom.* Percussive shock of a rocket from Gaza being shot down. *Boom. Boom. Boom.* Four booms this time.

It's not that it was exciting. That is not the right word, "exciting"; after all, the fear was so real. Every time we went to the bomb shelter, I had trouble regulating my breath. Maybe the word I'm looking for is "vital." I was here. Something was happening, and I was here for it. I was staying.

I THINK I'M IN LOVE WITH SOMEONE ELSE, I texted Eyal. Then paused for a second. Not long enough to make him actually freak out, just enough to make my follow-up text land. I'M IN LOVE WITH KIPPAT BARZEL, I wrote, using the Hebrew name for the antimissile system.

He wrote HAHAH so many times that it filled up two rows of text messages.

We had four more days until he came home from Hebron.

Nobody was talking about the possibility of a ground invasion. Not yet.

The English translation for *kippat barzel* is most commonly "Iron Dome," but that fails to capture the religious significance of the name. Literally, it means "Yarmulke of Iron." Like all the invasions named for biblical verses, it gives the sense of a war with the divine on our side. Holy war.

My parents were worried. My dad's voice was grave on the phone. "Listen, my dear, maybe you want to rethink this plan to stay," he said to me on a call he made using an international phone card. "Your mother and I can pay for your ticket." It would be a decade before he could afford to retire. In his restrained way, he was telling me he loved me. But how to explain to him and my mother that scared though I was, there was nowhere else I wanted to be? How horrible it would feel to watch all this from the outside—to be stuck refreshing a news feed in Montreal or New York while rockets fell on Tel Aviv. How to explain that it would feel like losing myself to be away from Israel? This place needed me here, or maybe I needed it, but either way I was exactly where I wanted to be—in the middle of it all, posting conspicuously nonchalant Facebook posts about meeting my neighbors in the building hallway as we waited out a rocket attack, all of us in our pajamas. Even now, I still feel that same vitality whenever the old antagonisms flare up and the rockets are falling. Many days I question my decision to stay in Israel, where it's almost impossible to find steady work, where the taxes are staggering and the bureaucracy maddening, where my Jewish heritage did qualify me for citizenship but still excludes me from the category of true Jew. But when the rockets come back, when there is something to survive, I feel once again that I am exactly where I need to be. I'm here, and it matters. It's important. "It's not so bad," I told my anxious father. "It's not as bad as the news makes it seem."

Invasion talk began. On an Israeli news show, a retired Israeli general was discussing the possibility that the prime minister would call up reserve soldiers—men who had finished their service but remained on call well into their thirties or forties. "We need to clear out the tunnels," the general said. He was referring to the secret passageways that Gazan resistance fighters burrowed to subvert the fortified border fence. "We need to exterminate them." Everyone on the show agreed: it's time to go in.

It's just talk, I promised myself.

So as to not make it real, I didn't text Eyal to ask about it. He would be home in three days.

In Hebrew class, Smadar brought up the Conversation Club again. I'd forgotten about signing up for it. "You should see an email," she said. An email would tell us the name of our assigned Hebrew conversation partner and where we should meet. "Check for the email."

When I checked, I found that I'd be meeting someone named Timor at a university cafe near the library.

It was a relief to think of befriending another Israeli. I didn't want to join the other foreign grad students for taco night at the Irish-themed bar near campus. ("You coming?" they always asked me, mostly archaeology students who were here to do terminal degrees. They celebrated the

Fourth of July together and always spoke English. "Maybe next time," I told them, until they stopped asking.)

Eyal would be home in three days.

That afternoon, I went to meet my Hebrew conversation partner at the university cafe. He was my age, and he was handsome. Curly dark hair, assured posture. He held a cappuccino cup that looked small in his hands. The way he leaned back in his chair was subtly commanding. I sensed that if you watched him long enough, you'd find that all the energy in the room was organized around him, that other men glanced at him before they spoke.

"Hi," I said sitting down. "Timor, right?"

He watched me sit. Then he spoke: "Allison." Not a question.

He had a way of watching that made me feel pinned in place. I was immediately uncomfortable, and the discomfort was exciting.

We shared a cheap, oily croissant and began to speak in Hebrew. The conversation plodded along—*How are you? Everything is* beseder. *How are you?*—in full, repetitive sentences for a few minutes. He struck me as someone who listens for what you are not saying.

"You're here for the summer?" he asked, although it was not quite a question. More like he was confirming a fact he already knew.

"I was supposed to be," I said. "But I decided to stay."

"To stay?"

"Yeah, I applied for a grant so I could do more graduate work here," I said. "And I got it, so here I am."

"*Wallah*," he said, sitting back a little. "That's impressive."

I felt encouraged. "My connection to Israel feels new," I said. "I didn't grow up in a Zionist household. So this is all new, and I . . ." I hesitated a bit; this seemed a little cheesy, but I said it anyway: "I don't want to lose it."

Timor didn't reply. Instead, he openly scrutinized my face.

I looked down, thrilled and overwhelmed.

I expected him to ask me about the rocket sirens: if I found them scary, if I was doing okay. But that's not what he asked. "You Jewish?" he asked me.

The familiar question. Since the day I'd arrived in Israel, I'd always answered the same way: *My father is*, which was a way of saying, *No, not exactly.* But that day, for the first time, I said, "Yes." I was startled, but I did not show it. "Yes, I'm Jewish." My boyfriend was in the army. What was more Jewish than that?

"From where?" he asked. I had come to understand that this question, when following one about Jewishness, meant not where I was born but where my family fled.

"Lithuania," I told him, which is true of my father's side.

He nodded.

Before he could ask any more, I pivoted: "What about you? You Jewish?"

He smiled appreciatively. *Haha, very funny.* Then told me his mother's side was from Germany, his father's from Poland. He made a joke about Polish mothers-in-law, but I couldn't focus on the words. My ears were buzzing.

Once at a pharmacy, I cheated the self-checkout kiosk by not ringing up a package of hair ties. It was a mistake, but as I was paying I realized the mistake and did not correct it. The rush of panic when I left the store was as horrible as it was delicious. *Did I do it? Did I really do it?* That's how I felt the first time I said I was Jewish.

It was my father's mother who told me about what she called "passing." A refined woman whose lipsticks were organized in their own drawer of her vanity. Women of all ages used to stop us—her granddaughters, off with her to do "the marketing" at her favored cheese shop, butcher (never kosher; she loved ham), and boulangerie—"Do you know your grandmother is a very elegant woman?" Of course we knew. We were pleased when we nodded yes. We felt entitled to our grandmother's beauty.

My grandmother was lining her lips with a plum-colored pencil when she told me that we—meaning, in our family—don't lie about being

Jewish, but we don't offer it. If someone thought she was Italian, she let them. This, she told me, was called "passing." Later, I would come to understand the word, belonging to distinct Black and trans experiences, was not mine to use. But the first time I heard about passing, it was my grandmother talking about letting it slide when she was misread as a gentile.

"Although you won't have that problem," she said, touching my chin to look into my mother's blue eyes. Either she did not understand or did not believe that by the time she was telling me this, Jews could be white. In her lifetime, she had become white—a body protected by the state.

And now she was gone, and I was passing for Jewish.

I pivoted. "What do you study?" I asked Timor in Hebrew.

"I study political science."

The courtyard was empty except for us. Two strangers at a cast-iron table. "You study for your second degree?"

"No, my first."

He was my age; I could sense that. I tried to figure out the math using a typical Israeli trajectory. Out of the army by twenty-one, maybe twenty-three if he did officer training. A year traveling, a year of bullshit bartender jobs. He could be my age and finishing his first degree. There was a small piece of chocolate-heavy croissant on the plate. He touched the rim of the plate with his hand. An invitation, but also a bit of a command. I ate it.

Timor spoke again. "I'm still in the army."

"Still!" I felt my eyebrows arch in surprise. Eyal couldn't wait to get out of the army, made fun of those who decided to enlist so much as a single extra year. "What do you do in the army?"

He spoke in English now: "You know what it is, *mod'in anoshi*?"

I puzzled it out. "'*Mod'in*' is 'intelligence,'" I said. I knew that from Eyal. "If '*anashim*' means 'people,' then '*anoshi*' must be an adjectival form . . ." I hesitated. It couldn't be "humanitarian," could it?

Timor's eyes were following something behind me. I turned to see two girls entering the cafe, young students, both in hijabs. The school had a fair number of Arab-Israelis, and this is why, Eyal's sister insisted, she had not been accepted for undergraduate study at the university. The Arabs, she said, had stolen her place; I remember thinking but not saying that where I'm from, they used to say that about Jews. Now, the girls glanced at us then quickly glanced away. Who was I in their eyes? Someone who thought they had stolen the spots of rightful Jews at the university? *I don't think that!* I wanted to exclaim. But what could I do? Together, Timor and I were two Jews watching two Arabs.

The words *mod'in anoshi* clicked into place. "Human intelligence," I said softly. "You are a human intelligence officer."

"Very good," he said.

He was not looking at me but behind me.

"As in, you work 'in the prime minister's office?'" I was recalling the euphemism I'd learned from the PR guy on our one date in Rabin Square.

His eyes flicked to me. He laughed. "Where did you learn that?"

"I heard someone use it," I said. He seemed amused, which I liked, so I kept guessing. "Like, interrogations?" I asked, thinking of it as a joke, expecting him to say, *No, of course not interrogations.* It seemed impossible that I would be sitting in front of someone who tortured people.

A subtle expression passed over his face then—just the shadow of an irritated frown that said, *Don't ask stupid questions.* His focus returned to the girls behind me. They must have been ordering their coffees. The Arab girls. Timor was watching me and watching them, but it wasn't the same. He saw me differently from how he saw them—these girls ordering their coffee. *This is fucked up*, I thought. *This is racist.* But even as I formulated these thoughts, a warm, cozy feeling was enclosing me. He was here to protect me. From them. Because . . . because why? Because I was special. "Do you work on a base?" I asked. My voice was faint. I was floating in a moment where nothing we said correlated to what I felt.

"No," he said, shifting his attention fully onto me again. "Not exactly." His hands were very still. Mine were nervous in my lap. "Tell me about your day," he said. "In Hebrew." He wagged a finger, joking and not joking at once. "Practice your Hebrew, Allison."

Even today, although so much has changed, Timor will sometimes pull out this line. Raising an eyebrow at me when he says, "Practice your Hebrew, Allison."

On an afternoon a few days before Eyal came home, Talia and I went to the beach—a usually crowded spot abutting central Tel Aviv. We chose it because there were restaurants nearby where we could take cover in case of a siren. The beach was quiet. We lay on our backs. I applied endless layers of sunscreen; she glowed like she was supposed to be here. For the first fifteen minutes I had trouble focusing on anything that Talia said. My stomach was raw and acidic, and I wondered if I'd eaten something bad.

"I love this song," she said, increasing the volume of the experimental Scandinavian pop music she had playing from a portable speaker. A girl-ish alien voice was intoning softly over a synth beat. Talia rolled her head back and forth to the beat, her face obscured by a bucket hat.

I barely registered her words as I rubbed my stomach. What was wrong with me? My hand felt foreign on my own body.

Inhale, exhale.

I realized Talia was saying something else. I tried to focus.

"It's hard for him," she said. "You know?"

"Sorry, for who?" My breath was too loud, louder than any music.

"At the call center, I mean." She must have been talking about her part-time job—some coworker at the call center where she worked some evenings. "It's hard for him," she said again. "To be an Arab-Israeli in Tel Aviv is hard right now." Pause, then when I didn't say anything, "Everyone is so scared."

Talia's politics were more nuanced than I understood at the time. Eventually, she would surprise me by pointing out the potential solidarity between Palestinians and Mizrachim. "If you want to understand the racism of European Zionism," she said to me later, "you have to start by looking at how Israel treats Jews from Arab lands." I remember being a little shocked by the critique, which sounded more like something my sister would say. *Then why live here?* I thought, and as if she had heard the thought she laughed. "Where else should my family have gone?" But that day on the beach, I could not process a word she was saying. "Sounds complicated," I said, which must have been the right thing to say, because her bucket hat nodded.

"It's really complicated," she said.

I sat up because lying on my back, I was having trouble getting air into my lungs. I tried breathing slowly, but it felt like my head was underwater. My stomach clenched, raw and green-feeling. And, oh, it wasn't something I'd eaten. No, this was terror. I was terrified. Any second. Any second a rocket siren could come and tear through the artifice of this day, this life. A terrorist could pop out of the sand, drag me back to Gaza. Rationally, I understood that the latter wasn't possible: the tunnels that Hamas built only took them a few kilometers at most from Gaza; they emerged in the kibbutz fields near the border fence, ready to detonate a bomb or kill a soldier. But in this moment, it all felt equally possible. If they could send mortars, why not fighters? Maybe there was a whole city under this city, tunnels filled with bombs and killers, all those Gazans we could not erase coming to get us.

I think Talia might have been saying something else about her Arab co-worker, but I spoke, loudly and impulsively, talking right over her: "Nobody has ever wanted to kill me before." I hated the hysterical note in my voice.

Talia sat up too, tugged at her yellow bucket hat. She didn't respond right away, I assume because she was startled. The sea was placid and shimmering.

"Hamas, I mean, the rockets," I said. "It's just weird for me."

"It's weird for me too," she said, nodding in a way that might have been a little resigned. "Although this happens before almost every election."

"What?" I didn't know what she meant.

"Yeah, the prime minister orders a missile strike before every election," she said, gesturing a delicate hand toward the sea. "That's why he keeps winning."

"Hamas has a prime minister?"

She laughed. "No," she said. "Well, maybe? I don't know. But I meant ours." She named the Israeli forever prime minister. "He's a genius at politics."

"But it's them firing rockets at us."

"Oh yeah, but we started it," Talia said. "We killed some Hamas leader."

"What?"

"Yeah, I think we blew up his car, maybe?" She was playing with sand now. Pouring grains from one hand into another. "I guess it makes sense," she said. "We have to stop them somehow."

I nodded, shocked at the cynicism. In time, I'd come to find this jaded attitude was common among Israelis: *Sure, there's a certain amount of farce in these hostilities, but what can we do?*

Talia continued, "He'll probably call an invasion soon."

For a second, I hated her. Eyal could not go to Gaza. It was impossible. It was . . . it was too real. "If that happens, I don't know what I'll do," I said, unable to even look at her. I picked at my toenail polish.

"You'll wait," she said. She said it simply and without smugness. "That's all we can do."

Her oldest brother had been in Gaza back in 2006. He was a combat engineer who had leveled houses in Beit Hanoun.

Eyal would be home in two days.

Talia was right about the assassination. I found the footage posted on the official Israeli army Twitter account. It began with an aerial shot of a car (circled in yellow) driving down what appears to be a normal city street. The images were blurry. Soundless in black and white, the video had the latent anxiety inherent to security footage—the sense of a crime about to happen.

We are looking at the car from overhead. Drone's-eye view. The car is circled in yellow. A target. We are following the target down what looks like a residential street, past parked cars and driveways. Then the car disappears. That's the missile. The video is silent. Something—a car door? a body? a body part?—flies across the screen, which is consumed entirely in white light. It looks clean and pure. It looks like an act of God.

Caption: WE SUGGEST ALL HAMAS OPERATIVES WATCH THEIR BACKS THIS WEEKEND. It was punctuated with a ghost emoji, the kind you'd use in a text message, as if this were all a joke. Or all a TV show, which in a way it was—death unfolding on screens, a war in frames.

This is happening in your name, I said to myself. *The power being exerted, the war games being played, the bodies shattered on-screen—you're part of this.* But no matter how hard I thought it, it didn't quite feel real.

The army Twitter is run by teenage girls. It's a good job, Eyal once told me. Easy hours.

My mother emailed me. *Is this true??* she asked, linking to a Canadian news headline: *Faced with Daily Rocket Attacks, Israelis Grow Impatient for Invasion.*

By way of response, I wrote only, *I hope not.*

One day until Eyal came home.

It took him forever to get home that Thursday. Initially, he was supposed to leave base at 9:00 a.m., but that became 11:00 a.m., at which point it seemed his commander might make him "close" Shabbat—an agonizing prospect that would hold him for an extra week—but finally that evening, he made it to his parents' apartment. I headed over right away.

He answered the door, freshly showered in sweatpants. The air-conditioning wafting out, he pulled me in. "You're just in time," he said, standing in the apartment vestibule to kiss my mouth and nose and eyelids.

"For what?" I whispered.

His mother called from the kitchen. "Is that Allie?"

He squeezed my waist. "Yes," he called back.

"*Yalla*, let's eat together." Then: "Koral, get *Aba*!"

Eyal looked at me and rolled his eyes in that indulgent way he had when he was annoyed—but not really annoyed—with his mom.

Two days later, I still had not gone back to my apartment.

"What should we watch?" I asked him. We lay in his twin bed facing each other, our heads on his single pillow. There was a hush in the room, as if we were waiting for something. But what? A siren maybe.

"What about that movie *Troy-ah*?" I could feel his breath on my face. Faint smell of oranges.

Bioethic-ah, metaphor-ah, Troy-ah.

I knew the film he was referring to—a slick and inaccurate rendering of the *Iliad* that I would never have willingly watched. But I also knew he chose it because he thought I'd like its proximity to our *Odyssey*. I told him it sounded perfect.

He brought his laptop to bed and clicked around until he found a pirated version online. He was lean as he hunched over his computer. His eyelashes were thick and full. My beautiful boy.

For the past two days, everyone had been on edge, his sister especially. She kept confronting him on small perceived acts of carelessness: he left the kitchen cabinets open, he left the bathroom floor wet after a shower, he left a light on in the hallway. "*Beseder*, Koral," he responded to her criticism, patience in his voice.

Nobody said, *We're scared our baby is going to be called down to the Gaza border*, but I assumed that's what was underscoring the tension.

His mom talked obsessively about Hamas, who had held power in Gaza for less than a decade at that point. She sat next to me on the couch when Eyal and I were reading our his-and-hers copies of the *Odyssey* to show me something on her phone. "Look at this," she said to me in English.

"*Nu, Ima*," Eyal said, looking up from his Hebrew translation.

But she shushed him. "It's important she see," she said in Hebrew.

On her phone was a video montage of people running for cover—kids, mothers with kids. "How many seconds? How many more seconds do we have?" someone shouted in Hebrew. A small boy ran holding his kippa to his head. These images were inter-spliced with photos of bombed buildings—balconies collapsing, gaping holes in living rooms like the one we were in. I knew that in the Israeli cities closer to Gaza, you only had a few seconds between hearing the siren and finding shelter, and, what's more, the antimissile defenses couldn't block every mortar. "This is what they do not show," she said, tapping the screen with a French-manicured nail. "In America, in Canada, on the news." On her screen, a mother was rocking a crying toddler in her arms as the camera shook.

"That's horrible," I said. "They look so scared."

"Hamas does this," she said. "We need to bomb them, bomb Gaza to dust."

Eyal was staring at his own hands, looking troubled. I understood that on a purely ethical level, what she was saying was wrong. I knew that I would be in the right if I said: *We cannot exert power over another people like this.* But that sentence felt purely hypothetical, unconnected to anyone I actually knew or cared about. Mostly, what I thought about—for the first time—was how if we did carpet-bomb the Palestinians in Gaza, then Eyal would not have to go in as a ground soldier. He'd be safe. "I understand," I said.

She leaned forward and kissed my forehead. Her lips were soft and dry. It was a shockingly tender gesture that my own mother has never made toward me.

In his room later that night, Eyal said, "You know, we made them live there."

"Made who live where?"

"The government made the Mizrachim go to the border places," he said. The terrorized people in the video must have been visibly (or audibly?) Jews from the east in ways I could not detect. Eyal was clicking around on his computer playing a puzzle game. "Like, forced them to live closer to the Arabs." He turned to me. "It's racist."

He was waiting for me to say something. But what?

"Isn't it?" he asked. "Isn't it racist?"

It startled me to realize he was waiting for me to act as some kind of moral authority. Me, whose own sense of right and wrong seemed to be changing with each beat of my heart. "That does sound racist," I said quickly, "to treat Mizrachi Jews like that."

He nodded, satisfied, and returned to his game.

The *Troy-ah* movie was a mess. All flesh and clash of weapons, gurgling blood, women hiding behind city walls. *They won't call you down, right?* I kept almost asking him. *They won't make you go, will they? To Gaza?* But I kept losing the question before it got to my mouth.

The city was burning when Eyal's phone rang. He paused the movie and sat up in bed. "*Allo*," he said, his voice a little deeper than when he spoke to me, which meant it was probably his commander, Avishi. But that didn't mean anything. That didn't necessarily mean anything.

The call was brief. "*Kibalti*," he said. Army-speak: *Got it, understood.*

After he hung up, he sat for a moment in silence with his bare feet on the floor. "I need to tell my *ima*," he said.

"Tell her what?" I asked. Already feeling my throat tight. "Tell her what?" I said again, louder.

"I'm going," he said. "My unit, we're going down to the border."

I covered my face with my hands. He kissed the crown of my head.

I stayed in bed while he went to the kitchen. Curled in a ball, I heard his mother cry out.

That night, I gave him the pages of letters that I had written while he was last in Hebron. These were the letters he would read while he was at the Gaza border, waiting for the call to go in.

He tucked them into a pocket of his enormous seventy-five-liter backpack. After, we lay together in his twin bed. I return to this memory. How these minutes were suspended. How everything was changing, had already changed, would never be the same. And yet, despite all that would unfold, we lay together concentrically as if held in the same womb.

Tomorrow morning, he would go to Gaza. He'd take a train to get there. Tonight, he was the little spoon. I hugged him from behind. "I will be here," I said. My nose pressed against the scratchy nape of his neck. Koral had buzzed his hair in the bathroom. She and his mom took turns.

That's when he jumped up to go to his desk.

The next day, we would hold hands in the car all the way to the train station. We would grip and regrip each other's fingers, as I remembered how he handed me his death letter stapled shut. A single word written on the front: אַתְּ. *You*.

Tomorrow, Eyal was invading Gaza. To get there, he would take the public train. But tonight, we made love quietly as the blind pug Charlotte clacked up and down the hallway. Eyal wanted me on top, maybe wanted to feel surrounded by me. He lay on his back, steadying my hips as I rode him to the rhythm of my own prayer. *Don't go, don't go*.

Eleven

So they waited. Eyal and hundreds of enlisted and reserve soldiers lived in makeshift encampments of tents and trailers down by the border fence, waiting for the call to go in. Eyal sent videos to me and his mother—soldiers snoring on cots, cheering as they opened boxes of donated junk food, or indistinguishable in tanks around the drooping fields of summer-dead sunflowers. The earth was red.

It was not inevitable that they would invade. Talia told me that a year prior there had been a dance with the same beats: we assassinate their politicians, they send rockets, so we send soldiers down to the border. "Last year, the boys just waited around for a while," she said. "Then they came home." I was cross-legged on her bed, wrapped in a soft synthetic blanket.

"Maybe this time too," I said, looking at her hopefully. "Maybe they won't go in."

The short pause before she answered felt like forever. "Maybe," she said.

∽ ∾

Sitting in a wheelless office chair stuck in the red dirt, Eyal unfolds the heart-shaped letter he keeps with him always. Any moment it will be time to patrol, but this second is his. Allie cut this paper heart out from construction paper. She wrote, *I am thinking about how when we are together— when I am alone with you—the room we are in becomes sacred. This room has been sacred with us in it.* The way she writes, he can hear her voice. He's folded and unfolded this letter so many times that the center of the heart is a soft crease, almost fraying. When he reads it, he feels for a second that he isn't a soldier but a whole person.

He quickly slips the note back into the pocket over his own heart as Avishi emerges from between two trailers. "Yalla," he says. They're going to join a regular infantry unit for a patrol. Later, the field intelligence unit that normally works this area is going to walk them through some surveillance maps of the current tunnel situation. Avishi is from the south. They aren't far from his home.

Eyal hoists his pack and joins the others. It is hot, and the ground is dusty. Avishi is carrying the contact radio, its antenna trembling like a live insect.

Hamas dig like insects. They burrow under the border fence, emerge in the fields of Kerem Shalom, grab a soldier, drag him back into the sewers of Gaza.

"How's the Canadienne?" Avishi asks, making conversation as if they are waiting for a bus.

Eyal thinks, *She keeps sachets of lavender under her pillow.* He thinks, *Her world is soft and yielding.* But what he says is, "Allie worries a lot."

Avishi nods. He's got acne on his cheeks, but it makes him look kind of tough, cool. "This is her first war?" he asks.

"Yeah."

In the fields, a man is driving a tractor with a sign taped to the back evidently painted by a child. THANK YOU TO OUR SOLDIERS. He can see the buildings of Gaza City peeking up in the near distance.

What would it be like to discover a new Hamas tunnel? To see a masked fighter emerge in these fields? What would Eyal do? If they came for him? He hopes he'd be brave. He imagines bravery as a sacrifice—

taking a bullet for someone else, for Avishi maybe. He's shot in the stomach and collapsing into Avishi's arms, like those paintings of Jesus all over Europe. Blood seeps across his stomach. Avishi cries out. Then it's two soldiers knocking at his parents' door. Enough, enough. He shakes his head to clear the thoughts. He's indulged enough.

Old water tower, rotting cement. Tired-looking Israeli flag. Fields of . . . whatever this is. What are we growing, anyway? He'd ask, but then Avishi would laugh and call him a city boy. Something brown and dry from the sun.

Over the fence, in the fields of Gaza, columns of dirt shoot up where the tanks have fired.

"Good morning, Gaza," someone says.

He remembers hearing about an elderly woman on a kibbutz not far from here who claimed to hear scratching sounds coming from under her floor. Nobody else heard, so nobody believed her. It was always weekday afternoons, when the younger people were at school or working. "Come on, Ima," her children must have said. "You're imagining things." She must have started to believe them when they told her it was all in her head, the deep, hollow scratching coming from under the floor.

Anyway, later that year the army found tunnels leading from Gaza into the heart of the kibbutz. They'd been digging right under the woman's kitchen.

He eats tuna fish while snipers take shots at Gazans over the fence. So far, only Palestinians have died. He doesn't know how to be here. It's true he's seen some chaotic shit in Hebron, it's true this won't be his first time seeing human brains, it's true he knows the smell of burning rubber well, but the enormity of the clash and all its machinery is making Eyal's body feel like it's made out of twigs. He finds himself receding into the back of himself. When he can't escape into Allie's letters, he retreats to another country: high school.

It wasn't much more than a year ago that he and Gil would walk together to a school that called itself a lycée to attract snobby parents. Backpacks sitting low, bouncing against their upper thighs. "You'll get scoliosis!" their moms said, but they did it anyway, carrying their skateboards under their arms.

Everyone had the choice of doing French or Arabic, in addition to English, and they both did French because that's what their parents said to do. Sometimes, if Madame was lazy (hungover, everyone surmised) and put on some silly French cartoon for them to watch—*Lucky Luke*, *Tintin*, *Asterix et Obelix*—he and Gil would sneak out to go skateboarding. Quiet streets and palm trees leading to the beach. People worked hard to make it to this neighborhood, but Gil and Eyal were born here—in adjacent apartment buildings with views of the sea—and it was boring. Neither of them was much good at skateboarding. Something held them back from being reckless enough to get truly good. So they just cruised around, half-heartedly attempting little ollies now and then.

They were in grade eleven when Gil asked Eyal to help him pierce his ear. "What do you mean?" Eyal asked. "Like, stick a needle through it?" They were walking home after school. Everyone was talking about the hostage who'd finally been freed from Gaza. Eyal had been a little kid when the Arabs kidnapped the soldier, snatched him from a kibbutz field where he was patrolling and dragged him through a secret tunnel to Gaza. All throughout high school he'd seen the guy's face on posters everywhere. Poor, emaciated motherfucker haunting the bus stops. Now he was free, in exchange for, like, a million terrorists let go from prisons. They talked about it in civics class. It was on the news. Maybe the guy had been brainwashed to become a spy. Maybe a Muslim! Maybe, maybe, maybe. But Gil and Eyal weren't talking about the hostages, they were talking about earrings.

"I have this stud," Gil said. "It looks like a real diamond." He stopped walking and held out his palm.

Eyal picked it up to take a look. An earring like a mobster would wear, and a stone that, sure, could have been a diamond. "Okay," he said, "but we'll need something sharper to make the hole."

"A safety pin?" Gil suggested.

Eyal agreed.

They met that night at the playground between their apartment buildings to do it. Gil brought the earring and the safety pin; Eyal brought a persimmon that he would stab the pin into. He'd watched YouTube tutorials that suggested an apple, but the closest thing in their house was a not-quite-ripe persimmon, pale and firm.

They were under fluorescent lights. It was October and warm. Gil sat on wooden steps intended for a child. Eyal stood over him. He held the safety pin in his right hand, the persimmon behind Gil's ear. "Stay still," he said.

"Your breath is nasty," Gil said, which made Eyal laugh, so they had to get into position again: pin in one hand, persimmon in the other, Gil's head cocked, Eyal kind of straddling him to get the right angle.

He was so close to Gil that he could see the whiteheads on his nose, and the nearly translucent hairs on his ear, surprisingly soft-looking. He gently pressed the prick of the needle into Gil's lobe and felt him flinch. "I'm going to do it on the count of three," he said.

"Beseder," Gil said, keeping his head still. He was making his voice deep and assured.

"One, two," Eyal said, but before he counted three, he stabbed right through the soft tissue. A completely nauseous feeling washed over him as he felt the pin go through.

Gil cried out. "Son of a whore, fuck fuck fuck!" He pulled away from Eyal. The persimmon fell on the asphalt. "You said on three!"

Eyal shrugged, stood back. Gil still had the safety pin through his ear. "Do you have the stud?" Eyal asked.

"I'll do it," Gil said. And he gingerly pulled the safety pin out. There wasn't much blood.

After watching Gil fumble and grimace for a few seconds, Eyal said,

"Bro, just let me," and he crouched by Gil to get the earring in. After, he had a smudge of blood on his fingertips. This was high school. He'd never touched another person's blood before. "Should we have brought hydrogen peroxide?" he asked.

Gil was gently touching his earlobe. "Probably," he said, without much interest. "Bro, how does it look?"

"You look like you run a strip club," Eyal said.

Gil laughed. "Perfect."

He kept that thing in his ear until it got too infected and he had to take it out. His ima freaked when she saw it, he told Eyal. "What are you?" she yelled. "A homo?"

He hates to imagine Allison losing her virginity, but sometimes he does. She wouldn't have been scared. He's never asked her about it—because then she might ask him about his first time, and, well, they both knew . . . but he feels certain she wasn't scared. He can imagine the way her jaw jutted slightly out. He associates that expression with her hunger for life. The way she runs toward the sea and jumps straight in, Ima and Koral exclaiming at her bravery. Sometimes Allie makes a show of being cute. He doesn't mind. He likes that it's for him, the little pouts and the flowers pressed into letters. But that's not when he wants her most. It's when she's running into the waves or when she's reading a book with intense focus or when she's riding him hard with her nails digging into his shoulders, her hips rolling over his cock and her jaw set, determined and unafraid.

Her first time, she must have been more interested than nervous. Here was a new way she would come to know—not the person (the man? The boy?) she was going to have sex with—but herself. She might not have told him, whoever he was, that he was the first. Eyal could imagine that. He could imagine her keeping her virginity a secret, hoarding its power for herself. She was not afraid, he's sure of it, and yet there must have been a moment of shock. When he was really inside her, irrevocably inside her that first time, there must have been a jolt of pure awe that told her she was changed. And it wasn't him. It wasn't Eyal that gave that to her.

∽ ∾

Timor pulled out a chair at the cafe table and sat down. "Where is your boyfriend?" he asked.

I felt my head jerk back in surprise. We were on the patio, same sunken cafe that felt like it was at the bottom of an empty swimming pool. The whole campus was built like a bomb shelter. We were speaking in Hebrew. After twenty minutes, we'd switch to English. Mutually beneficial language exchange.

He must have seen my confusion—how did he know about Eyal?—because he added, "The boyfriend you mentioned. He's in the army?"

I was sure I hadn't mentioned Eyal to Timor. In fact, I'd felt a little guilty after our first meeting, wondering if I'd omitted mention of my boyfriend because Timor was handsome, charismatic, and my own age. I cocked my head. "I didn't mention him."

Timor seemed only amused, not alarmed. "I know," he said. "Your Hebrew teacher told me."

I could easily see that. Smadar touching Timor's shoulder warmly and in confidence: *She has a soldier.* I inspected a nail where my pale pink manicure, self-administered, had chipped. "Eyal is *b'gvul 'aza*," I said, echoing the words I'd heard on the news again and again. The Gaza border.

"Eyal," Timor repeated.

"I am scared," I said, or I thought I said, in Hebrew.

Timor frowned for a moment until realization smoothed out his brow. "Oh," he said, "you mean, *I'm scared.*" He spoke in English.

"What did I say?"

"You said, *I'm scary.* Try again."

I tried again. "I'm scared that he will go into Gaza." There was a lot I seldom said aloud. But to Timor, someone who was part of Eyal's world, it seemed simpler. "I know it's not what he wants," I went on. "For this to be his life." Eyal spoke so longingly of life after the army. On the advice of the bioethics professor he'd written to, he was looking for Israeli programs where he could take both philosophy and biology classes.

Timor inspected his paper coffee cup. I'd never seen him use the sippy lid, and he did not use it now. So protective of his aloof dignity. "It's complicated," he said in English.

"It's not that complicated," I countered, feeling a possessive surge tighten my chest. "He wants his real life to start; he doesn't want to invade anyone."

Timor looked up at me. Such striking bone structure. On Facebook— he'd added me, a thrilling surprise: *he found me*—I'd seen photos of him working out shirtless. He was muscular, yes, but incredibly lean, almost emaciated. "Boys want war," he said. His lack of insistence or conviction made it seem that much more true. "Boys want war because it's exciting."

It was almost cinematic how a rocket siren punctuated this conversation. "Fuck," I said aloud. Then, "Sorry!"

Timor laughed. "*Yalla*," he said, unhurried.

The siren was a rising and falling pitch up and down my spine. *War*, it said. That's what I heard. *War.*

Timor didn't bother going to the bomb shelter, so I didn't either. Instead, we stood in an interior hallway—no windows—and watched one of the countless stray cats on campus sniff a garbage can.

I remembered the memorial sirens I'd heard only a few months ago, back when I first met Eyal. Funny to think they issued from the same speaker system, one that laced invisibly through the entire country. All over the cities, on the roofs of buildings, on the telephone poles of highways, in the high corners of municipal offices—hidden mouths that caused us all to stand still or to run for cover, depending on the occasion.

The English word "siren" comes from the mythological Sirens encountered by Odysseus—those taloned sisters whose songs tempted sailors to their deaths. These are the realms of pleasure and danger. In Greek, a "*seiren*" was a deceitful woman, perhaps coming from the word for "rope," "*seira*," as in "one who entangles."

I was beginning to feel that the sirens were Israel's true national anthem—summoned forth from concordant spasms of fear and memory. So much came down to the sirens, hidden but unavoidable like the helicopters I always heard but never seemed to see.

Text from Eyal: WITH YOUR LETTERS IT'S LIKE YOU ARE HERE. Pause. OR BETTER: I AM THERE.

༄ ༄

Eyal has tucked her letters into his bag along with a toothbrush and extra socks and body wash and running sneakers and undershirts and boxers and granola bars. Scared that someone would find them, he folded the pastel pages into a plastic container meant to hold a bar of soap. Only when he is sure he is alone does he take out her letters, often in the dark, although down here it is never really dark.

He touches the pages, which are soft, somehow they are soft, of course they are. He only reads a little at a time. Make it last. But he permits himself to riffle through the pages, watching the words that repeat. *Together, missing, praying, me, us, you, you, you.* He savors the places where her pen pressed down hard on the page. Tonight, he will sleep on a cot with his boots on, ready for the call.

He remembers how Aba didn't want to sign the form. The famous form that parents must sign when they have only one son, and that son wants to go into a combat unit. His father did not want to sign it. Or at least, he hesitated with the pen. "The life of your only son," he said softly, reading from the form. Just a formality. Eyal wondered if the girl warriors, few as they were, had similar forms. He sensed they did not. It was different to be a son. An only son. Fruit of your loins.

His father hesitated with the pen. He'd been a warrior. Now he is a balding man with a struggling pharmacy, but once Aba jumped out of planes. Eyal is not a paratrooper. He knows that people assume his aba must be disappointed. But it's not like that. Eyal did well in school despite skipping French class to skateboard. Like, really well. An intelligence unit, he and his parents agreed, would lead to more opportunities after the army. That's what they said. Eyal suspects that for his father, there's more to it than he can say.

Aba has a photo in his wallet: three soldiers not much older than Eyal is now. They are standing in front of an army Jeep, exuding a nonchalance that Eyal recognizes as his own—practiced. Pants sitting low on their hips, sun in their eyes. One is Aba. Eyal can't remember which of the other two is dead, but knows his body never came back.

"Are you going to sign it?" Eyal asked. Not so much impatient as afraid of the welling significance of the moment. It was night and they were in the bright kitchen sitting at the little table they used for family meals when it was just the four of them. His mother was in the living room, on the couch with the dog, pretending not to listen. This was between a father and his son.

"I love you," his father said, shocking Eyal. He signed the form.

He remembers how after he spent that first night at Allie's, ignoring his father's texts and phone calls, Eyal expected an argument when he got home early the next morning. Quietly opening the front door of the apartment, he'd braced himself for a lecture on responsibility. But his father had looked tired sitting at the kitchen table with a cup of black coffee. "I was worried," Aba said. No anger in his voice.

"I'm sorry," Eyal said. He meant it.

"Go on," Aba said. "Get your things and I'll drive you to the station."

It's night before Eyal has time to really read. He should change his socks. He's worried about getting foot fungus again. Leaning against his pack, reading with a mini-flashlight. The air smells like a porta-potty.

It's 3:17pm and I am pretending to take notes in the class I'm TA-ing for. (She'd taught him this acronym: "teacher's assistant.") *Today, my most important lesson didn't happen at the university, but at lunch in a convenience store off campus. I went to get a Coke—it's half the price outside the university gates. The shop was one of those tiny stores crammed full with dehydrated soups and dusty bottles of white vinegar. The man behind the register was praying. He held a prayer book to his face, bending and swaying. His words were indistinct, flowing. I clinked through the bottles in the fridge to find a cold one. I wasn't sure what to do when I brought the bottle to the counter. There was no price sticker on the top or bottom. I didn't want to interrupt his prayers. He was young, this man. As young as me but not as young as you. Something about him made it seem that he had recently become more religious. What was it? Maybe his earring? Maybe his scruff? Maybe that, as I listened more, I heard that he was praying more slowly than I'd thought. I could make out specific words: "baruch," "shamayim," "noten." Should I go back to the fridge? Check for the price on another bottle? Or maybe just leave ten shekels? Surely, that would be enough. Then I heard one word very clearly: "sheva." Our eyes met, and he nodded. "Sheva," he said again, between blessings. I left the seven shekels on the counter and took my soda.*

Eyal rubs his thumb over the place where, in the margins, she's drawn a vine of flowers that weaves between the lines of the paper. Oh, to be inside a letter that she has written. If only he could escape this brutal place by slipping into her writing, into her dreaming, into a world where everything is delicate and profound. When she is sleeping—napping in his bed or on a blanket in the park—he is pulled apart by two conflicting urges. Either let her sleep. Let her dream. Lie next to her and listen to her breath, steady as waves. Or wake her. Take her warm and sleep-baked body in his arms and rouse her with his mouth and hands so that she wakes up into pleasure, moaning half asleep into his mouth, clutching him, awake now, her hands searching his back and scalp.

What he loves most is when she seems to forget that she is writing to him at all, and instead writes to herself. Reading about her earliest memory of crying—from a beesting—was almost like reading her journal. "The bee flew up my dress and stung me its secret," she wrote. "They only get to tell it once." He liked that. *Stung me its secret.* He understood that the sting was the secret. After they tell it (sting), they die. Metaphor-ah. She rereads the *Odyssey* year after year "because each time I read it, I've changed, and it becomes a different story." She wrote a letter from the beach once, crying over a poet he'd never heard of. Salty sea and salty tears. It's as if her mind is a foreign country, and sometimes she lets him visit.

Occasionally, she'll write about her sister. "Anything she has seems to cost me something," she wrote of Erica once, "as if it was supposed to be mine, not hers." Then something crossed out that he could not read, no matter how he tried. Then: "I hope you don't think I'm horrible." She was trusting him to love her even if she was a bad sister. He treasured that.

He's gotten off to the image of her touching herself. She let him watch once as she rubbed herself in pleasure, her eyes closed tight as her head lolled against the pillow. She pressed gently on her own clit, her breath getting gaspy as she got close. God, just remembering that, he's hard—the privacy she had with herself in that moment.

"What did you think about?" he asked after.

"Of you," she said dreamily. He didn't know how to explain to her that it was okay, really okay, if that wasn't true.

೧೨ ೧೨

One morning, the sirens interrupted the master's class I was TA-ing. I liked the professor, the one who had agreed to sit on my dissertation committee. He was a wiry man prone to delightful tangents on ancient grammar. Modern Orthodox in khakis, hiking boots, and a yarmulke, he had made *aliyah* from Brooklyn. My job was to sit there and nod; sometimes, I marked their quizzes. "The brain is lazy," he said, his hands slight and expressive, "or you could say, *effective*." That is why languages simplify over time. Once, Hebrew was far more inflected—meaning each word in a sentence was marked to indicate the part it was playing. (In English, we rely primarily on word order: *The fish ate Jonah* means something very different from *Jonah ate the fish*.) "The Arabs, they still have precise inflection," he said. "But only in the literary form." Nobody in the class spoke Arabic.

Someone's hand was raised to ask a question when those thin, haunting notes called out. We froze.

"*Nu*, again?" the professor said. "*Yalla*, leave your textbooks."

A hefty young man—a pastor, if I recall correctly, some Evangelical from the American south—who had doubled over in his seat as if on a crashing airplane, now sat back up, looking around to see if anyone had noticed. I pitied him. *These Americans aren't used to it*, I thought. As if I were used to it.

In the basement bomb shelter, a few dozen students and teachers stood around with notebooks and laptops.

The fluorescent lighting made everyone look a little green.

Silence. There was always a pause between sirens and impact. We waited.

Boom. There it was. A rocket being shot down. "*Ima-leh*," someone gasped. *Boom.*

A few feet away from me, a girl I did not know was crying. "Are you happy?" she said in Hebrew. A friend was comforting her. *Shh, shh.*

Boom, boom, boom. That made five booms total.

"I asked if you're happy. Are you happy?" the girl shouted tearfully, her nose congested. I looked at her then looked away, puzzled. She was speaking in the general plural. Was she talking to us here? Or was this some imagined address to Hamas in Gaza?

I glanced around the bomb shelter. In a few more seconds, I had processed the scene. The Israeli girl was yelling at two Arabs. I hadn't noticed them before—a willowy girl in a plum-colored hijab standing close to, but not touching, a young man in fitted jeans. Arab-Israeli students.

"Terrorists," the crying girl said, her voice muffled into her friend's shoulder.

Someone clucked with disapproval. Nobody intervened even though everybody witnessed. My professor was talking quietly to the American pastor about translations of Genesis: "The opening line is deceptively tricky to parse."

I didn't know what to do. Help, somehow? What could I do that wouldn't make it worse? Should I approach the girl in hijab to say, *Hey, we met at Sarah's, right?* A tactic any woman knows to save another woman from harassment. But would the boy with her react badly to my approach? And what would my professor think? What would it mean to be seen as sympathizing with the Arab students? No, don't think like that. Why was I hesitating when the right action was clear? If I kept agonizing, the moment would pass.

I took a deep breath and began walking across the bomb shelter toward the girl in purple, not sure of my plan. Maybe just say, *Are you two okay?* She looked up. She saw me moving toward her. We made eye contact, and before I could smile reassuringly, she flinched, whispered something to her friend who quickly stepped in front of her. There was another boom. I pretended to look at my phone, regrouping mentally.

She'd flinched. He'd shielded her. I opened and closed my Instagram feed just to do something with my hands.

He'd shielded her. From me.

The realization was unbearable: they were scared of me. Of me. When I looked up, they were gone, even though the booms were still coming.

ᔰ ᔰ

Tonight it's flares into the sky over Gaza City. The tanks are firing across the fence. Orange flashes and the ground shaking. When Eyal checks his phone, his ima has sent him another prayer: a psalm of protection, animated with graphics of pink hearts and blue stars of David.

Soon, Avishi will come out of the trailer and tell him that it's time. Their unit does this night after night. Painting one another's faces with green and black and brown. There's been another tunnel identified. This time, they'll take the cramped surveillance tank and monitor the tunnel mouth for as long as it takes. Hours, days. Waiting for the fighters to emerge so they can pick them off. It's not his team that goes into the tunnels, detonating bombs to collapse them. He's never been inside one. What does he imagine? A gaping mouth leading deep into the putrid stomach of Gaza. They don't get enough power to run a sewage treatment plant. It's a tactic. Eyal understands this. It's a tactic: give them just enough to survive, then kill them.

Twelve

Today was a day of unlikely connections, I typed into my laptop, which I balanced on my thighs. I was propped up in bed, drafting another Facebook post.

It started, of all places, at a beauty store in the mall.

Since beginning to date Eyal, so much younger, I'd developed more than a passing interest in anti-aging products. This was how I'd ended up on the email list for several skin-care shops in Tel Aviv and learned that a shop near the university had begun carrying a line of products from Korea—ecstatically reviewed masks and serums. Some products famously contained snail mucin, like from actual snails.

It's a small shopping center, I continued in the draft of my Facebook post. *After the middle-aged security guard checked my bag—"Neshek?" he asked without any interest in the answer. Weapon? Are you carrying a weapon? "Eyn," I said: none—I walked past the Magnolia jewelry shop and past the Nespresso shop.*

I'd come to this mall once before with Eyal and his mom. They wanted me to try a crêpe place they said was the best in Tel Aviv. "So good, right?" his mother had said, watching me eat a crêpe with real Nutella, not the Israeli replacement. They were crêpes; they were fine.

How good can a crêpe be? But I couldn't bear to disappoint her. "So good," I'd exclaimed, my mouth a little full. "So, so good."

At the skin-care shop, the products I'd come to check out were displayed near the front of the store: a large cartoon cutout of a snail surrounded by brown glass bottles.

I didn't say this in the post I was typing up, but I spotted the two Arab girls immediately. For the past few days, I had been revisiting that afternoon in the bomb shelter: the panicked look on the hijabed girl's face when I moved toward her; the boy with her, stepping out in front. I was only trying to help! But he was protecting her. Protecting her from me. Maybe that's why I spotted the two Arab girls in the shop so quickly—standing by the display, examining the testers. Unlike the girl in the bomb shelter, neither was wearing any visible ethnic markers, no hijab or keffiyeh. What conveyed their Arab-ness was something I couldn't quite articulate—not just of how I was coming to see others, but also how I was seeing myself in relation to them.

As I poked around the test products, I noticed two Arabic speakers—young women standing next to me.

This was the wording I chose—*Arabic speakers*—to convey their identity. It was not exactly untrue, but it was a kind of narrative simplification, for I had not heard them speak at all, Arabic or otherwise. (I am not sure they would have felt safe to speak Arabic in a North Tel Aviv mall.) What is true is that we, all three of us, stood at the display of snail mucin products, dabbing colorless, viscous serums on the backs of our hands and wrists.

What had agitated me most in the days since the bomb shelter incident was the realization that I did not know a single Arab-Israeli. (*Palestinian*, Erica would correct me. Fine: I did not know a single Palestinian. The word I used did not change the truth.) For all my months in Israel, I had never spoken to a Palestinian beyond, perhaps, thanking a busboy at a cafe. Now I glanced at the Palestinian girls next to me.

All of us were dressed similarly, in jeans and sneakers, but each of us had her own flavor. One girl wore a black T-shirt with cutoff sleeves—chic and punk; her friend opted for a more business-casual blouse.

I don't understand what possessed university-age girls in those years to wear cheap, bright blazers and polyester collared shirts like Midwestern junior executives. Then again, these girls might have judged me for dressing immaturely, with a sweetheart neckline and a bow securing my ponytail.

The products had a gooey consistency. At varying times, the three of us giggled. The punk-chic girl seemed especially friendly, even exchanging a shy smile with me. When her companion pointed out another product, they whispered together; then I really did hear their Arabic. A language like bubbling water. I inspected the back of a brown glass bottle.

Just say hi, I urged myself. But remembering the girl in the bomb shelter—her fear—I could not bring myself to do it.

When a sales associate in a black apron walked by, the chic-punk-looking girl called out to her in Hebrew.

She had to call out twice—"Excuse me, hi, excuse me!"—before the salesgirl came over. "Do you know if there's any artificial fragrance in this?" she asked. Her Hebrew had the telltale music of an Arabic speaker.

"I'll check," the Israeli shopgirl said briskly. She was about Eyal's age, young, with long brown hair that lightened at the ends into a pale blond.

I felt nervous. Why did I feel nervous? Nobody was calling anyone a terrorist. There was no tension between these girls. Was there? Had the Israeli girl been more curt than brisk? Involuntarily, I recalled a clip circulating online in which pretty, teenage girls hold up Hebrew signs at a pro-invasion march somewhere in the south. The signs say, DEATH TO ARABS. The girls are in jeans and white tank tops. Their hair is straightened. "Leftists, go suck a dick in Gaza!" they yell, giggling. It was these girls themselves who had posted the clip. Odd how, when I saw this clip, I understood the words were bad—I could say to myself, "That was racist"; saying *Death to Arabs* is racist—but also, I understood the feelings behind the words. There are rockets falling on our cities; our brothers and boyfriends are down south. It wasn't hate so much as fear. I could not explain any of this to someone who did not live here, so I did not mention any of it in my Facebook post.

The girl in the apron came back. "None," *she said to the Arab girls in Hebrew.* "There's no artificial fragrance." *Then she turned to me.* "La'azor lakh im mashu?"

I froze.

Usually, it was a delight when Israelis spoke to me in Hebrew. In fact, sometimes when they spoke to me in English I answered in Hebrew. "I need to practice!" I tended to insist, and they usually relented with a laugh, saying, "Okay, *yalla, b'ivrit.*" Only now I felt—what's the word? Not "fear," but a fearsome feeling, almost repulsive. Let's call it "discomfort": I felt *uncomfortable* to be seen as Israeli when these Arab girls were watching.

Apparently I had not answered her, because she switched to English. "Oh! Sorry!" *she said, her* "r"*s soft and her* "o"*s round.* "I can help you to find something?" *She looked embarrassed but brave. She had baby fat in her cheeks and a proud chin.*

I felt the Arab girls looking at us. I wondered if they were recalculating who I was, how I fit into the narrative of this place. The repulsive, fearsome feeling lifted. "Oh, I'm just looking, thank you," I answered in English.

"*Beseder*, if you will need anything you call to me," the Israeli said. I liked her, liked imagining she'd said she was fluent in English on her job application. Close enough.

I nodded. Had I spoken in Hebrew, I would have been placed on one side of a boundary alongside the Israeli girl, the Arabs on the other side. But because I'd spoken in English, that boundary was porous to me.

I couldn't begin to articulate any of this in the Facebook post I was drafting. Instead I wrote, *When she left, there was a silence that encompassed me and the Arab-Israelis girls together. If I wanted to connect, it would have to be now.*

"I've heard great things about this product," I said in English, suddenly unsure if they spoke English—fuck. But also, unwilling to speak Hebrew lest that creeping discomfort descend again.

It was the chic-punk girl who responded; her business-casual friend (a cousin, I would eventually learn) did not acknowledge me. "As have I," she said, her English formal to the point of sounding British. "I adore these Korean skin-care brands."

"Same!" I exclaimed. Then, before we lost momentum, "I'm Allie, by the way. I'm a visiting student at the university."

That's how I met Aisha and her cousin, both of them students at Tel Aviv University. We looked around the shop, talking about skin care.

"What do you think about chemical exfoliants?" I asked, picking up a bottle of alpha hydroxy acid toner.

"Obsessed," Aisha said. "Although I use the French one."

"Wait," I said, turning to her. Her skin was indeed luminous, but the product she was referring to was like ninety American dollars for the tiniest bottle. "Not *the* French one."

She smiled, pleased. "It's a good investment," she said.

"Aisha," I whined, trying out her name, "I'm envious."

I was talking about skin care. But I was talking about skin care with an Arab. It gave the conversation an exciting sheen, almost dangerous. The word that comes to me, although I would never admit it, is "exotic."

In the end, we decided to take a few samples rather than buy a full-sized product that day.

At the counter, Aisha spoke in Hebrew to request our samples. I stayed silent, except for the odd "Thank you." Her Hebrew was better than mine, I reasoned. I didn't even know the Hebrew word for "sample." This wasn't lying, not exactly. To avoid speaking Hebrew so as not to alienate Aisha was not exactly lying.

I tried to smile at Aisha's cousin, but she avoided my eye.

After the three of us left with our samples, we were a kind of trio.

The closeness was undeniable: our walking was synched; our exchanges felt more familiar, with less explained and more understood. "Excited to smear on some snail mucin," I said.

"Get it, girl," Aisha replied.

We had a rhythm now. If the salesgirl hadn't spoken to me in English, or if I'd answered her in Hebrew, this dynamic would not have been possible. I was finding that I lived in a place of boundaries—some physical, enforced by walls; others invisible, enforced by language or even just an accent. But I was also finding that these boundaries did not always apply to me.

I decided to be bold. "We should get coffee sometime," I said to Aisha.

"Yeah," she said, "we should."

Under fluorescent mall lighting, I typed my name into her phone.

Unmentioned in my Facebook post was how Aisha's cousin did not look up from her phone as Aisha and I exchanged numbers. How I'd had a sudden fear that this quiet girl had found my Facebook. My account was set to private—the content not visible to anyone who was not in my network—but in my fearsome daydream, Aisha's cousin was looking at photos of me and Eyal. She was seeing captions written in Hebrew, she was seeing me with a soldier, she was reading my sympathetic posts about memorial and narrative. There it was again, the unnameable revulsion I'd felt when the Israeli shopgirl spoke to me in Hebrew.

"Do you have Facebook?" Aisha asked, as she took back her phone.

I was startled but tried not to show it. "Totally," I said, "you should add me." I somehow knew that I would edit my profile before accepting her request—limiting how much of my online life she could see.

And so in a North Tel Aviv mall, on a day without rockets, connections were—

—I stopped typing. My laptop was hot against my thighs. I still had not accepted Aisha's friend request on Facebook. What was my plan? Obviously, she could not see this post: I'd benefited from a misunderstanding that I'd failed to clear up. At best, she'd find me creepy. Even if I restricted her access to my profile such that she couldn't see this post (should I publish it), wouldn't it be unsettling for anyone else reading? Wouldn't they wonder if Aisha was reading it too? Just the threat of her presence was spectral, calling the whole narrative into question.

This was all too complicated! My cursor was still blinking on the unpublished words of my Facebook update. COMMAND+A. The text highlighted. DELETE. I erased all that I had written.

Instead of posting anything, I went through my Facebook profile as Aisha would see it. Long posts about life in Israel, about learning Hebrew, and coming to live by the rhythms of Jewish life. Photo of me and Talia waving mini Israeli flags on Independence Day. Photo of me and Eyal. He in uniform, I on his lap. The comments are ecstatic. His mother and all her friends, leaving Hebrew expressions of delight. LOOK AT THESE BEAUTIES! Kissy-face emojis. These images were precious to me. I was loved; I had been absorbed. But now, imagining Aisha seeing them, I again felt that repulsive, almost frightening feeling seeping cold into my gut, and oh, I knew it.

I knew what the feeling was. Shame. I'd been unable to name it before, but it was shame. When I imagined Aisha going through my Facebook, seeing my life in Israel, it was shame I felt.

Here is a life that excludes you. Here is a life that was built on what we took from you, what we will never ever give back.

Almost immediately, I was arguing with Aisha, as if it was she herself who told me I ought to be ashamed. *What do I have to be ashamed of? I'm supposed to be ashamed that I love my boyfriend? That I love living here? In the Jewish state? I have nothing to be ashamed of*, I thought defiantly.

Yet I Googled a step-by-step guide to limiting someone's access to my Facebook profile. I adjusted the controls such that photos of me and Eyal—or me doing anything particularly Israeli-seeming—could be viewed by all groups *except* a group I called "university friends," which was really a euphemism for "Arabs," because it would only ever have one member: Aisha. The result was a version of myself curated only for her. No soldier boyfriend, no Israeli flags, no links to articles about Israelis in the south pummeled by Hamas rockets, no posts that I had written in a tentative and imperfect Hebrew, cheered on by Eyal and his friends for my progress in the language, and, for good measure, no photographs of me in a swimsuit.

Not so different, maybe, from the way I curated myself for Eyal. Softened and reduced in ways I thought he would like. Now I was two people: the one who wrote letters to Eyal and the one that Aisha saw on my Facebook page. Two versions of me: and neither of them exactly true.

The *Odyssey* is filled with liars: Penelope spends each night unweaving a burial shroud to secretly buy herself time; Athena cannot resist changing her form when appearing to the mortals whose lives she's manipulating. But no one lies more than Odysseus, he of many schemes. He lies about where he is from, where he has traveled, what he has seen. He lies about his own name.

When he tells stories of his wandering, he speaks in the third person—as if he himself were not Odysseus, revealing and disgusting himself at once.

"He knew how to speak lies that were like truth," the poem tells us. This is to say, Odysseus is a writer.

I accepted Aisha's Facebook request.

When I sat down with Timor that week, I struggled with a question that I was not sure how to phrase. "Does being a soldier change how you see?" I asked him.

"What do you mean?" Timor asked. "Change how you see what?" He always sat leaning back in his chair with his legs spread. Relaxed and proprietary. A cafe worker came by to clear away the cups, but Timor did this thing he knew how to do, kind of shook his head and moved his fingers—so slightly you'd barely notice—and the cafe worker walked away.

"I mean, a soldier *ba-sadeh* sees things a certain way," I said. I was speaking English, but I used the Hebrew I'd learned from Eyal—*ba-sadeh*, "in the field," that nebulous zone of combat.

"*Ba-sadeh*," Timor repeated, sounding amused. "Okay."

"But on a mission, a soldier sees differently," I persisted, feeling self-conscious to be telling a soldier about being a soldier. "Right? Each Palestinian is a potential threat?" I waited a beat for him to contradict me, but he did not. "So when he comes back home, isn't that still how he sees them?" Pause. "Palestinians, I mean? All as potential threats."

"As opposed to what?" Timor said.

For one single moment, I missed my sister—how she would occupy this point of view so I didn't have to. "As opposed to people, Timor."

He was inspecting the underside of his empty cup. No reaction.

"And isn't that dangerous?" I felt lost in my own sentences. "For the soldiers, I mean. To see people that way." I'd heard academics in New York talk about "self-traumatizing perpetrators," which was to say the trauma of oppressing; I'd heard other academics insist that focusing on this kind of trauma was a further erasure of the oppressed.

Timor's face betrayed no emotion when he said, "It sounds like you are talking about yourself."

This unraveled me. "I don't think that I—wait, am I? Maybe you're right. Maybe the way I see is changing." I was fumbling. "What does it mean to see, anyway? When is it an act of violence? Or am I abstracting violence beyond reason?" I began peeling the rim of my paper coffee cup, even though the cup itself was half full. "Then again, who cares about reason?" The rim of the coffee cup was a flap now. "But anyway, to not see an individual when you see a Palestinian, it feels dangerous. I mean, dangerous for"—I hesitated—"I don't know, the soul?"

Timor laughed.

I looked up. "What's so funny?" I asked, a little relieved. He was such a serious man, it was nice to see him laugh.

"I was just thinking," he said, putting down his cup, "you'd be easy to interrogate."

I spilled my coffee.

Eyal's mom sent me a link to an article about a four-year-old Israeli boy killed by a rocket that landed on his kibbutz.

I posted it on my Facebook wall, making it visible to everyone but Aisha.

I texted Eyal, knowing it might be a while before he saw the message, but wanting to feel close to him. PLEASE KNOW THAT I LOVE YOU AND I SUPPORT YOU. THANK YOU FOR GUARDING OVER US.

∽ ∾

Because it's so brutal to find a charging outlet, Eyal has got his phone on airplane mode a lot of the time, even when he's allowed to have it on him. It's satisfying to turn his data back on and watch the messages spill in.

He knows he should be happy at Allie's message: PLEASE KNOW THAT I LOVE YOU AND I SUPPORT YOU. THANK YOU FOR GUARDING OVER US. She's sweet and appreciative, yes, and her gratitude brings meaning to this chaos, sure. So why does it make him so sad? When he read it, he felt a sense of despair and loss. Was it because she could be any Israeli saying this to any soldier? *Thank you for guarding over us.*

It is night. At the border fence, the snipers are shooting Arabs again. Everyone was antsy today because of news about that toddler who died. "Let's go already, yalla, send us in."

You can't say you're scared to go in. You can't even think it. There's no way to survive if you let yourself think such a thing. The closest he can come is attributing that emotion to Allison. *Allie is scared for me.* That he's allowed to think. *Allie is scared that we'll invade. Allie is scared that I'll get hurt, that someone I love will die, that I'll have to kill an Arab and live with those feelings forever. Allie is scared.*

But that's not what her text message says. *Thank you for guarding over us.*

He thinks about his ima and sister, taking him down to the apartment building's bomb shelter. He couldn't have been older than five. Aba was still going to reserve duty then, so it was little Eyal in the shelter with all the women of the building. Mothers and sisters, grandmas and a few grandpas. Koral made it a game that they would curl themselves up like little seeds until they heard the boom of the rocket, then Koral would open her palms and say, "Boom!" And Eyal would imitate her. *Boom!* It was a game. He imitated his sister, and he was not scared.

Suddenly, he misses them. His annoying sister. His meddlesome mother. He misses them. He misses the version of himself he was—a child protected by the tiny blond women of his family.

HEY, he texts Koral.

She writes back right away. WHAT'S WRONG?

IT'S FINE, he writes back. JUST SAYING HI.

WE MISS YOU, Koral says. IMA IS PRAYING ALL THE TIME.

He doesn't say he misses them too, but hopes she knows. TELL HER I'M OKAY, he writes. TELL HER I LOVE HER.

In the dark, he hears gunfire.

Thirteen

After we added each other on Facebook, Aisha and I interacted tentatively online. We liked each other's profile photos. She posted a link to her favorite homemade face exfoliant recipe—just fine salt and olive oil, really. I commented on the post: BUT IS IT AS GOOD AS SNAIL MUCIN?? She liked the comment and responded to it with a laughing emoji.

Secretly, I went through every single one of her hundred or so photos—or at least, the ones she had left visible to me. Some were obviously taken in Tel Aviv: Aisha on the boardwalk looking chic in a leather jacket with a cropped shirt underneath; Aisha posing with a carton of strawberries in the open-air Carmel Market; Aisha and a friend candidly sharing a cigarette at the port of Jaffa (in the background, two soldiers). In these images, there was something wry in her expressions. "Amused" is maybe the wrong word. *I'm here but I'm not here*, is how I read it at the time. After knowing her longer, I would come to read the expression a little differently: *I'm here because you cannot erase me*.

In status updates in Arabic and English, she referred to herself as a "48 Palestinian," a term I'd never heard before. It took me a few seconds to process it: 48, as in 1948, as in this land before the modern state of Israel, as in had Israel not been founded she would have been a citizen of Palestine, not of Israel. She was declaring not a legal status (her ID was Israeli) but a spiritual one. Huh. I felt a slight tingling of discomfort.

Interesting to consider that Eyal's maternal grandfather could have technically called himself a 48 Palestinian. Why not? No doubt his official documents had listed his birthplace as Mandatory Palestine. Had I said that to Eyal's mother, that her father was a 1948 Palestinian, I truly believe she would have slapped me. Not that she was a violent person! Not once. But her entire self-concept was built around not being an Arab; for me to essentially call her father one—what could she do but strike me?

I was especially interested in the photos that Aisha had posted from her home in the majority-Arab city of Nazareth. Like Aisha, the city was technically Israeli, but belonged to a different world. These photos were softer than her Tel Aviv shots: Aisha holding a baby, the background looking like it might be a construction site—slabs of marble and bags of un-mixed cement; Aisha sitting with an elderly woman who had her hair covered by a loose scarf—a grandmother?—under a tree, the two of them holding hands; Aisha on an overstuffed couch surrounded by other women, some younger, some older, all of them seeming to be talking and laughing at once. These were glimpses of a life that was very far away from me. *Let me in*, I thought.

WE SHOULD GET COFFEE! I messaged Aisha at the beginning of the week.

FOR SURE! THURSDAY? she wrote back.

THAT WOULD BE GREAT!!

I could tell we were both invested because of all the exclamation points we used. As it happened, she suggested we meet exactly one hour before my regular meeting with Timor. *Could you do earlier?* I asked, but she had a class. Nervous that she would change her mind altogether, I made the tight timing work by suggesting the cafe where Timor and I usually met. That way I could go from one meeting to the other.

At the Gaza border, I knew, Eyal and his unit were patrolling and sur-
veilling while the air force bombed Gaza City. It seemed impossible that
ground soldiers would actually go into Gaza. In my heart, I thought that
someone would intervene before it got that far. Who? An adult, maybe.
Someone to tell the boys to stop playing their war games and come inside
for dinner.

A pretty American undergraduate in my Modern Hebrew class—
distressed jean shorts, sunglasses on her head—asked our teacher about
the invasion. "Why won't the prime minister—"

"*B'ivrit*," Smadar cut her off gently, adjusting a shawl that was vibrant
with impressionistic blossoms in red and yellow.

The question became simpler when the girl attempted it in Hebrew:
"Why aren't we in Gaza?"

It was a question you could feel in the air. When would they stop waiting around the border fence? When would the invasion start? I thought
about the words Timor had said to me: *Boys want war.*

Smadar hesitated before answering. It was rare for the class to broach
what I want to call "politics," although I suppose everything in that class
was tacitly political. Our textbooks were filled with stories of Jewish immigration to Israel, the inventive Zionist spirit, the history of Tel Aviv;
I didn't even know how to spell "Palestine" in Hebrew. Smadar leaned
against her desk. She had three children who had all served in the army,
and four grandchildren who one day would. "Look," she said in Hebrew,
speaking in the plural imperative, speaking to us all, "it's a balance."

"My boyfriend says they only understand *koakh*," the girl said, her
American accent making it sound like she was chewing gum even though
she wasn't. The word she used could mean "strength" or "power," but in
this context it clearly meant "force." The Arabs only understand force.

Her comment made me uneasy. The words formed a ledge. What would happen if I fell off it? How could I tell if I already had?

I don't know why I thought Smadar would share my sensibilities, say something like, *Yikes, that's a little racist.* Or maybe: *This isn't a game.* Or maybe: *Please be more sensitive—Allie's boyfriend is down there.* But Smadar nodded her head. "*Nakhon, nakhon,*" she said, her voice arcing in that musical way it had. *That's true, that's true.* "Is he at the border?" she asked. But not to me.

The American girl nodded. "Yes, he's been there forever," she said, adjusting the sunglasses on her head.

Smadar nodded. "He's guarding over us."

Of course I wasn't the only foreigner dating a soldier. But I'd imagined I was the only one, hadn't I? I'd imagined I had special access to a deeper inside than anyone in this room, and I was wrong.

Inland from Gaza, east of Tel Aviv in the so-called West Bank, a Palestinian stabbed a young Israeli father to death on a settlement. The soldiers on the scene killed the Palestinian. Later, the army demolished his mother's home.

"Why did I decide to do summer classes?" Aisha moaned.

We were drinking coffee at the campus cafe, where, in an hour, I'd meet with Timor. We were seated outside, despite the atrocious midday heat. The area was shaded, not that it made much of a difference. Heat rose up from the ground. I thought of Eyal, sweating in all his gear, patrolling for tunnels. I had to stay vigilant about avoiding any mention of my army boyfriend. "Is it cooler in Nazareth?" I asked. When I imagined the city, it was basilicas and crosses on a hill. White light, white stone, doves in the olive trees. An uncontested version of Jerusalem.

"Yes, ours is a much more temperate climate," she said. So exact with her words. "I go back most weekends."

I watched one of the campus stray cats stick its filthy face inside an abandoned disposable coffee cup. *I know*, I could have said. *I've seen every photo you've ever posted online.* Her Facebook albums were filled with photos of family gathered around a low table for tea, women holding various toddlers, a grandmother surrounded by granddaughters. Normal but also foreign. But I didn't say any of that. "In this heat, I almost miss the Canada cold." I was talking about the weather, sure, but I was talking about the weather with an Arab. "Have you been?"

"To Canada?"

"Yes."

"Maybe one day," she said mildly.

I wondered if I was boring her. I started to ask another question, and just as I did she started to say something. We both apologized, holding up our hands. *You go. No, you go.*

"Please," I said, gesturing toward her.

"What I was going to say," she said, "is that it's great for me to practice my English."

"You speak perfectly," I said. Was this awkward? Was I making this awkward?

"No, no." She waved away my compliment.

"Did you say you study political science?" I asked.

"Yes," she said, "it's a consequential discipline here."

"A *consequential discipline*, wow," I said. "I think your English might be better than mine."

I meant it as a compliment, but from her uneasy laugh, I could tell I'd come off as condescending. Maybe it was both a compliment and condescending.

"And you? What do you study?" she asked.

I didn't want to tell her that I studied the ancient rabbis. That seemed too Jewish, and more importantly, too Zionist. Instead I said, "I study poetry."

"Here?" she asked. "In English?"

"Ancient poetry," I said, a variation on what I'd told Eyal the day we met. *Metaphor-ah.*

"In English?"

"In translation." I felt myself stepping carefully, avoiding the facts that might cause Aisha to second-guess a friendship with me. How could I jump back to the feeling from the mall? The feeling of closeness with her? "Wait, is this weird?" I asked, leaning forward quickly such that Aisha ever so slightly leaned back. "Do you use a mud mask?"

She looked at me quizzically. "A what?"

I was acting weird. Oh my God, I was acting so weird. I wished I could start the conversation over. If she left, would I ever speak to a Palestinian again? Would I be just another girl in jean shorts in Hebrew class, casually racist and uncorrected by anyone? "Sorry!" I exclaimed. "Sorry, is that weird? I'm just looking for a good facial. My skin feels dull."

"Oh," she said, drawing out the word. "Do I use a mud mask." She touched her cheek lightly. "No, I order masks from a spa in New York."

"That has to be what I miss most about New York," I said: "The spa treatments." This was a slight exaggeration: I'd had exactly one facial when my comprehensive exams had me breaking out. It cost the equivalent of one month's worth of groceries. I hadn't known how much to tip, which mortified me.

Now it was Aisha's turn to lean forward. "You lived in New York?" She looked excited. "But I thought you were Canadian."

"I went to graduate school in the city," I said, hoping my word choice sounded urbane.

"It's my dream," she said.

"You look very New York," I said. And it was true. I could easily see her there. Thin with perfect skin and a chic-edgy look that clearly, I realized now, she had modeled on the city's uptown-downtown feel: the zip-up black ankle boots and cutoff T-shirt with perfectly fitted jeans. She dressed for a life somewhere else.

"As if," she said, but she was gratified, I could tell.

We talked about spas and department stores. We talked about Brooklyn and subway routes. I told her how much I missed authentic, hand-pulled noodles. All the Asian food in Israel was made by Israelis who had visited Asian countries, I complained. There was no mechanism for immigration here if you weren't Jewish or married to a Jew.

She nodded significantly. "Believe me," she said, "I know."

Whatever discomfort I felt by her alluding to her subjugation, I pushed it down. We talked about Central Park.

It wasn't until Aisha got up to use the washroom that I realized I should check the time.

Timor would be here in four minutes.

Shit, I thought. *Shit, shit, shit.* The idea of them overlapping was unbearable. He'd greet me in Hebrew. Aisha would be confused, like, *Oh, I thought you didn't speak Hebrew?* And I'd have to say something along the lines of, *Oh, I'm really bad at it.* I'd be feeling like a creep, of course. How could I explain that I didn't mean to lie, just failed to clear up a misunderstanding? Meanwhile, Timor would be watching all this unfold, understanding something about me that I didn't want him to understand, maybe that I didn't want to understand about myself.

As so often happens when I panic, I remained frozen. Sitting in the uncomfortable cafe chair, I waited for Aisha to return from the washroom.

By the time she got back, we had two minutes.

"I have to get to class," she said, packing up her books.

I tried not to look too relieved. "Great!" I said. "I mean, sure!"

"Are you around next week?" she asked.

"Totally." I nodded, eyes wide. *Go, go, go.*

"Great," she said, slinging a backpack over her back. "I'm in Nazareth this weekend, but back Sunday."

Timor would be here in one minute. "I'll message you," I said, thinking, *Please, please let Timor be late today.*

"Sounds good," she said, checking her phone as she began, to my relief, to walk away.

As she left the cafe, I watched her pass Timor on his way in.

"A friend of yours?" he asked me as he took his seat.

"I think so," I said.

"What's her name?"

A brief wash of doubt: What did it mean that Timor was an intelligence officer? When was he in the army and when was he a civilian? And what did that mean for someone like Aisha? But I wanted to announce that I had a Palestinian friend. I liked what it said about me. So I answered: "Aisha."

He nodded. "Aisha," he repeated. Then he said it again, only this time he emphasized the first letter: *"A'aisha."* He pronounced her name as an Arabic speaker would: voicing the initial letter, ayin, as the throaty pharyngeal fricative it is in Arabic. Long, long ago, Hebrew sounded like this, but in Modern Israeli Hebrew, consistent with the European-influenced Hebrew of Ashkenazi diaspora, the letter ayin has assimilated to be a glottal stop—the sound of obstructed air, identical to the letter aleph. Timor's pronunciation of "Aisha" was a joke. The humor was premised on difference. They talk one way, we another. If I laughed, I was accepting a boundary between Jews and Arabs. The boundary itself was fictitious; after all, for thousands of years, Jews living in Arab lands kept the ayin intact—Talia's ancestors, for instance.

It was a joke. Also, it was a test. Us and them.

I laughed.

I began to find that I was always looking for Aisha around campus. I sat at a cafe, reading articles about the influence of Middle Persian narratives on rabbinic storytelling and, every few paragraphs, looking up to scan passersby.

Certain features of the campus began to announce themselves more forcefully. The unambiguous Israeli flag. The names of buildings in Hebrew and English only. As if I were seeing this place through her eyes, which, it turns out, I found incredibly unpleasant. She passed over each moment like a shadow.

Talia told me about an upcoming protest against the invasion, although she herself would not be going. "It's too dangerous," she said.

We were both sitting on her bed. The room filled with the soft, steady electronic glitches and hitches of a new music project. Inspired by the cassettes of Mizrachi music—the ones that had circulated in the poor neighborhoods where Talia would have grown up had her parents not "got out"—her new work had the distant, textural feel of cassette tape played until worn thin. There were snatches of older women speaking in Arabic, the trilling *mawwal* introductions to Arabic-style songs, samples of men singing Hebrew with Arabic accents, as if her music was an attempt to give herself memories of a childhood she had not had. Recently, she'd told me she was thinking about studying Moroccan Arabic. I asked if she could have learned it in the army, and she said, "But that's different—it's the Palestinian Arabic not Darija, and anyway, they aren't teaching you to connect with your roots, they are teaching you to be a weapon." That's what she said: "They are teaching you to be a weapon."

Now, Talia dipped one of her long, cylindrical cookies into milky coffee. "It's fine to criticize the government," she told me. That's fine, sure. But you criticize the army? The average Israeli can't accept that. "The army is a holy cow," she said, translating directly from the Hebrew. A golden calf is the reference point—the idol that the sons of Israel worshiped in the desert. People love the army like it's blood, she told me. It's their whole identity. Timor had told me that the army breaks you down and then rebuilds you. And that's forever. I don't think I could be broken down like that, I'd told him at the time. He hadn't hesitated even for a moment before answering, "Of course you could."

"What did you do in the army again?" I asked Talia.

"I taught exercise classes," she said.

"You?" I exclaimed. This girl laughed at me every time I went for a jog.

"Hey, I was very *sportivit* back in the day," she said, nudging the open packet of cookies toward me.

I wanted to ask her what she thought I'd have done in the army, but it seemed somehow too revealing that I wanted to know. I took a cookie. "So should I go?" I asked. "To the protest?"

Her eyebrows shot up. "That's hard-core," she said.

"I'm just kidding," I said. "Can you imagine?" I bit into the cookie. White chocolate—too sweet.

"Ah, okay," she said. She closed her eyes and leaned against the wall. Her hair was dark and curly, almost but not quite tangled. Like Aisha's, I realized. She had the same hair as Aisha.

Sometimes, when I tried to touch myself to thoughts of Eyal— remembering his hands, his mouth, his devotion—it was Timor who swirled into my fantasies. The first time it happened, I stopped. But the next time, I let myself keep going. I imagined Timor holding me in place, seeing right through me, seeing down to my core and knowing everything I ever tried to hide from myself.

We stood facing each other. Standing. Not too close. Not even within arm's reach. Me fixed in place by his power alone.

"I want—" I'd try to begin.

"I know." He'd cut me off. Taking a step toward me as I took a step back. Ancient, primal fantasy. Hunted. "I know because I've watched you."

"You have?" My voice scratchy, a little breathless.

"You know I have." Another step.

Me, helpless, taking another step back, finding that I've bumped into a wall behind me.

Another step. "You know I have because you've felt me." He could reach out and touch me, but he doesn't. He stops to survey me. From head to toe. Taking me in with a possessive satisfaction. He doesn't have to say it aloud: *I have you right where I want you.* "You like it, don't you?"

I nod.

"Turn around," he says.

I do it, slowly. Only when I'm facing the wall do I feel him behind me. His breath creeping into my ear. "I see you take the bus to campus every day. How you look up from your book sometimes and you are smiling—something has pleased you. I watch men watching you and think about how, if they even try to talk to you, I will kill them." He touches my neck so gently. *This is love. Isn't it? Isn't this love?*

I came as hard as I had ever come.

In the fantasy, there was no sex, and yet I was opening myself up to him. Was that what I wanted? To confess what I was too scared to say? But what was I too scared to say?

I'M SCARED, I texted Eyal.

DON'T BE SCARED, he replied.

I wanted to pick a fight—to do something that would alleviate, if only briefly, the agitation of waiting: Would they call the invasion? Or would he come home? Instead, I told him that I was going to text his mom to see if I could go to their apartment. I MISS YOUR BED, I wrote. MAYBE I'LL TAKE A NAP THERE.

He replied with a voice memo in English. Always, he sounded tentative in English—like someone tiptoeing through the wreckage. "It is comforting," he said, "to think of you there." Pause. Then, a second voice memo: "Also sad. Sad without me."

An unexpected source of comfort emerged in those days: how Eyal's family treated me less as a guest and more as one of their own. Whoever answered the door would give me a quick hug, then go back to whatever they'd been doing, and I would slip in and do my assigned reading at Eyal's desk. Later, I'd join them to watch the news. We might eat together. "Can someone take the dog out?" his mom often asked after dinner, and I always volunteered.

My parents back home were cautious when they inquired about Eyal. "Any news on the probability of an invasion?" they asked over the phone. "How does he feel? How do you feel?"

There is a lack of ideology in my parents that I have come to admire. Neither of them would die for any cause: not justice or love, and certainly not God. I do not know if this is selfish or enlightened or both. My sense now is that, at the time, my parents worried if they revealed any moral outrage at the potential invasion of Gaza, they might push their eldest daughter further into what they considered a kind of extremism, so they asked personal, almost deferential, questions: Do you miss him? How is school? Who is walking his dog?

Only Erica was more direct, of course she was. Over messenger, she sent me article links that I was sure Cee had sent to her: a report by Al Jazeera on PTSD in Gaza; profiles of the Palestinian children killed in Israeli air strikes.

I DON'T HAVE THE CAPACITY TO THINK ABOUT POLITICS, I replied eventually. I'M WORRIED ABOUT EYAL. It felt good to say to Erica and Cee—two people commenting from the sidelines, loving no one.

Later, Cee tweeted: CRAZY HOW A CONVERSATION IS SUDDENLY "POLITICAL" WHEN IT INVOLVES A BODY THAT IS NOT WHITE OR CIS.

I rolled my eyes when I saw it on my timeline. I could just imagine Erica repeating my words to Cee—"She said she doesn't have *capacity*"— her voice derisive. And then Cee tweeting their little judgment of me.

Once a week, I attended a dissertation workshop, held in a small class-room filled with display cases of excavated pottery. "It's crazy what's happening down south," one German theology student said to another. When the war came up, it was something surreal and novel—a backdrop to the anecdotes my classmates would one day tell about graduate school.

It was at least a small solace that Eyal still had his phone, for now. For now. When I texted him, I tried to offer a little bit of softness and magic. From flowers I found growing in a little patch of Tel Aviv wild, I wove a dainty garland. Yellow flowers with nearly translucent petals. They would droop within an hour of being picked. It wasn't until I put on the garland— already taking photos of myself to send Eyal, trying to look ethereal— that I felt the ants on my scalp. I threw the flowers to the ground, but it was too late. Ants in my hair, on my scalp, crawling down my neck, one in my ear. They must have been hiding in the dark filament at each flower's center. For days after I found ants on my pillow, curled in death.

Aisha and I walked around campus with iced coffees that she had insisted on paying for. We were talking about our favorite neighborhoods in New York.

"I love the West Village," she was saying, stirring her drink with her straw.

"You have great taste," I said. I took a sip from my drink. "Also, expensive taste."

"That's what my dad says." She smiled shyly. "You lived in Brooklyn, right?"

We walked under date palms, the shadows flickered pleasantly.

"No, I wish," I said. "I lived on the Upper West Side, just south of the university." Bagel places, shawarma places, Indian places. One eternal late afternoon—the day feeling lost before it began. That was my New York. "But I love parts of Brooklyn."

"DUMBO?" she asked. "Those cobblestones are so romantic."

"Such a hip area," I affirmed. I had a memory of puking out of a cab onto those cobblestones, but I didn't tell Aisha this, of course. I wasn't sure of her stance on alcohol, and maybe more than that, I didn't want her to think I was a lesser person. Dirty. Instead, I said, "I used to love seeing plays at St. Ann's Warehouse." I noticed that in my word choice, I was placing New York in the distant, perfected past. I wondered if Aisha noticed too.

But she was responding with some excitement. "When I visited, I saw Karen O there!" she said, referring to that era's indie rock matriarch.

"No shit!" I exclaimed. Then, glancing at her, "I mean, wait, sorry for swearing."

She laughed. "You're totally fine."

So I repeated, "No shit!" Which made her laugh more. "I can't believe you got tickets." I knew what she was referring to: perhaps the coolest show of that year, a kind of psycho-opera with a chorus of women. *I was young. I was clean. I was only seventeen.* I wondered if Aisha was a virgin, then felt gross for wondering. We knew so little about each other beyond our similar taste.

"Maybe next time I visit, you'll be back in New York," Aisha said.

Something dropped inside me, like a stone falling, falling, falling into a deep well. "Maybe," I said.

"When do you go back, anyway?"

It was a fair question: I'd already extended a year, but the way months passed, it would be over soon enough. *Just make* aliyah, Eyal's mom said, Talia said, my advisor said. They were using the Hebrew word for a Jew immigrating to Israel. Literally, *Just make the ascension.* "In the spring," I answered Aisha, the stone inside me still sinking.

"Oh, you're here for a while," she said, recalibrating something.

"I think about . . ." I caught myself. I had been about to say, *I think about making* aliyah. But the ideology of the wording felt suddenly obscene. Only Jews make *aliyah.* "I think about living in Brooklyn," I redirected, "when I move back."

Aisha began talking about bagel places. I bit my thumbnail, feeling dishonest.

Timor met me in jogging shorts and a T-shirt. "I just came from my workout," he explained. The scent of his sweat was faint and not unpleasant. Salty and new.

We drank iced coffees in the heat of the courtyard.

"Will you go to Gaza?" I asked, a little suddenly.

"Not this time," he said.

"So there will be an invasion?" I pressed.

He hesitated. "I don't know."

I didn't believe him. "I haven't heard from Eyal all day." It was coming, wasn't it? The soldiers storming into the tangles of Gaza City just beyond the border fence.

Timor shrugged. "He's busy." He took a sip of iced coffee. Odd to see someone with such a commanding presence drink from a straw, the way it had also been odd to find that, when he had to go to the bathroom, he said, "*Yesh li pipi*," literally, *I have peepee*, and the way it would be odd when I eventually learned that, like many Israelis who extend their army service, he still lived with his parents. "How is your friend Aisha?" he asked. "Aisha with the snail cream."

My mind snagged on what he said. "I told you about that?"

"You did," he said, unbothered, playing with the straw of his coffee. "Cute story."

I had wild, uncertain thoughts. The army was reading my emails and text messages. The army was watching how I interacted with Arabs. Surveillance was everywhere. Just knowing that was enough to make me want to be careful. But then, I had told Timor, hadn't I? About the day at the mall? I was almost sure I had. "She's cool," I said. I looked for the right word. "She's normal."

"Will you go to Nazareth?" he asked.

This was not something I had even once considered. But as Timor said it, the possibility seemed real.

"Maybe," I said. "If she invites me, I mean."

"Guard yourself," he said.

"Why?" I laughed. "Not all Palestinians hate us, you know."

"Of course they do," Timor said. He said it again. "Of course they hate us."

I opened my mouth to speak, then closed it.

"That's the cost of a Jewish state," he said. He was not angry. "They hate us." He blinked slowly, unhurriedly. "They hate us, and it's worth it."

Fourteen

When the ground invasion began and the troops stormed the fence separating Gaza from the rest of the world, there was no fanfare in Israel. No grand announcement on the radio, no siren like the one that called out danger and memorial. It was announced on Twitter. OUR SOLDIERS ARE NOW ENTERING GAZA: THE WHOLE NATION STANDS BEHIND THEM, the IDF Twitter posted, along with a photo of one soldier painting another soldier's face a camo green.

A Twitter account with no profile image replied: KILL THEM ALL!!

They can't all go in, I pleaded with myself. Some people must stick around the border fence to patrol for tunnels, right? They can't all go in. ARE YOU THERE? I texted Eyal. No reply.

He had stopped answering texts. My calls went right to voice mail. I knew that if—that when—he went in, he would have no way to tell me. He was forbidden from sending messages that could be intercepted and interpreted. No lengthy goodbyes, no *I love you*s, not even a heart emoji. And still I did not believe he was actually in there.

News sites showed images of tanks rolling over fences.

"Are you getting through?" I asked his sister on a phone call. It was afternoon, and I was still in bed, lying on top of the covers, counting my ribs.

"Come over for dinner," Koral said, not answering my question.

"Okay," I said. Then I asked again, "Are you getting through?"

"No," she said.

"I don't think he's in Gaza," I said. "I just have a feeling."

Koral hesitated. "You know, he loves you very much."

We made plans that I would come over that evening.

At Eyal's house I watched the news with his parents. His father paced around the apartment made cramped by the imposing leather sectional that curved through the living room.

Earlier that day, four soldiers had died in a booby-trapped Hamas tunnel. Their names and photos were on the screen. Then weeping mothers, weeping girlfriends. Then an ad for cell-phone service, an ad for corn snacks.

The four of us stayed huddled on the sofa, watching a news special on wounded Israeli soldiers. The program featured one young man, an infantry soldier, who had returned from Gaza blind. Eyeless in Gaza. There were long shots of this young man playing piano in the hospital. The camera zoomed in on the bandages wrapped around his face, then dropped down to the hands he could not see, spread across the keys. In the background, long-haired girls in the uniforms of army social workers clung to each other, weeping. He was playing a wistful pop song with simple and mournful lyrics that we all know; it is a song about saying goodbye to love.

How did they get a piano in the hospital? I wondered. Whatever I was actually feeling, I couldn't let myself feel it yet.

Eyal's mother was crying, and Koral was holding her hand.

We watched news footage of Israeli planes dropping bombs on Gaza City. When a building collapsed, it brought up a chalky white dust with it. *Where are you?* I thought about Eyal in there, waiting for the rubble to clear so he could advance. *Are you safe? Are you thirsty?* This was as far as I could let myself go.

"The problem is," Eyal's father said, "that we never go far enough with Gaza."

Koral said, "Do you think he packed enough socks?"

I said, "He could still be patrolling the kibbutz for tunnels."

His mom didn't say anything.

None of us seemed to hear the others, but we all wanted to be together.

Before I left their apartment that night, I took Charlotte on a walk. The dog puttered around the apartment complexes of Eyal's neighborhood. Playgrounds and abandoned construction material. She panted intensely as she hunched to poop.

I texted Eyal: TAKING CHARLOTTE FOR AN ADVENTURE!

It was a cool night for summer, the sun already set. I had forgotten to bring a plastic bag. I looked around. Nobody was there to see as we wandered away, leaving our mess behind.

On the bus ride back to my apartment that night, I heard a young American, she couldn't have been much older than Eyal, on her phone, complaining to a friend. "How am I supposed to get married," she said in English, "when my rabbi has been called up to reserves?"

She had red hair, so smooth it must have been straightened with a keratin treatment. Her fingers were stacked in slim, elegant rings. She waited for someone on the other end to say something. "Yeah, they sent him to Gaza." She played with her hair. The bus was nearly empty. "Exactly!" she said into her phone.

A Palestinian laborer boarded the bus. Dusty boots.

"No, I swear. My rabbi got called to Gaza. Also, my weed guy." She paused. The man paid his fare and walked to the back of the bus. The girl glanced at him as he passed. "What?" she said into her phone. "No, no. Two different guys. Both in fucking Gaza."

Our bus was on the highway, driving south past the park where, once, Eyal and I had lain on a blanket, mythologizing our love. It hit me then. Whatever understanding I'd been keeping at bay, it came crashing down as the bus drove past that park.

He really was in Gaza. Whatever was there, he was in it.

On a bus speeding down the highway, by the rivers of Tel Aviv, I wept.

I couldn't get out of bed. I lay under a sheet, holding my phone up to my face. The army Twitter posted the names of two more soldiers who died in the invasion. THEY FELL DEFENDING OUR HOMELAND, the tweet said. Twenty and twenty-one. Photos of them squinting happily toward the camera. Somewhere in Israel, someone was opening up their stapled death letters.

Get up, I told myself. I had class. I did not get up.

Instead, I wrote him letters that I could not be sure he would ever read. In these letters, I remembered. *What I wouldn't give now to lie with you in the sun, letting a day slip by in pleasure and exhaustion.* How many hours had we spent drifting in and out of consciousness on empty beaches, in parks, on the couches of his cousins? We'd squandered the time, luxuriated in it. Or so it seemed to me now. *Your head lolling toward mine. Our fingers entwined, our legs entwined.* Back then, the only impediment we could imagine was my leaving.

We made every room the golden room.

Once, as we lay in his twin bed, I recited for him the Donald Hall poem "Gold." *We slept and woke / entering the golden room together.* I had spent a few days practicing, making sure I knew it by heart so that I could impress him this way.

"The golden room," he repeated, touching the back of my knee.

"The golden room." I kissed his fingertips. How I wished I had written those lines! I almost told him I had.

He asked me for a copy of the poem, so I wrote it out by hand on a piece of notebook paper that he folded into one of the many pockets of his uniform. Maybe it was with him now.

The night before he left, he had pressed his forehead into mine. I could feel the bones of his skull. "I will come back," he whispered. His fingers were strong at the back of my neck. He said it again, "To you. I will come back to you."

But where are you now? I asked my damp pillow.

Sometimes I cried; sometimes I slept. In the *Odyssey*, Penelope weeps for her husband until the goddess Athena gifts her with sleep. Sometimes she dreams of the man who is so far away.

"I named it the golden room," Eyal had told me on a rare phone call before the invasion.

"Named what?"

"A place we are watching." A place under surveillance, this meant. Perhaps somewhere suspected of being used for rocket launches or interrogations. Perhaps a tunnel entrance used by Hamas fighters to get under the border fence.

"Why did you get to name it?" I asked.

"We take turns." In the background, I could hear artillery. A firing range, I told myself. "My commander thought I was crazy. Such a pretty name for an ugly place." By this time we switched so easily between Hebrew and English that I can't remember which language we were speaking.

"The golden room," I repeated.

Some tunnels were intended for explosives, others were for kidnapping.

Eyal said the name would appear on surveillance maps and intelligence briefings.

Now, alone in my bed, I wrote to him: *There are tunnels inside me.*

I stayed in bed a full day and night. Asleep. Awake. Asleep. Awake. Asleep. Asleep. Asleep.

I tried to touch myself—just for the comfort and release. *He's lying on top of me*, I promised myself. *His skin is warm. His voice in my ear, heaving in pleasure,* You feel so good, you feel so good, fuck, baby, you feel so good. But shortly into my rubbing, I became too sad. I knew I could not withstand the crisis of an orgasm. I stopped touching myself and fell back asleep.

Aisha texted me. BACK FROM NAZARETH! WALK THIS WEEK?

I couldn't bear to see anyone, especially her. THIS WEEK IS NUTS!! I wrote back, always with so many exclamation points. NEXT WEEK?

SOUNDS GOOD :)

I texted Timor to say I wouldn't make it to our regular meeting time. With him, I was frank: I'M TOO OVERWHELMED, I JUST CAN'T . . .

TAKE CARE OF YOURSELF, he texted back.

I reread letters from Eyal. On a translucent packet of medic's gauze, empty of its supplies and torn in half, he had written, *I dream you are sleeping. Night after night. I can't wake you up.*

His writing was soft in pencil like a whisper. *I wait with my head on your back, listening to you breathe. Sad but somehow satisfied.*

Where are you, where are you, where are you, I moaned into my pillow.

Talia knocked on my door. "This came for you," she said, stepping into my room with a takeout bag. Then: "Whoa."

My room was littered with water bottles, the windows closed, and me in bed in the middle of the day.

"Are you okay?" she asked.

I didn't know how to answer the question. I was embarrassed to be seen like this. My room probably smelled musty. I needed to get up and tidy, but everything felt too overwhelming. To Talia I said, "I didn't order anything." I'd been living mostly on cereal.

She read from the receipt stapled to the plastic bag. "You know a Timor?"

"Whoa, I . . . yes," I said. "He's a friend from school."

She put the bag down on my side table. "I'm coming back to check on you," she said.

In the plastic bag was a paper bag, and in the paper bag was an enormous plastic container of salad. Green, healthful, overflowing with sliced veggies, crumbled cheese, and nuts. No note.

I texted Timor: THANK YOU.

Response: DON'T FORGET TO DRINK WATER.

I took a sip of room-temperature water from a bottle. Empty ones littered the floor around my bed.

Talia came back as I was finishing the salad, shoveling in mouthfuls with a plastic fork. She opened the windows in my room. Light and air poured in. It made me feel ill. Too much world. Too much world filled with too much uncertainty. *Eyal, where are you?* "How do I live like this?" I asked. "With all this worry?"

Talia sat on the edge of my bed. "Come home with me this weekend," she said. "Come for Shabbat with my parents."

I hesitated. "I'm not sure," I said, suddenly aware that I hadn't showered in two days.

"Come be around people," she said.

She'd invited me before, but I'd always demurred, because I knew her family was observant. Not cloistered like the Hasidic Jews I'd seen in cities, with black hats and curly *payot*, but religious enough to have two sets of dishes: one for meat, the other for dairy. What if I messed their kitchen up? "I've never done a religious Shabbat," I said.

"Totally *beseder*," she said. "We're more *masoriti* than *dati*, you know?" I knew that one: more traditional than Orthodox. She was already on her phone, probably texting her mom. "We'll leave around noon, okay?"

"Won't we go tomorrow?" I asked. "On Friday?"

"It is Friday," she said.

I'd been in bed for three days.

In the shower I tried not to think about Eyal. The water felt good.

Talia said we'd be getting a ride from two guys who lived near us in Tel Aviv and were, it turned out, driving to somewhere near Talia's family in the suburbs outside Jerusalem.

"Friends of yours?" I asked. I was packing my bag while she sat on my bed.

"Oh, I don't know them," Talia said.

"Is that safe?"

"Of course," she said. "They're Jewish."

That afternoon, we piled into a tiny European car that seemed to be made of plastic. In the front were two young men who had, in the kibbutznik style, cut the crew necks out of their T-shirts to make them sit more freely. The boy in the passenger's seat wore a knitted kippa; the one driving had wild hair and a sunburn across his nose bridge. The car was filled with blankets and musical instruments, hand drums and guitars. "*Ahlan*," they said to us as we climbed over the chaos to get in.

"*Ahlan*," we echoed. This is in fact an Arabic greeting that has entered Modern Hebrew.

I listened while Talia and the guys played the game where they figured out who knew whom from which neighborhood, whose brothers had served in the same army units. She idly twirled her nose ring as she spoke. The guys had a sweet, boyish energy. I didn't feel like engaging, but I was glad to be in the car with them.

"And what about you?" the one driving asked me, looking in the rearview mirror.

In Hebrew, I told them that I was from Canada. "But I'm living here now."

Talia glanced at me but didn't say anything.

"You have family here?" the boy riding shotgun asked.

"No, they're all in Canada," I said.

"They must be proud of you," he said.

"They find it a little weird," I said. "Almost extreme." Posts about the invasion had dominated Erica and Cee's Facebook pages. Cee had shared a pie chart showing that the States' military aid to Israel was 3.7 billion American dollars a year. Erica reposted op-eds from leftist rabbis. NONE OF US ARE FREE, one of them said, UNTIL PALESTINE IS FREE.

The boy driving turned around in shock. "Extreme for Jews to live in Israel?" His nose was peeling a little from the sunburn. His eyes had a softness.

I shrugged, and he turned back to the road.

Outside the car, the fields around Tel Aviv were edging into the forests of Jerusalem. We were driving inland, even farther from Gaza. I zoned out while the others in the car kept talking. Unless I was paying full attention, the Hebrew drifted over me. The last time I'd been to Jerusalem, it was with Eyal. We'd explored strange churches.

"She's worried about her boyfriend," Talia said, jostling me out of myself.

"Sorry," I said. "What?"

"He's in Gaza?" the boy in the passenger seat asked.

I nodded.

"My little brother is too," he said. "Eighteen years old."

"I'm sorry," I said.

"Why sorry?" he said. "It's important what they do."

I nodded. "You're right," I said. "But it's so hard."

Talia squeezed my shoulder.

Ever so slightly, we inclined up a hill. Seven hills surround the city. *As the mountains enfold Jerusalem*, the psalmist sings, *so does the Lord enfold His people.*

We dropped the religious boy off at a settlement. I'd never been to a settlement before and had not noted where we crossed from one kind of territory into another. When I thought of settlers, I imagined the screaming women from Erica's articles: righteous and violent.

And now, here I was, turning off the highway and pulling up to the gates of a settlement, the guard waving us through without even bothering to check IDs. It was just another gated community with houses in interchangeable models, only there were soldiers all around. Hard to tell who was working—guarding, I suppose I mean—and who was just waiting for a bus, just existing. They all looked like Eyal. All of them looked like Eyal.

I'm on a settlement, I thought. *I'm on an illegal settlement.* It didn't seem real.

As we drove through the neat settlement streets, the boys and Talia sang along to a much-loved song on the radio. *It's Friday*, the song went in Hebrew, *Friday has arrived and it came just in time.* They knew all the words.

We pulled up to a house with a woman out front taking laundry down from a drying rack, her hair colorfully wrapped. She waved as the boy in the passenger seat got out of the car.

He leaned in the window after closing the door. "Allison," he said. He pronounced my name the same as Eyal. "The soldiers watch over Israel, and Hashem watches over the soldiers." He used the religious Jews' term for God, literally *the name.*

"Thank you," I said. I meant it.

"Shabbat shalom," he said to everyone in the car.

Talia switched seats to sit up front with the sunburnt boy. They chatted softly while I looked out the window at a tall concrete barrier along the highway. It was painted almost charmingly with a pastoral mural: fields and arches.

Talia's house was overflowing. Her older siblings had brought their kids; her younger siblings were kids. Her mother moved swiftly around the kitchen, adjusting dials and peeking under aluminum foil, her hair covered by a scarf, giving instructions to a sporty-looking high school–age girl (Talia's youngest sister) in a long stretchy skirt and soccer jersey who was holding a baby (Talia's nephew). "Shabbat shalom, *Ima*," Talia said.

"*Chayim sheli*"—*my life*—"Shabbat shalom," her mother said, rushing toward her for a hug. She turned to me. "And this is Allison?"

"Shabbat shalom, " I said, "thank you for inviting me."

"Oh, *baruch Hashem*, you speak Hebrew," she said laughing. A fit woman, she worked as a nutritionist.

"I told you," Talia said, a little proudly.

The kitchen was big but not fancy. Lots of counter space and, as I'd been prepared to see, two sinks, although just one dishwasher. A narrow window above the sinks looked into a small backyard that was, I would find, AstroTurf. All around were identical houses and duplexes.

Talia gave me the tour. Picking up children on the stairs to give them kisses and tickles. In her childhood bedroom, traces of a teenage Talia lingered. There were posters on the walls: the ones I recognized were of alternative bands from the '90s—Mazzy Star, My Bloody Valentine— gauzy, moody rock that, growing up in the 2000s, you only knew if you were cool. Their albums had come out before Eyal was born. The posters in Hebrew I did not recognize. "Who's this?" I asked, tapping on the image of a woman drawn in the silhouette of another woman.

"That's Zehava Ben," Talia said, as if I should recognize the name.

"A singer?" I asked.

"Wow," Talia said, sighing a little, "it's so much to explain. Basically, she's Mizrachi; her parents are from Morocco." She came over and touched the poster gently. *Zehava Ben Sings Arabic*, it said, in Hebrew. "She put out this album covering classic Arabic songs and, like, you have to understand, this was revolutionary."

"Was it popular?" I asked. Aisha had told me how uncomfortable Israelis got when they heard Arabic.

"So popular," Talia said. "She performed for them in Jericho. They loved her."

It took me a moment to understand that "they" were Palestinians. A Jewish Israeli with roots in Morocco, performing Arabic love songs for Palestinians in Jericho. How hopeful everyone must have been in the years before Rabin was assassinated.

"Later, her management—these Ashkenazi guys—stole, like, all her money," Talia continued. "It's really sad." She turned her attention to a pile of CDs, began sifting through them.

I lingered on the poster. So much promise. All this in the years before the separation barrier went up. "It's crazy we were on a settlement," I said.

Talia paused in inspecting a CD case, looked up at me quizzically.

"Before, I mean," I clarified. "The boy we dropped off."

"But, Allison," she said, "you're in a settlement now."

"What?"

"We're over the green line," she said. "So, yeah, this is technically a settlement."

We'd been driving along the separation barrier to get here—the eight-meter-high wall that scars the West Bank. Why hadn't I seen it for what it was? It disguised itself with that mural: painted scenery, blotting out the Palestinian villages we were passing.

"I thought you were—I mean . . ." I faltered. Talia had always seemed so liberal. Hadn't she? She had a nose ring, gay friends, critical feelings toward the country's status quo.

"It's just a suburb," she offered. "My parents got priced out of Jerusalem."

I nodded. The divisions I'd assumed between extremists and normal people were fading.

"Too many European Jews buying vacation homes," she said. Later, she showed me how, from out one of the high windows, we could see a curve of the famous separation barrier. Dark gray concrete, cutting through the land like an invasive thought. What you call it depends which side of it you're on: security barrier, apartheid wall.

After the sun went down, those who had gone to Friday night services came home. They came home singing, and we sang with them. *Shalom aleichem* (*peace be upon you*), *malachei ha-sharet* (*ministering angels*). Songs of praise for the two angels who, the tradition goes, escort worshippers home from synagogue. The lyrics were repetitive; I caught the chorus where I could. To me, the song's haunting minor key suggested it was an ancient melody, maybe brought to Israel from the East by one of Talia's relatives, but no, she told me later, it was written by a twentieth-century rabbi in Brooklyn.

The table was covered with a feast that looked like an American family's Thanksgiving. Roasts, piles of chicken thighs, heaps of rice and salads.

For the first time since the invasion began, I did not feel alone.

That night I accepted whatever was given: second helpings of fluffy yellow rice, seasoned meat, salads glistening with oil. It had been days since I had a real meal. In bed, I'd eaten cereal from the box and chugged room-temperature water. Now, I ate it all.

"She can eat!" Talia's father exclaimed. He was a serene, agreeable man who said little at the table but seemed to take supreme joy in watching his family members enjoy themselves. He worked in some kind of chemical lab, Talia had told me.

There were nine of us at a long table, covered in a vinyl tablecloth that I would come to find was typical in observant households. Talia's eldest brother and mother seemed to share a special rapport, chatting in a Hebrew that was a little too fast for me about something to do with a client of theirs.

"He works at her clinic," Talia explained to me softly.

Next to Talia's brother, his wife—a sturdy, freckled girl that by then I knew enough to identify as Ashkenazi, like me—was convincing a young toddler to eat a vegetable.

"How did your parents meet?" I asked Talia. I love a love story. Eyal's parents met at a nightclub while she was on a date with another guy.

"They met at university," Talia said.

Her high school–age sister leaned across the table. "*Aba* tried to start with *Ima* for weeks," she said, munching on some kind of green bean. "But she ignored him."

"At least at first," Talia added. "It was lonely there, you know? Very Ashkenazi."

I watched Talia's father as he surveyed the table with obvious pleasure. "They were in the minority?"

"Totally," Talia said. "At the university, my parents were careful of how they spoke, what they ate, how they dressed. They were lonely from themselves, you understand?"

What she described made me think of Aisha at an Israeli university, although I wasn't sure about invoking a Palestinian at this table: how that would be read, responded to. Instead, I said, "They must be so proud of you." I kept my voice down so her parents wouldn't hear me at the other end of the table. "Your music career, I mean."

She glanced at her father, smiled privately, maybe a little sadly. "They were worried at first," she said, "but they've come around."

"Worried?"

"My mom used to tell me not to use so much Arabic in my music," she said. "Safer to . . ." Talia hesitated, looking for the word in English. "Became part of the group? What's the word?"

"Assimilate!" Talia's sister piped up.

We both looked at her in surprise. "How did you know that word?" Talia asked her in Hebrew.

Her sister shrugged, shy now, looking at her green beans. "I read it."

"*Yafe*," Talia said. *Nice.* She hesitated again. I could tell she was deciding between the long and short versions of a story.

What was the long version? Something to do with the parts of herself she could feel calling out from Yemen, from Morocco. Something to do with the Arabic that her parents never once spoke to her, because you can be taught to hate parts of yourself. And how Talia herself felt, at times, lost: unsure what to let go of and what to reach toward, trapped between the Ashkenazi status quo and the Palestinian villages on the other side of the wall.

But she decided on the short version. "My parents want me to be happy," she said at last.

The house was quiet as I lay in Talia's childhood bedroom. I fell asleep thinking about Eyal.

I had still not read his death letter, the one he gave me the night before he left—stapled shut and only to be opened if, if, if. It sat waiting in the small red jewelry box where I kept my earrings and necklaces, a folded piece of paper under heaps of tarnished silver. I was far too superstitious to open the letter. (How would I forgive myself if something happened to him then?) But I thought of it often.

On the front of the note, instead of my name he had written "you" in Hebrew—אַתְּ—"*at*." A gendered pronoun. First letter aleph, which is also the first letter of the Hebrew alphabet. Aleph, a beginning. *In the beginning.* Although the Bible begins not with an aleph but a bet—second letter of the Hebrew alphabet: *B'reshit bara. In the beginning.*

To the rabbis, Torah is perfect—handed to Moses directly from God. There are no mistakes and no coincidences. So what does it mean, they ask themselves and us, that the opening line of the Bible begins not with the first letter, aleph, but with the second, bet? Would aleph not be a truer beginning? They contemplate the shape of the letter bet, how it opens to the left, i.e., the front if you are reading right to left: ב. Just as the bet is open only to the front, they surmise, so too can we not know what came before, what is above, or what is below.

Actually, *in the beginning* is a subpar translation, most modern scholars would argue, because it fails to capture the particular morphology of the Hebrew. A truer translation: "When God began to create . . ." This is to say, Genesis opens when creation is already underway. In medias res, some call this.

Privately, I believe the Bible knows what any storyteller learns eventually: you never start at the beginning. As a graduate student, I learned to keep such fanciful ideas to myself: *The Bible knows.* In my discipline, you have to be careful about coming off as fanciful or unprofessional. If you want to talk about what "the Bible knows," become a rabbi or study comparative literature. If you want to be a philologist, learn Middle Persian and stay in your lane.

When I try to tell myself the story of Eyal, where do I begin? Meeting on the bus? Texting on Memorial Day? Writing letters? Holding hands in the car on the way to the train station? Graphically, the "E" of "Eyal" is not so different-looking from the "ב," is it? These are letters that face forward in their respective alphabets: left to right, right to left. They know only what lies ahead.

No matter where I open my telling, the true starting point will always be the end—the place I speak from, as someone who was altered by the violence committed in my name.

That night at Talia's, I fell asleep with my phone under my pillow. Outside, the West Bank separation wall curled around us in an embrace.

Fifteen

He loves to think of her sleeping. He imagines they are lying on his twin bed, their foreheads touching, as he listens to her breathing. She is so docile when she sleeps, so completely withdrawn into herself, not unlike the way she shuts her eyes in pleasure when she's getting close—*Please don't stop.* If only he could follow her into her dreaming.

Someone is pissing in the sink. Eyal lies on the hard tile floor of the building they're holding down. It's his turn to rest, just a little. Around him, dust and glass. Around him, walkie-talkies and, in the distance, mortars. Chaos.

Eyes closed, he is clinging to Allie. How when he is with her, the world feels bigger and filled with possibility.

In early summer, they'd taken a day trip to Jerusalem. He wanted to borrow the car, but Aba said no.

The train was filled with religious children who ran up and down the aisles with snacks. "Ima!" they screamed, always screaming for their mothers, who were Allie's age.

He and Allison sat in seats facing each other with a small plastic table between them. He touched her sneakers with his sneakers. Always surprising for him to look down and see he wasn't in his army-issued boots.

She pressed her forehead against the cool train window. He wanted to see what she saw, feel what she felt. "Are you excited?" he asked.

When she turned to him, her eyes were jewels. "Yes," she said, "I love the Old City."

The train continued slowly through the valley.

"Why?" he said. He thought of Jerusalem as an anxious place. Everything heavy, too heavy with religious significance. Every inch of soil was contested. Blood-soaked. How could a place be holy if people killed for it?

"I love it because it's another world," she said.

No, he'd wanted to say. *You're* from another world. She had told him about winters in Montreal. He had images of her walking home from school with Erica. Two girls in snow pants disappearing into snowbanks.

From the train they caught a Jerusalem city bus, which dropped them just outside the Old City. She was in light, long layers that trapped the sunlight. She took his hand and led him through the ancient gates—down the slippery stone path of the medina. The shop overhangs were low. The stone was white. Once, his grandfather had been from here. But this was not Eyal's world. The last time he'd walked through an ancient city center like this, he'd been with his unit in Hebron, securing a perimeter before an arrest. Nighttime, and each guy had facepaint on. He hadn't thought he was scared—he stayed focused on each task, each step, when to scan the four corners of his vision, when to crouch, when to tap someone on the shoulder, when to advance. But when he got back to base, after a ride in the back of the Jeep, everyone tired but happy and the prisoner in zip ties, his whole stomach turned and he had rushed to the toilets to let loose a putridly orange shit that seemed to him like the embodiment of fear. Now he was wearing civilian clothes and listening to his Canadian girlfriend talk in English about "the Ottoman period."

She sprinkled the whole world with her wonder. Each Arab shopkeeper called out to her, "Welcome, welcome!" They were selling trinkets, pomegranates, Jesus sandals. "Welcome, welcome, where you from?"

She laughed when she answered, "Canada!"

"Canada!" they exclaimed. "Come in, come in, Miss Canada."

"Thank you," she said, smiling openly and never pausing. An expert in politely brushing people off.

They approached three border police guys holding down an intersection where a narrower alley sprang off from the main thoroughfare. He could imagine this being a hot spot. They were stationed next to a bread vendor who ignored them. All three in heavy gear, they scanned each passerby. Allison was explaining about the churches of Jerusalem. "There's a shrine at every point in the story," she said. "Where Jesus fell, where he wept, where he died." He wondered what the border patrol guys saw when they saw him with her. A tourist? A foreigner like her? Or could they tell, just by looking at him, that he was Israeli? Could he tell if he saw himself? It should have been him, standing at a hot corner, waiting for Intifada Three to spark up. But here he was about to visit a church with a girl whose mother was a goy. That's how she knew about the churches, he figured.

She was talking about a queen of Byzantium now. "Some call Helena the first archaeologist," she said lightly, "because she always found what she was looking for." She squeezed her hand in his. "That's a joke." Her cheeks were flushed.

"You are so cute," he said, almost pained by how true it was.

In the church, it was very quiet. She had led them through a sunken entrance of carved stone, almost underground. Through a muted chapel with a low ceiling, long candles melting in troughs of sand, giving the air the mournful scent of roses. There was a priest all in black with a hat like a mushroom, whispering to an old woman who clutched a teenage girl's hand. Both woman and girl had their hair covered. The girl looked at him and Allison as they passed, startled eyes and a faint brush of dark hair on her upper lip.

"Can we be here?" he asked Allison as they hurried through the dimly lit room, the shadows on windowless walls. He had never been in a church before.

"Sure," she said, so chipper and bright. "If anyone asks, we're here to pray." Before entering the church, she'd tied a square scarf over her head.

Allison led him past one dim room and into another, this one with a high vaulted ceiling. The air was blurry with incense, the light faint. Again, the troughs of tall thin candles with their smell, so sweet and nostalgic. He had the feeling of being deep inside an ancient stone. The room was cluttered, like a dragon's den in a fantasy story. Crystal chandeliers lining the ceiling, statues of weeping virgins were decked out in crowns and necklaces, paintings of nameless saints were covered in gold.

They passed a cluster of kneeling pilgrims. One man had a huge wooden cross on his back. A woman with a scrunched face was reaching her hand into a hole in the floor. She wept. Her arm disappeared to the elbow as if she was probing an endless shower drain. The hole was ornate, decorated in what looked like wrought gold.

He was aware that the sentences that came to him in this place— words in English, "wrought gold," "nameless saints," "vaulted ceiling," "weeping virgins," "kneeling pilgrims"—were not from his own mind or experience. They came from Allison. These were Allison's words, slipping into his brain. Or maybe not Allison's. Who could say in this strange place? Maybe he'd entered the dream of that startled-looking girl in the first room. He was as far outside of himself as he had ever been. *Where am I?* he thought. *In what country, in what century? In whose life? Whose dream?*

They stood to the side as a procession of monks, their robes dark and swishing, their faces obscured by peaked hoods, walked through the room chanting and swinging a silver incense burner. The kneeling pilgrims crossed themselves like in a movie. The monks did not pause before they disappeared behind a smoke-faded tapestry in the back of the room. Allison watched them disappear. "Come on!" she said, her face animated.

He remembered how in history class, they'd learned about the Jews of Spain. They converted to Christianity, and it didn't save them. The inquisitors tortured them to death anyway. "It's because we are not merely a religion," his teacher had said, a woman who brought her own lunch and ate it at her desk each day. "We are a people."

"I don't know," he said, but Allison was already pulling back the tapestry, so he followed her. No sign of the monks, only narrow and well-worn stairs that circled upward. They climbed up, the only sounds were their footfalls and breathing. He thought they might emerge once again onto the street. He hoped they would. Return to Israel instead of the stuffy, choked air of this Christian century. But instead, they came into a clean and well-lit room. High windows let in clear sunlight. Instead of pews—Allison had taught him this word, "pews"—there were long wooden tables and benches, like from the black-and-white photos of his grandma's kibbutz.

They were the only people in the room. The white walls were decorated with paintings in gilded frames. *Gilded.* Paintings of a woman and child, paintings of men in robes, two fingers raised to God. They were almost ancient, she said. He could tell from how the proportions on the body were a little wrong. "For eight hundred years," Allison said, "these icons have lived here." She said that comparable works from the same era were locked away in climate-controlled museum archives, preserved behind inches of protective casing. Priceless. But these paintings didn't even have glass in the frames. Black marks like fingers—smoke stains, Allison said—reached up the canvases. Dust filtered through beams of sunlight. "They are desecrated," she said. "Desecrated by love."

Across the room, a woman dressed in a gray cocoon came in lugging a metal folding chair behind her. It squeaked on the stone.

"A nun," Allison whispered, squeezing his hand.

The nun set up the chair under a painting of the woman and child. "See," Allison whispered, "how Mary looks at Jesus and Jesus looks at us." Jesus was apparently the baby. "It is a cycle of glances," she went on. "I wrote a paper about it once."

The nun did not acknowledge them. She had supportive sneakers like old women wear, but when she stepped up on the chair, Eyal saw that she was young. As young as him. At first, he couldn't tell what she was doing as she stood on the chair to face the painting. Then out from her robes she pulled a feather duster, like from the *Beauty and the Beast* cartoon. Allison squeezed his hand again. On her tiptoes, the nun could only just reach the highest part of the frame. She dusted with care. Before stepping down, she paused and, very slowly, leaned toward the painting. Eyal thought she was inspecting it for damage, but no, he saw now that, no—she was kissing the canvas. Allison gasped. The nun kissed the virgin's feet.

If he makes it through this night, if he makes it home from Gaza, he will tell Allison everything he has seen and felt. She will listen. She will hear him, and he will not be alone.

Tonight they won't stay inside Gaza. Ruined buildings. Tire smoke. Glass. Sewage. They come back through the fence to the trailers. He's almost too exhausted to eat but knows he should, so he sits with Avishi and they eat the rations. Greasy pasta bits and a few beans in a can, some fish mixed in that must be tuna, who knows. He can't taste anything but salt and oil. His hands are filthy. "Get some sleep," Avishi says, and that's the last thing he remembers of the first day.

After the church, Allison wanted to go to the Kotel. "It's nice to check in," she said, taking his hand again as they followed the little green signs toward, in English, the Western Wall.

"To check in with the Kotel?" he said, laughing and squeezing her hand.

She waved a pointed finger upward. "It's the holiest place we have."

"Allison the rabbi," he said. He was teasing her, but he was relieved that she wanted to go to a Jewish place. Somewhere familiar after that other world.

At the Kotel, they went through the metal detectors. He hadn't been here since high school. A rabbinical decree was framed above the X-rays: THESE MACHINES DO NOT VIOLATE SHABBAT. "Give me your backpack," he told her as they approached the checkpoint. By now she knew the routine and handed it over without asking why. When he flashed his combat soldier ID, the guards let him through without holding them up. They walked past the tables of old women who enforced modesty by handing out scarves to women who had not thought to cover their shoulders. But Allison had.

The wall rose up in front of them. You'd never guess that it's all that remains of the Temple—these white stones with doves nestling in the cracks. Men on one side, women on the other, a large divider between the two, and everyone praying in plastic chairs or standing with their faces to the ruins. Beyond the wall rose the golden Muslim dome. Beautiful and sinister. When the messiah comes, that's where the Temple will be. "I'll be right back," she said, and squeezed his arm. They did not kiss here. She went to the women's side, disappearing into a sea of swishy, modest skirts and head coverings.

He didn't know what to do, so he went to the men's side. There were little huddles of guys praying and chatting. There were fathers holding their sons' hands. The last time he had been here, he was just back from a school trip to concentration camps in Poland. After two days of crying and barbed wire and piles of shoes and inherited memories of bloody feet and that one girl who gave her boyfriend a blow job in the crappy hotel, they had flown home, and how good it was to see Israel again. The buses took them straight from the airport to the Kotel. His family had been waiting for him with an Israeli flag to drape over his shoulders. Three years later, he was a soldier.

He always forgets how tall the Kotel really is. He wedged between two Golanis his age, both praying intensely, one shouldering a bulky M203 attachment on his M16. Eyal pressed his face into the ancient stones, cool and smooth. All over were notes, folded and stuffed into crevices above and below. Some of them high, some close to the ground. Some had fallen out. Others were wedged in tight. *What happens to them?* he wondered. *Where do these pieces of paper go? Do they stay in the wall or does someone clean them out each night?* His ima had come here after he enlisted. She wrote his name on a piece of paper, rolled it up, and wedged it into a crack in the wall. Maybe it was still here. His name, her prayer for him. Keep my son safe. A love letter to God.

He could hear the prayers of men next to him, behind him. He touched the wall. Jews all over the world prayed in this direction. Some of them right at that second, no doubt, were praying toward this wall. He thought about his grandfather forming a kippa with his hands, his father signing the combat soldier release form. Most of the time, he thinks of himself as set apart from his unitmates, but he still remembers the day when they became more than just a bunch of guys grouped together, when they became a team. It was when they completed the fifty-kilometer hike that ended with each of them receiving their beret. They began at night. Everyone with camo paint on his face, laden down with gear, knee-pads, weapons, vests. Before they set out, they went around in a circle to talk about why they had chosen to be a warrior. To protect my family. To guard Israel from Arabs. Because my father was a warrior. Eyal had wanted to answer in a way that was special, but the truth was his answer was the same as everyone else's. The march had almost killed him. Or that's what it felt like. All night they went, all night. Along the highways through the desert of Judah. It was dawn when they reached the rocks of Masada, the fortress where ancient Jews had died rather than surrender. By then he had wept from exhaustion. He had carried a stretcher when he thought his shoulders would crack. He had held up and been held up, and he was still going. They were still going, all of them, a single unit, a single animal. When they reached the spot where the beret ceremony would be, they huddled without anyone having to give the command. They moved by instinct, all together, into a huddle, sweat and bloody broken calluses and panting. "We are one now," Avishi said. They were all breathing together. In the huddle, he was not sure where his body ended. He's never gotten that feeling since, but it was magical that once. His body, every body. "We are blood now," Avishi said softly. The quietness of his voice was electric. "Look around; these are your brothers." Someone cheered. Avishi said it again, a little louder: "I said these are your brothers." Eyal felt grief and joy rising up in his spine. The last time, Avishi shouted: "These are your brothers." And they all cried out together, heaving in the circle, arms holding one another tight. When he thinks about God, he thinks about that feeling of oneness. "Hear, O Israel, the Lord is One," a man intoned toward the wall.

At the Kotel he did not pray, but he closed his eyes and touched the cool stones. He felt the place that Jews prayed toward and thought, *I'm guarding over you, over all of you.* Then, following tradition, he walked away from the wall backward. He did not turn his back to the holy place, but faced it as he gingerly stepped back. He had to be careful not to bump into an old man in a plastic chair. It was a little like a game, wasn't it? Religion always seemed a bit like a game.

He waited for Allison at the fountain where they had separated. He didn't see her for what felt like quite a while. When he did catch sight of her, she was walking backward and holding hands with a religious woman. *Do they know each other?* he wondered. They walked backward, step by step as he had done, to leave the sacred place with respect. The woman was in a long skirt, hair covered. Hard to tell her age. When they turned around to walk normally, Allison pointed at him, and he, unsure what to do, waved. He watched as Allie leaned in and hugged the religious woman. A long, significant hug. Then they parted. Allison bounded toward him.

"I made a friend!" she exclaimed, her face glowing.

"You just met?" How did she do this? Like a butterfly in the world.

"She helped me pray," Allison continued.

They began walking together toward the exit. "She's Israeli?" he asked. Allison told him yes, a nice Israeli lady. He had a passing fantasy that he was Allison's father, asking her how school went that day.

From there, they'd walked to a Korean restaurant outside the Old City walls. He hadn't known Israel had a Korean restaurant. She ordered a dish with pork, pale strips edged with fat. He got the simplest chicken-and-rice item he could find. He watched with fascination as the pig meat crackled and sputtered on a kind of hot plate. The smell was heavier and sweeter than lamb. "Can I try?" he asked as she munched away on mouthfuls she made of rice, pork, and a red pickle all wrapped in a lettuce leaf.

The restaurant was filled with Asian people. She'd told him there was a sizable population of Evangelical Koreans in Jerusalem, and he had nodded like he knew the word "Evangelical."

"Of course you can try," she exclaimed, her mouth full. She passed him one of her lettuce rolls.

It was salty and almost familiar. "It's different," he said.

"This style, you mean?"

"Different than I imagined."

She stopped chewing. At the next table over, a group of foreigners were laughing happily. "Please don't tell me," she began to say.

He looked away guiltily.

"Please don't tell me," she started again, "that you just tried pork for the first time."

"Why not?" he said, trying to sound unbothered, masculine. Trying to sound like Aba.

Then she burst out laughing, raspy and joyful. God, he loved her mouth. She said, "Your mom is going to kill me!"

He took another bite of pig. So much fuss over a little scrap of meat. He wanted to say, *I can make my own choices*, but knew that wasn't exactly true. Not yet.

"Please don't tell her," Allison pleaded. She was smiling, but he could see she was truly a little worried. "Don't tell her I corrupted you."

She paid for the meal.

Someone taps him on the shoulder. "My brother, my brother, it's time to get up."

Sixteen

The army Twitter posted cheerful infographics about Hamas's "practice of using their civilians as human shields" by launching rockets from residential apartment buildings. The images were cartoonish in primary colors.

"My heart breaks for what is happening," a popular American newspaper columnist wrote a few days later. "Hamas must stop the practice of using their civilians as human shields." She included the same army infographic.

Several of my Jewish friends from Montreal retweeted a South African model with a popular YouTube channel: *Why is Israel criticized for defending its citizens? No other country in the world would be expected to do nothing when they are violently and repeatedly attacked by deadly rocket fire.*

Dear Allison, my father wrote to me in a characteristically formal email. *Your mother and I read the news and worry. Are you still spending your afternoons in bomb shelters? Please check in, we'd be grateful.*

With my laptop in bed, I responded to his email. *Dad*, I wrote, *Thank you for checking in. It's been so hard, but at times it's been beautiful. A few days ago, I went to Shabbat dinner at my roommate's parents' place. It's on a settlement, but you would never guess it. I experienced such warmth there. We ate and we sang. It was the most normal I've felt since the invasion began. I worry so much about Eyal. Please keep him in your thoughts.*

At the last second before sending, I copied Erica on the email, then sent it before I could reconsider.

I lay in bed, waiting to see if Erica would respond. It was evening in Israel, early afternoon in Montreal. Earlier that day there had been air raid sirens. Now, just balmy quiet.

When Erica replied, she too replied all. *Allie, I feel your pain and your fear. I really do. And I want to make space for it. But let's not forget that in Gaza, they do not have bomb shelters to run to. Let's keep Palestinians in our thoughts. Let's not dehumanize anyone.*

This was all for Cee. I could tell. Look! She'd even copied Cee. I replied all right away. I didn't give myself time to process, but instead let the anger pound the words out of me. *No other country in the world, Erica, would be expected to do nothing when they are violently and repeatedly attacked by deadly rocket fire. A country of Jews can't defend its citizens?* I wasn't sure exactly where these sentences were coming from, what was from me and what I was repeating from someone else, but I didn't care. *If anyone "dehumanizes" Palestinians, it's Hamas and their practice of using their civilians as human shields.* Hunched over my laptop, I kept writing. *So, "make space" for that.* I was directing my message at Erica and Cee, yes, but also at Aisha, also at the vegan law student I'd once been on a date with—at anyone I felt was trying to wrench me out of my life in Israel. I didn't want to feel guilty. I didn't want to feel responsible.

I clicked SEND. Reply all.

I imagined my mother as a recipient on this chain, watching her daughters bicker. She must have been relieved that finally—at last—she was not the bad guy.

I could feel my heart in my ears as I refreshed my inbox, waiting to see what Erica would say. But she didn't respond that evening.

Erica's words stuck with me. *Let's not dehumanize anyone.* Fuck her.

I texted Aisha: HEY!! SORRY ABOUT LAST TIME, STUFF WAS NUTS. I hadn't spoken to her since the invasion began. COFFEE THIS WEEK??

She responded with an emoji of two girls dancing.

We made plans.

This time, I tried to pay for our coffees. No luck, however. By the time I ordered my drink, the barista already had Aisha's card. "Oh, come on," I complained in English after ordering my iced coffee, also in English.

Aisha smiled. "It's a Palestinian thing."

I felt a prickle of alertness as I became sharply aware of the drab little cafe, the students at tables, the baristas pulling espresso shots. Why suddenly so vigilant? It was her saying the word "Palestinian," I realized. That's what made me nervous. Nobody seemed to notice.

Aisha and I left the cafe to find a bench in a shady spot.

"Did you crop that shirt yourself?" I asked, quickly adding, "It's so cute."

She was wearing an oversized Nirvana T-shirt, cropped just enough to show flashes of her belly button when she lifted her arms. "Yeah," she said, looking down at her own shirt, "but it's a little asymmetrical, so don't look too hard."

I had wondered if she would bring up the invasion, but we talked about crop tops, which led us somehow to Botox and fillers—whether we'd get med-spa treatments in a few years (fillers yes, Botox no, was our consensus).

Walking in the shade of date palms with Aisha, I thought about Erica. She was off repeating leftist slogans, imagining herself superior to everyone, but which of us was friends with a Palestinian? Me. "Do you have any siblings?" I asked.

"Of course, two brothers and a sister," she said. "I'm the second, af-ter my oldest brother." She took a sip of her iced drink. "My sister is the youngest, not even in high school yet." I thought back to Aisha's Facebook posts, placing the younger sister mentally—a sweet girl in a uniform. "But my cousin—you remember her? The one from the mall?"

I nodded. "For sure." The quiet one on her phone who I sensed didn't trust me.

"We're the same age, so we were raised like sisters." Aisha tousled that dark curly hair of hers, so voluminous against her petiteness. Barely one hundred pounds, I guessed enviously. Dark jeans, cropped band tee, and those black buckle boots she wore everywhere. "I'm so lucky she's here," she went on. "I'd be lonely without her."

"But isn't that what uni is for?" I asked. "Making new friends?"

She stopped walking and looked at me for a long second. We were standing next to an expansive lawn, where students in groups of two or three sat in the sun with their backpacks.

"Right?" I said nervously. I didn't know what she was getting at. When I tried to imagine her life, all I could really imagine was her look-ing at me. Did she hate me? Did she want me to die in a rocket attack? She only existed in relation to me; at times, I fear this is true of everyone I have ever tried to love. "I guess it's complicated," I said.

"It's not complicated," she countered. "For them, my existence is a problem." She laughed—a single, derisive exhale. "It's not complicated at all."

By "them," she meant Jewish Israelis. *Then why come study at this uni-versity?* I thought with a measure of bitterness that caught me off guard. I metabolized it in time to say, instead, "Did you consider studying else-where?"

"Where?" she said, exasperation leaking through her poise. "The only passport I have is Israeli. Where?"

"I didn't think of that," I said. Cut off from Palestine, cut off from Lebanon. So much I hadn't considered about her life. We paused. In the

silence, I felt the hugeness of the gap between us. No talk of beauty products or New York spas could bridge it. Aisha must have felt it too. By the
way she checked her phone, I could tell she was about eight seconds from
saying she had to go. I'd never see her again; I'd lose her. "I have a sister,"
I offered.

"Oh," she said, not looking at me.

Yeah, I thought. *A sister you'd like a lot more than you like me. Unless you're
homophobic, I suppose.* "We're not close," I went on.

She looked at me. Maybe a little interested. "Oh?" This was not what
she had expected.

"We disagree a lot," I said. I could feel myself groping toward something, the way you feel along the wall for a light switch. "Like politics," I
went on. There it was. "She's very pro-Israel," I said. I found it.

"Oh, wow," Aisha said, nodding meaningfully. "So she's a Zionist."

"Totally," I said. "She's a Zionist." I was scaring myself but not enough
to stop.

"Is that how you were raised?"

"No, that's the weird thing!" I exclaimed. "Not at all." Now I was
Erica. I was Erica talking about me, talking about my weird straight sister
who had decided to become part of an ethno-state. "Maybe it's her boyfriend's influence?" I offered. "She's dating an Israeli."

"Damn," Aisha said. "And do they live here?"

"No, they just post one-sided shit on Facebook," I said. Now I was
myself again, talking about Cee and Erica. "They sit in Montreal and
make commentary from the sidelines." That part, at least, was true.

"To be honest, I wasn't sure about your politics," Aisha said. She
seemed relieved, newly at ease. "Although," she added quickly, "I mean,
I knew not all Jews are Zionists."

"I've tried to talk to my sister about it," I said. I'd never lied like this
before.

"*Wallah*, about Palestine?"

"Yeah, and about her own . . ." I hesitated. What did Erica say in that post about the Occupation? "About how when we dehumanize Palestinians, we dehumanize ourselves," I recited. Odd that in lying, I was voicing a truth I'd kept hidden from myself—our own humanity hung in the balance. Turns out, part of me believed that.

"Exactly," Aisha said. "Yes, exactly." She had an animation I had not seen in her before. "It's so hard to get people to see this." She was gesturing with her plastic coffee cup, the ice cubes long since melted.

"I know!" I exclaimed. I could feel Erica in me. Closer to her than I'd felt in years, in decades. I felt the simplicity of her politics. I felt the grace of that simplicity: where there is power, distrust it. "Like, who are the real terrorists, you know?"

Aisha was silent then, looking intensely at me. Did I go too far? Maybe I took it too far.

But she spoke quietly. "Coming to school here is so hard," she said softly. "I'm angry, sure, but mostly I'm lost."

I nodded.

"You know this campus was once a Palestinian village?"

I shook my head. I had learned in Hebrew class that Tel Aviv was an uninhabited swamp until Jews drained it and built a city, built a home for refugees.

"It was called Sheikh Muwannis," she said. "But now it's called Ramat Aviv."

I suppose this is what a conquering force does. It enters a place and erases the names. Eyal himself did a fair amount of renaming in the army. The golden room. To Aisha, I repeated the name of the disappeared village: "Sheikh Muwannis."

She nodded. "Sheikh Muwannis," she confirmed.

We said it like a spell that bound us together. Secret name.

"This is one endless invasion," she said, her voice low. "They never stop. The Zionists never stop."

We stood so close that I could see her heartbeat in her neck. A new intimacy was pulsing between us, lighting us up. It scared me.

"I have to go to class," I whispered.

"Let's talk soon," she said. She squeezed my arm gently.

It was the first time we ever touched.

That evening, Erica finally wrote me back. Her email was brief: *Hey, can we talk?*

Sure, I wrote back, *call whenever*. I assumed she was going to apologize for her insensitivity before.

When I picked up the FaceTime call, I saw that, of course, she was sitting with Cee on a couch framed by the green tendrils of houseplants. It was afternoon where they were and night in Tel Aviv. I was in my bedroom lit softly by fairy lights. "Hey," Erica said. Her hair was shorter than I remembered. Cee's hair was still buzzed. Weird how much Cee looked like Eyal. Buzzed and boyish. Why hadn't I noticed that before?

"Hey," I said, more curtly than I had intended, but whatever.

"I just wanted to clear the air," Erica continued, glancing at Cee who nodded encouragingly. "Some of our exchanges have been a bit, um, disturbing?"

She said it like it was a question but it wasn't a question, so I didn't respond.

"Sometimes the way you talk, it just . . ." She hesitated. Cee took her hand. "It feels like you've been . . ." She took a deep breath. ". . . radicalized."

"Radicalized?" I spat out the word. "What do you mean, 'radicalized'?"

"I mean you're off visiting settlements," Erica began to say.

"They're normal people," I said, thinking of Talia's parents—the cozy warmth of their home, so at odds with the cold edge of the conversation I was in now.

Cee spoke next. "It's weird to hear you repeating Zionist talking points," they said. Their voice was so whiny.

I lunged at this. "Oh, so it's radical to be a Zionist? It's radical to not hate Israel?"

Erica's voice was soft. "Ideology is scary, Allie," she said. "It can change how you see, and even . . ." She hesitated.

Cee finished the sentence. "Even how you value lives."

"I have Palestinian friends," I countered, although "friend," singular, would have been more accurate. "How can I—"

Cee cut me off: "How can you be racist? Are you seriously making that argument? That a Palestinian friend somehow overrides your Zionism?"

A vicious thought came to me: Cee would have no value in Israel. Not a Jew, not a man, not a woman. In Israel, I mattered, and they did not matter. That's what I thought: *I matter, and you don't.* And it comforted me. I'd never admit this aloud—not even to another Israeli—but the thought comforted me. To Cee I said, "Where should we have gone?"

"What?" Cee looked lost. They touched their nose ring.

"During the Holocaust," I said. "When Jewish refugees were being turned away." I did not expect to feel so much pain in my chest.

Erica touched Cee's thigh. A moment of tenderness I envied. "Allie, we're talking about today, right now," she said, her voice pleading. "For every Israeli killed, there's, like, ten Palestinians in Gaza killed."

I knew this, and actually, I knew it was more like eighteen Palestinians killed, but I held firm. "Sorry not enough Jews die," I said, bitterness spilling over in my voice.

Erica looked at Cee, desperate and unbelieving. "Allie, they don't even have bomb shelters. We have to—"

I cut her off. "The person I love is at war," I said. "To you, this is theoretical. It's a debate." I took in a shuddering breath.

Erica looked stricken.

"You have no idea what this feels like," I said. I ended the call by closing my laptop forcefully.

Only once did I see images of what was happening inside Gaza. I was visiting Eyal's parents again. His mom and I sat on the couch, watching the news, which suddenly was showing images of crumbling, disastrous wreckage. Whole apartment buildings emptied, disintegrating before us. "Oy, where is that?" she asked in alarm. She examined the screen. A man was crying. An adult man, crying in the ruins. "Oh, it's just Gaza," Eyal's mom said. Then she changed the channel to an Israeli reality show about vacationing at the Red Sea. Where the crying man's face had been was now a woman, laughing with a bright pink mouth.

"Her, I like," Eyal's mom said. "I hope she wins."

A nauseous wave of claustrophobia came over me. *It can change how you value lives*, Erica and Cee had said. Now, here I was watching whole families die.

I have to get out of this house, I thought. Nobody was keeping me here, but I felt trapped. *I have to get out of this horrible house.* I didn't get up. Instead, I texted Aisha: HEY, HOW ARE YOU DOING?

THINGS ARE INTENSE, she replied, BUT I'M OKAY. Her message was like air. My panic settled.

SO INTENSE, I wrote. I waited a few moments, but she wasn't writing back. The TV was so loud. This was my life. I was choosing this life, which seemed suddenly intolerable. MY SISTER IS SAYING CRAZY SHIT ABOUT THE INVASION.

REALLY? LIKE WHAT?

YOU KNOW, ABOUT LIKE ISRAEL'S RIGHT TO DEFEND THEIR CITIZENS. ALL THE ZIONIST TALKING POINTS.

Aisha sent an emoji rolling its eyes. DO YOU RESPOND?

I TOLD HER THAT GAZANS DON'T EVEN HAVE BOMB SHELTERS. I tried to remember what else Erica had said. It felt true. I was lying, but it felt true. At least, partially true. IT'S JUST SUCH A DISPARITY IN POWER.

THAT'S REALLY POWERFUL, ALLIE.

I sent a heart emoji.

She wrote again: REALLY IT'S SO SO POWERFUL THAT YOU HAVE THESE CONVERSATIONS WITH YOUR FAMILY. Pause. THANK YOU.

Eyal's mom had changed the channel. Now it was a cooking show. "I'm going to head home," I told her.

"*Beseder*, my dear," she said to me, stretching toward me for a hug.

Such a tiny woman. When I hugged her, I felt the delicate bones of her back.

When I got home that evening, Talia was frying eggs for dinner.

"Do you want one?" she called out to me from the kitchen.

"Sure," I said, coming in to take a seat at our tiny table. "Thank you."

When a text alert dinged on my phone, I thought—just for a desperate instant—that it was Eyal. But it was Aisha: WOULD YOU LIKE TO COME VISIT MY FAMILY IN NAZARETH? Pause. I'D LOVE FOR YOU TO COME.

This is what I had wanted, wasn't it? By playing the part of Erica? This is what I had wanted, but I hesitated. Nazareth was about one hundred kilometers away from Tel Aviv, technically in Israel, yes, but majority Arab. Another world.

Aisha was texting me about bus routes. Talia was asking me a question. "Sorry, what did you say?" I asked.

Talia put down a plate of eggs in front of me, then sat down with her own.

"You're the best," I said. "Thank you." Talia always used something in her eggs to make them taste a little more flavorful, and I always forgot to ask what it was. My phone lit up with another text from Aisha. "Is Nazareth safe?" I asked.

Talia looked up. On her plate, an egg yolk was running. "Like, the Old City? Not the Jewish settlement?"

I didn't know what she meant, but I nodded.

She considered this. "It's mostly Arabs and tourists," she said. "But you'd be fine. You seem like a European tourist." She took another bite of her eggs. "Are you going?"

"I think I might."

"I'm a little envious," she said.

"Envious?" That was not a response I had been expecting.

"That you are less"—she looked for the word—"restricted than I am."

"Because I don't seem Israeli?" I offered.

"It's more than that," she said. "It's like, I'm too Arab for Israelis and too Israeli for Arabs." She paused. "I've been thinking a lot about Yemen."

At the time, the endless civil war had just begun. "About the war?"

"No, about community," she said. "Sometimes I wonder if they have forgotten about us."

I felt a little lost in the conversation. Yemen didn't even recognize Israel as a country. "Forgotten about Israel?"

"No, about us," she said, agitation in the corners of her words. "For generations my mother's family lived in Yemen—Jews in Yemen for hundreds of years, for thousands of years." She was moving food around on her plate. "And I wonder if the people of Yemen have forgotten about us, the Jews who were part of them."

The weight of Talia's yearning hit me. I didn't know her at all, did I? Not really. Not what she was carrying in her heart. For two thousand years, Jews had prayed toward Jerusalem, prayed to return. But growing up in Jerusalem, Talia had prayed with lost homelands in her heart, forever separated. "I'm going to go," I said. "To see Nazareth, I'm going to go."

I responded to Aisha: I'D LOVE TO! I'M HONORED!

Aisha had texted me again: HOW ABOUT SUNDAY?

I do not think of myself as a passive person, and yet I understand that for the most part, life happens to us. What we call decisions are just a series of reactions. Only on occasion do we truly take action—make a movement against the flow of our lives. YES, I wrote, SUNDAY IS PERFECT.

Talia got up to put her plate in the sink.

"I'll do the dishes," I said, looking up from my phone. "You cooked!"

She waved me off, began doing dishes.

IS THERE A BUS? I texted Aisha. In Israel it was a weekday, which meant the buses would be running regularly, but neither of us had classes that day.

YES, she replied. She began texting details of the route.

I'd take the bus to Nazareth. Two hours, bring a book or a podcast. "I'm going on Sunday," I said, speaking loudly over the running water.

Talia turned off the tap. "That's great," she said. Then she added, in a way that seemed compulsive and almost against her own will, "But guard yourself." She sighed, as if to say, *It is what it is.* "Guard yourself," she repeated.

Seventeen

We hid in caves," Aisha said. She was translating for her grandmother, who spoke only Arabic. The two women sat side by side on a plush couch. Thick fabrics and heavy furniture overwhelmed the relatively small sitting room where we had come to visit Aisha's grandmother. I could not detect air-conditioning, but the room was cool, perhaps because it was semisubmerged.

Aisha's grandmother—wrinkled but solid-seeming—spoke again in Arabic and, after listening, Aisha spoke in English: "After the Zionists massacred Der Yassin, we hid in caves."

Her grandmother gestured toward me, asked a question. Aisha responded to her grandmother in Arabic. I waited during this brief exchange. Then Aisha asked, "You know it, right? The village of Der Yassin?"

I nodded, although I did not. Aisha's cousin—that watchful girl—was also there, sitting in an overstuffed chair, observing me as I ate their fresh figs, their date cookies, drank their black coffee. I hadn't seen her since that first day at the mall.

The grandmother resumed her mournful recounting as Aisha translated: "They came at dawn, when the village was sleeping." Her grandmother's hand was in her hand. Darting between the two languages, Aisha was like someone pouring water from one vessel into another. "Two hundred and twenty-four people," Aisha articulated the number clearly. They killed in horrific ways: babies ripped out of dead mothers, mutilated body parts everywhere. "A tactic," Aisha said, "to spread terror to the neighboring villages."

Aisha nodded at me, and I nodded back, as if I could absorb any of this.

"After the massacre," she continued, "we understood that it was to be an ethnic cleansing, although we did not have those words yet." *Ethnic cleansing.* "My mother," Aisha said, then clarified, "*her* mother," squeezing her grandmother's hand, "carried what she could." The grandmother gestured with one hand to illustrate a phantom burden on her head.

From the other side of the room, Aisha's cousin joined in, helping Aisha with the translation. "My sister left all her dresses," she intoned.

"Such beautiful dresses," Aisha echoed.

"We ran for our lives," the cousin said.

Here was the story of how the family had come to Nazareth, a few years before the grandmother herself was born. A story passed down. I took another fig.

What am I doing here? I asked myself. Imitating Erica? Or is it more than that? Trying to listen? Trying to . . . grow. This was not what I had expected from my visit to Aisha's home. I had imagined newness and hospitality, the unfamiliar and (that forbidden Orientalist word) the *exotic*. On the bus ride from Tel Aviv to Nazareth, I'd sat alone by the window. The route was pastoral in an indistinct way. Red-roofed homes surrounding the highway, summer-dry fields, and, closer to Nazareth, pine trees. I alternated between napping and reading until the bus arrived. Aisha met me in the station parking lot. She was leaning on the hood of her car. We greeted each other warmly. "I'm so glad you're here," she said. As I got in her car, I wondered if the people around the bus stop noticed. Who did they see when they saw me? A Christian tourist? A secular Arab?

Arriving at Aisha's home had indeed felt like entering a different world. The city streets were dirty and chaotic with trash, but once inside the gates to her yard there was cleanliness and order. It must have been this way behind each compound wall, behind every sturdy front door: each family, its own little country. I was excited. I used my phone to take photos of the olive saplings in the yard; the evil eye pendant on the chicken coop; the zucchini piled on the kitchen table, ready to be hollowed out and stuffed with meat and rice.

For the first half of the day, I had sat with Aisha, her mother, and her cousin in an airy, modern-feeling sitting room. Aisha's house was all modern angles and marble. I half expected to catch a glimpse of the sea out of a window, as if we were in a high-rise on the Tel Aviv coast and not a single-family home all this way inland. Aisha's mother brought out a tray with tiny, delicate cups of black coffee.

Aisha's cousin politely refused coffee. "Not for me," she said. "I only drink tea." One hand rested elegantly on her sternum. She wore delicate gold rings on her fingers. I could imagine her wearing enormous Chanel sunglasses, sitting in an armored SUV.

"Only drink tea," Aisha mimicked her cousin, making her voice unnaturally sweet and high. She sat on the couch in jeans and a cuffed black T-shirt, her elbows resting on her knees, feet firmly planted.

The cousin said something in Arabic, and although I did not recognize the words, I knew the cadence well: teasing without malice. Any girl can recognize it. The cousin's voice dipped and arched triumphantly as she imitated Aisha's more masculine stance.

Aisha laughed, held up her hands as if to say, *Have mercy.*

"Girls!" Aisha's mother exclaimed, but clearly she was amused. Her hair was short and dyed a dirty blond that suited the colors she wore—a silk shirt of pale blues and purples, hanging from a maternal torso. She was a little embarrassed speaking to me in English. "For lunch we have chicken," she said, her words halting as she glanced at her daughter. "It is okay for you?" Then she laughed, covering her mouth with her hand and saying something quickly to Aisha, although I caught only two words: "*ibrani*" (Arabic for "Hebrew") and "*tarnegol*" (Hebrew for "chicken") and

I wondered if perhaps she was lamenting that I did not, at least, speak Hebrew.

"Chicken is wonderful!" I exclaimed.

The cousin was looking at me hard—of course she was. "Do you really not speak Hebrew?" she asked. "It would be easier for my aunt, you know"—she gestured toward Aisha's mother—"to speak Hebrew." Her eyelashes were very long.

"No," I said regretfully. "Sorry." The language barrier I'd insisted upon was snaking through the room invisibly. "I'd love to learn Arabic," I offered.

The cousin did not take me up on my diversion. "You've been in Tel Aviv for a year, and you don't speak Hebrew?" I heard accusations in the question: *Aren't you one of them yet? Don't you love a boy who is brutalizing Gaza? Isn't that your life?*

I hesitated. Aisha answered for me. "She studies *poetry*," she said, emphasizing the word as if that explained anything.

The cousin let it drop.

Lunch was a feast. Glistening chicken quarters served over stewed greens, a little gummy. Aisha and the others laughed as I repeated the name after them. *M'lukheye.* "No, no," Aisha corrected me. *"M'lukheye!"*

"That's what I said!" I protested happily.

But after the meal, we did not stay at Aisha's home. Soon, we had gathered ourselves into the car. Aisha's mother drove us all to her own mother's home, not far away, in an older part of the city. We walked down the steps into this low-ceilinged room. Perhaps this is where they spent afternoons in the summer months. Here, the grandmother had been waiting with more coffee, more tea. The introductions and questions were conducted through Aisha, with a bit of help from her cousin: "And what is she doing here?" Aisha glanced at me, then answered, "She studies poetry."

It was the cousin who initiated the recounting of family history. "*Ya Teta*," she addressed her grandmother. The women had a brief exchange. To me she said, "Our *teta* will tell you about how we lost our home." And so I began to hear the other side of 1948—the others' side, othered side.

"She says, 'I still remember walking through the fields in the morning,'" Aisha translated, her eyes closed. "'The smell of the earth at dawn.'" I wanted to go back to before, when I was seeing a secret glimpse of Aisha's life. How she was with her mom. Who they were when I was not there. In a Facebook post written in English, Aisha had spoken to an imagined Israeli addressee: *Why are you so obsessed with us?* she wrote. She listed the apparatuses of intelligence gathering: hidden cameras, intercepted cell-phone data, scrutinized Facebook posts (*like this one*), secret interrogations, informants listening to phone calls and seeing through hidden cameras and collecting stories from unwilling men locked in rooms with a single chair. She was referring to explicit surveillance, but in a way, she could have been speaking to me.

"The key to interrogation," Timor once told me, "is intimacy." My whole body had buzzed. I was not supposed to hear this; I was not supposed to know people who did this. Torture. Wasn't he talking about torture? I felt then like a girl who put her hand in a lion's mouth, only to find that the lion would not bite her. Timor was a weapon, but not one used on me. It is a relationship, he went on, what happens between the interrogator and his subject.

My relationship with Aisha was built on deceit. I'd imitated Erica to the point that Aisha thought of me as someone who advocated for Palestine. Someone safe. But the intimacy was real, wasn't it? That's what I told myself as Aisha expressed our intimacy by giving me access to the women of her family: their food, their memories, the inner rooms where their lives played out, their pain. *Why are you so obsessed with us?*

"This is all we have left," Aisha said as the grandmother gestured toward a chalky white millstone resting on the low coffee table. It had been used to grind grain. Its shape reminded me of a funnel cake. Aisha's great-grandfather ("*Allah yerhamo*," they said after his name, a benediction for the dead) salvaged it from his village as the Jewish army swept through the land. Eyal's grandfather was in that army.

How did anyone carry the millstone? It was sizable, like the bigger wheels of cheese I associate with European markets, so solid and dense-looking that I expected it to crack the table, sink through the floor, and pull us all into the ground with the impossible weight of the past.

I ate more figs.

∽ ∾

He's watching an Arab through his scope. Someone picking through what is left of a bombed building. Or that's what the Arab appears to be doing. You have to be careful. You never know where fire will come from.

Eyal is on his stomach, positioned out a busted window. The after-noon air is hot, and they are near the sea, but all he smells is the caustic burn of tire smoke. The Arab, a thin man, is leaning over the chunks of concrete and glass. His clothes are loose and torn. Groping through the wreckage, he seems like a man wrist-deep in a river looking for his own reflection.

In Eyal's breast pocket is a crumpled letter he will never give to her.

Where to start? I'm writing this when I should be sleeping. I'm on the floor of what I guess is a kid's room. I didn't get the bed but I got a pillow. Two days we've been here. The apartment was empty when we rammed in the door. Everyone in this building has fled. I've never been in an Arab's house before. It's cluttered with stuff. Plastic over the dinner table. Fancy photo frames that we turned facedown. Photos of covered women and men trying to look serious. I'm tired. All day, exchanging fire when the air force isn't bombing. You probably

know more about the fallen than I do. You probably already know their names.
But I do know that there have been deaths in infantry units.

Actually, we smashed the photos, is the truth.

A sentence crossed out, scribbled over to the extent that you'd have to hold it up to the light to make out the words. *I'm lost.*

"He's still there, the Arab?" Someone has a hand on Eyal's shoulder.

"Still there," Eyal confirms. "What do you think he's looking for?"

But when he turns, the person is already gone. The hand no longer on his shoulder. But it was there. He's almost sure there was someone there.

He remembers his grandfather's stories. Sneaking past the British and into Arab villages to count the number of houses, the number of goats. What he did there was unclear. Something with a radio, sometimes hiding a gun in a feedbag. By the time the war really started, he said, talking about 1948, the villages were empty.

꩜ ꩜

"They killed the women with the children," Aisha's cousin was saying, translating for her grandmother. Look at what they are doing now, right now, in Gaza. "Have you seen what they are doing?" her cousin asked. Both she and her grandmother were looking at me, and I nodded, not sure which woman to make eye contact with. "You've seen? You've seen the murders in Gaza?"

I nodded again. "Horrible," I said.

Aisha cut in here. "Allie has been educating her family about Gaza," she said in English. Then she said something else in Arabic that I did not understand, and her grandmother nodded, lifting a hand up to me.

From here, Aisha picked up the telling again. "She is saying, my grandmother is saying, that it is a straight line." She separated her hands to show two points on an imaginary line. "Between 1948 and what happens in Gaza, it is a straight line."

"It's about control," her cousin said. "Control the land, control the water, control the air, control our bodies."

The grandmother's voice entwined with Aisha's and the cousin's. A story of brutality and loss. Power and injustice. Not a line but a circle. Now the youths being shot down in Gaza, being buried under rubble in Gaza. Tunnels under the border fence penning them in, tunnels choked with corpses. "Horrible," I said. "Heartbreaking, so heartbreaking." I repeated the words as if they were talismans that would protect me. Horrible, heartbreaking, sad. So sad.

"They take the bravest," Aisha said, in a slightly lower and more intimate pitch, "and in every generation we have more fear." It took me a moment to understand that this was Aisha speaking in her own voice, telling me about her own fear. "They kill us and cannot bear to see the evidence of their crimes. Did you know that the bodies of martyrs are returned with their organs removed?" This could not be true. I knew this could not be true. When I looked it up later, it was true. "The Israelis are obsessed with us. It's perverse, their secret desire that Palestinians love them even as they kill us. What is this obsession that the boot has with the neck?"

Aisha's mother stood in the doorway nodding.

The grandmother's mouth was still moving, but I could not hear a sound. I felt like I was falling into the dark hole of that mouth. Into the dark cup of sweet-bitter black coffee, which Aisha's mother refilled every time I drank. I was falling with the millstone into the past that is always happening, that never stops happening. For the rabbis, history is one simultaneous cacophony: Moses is ascending to Sinai as he is dying as the Temple is being dedicated as the Temple burns as our sages are expounding on what Moses received at Sinai as they are being martyred by the Romans as all of us every Jew who ever lived or will live is standing at the foot of Sinai waiting to become Jews. All at once.

In my stomach, the black coffee and figs were churning. Clenching, cramping. The family was sitting around solemnly. "What does being a settler do to a person?" Aisha was asking. "How must it warp their minds?"

"Like in Hebron," I said. On this point—the extremity of the settlements—Aisha and I probably actually agreed. "They are crazy—" I started to say.

Aisha's cousin cut me off. "All of Israel is Hebron," she said sharply. "All of Israel is a settlement. This is Hebron, right here, right now. This is Hebron." She gestured around the room.

Three generations of women looked at me.

It was hard to regulate my breathing, which was too fast. I pressed my legs together, cold with sweat.

"Ask your Zionist sister this," Aisha said. "What is the Jewish state doing to the Jewish soul?"

"I'm so sorry," I said, and Aisha looked at me cloudily for a moment, as if roused from dreaming. "I'm so sorry, but where is the washroom?"

Aisha blinked.

I tried again: "The toilet?"

"Oh!" she said. "Yes, of course, of course." And she led me down a hall.

"Your grandmother is amazing," I said, slipping past the flimsy teakwood door before she could say anything. "So amazing."

I closed the door and could barely get my jeans down fast enough as I sat down on the toilet. The relief was immense and immediate. A loose and relentless shit that made me feel my stomach was falling out. I worried that someone outside the door would hear the crack of my insides. After I wiped—hesitating before folding the used toilet paper in clean toilet paper and throwing it all in the little plastic trash bin—I stood to flush, then sat down again in case more came. How orange it had been. I felt a light sweat on my forehead. I'll leave. I closed my eyes. It's too much. I'll just leave. "Where are you?" I whispered to Eyal. My lover was at war, and where was I?

～～

When Eyal has a break, he wanders around the apartment. Everyone catches sleep when he can on the couches and the floor. Some guys take beds, but that makes Eyal uneasy for reasons he doesn't want to interrogate.

He wishes he could take a souvenir from here. But what? It all seemed foreign at first—Arabic calendar, Dome of the Rock fridge magnets, some weird sword art—but the more time he spent in this home, the more he recognized. They had the same spoons as his family, same water glasses. Same map of Israel, except they call it Palestine. They have Israeli milk in the fridge, Hebrew lettering and everything.

Every few minutes he reaches for his phone, only to remember he doesn't have it. His phone is on the other side of the border fence, sitting in a plastic bin with all the others. His name and army ID number written on a piece of masking tape. Also, the phone's passcode, just in case.

～～

I took my place back on the couch. Aisha's cousin watched me steadily. "You found the *sherutim*?" she asked, using the Hebrew word.

I kept my face neutral, not wanting her to gauge I'd understood. "The bathroom?" I clarified with excessive politeness—a Canadian's approach to signaling disdain. "Yes, thank you so, so much for asking."

Aisha was looking at her phone. "They are dropping more bombs," she said, the fingers of her left hand tracing across the screen elegantly.

After an exchange in Arabic, the grandmother produced the TV remote from between the couch cushions. Aisha's cousin was the one to turn it on and find the Arabic news channel. On the screen, buildings were tumbling down. White dust everywhere. "Haram," Aisha said.

Her cousin and grandmother and mother all echoed: "Haram, haram."

It was early evening now. As well as the figs and coffee, I'd eaten from plates of Ramadan cookies—left over from the holiday not long ago. Crumbly and round, stuffed with dates. On the TV, a pretty newscaster was intoning gravely in Arabic. Men were carrying a stretcher out from the rubble. The body on the stretcher was mottled with blood. A man pleaded with the camera.

Aisha's mother spoke quickly to her mother. Aisha jumped in too. I wondered if they were discussing something on-screen. The grandmother gestured toward me. Oh God, they were talking about me.

Aisha's cousin leaned in toward me. "They're talking about dinner," she said. "We are going to eat in here, so we can stay with Gaza." She added something to the discussion in Arabic, which seemed to satisfy Aisha's mother, who left the room, presumably to bring in the food. "Sorry," Aisha's cousin said, loudly for everyone to hear, "next time we'll negotiate in English." Pausing, she cocked her head. *"O b'ivrit?"*

"Just English," I said, and then in the most heavily accented Hebrew I'd ever offered: *"Rak Anglit."* She wants to trick me, I thought. She wants to trick me into revealing who I am.

"At bemet lo medaberet ivrit?" her cousin tried again. I understood her perfectly: *You truly don't speak Hebrew?*

Go suck a dick in Gaza, I thought as I smiled blankly.

ᕬ ᕬ

When he sleeps, memories of sensations rise up like cities from the sea:

The elation and—oddly—enormous loneliness that welled up in him the first time he entered her without a condom.

The shock of sleeping over at Gil's and hearing his parents do it in the morning. Gil turning up the TV. Eyal sensing Gil's exclusion from his parents' love and being relieved, for the first time, that he was the center of his parents' lives, that his parents loved him more than they loved each other.

The satisfaction of finding calluses on his hands after basic training. Numbness and pride.

There are two pages to the letter in his pocket. The second page he might give her. He hasn't decided yet. It doesn't matter. Back home, he knows his dad is sleeping. His sister is sleeping. His mom might be awake. She stays up and worries, he knows. *Ima*, he thinks, *go to sleep*. He remembers running toward her at the end of each school day. Burying his face into her stomach.

I don't remember falling asleep. When I woke up with the sound of the bombing I was certain that I was in my own bed. But I was on the floor of this kid's room. I guess he likes Spiderman because that shit is everywhere. On the blankets, the pillows. Even the curtains. All night the air force was clearing space for us so we can move forward. Boom, boom, boom, boom. The floor shook. I don't know how I slept at all.

He doesn't tell her about how the guys peed on the kid's bedroom wall, because then he'd have to say aloud that he did it too.

∽ ∽

On the TV screen Israeli soldiers peeked out from wreckage. Green helmets and the muzzles of guns. That's all I could see of them. That's all they were. Weapons. *Where are you?* I thought. Quick cut to a man on the screen holding an infant close to his chest. Covered in white dust, screaming.

Aisha's mother came in with plates of food. Olives in a small dish. Lightly oiled breads with herbs rolled into them. Folded meat pies I could not get enough of.

"Have some more," she said, pushing a plate of figs toward me, their bodies split to reveal pink, trembling insides. I remembered my sickness earlier and declined the fruit.

Aisha told me that a human rights group tried to pay for radio time to read the names of Palestinian children killed in air strikes this year, but the Israel Broadcasting Authority would not allow it. "Heartbreaking," I said. Again and again, "Horrible, heartbreaking."

Evening was slipping into night. More than once I thought I should go, but I stayed rooted to the sofa. *Where are the men?* I wondered. *The brothers, the fathers, the uncles?* On the television, they showed footage of the man and the baby again. Aisha was crying. *The men are in Gaza,* I thought, even if that was impossible. *Their men are in Gaza. My man is in Gaza.*

৶ ৵

He's on his belly again, watching through his scope as the Arab—the same Arab—returns to the wreckage. What is he looking for? Many times, he picks something up with great urgency. Inspects the object closely but, invariably, sets it back down with a care that seems unnecessary. The Arab is in a loose, tan-colored shirt and pants that are not jeans. Eyal can tell he's older because of his posture and the distribution of his weight.

৶ ৵

It was the second time that I went to the bathroom—just pee, mercifully— that Aisha's cousin caught me in the hallway. My first thought when I came out of the bathroom and saw her: *Fuck.* She was leaning against a wall. Her fingers nervously tapped one another, and I felt certain she was going to say, *I know what you are doing. I know what your boyfriend is doing.*

"I need to ask you something," she said to me, her voice low.

I braced myself. "Okay," I said, trying to figure out how, if she attacked me, I'd get by her. I could feel my stomach clenching. The animal of my body needed to flee. But I stayed still. Before coming here, I had gone through my phone contacts and changed all the names from Hebrew to English. Eyal and his family, Talia, Timor. I rewrote each name in English so that if a notification popped up on my phone—Eyal's mom asking if I was watching the news, Talia asking if I was okay, our meddle-some landlady asking if we had paid the power bill—the contact name would not appear in Hebrew; it would not give me away.

"Do you have a boyfriend?" she asked, her voice low.

My palms prickled. I knew it, I knew it. She'd found me out. She'd found Eyal on my social media. Or she'd seen us in Tel Aviv. She'd seen me in his sweatshirt. She knew. She was about to confront me. Here it was. "Yes," I whispered.

Her eyebrows were heavy. "Will you continue your education," she said, "after marriage?"

It took me a moment to process that this was a question about whether or not I would quit school were I to become a wife.

Before I could answer, she clarified, "I mean, will you finish your degree?" She bit her lip nervously. "Will you?"

I opened and closed my mouth. I would never be able to see this girl, would I? Truly see her. I could only ever see my own fear, or maybe I mean guilt. "Yes," I told her, accepting the hypothetical. "Yes, when we get married, I will continue my studies."

She nodded and reached for my hand. She squeezed. "That's good," she said. "That's so important."

We walked back to the TV room together and sat in our opposite chairs. She smiled at me from across the room.

∽ ∾

Eyal watches as the Arab holds an object no bigger than his own palms up to the fading light. He inspects it. Close to his face then held up at a dis-tance. There is some agitation in him now, like he thinks he found what he sought but he has to be sure, needs to be sure. What is the object? It is round and between the man's two hands. A cell phone? A clock? A bomb?

The man inspects it with care, uses his sleeve to rub the surface in the exact same way Eyal's mom cleans off her iPad, and he knows—somehow by this gesture alone—he knows that the man has picked up a framed photograph. He has come looking for photos. Maybe that is all that remains.

The picture frame glints metallic. The man needs to move. The Arab needs to move. That's a dangerous glint, the silver of the frame. Inside, a photo of his family, the Arab's family. Or not. Inside, a photo of Eyal's family. Of Eyal's grandfather, his late grandfather, hiding guns in feedbags. No. Saba spoke Arabic. No. That's insane, no. *Move*, Eyal thinks toward the Arab. He's a figure in a thermal imaging scope, a figure on a security screen, a figure in black-and-white footage. He's not a human, just a shape. *Move*, Eyal thinks. Also, *Don't move*. Also, *Die*.

೧೨ ೧೨

It was night by the time I got on the bus back to Tel Aviv. "Stay over," Aisha and her mother had cajoled sweetly, but I made up an excuse. Something about homework. In truth, I was too far away. I had come too far and I wanted to go back. I wanted to go back to my dingy kitchen, where Talia might be heating up leftovers from her mom: some kind of yielding, flavorful meat. I wanted to text my boyfriend's family in Hebrew to ask if there was any news. My heart was tired. Tired from trying to find space for Aisha and her family. I wanted to go back.

The girls hugged me; the women gripped my hands. I left.

೧೨ ೧೨

The man in the rubble is holding the frame close to his chest now, rocking, rocking. He is rocking the frame the way you would comfort a crying child. *Hush, hush*, he could be saying. *Oh, I have not protected you from a world that sought to destroy you. Oh, my darling. Oh.*

Eyal isn't the only one who shoots. You can't say for sure, he can't say for sure, whose shot it was. He doesn't know. It would be impossible to know. He can't know. But when the Arab is hit, he doesn't make a sound. He falls without a sound like the coming of night.

∽ ∽

After a cab ride from the Tel Aviv bus station, finally back in my room, I lay atop my bed, fully clothed with eyes closed. I thought about Aisha's grandmother and mother, her dead neighbors, dead babies in Gaza, the contorted faces of men screaming for war, Eyal's rifle under my bed, the buildings crumbling on TV. What I wanted was for there to be a rocket siren now. Right now. A siren would crack the world open. That's what I wanted. No more questions about history, justice, or power imbalances. Let it all evaporate. When the sirens were singing, I did not have to ask myself how I was changed or if I could ever change back. There was one imperative: find shelter. To be afraid was to be blameless. It felt simple and clean. It felt good.

In Book 12 of the *Odyssey*, the Sirens tempt Odysseus with understanding. He is a man who knows many things, but not how to come home from war; this is to say, perhaps, that he does not understand what war has done to him. The Sirens capitalize on his not-knowing: to lure Odysseus, they promise to tell him what befell him during the Trojan War.

In the Greek, the passage is dominated by the verb ειδω ("*eido*"): "to know," or sometimes, "to see." *We know*, the deadly Sirens sing. *We know, we know.* All around them are the bones of dead men and ruined ships. *Sail toward us and go away a wiser man.* They are lying. To sail toward them is death. Their voices rise up in an irresistible chorus. *We know, we know, we know. We know what happened at Troy.*

That night, like a girl in a fairy tale, I got my wish. The siren rang out, seeming to emanate from my own belly. I scrambled out of bed to find my shoes but, worried I was running out of time, ran into the building hallway in socked feet. Talia had told me that some of her earliest memories were from bomb shelters. Tonight she was at her parents' home.

In the hallway, my landlady's preteen kids yawned sleepily while we, the adults, counted the booms of rockets being shot down. Four, five, six, seven. "*Sheva?*" asked my landlady. She'd been especially annoying recently, asking me and Talia prying questions about our water bill. But in this moment, I loved her. "*Sheva*," I confirmed—seven. Seven rockets.

"How are you doing?" she asked in Hebrew. "You're scared? Where is your soldier?"

"It's a little scary," I said. "He's in Gaza."

"*Bo'i*," she said. *Come here.* She hugged me firmly. Her breasts were huge in her oversized sleeping shirt.

I felt my body relax. A mother. Mothers everywhere in this country.

"*Yihyeh beseder*," she said, same as Smadar had said that first day. *It will be okay.* Her scent was sweat and lilacs.

∽ ∾

Eyal leans against a wall with his forehead on his knees. Curled like a fetus. "Allison," he says. He says her name once. As if it were a magic word that could take him away from here.

Eighteen

When Eyal came back from war, I went with his parents to pick him up at the train station. I'M HERE, he'd texted us in the group chat. But outside the station we didn't see him. Even as he was walking toward us, we didn't recognize him—the lost-looking soldier with a dark wash of beard. He stood in front of his mom. "*Ima,*" he said, putting his pack down. His uniform was covered in red dirt from the south.

She screamed.

Then she and Koral were touching his face. "He's so thin," his sister said to his mother. Their hands were in his hair, longer than I'd ever seen it. Commuters navigated around us.

His father was watching, looking shocked. Eventually, he stepped forward to hug his son. "What a smell," he said, tearing up.

When it was my turn, Eyal pressed his forehead into mine. I touched his neck, which was grainy with some kind of chalky rubble. His smell was pungent, covered up by a harsh body spray that I imagined him borrowing from another soldier on the train. "My love," I whispered. "You came back to me."

He seemed almost afraid to touch me. His hands hovering above my ribs when he whispered, "Am I here?"

At his family's apartment, he showered for a long time. Often we showered together, even when his family was home, but this time he showered alone. He left the tub lined with red sediment.

His mom loaded his filthy uniform into the washing machine, careful to check the pockets first. Folded pieces of paper, small corner of concrete rubble, torn photograph of no one in the family, old-looking bullet casing. She made a small pile of these items—not sure what was souvenir and what was trash—then washed the war off his clothing.

In the kitchen, Koral was making him a plate of his favorite foods. Grilled cheese and baby carrots. Charlotte the pug snorted at her feet, hoping for bits of processed cheese.

His father sat stunned on the living room couch.

I wandered from room to room, unsure where I belonged.

After he came out of the shower, we all sat in the kitchen watching him eat grilled cheese, which for some reason everyone in Israel calls "toast."

He seemed embarrassed. "None of you are eating?" he asked.

We shook our heads. It felt so good to see him chew. He looked young and clean again. He had shaved. "Do you want more?" Koral asked when he finished.

He shook his head no, took my hand, and together we went to his room.

In his room, he paced with the agitation of a caged animal. I sat very still on the bed. "Is it weird being home?" I asked.

"Yes, it is so weird, yes, exactly, yes," he said, his eyes bulging with what I think was gratitude that I understood. He sat down next to me and lunged into me for a kiss. Our teeth clinked like wineglasses. Then he sprang back up and continued his pacing. We had been waiting so long to see each other, perhaps it was a shock to find that our reunion was not, in itself, a resolution.

I laid my head down on his bed's single pillow as he continued to pace. After a moment, he lay down next to me, into the curve of my body. Little spoon. I could feel his back expanding with his lungs as he breathed.

"Allie," he said softly.

"My love," I replied.

"It was not . . ." he hesitated.

I waited. My forehead pressed into his spine. Fear was in the room, pooling in all the corners.

"It was not good there," he whispered.

I squeezed him. "It's okay," I said. "You're okay."

He shifted around to face me, then pulled me toward him, but instead of kissing me, he tucked his chin over the crown of my head. "I don't know," he said, holding me close. On his Adam's apple were hairs he had missed while shaving. I felt an unprecedented wave of repulsion as he spoke. "I don't know if I am okay."

I wriggled up so I could see his face. He needed me to ask him what happened. I understood this. He needed me to ask him what happened there. But I couldn't. I was scared. What if I didn't know what to say? What if something bad had happened to him, and I somehow made it worse? What if he needed something from me I did not know how to give? "Shh," I said. "Shh, shh." Rubbing my hand on his back.

I was torn from sleep that night. Eyal cried out, thrashing under the blanket. I grabbed him from behind, squeezing his body tight until he stilled. "Shh," I said. "Shh, shh."

The army had given him a week to recover before he returned to his pre-Gaza duties. On a weekday afternoon, we went to the beach. A luxury. We lay in the sand together. The air was hazy with heat. My head was on his shoulder. His body was an abstracted expanse of skin over muscle. Little grains of sand gathered in his belly button.

"It was not good there," he said.

I couldn't see his face.

"We were in their homes."

I closed my eyes against the relentless noon sun. A total exhaustion began to take over. Sleep was creeping up on me. "They had the same microwave as us, same cups," Eyal said. But the words were distended. Each one giving birth to a starburst of dreaming. I could hear him, but I could not hear him. Aisha's grandmother was saying, *We hid in caves.* I was reaching for a plate of figs.

Eyal's voice was a trickle. *When he fell.* I was holding a framed photo no bigger than a man's palm. *When he fell, he didn't.* All around me was wreckage. Inside me, also wreckage. From a window above me, movement. And I knew this was Gaza, the brutalized city. I held the photo to my heart. My babies. Gone. My babies. Let them come. Let the soldiers come. What more do I have to lose? *When he fell, he didn't make a sound.* Our mothers mourn us as they birth us.

I was dreaming. I dreamt that Eyal and I were at the beach in the noonday sun. Only it was night. It was noon and it was night. The ocean breathed heavily, waves rolling in like a sigh. "Allie, please wake up," he said softly as I was pulled even deeper into my sleeping.

I think I must be dreaming now, sleeping lightly in a bed that is soft against the winter-damp air. All around me, letters and journals, the read and the unread.

Or maybe I am still on the beach with Eyal. Dreaming of the last decade as the sun moves across the sky.

I do not know how long I slept, but when I woke up the sun was behind a cloud and I was alone in the sand. I sat up on my elbows, looking for Eyal. He was at the water's edge with his back to me.

To myself but really to him, I whispered, "I'll try to do better."

"He'll get some kind of counseling, right?"

Talia and I were cleaning the small patio behind our apartment. "What?" she said as she dumped a bucket of soapy water on the patio tiles.

"Eyal," I clarified. "He'll get some kind of counseling, right?"

Talia began pushing the water around with a kind of long-handled squeegee. I was meant to be scrubbing the bird and bat shit off the wall with a rag, but I was watching Talia.

"Counseling?" she said. The soapy water was already black with filth as she corralled it toward the hole in the floor that would let it drain onto the street.

"Like, a psychologist," I said, in Hebrew so there could be no confusion.

"Oh," she said, pausing for a moment. "No, probably not."

Without telling him, I texted Eyal's mom. DOES HE NEED HELP? I asked. I didn't want to betray him by telling her how he'd cried out in his sleep. But I also imagined she must know. Didn't she hear him?

HELP WITH WHAT, CUTIE? she texted back.

LIKE, FOR PTSD? I used the English word because I couldn't find an equivalent in Hebrew.

My phone rang. She was calling me. "Listen," she said as soon as I picked up, "my love, I know you're worried."

"Yes," I said faintly.

"But we don't have that here," she said.

I felt relief. "We don't?"

"No, it just takes a little time." She paused. "For a year after Eyal's *aba* came back from Lebanon, I couldn't cook chicken in the house."

"Really?" I held the phone under my chin and chipped away nail polish from my thumb.

"It was the smell," she said. "It reminded him of something."

"Of what?"

"I don't know," she said. "But now we eat chicken all the time."

Timor suggested we meet at a hidden botanical garden near campus. We walked through a tropical greenhouse, the air hot and damp, wide green leaves canopying over us. It was our first time meeting outside the cafe.

"Do you know people who"—I hesitated—"who changed because of the army?" I hadn't worded it clearly. "Changed" could mean anything, but I trusted Timor to understand what I was getting at. Steam was hissing from an invisible vent; water droplets tapped on the huge leaves overhead.

"It's hard for him? Eyal?" Timor was leaning against a metal railing. A yellow lily unfurled toward him.

I nodded. "It's very hard for him. He . . ." I hesitated again. I didn't want to betray Eyal by telling how he cried out at night. How once, at least once, he had actually wet the bed, and we had quietly loaded the washing machine in the predawn hours. "It's okay, it's really okay," I kept saying. But was it okay? To Timor I said, "He has trouble sleeping."

"Okay, which *gdud* is he in?"

"Which what?"

Timor smiled down at me. Even leaning against the railing he was taller. "I think the English word is 'battalion'?" he said. "It's a number." We were the only ones in this greenhouse.

I didn't know. What kind of soldier's girlfriend was I if I didn't know? I shook my head.

"Okay, no problem," Timor said. "You have a photo of him in a unit sweatshirt or T-shirt or something?"

Of course I did. I went through my phone until I found a photo of me and Eyal: him in one of his unit T-shirts cut into a tank top, me in a sports bra and shorts. We were about to go on a run.

Timor took my phone. "Cute," he said, mostly to himself. Then he was back in focus. "I'll talk to someone."

"Will he get in trouble?" It was almost as if Timor and I were Eyal's parents, conspiring behind the scenes to take care of him.

"No," he said.

"Will he be okay?"

"Sure, he'll finish the army, spend a year in Nepal or Peru." Timor's cadence was relaxed, almost bored. "Maybe take some mushrooms, lose himself, find himself," he continued. "Then come home and go to Technion and study biology."

I nodded. The full force of Eyal's youth hit me then, in a way it hadn't since the day we first met. He and I always talked about the army as an impediment to our love—it kept us apart, stole him away for weeks at a time. But really, I saw now, its structure was what allowed us to be together at all. And when it was gone? What would happen then?

"Don't worry," Timor said.

We continued walking through the garden.

Eyal got a text from his commander, informing him he was getting an additional week off.

Eyal wanted to ask why, but I tugged at his elbow. "Who cares?" I said. "Let's just enjoy it."

Later, I texted Timor: THANK YOU FOR DOING THAT FOR EYAL.

He responded, I DID IT FOR YOU. Butterfly wings tickled my lower belly.

Eyal and I were unaccustomed to so much time together. During the week, I was often at campus: in Hebrew class, TA-ing, or researching in the library.

Eyal's friends were mostly at the army. When he texted me from visits with family—the stuffy home of his paternal grandparents or the suburban pool of an aunt—he seemed bored and agitated: THEY ASK ABOUT ANYTHING BUT GAZA.

We went to the movies in a huge suburban theater off a highway. Most of the films were American with Hebrew subtitles, except the children's movies, which were dubbed. His sister dropped us off, looking ready for a long weekend in aviator sunglasses. She was off to meet her boyfriend, soon to be fiancé, for a drive up north to a winery. It sounded wonderful. Vineyards, infinity pools, cheese plates. "What movie are you seeing?" Koral asked us as she pulled into the theater parking lot.

"The new Marvel movie," Eyal said.

"Oh, there's a new one?" she said as she put the car in park, her voice a bit condescending, almost maternal.

"Yes." Eyal squeezed my leg and rolled his eyes at me.

In the dark of the movie theater, his knee bounced anxiously. Not long into the movie, he whispered in my ear that he was going to the restroom. I nodded okay.

I'm not sure how long I was alone in the theater. The movie was hard for me to follow. Everything was exploding, and everyone was always saying goodbye. After a while, I went out to find him.

He was sitting outside the theater, on the curb, not far from where

Koral had dropped us off. I sat down next to him. Beyond us, the highway, and beyond that, fields.

"It was a boring movie anyway," I said.

He put his head on my shoulder.

I felt tenderness, resentment, and terror all at once. I did not know how to help him.

"What if we went to Canada?" he asked.

"To visit?"

"No, I mean next year, when you're done here."

"I'm not . . ." I tried to find the right words. "I'm not from there anymore."

"Okay, America, then. Could I apply for university in New York?" He bit at his thumbnail, not looking at me. "Could you help me?"

"But I want to stay here," I said, and as I said it, I knew it was true. "I want to stay here," I repeated.

He nodded, still biting his thumbnail.

I touched his hand gently to take it from his mouth. "Look, you'll be done with the army soon," I said. "You can take your trip."

"My trip?"

"Nepal, Peru—have you thought about it yet? Maybe you and Gil together?" I sounded like I was suggesting a playdate.

"I haven't thought about it yet," he said quietly.

Eyal stayed at home when I went to campus for class. I MISS YOU, he texted me when I was TA-ing for my thesis advisor.

I'LL BE BACK THIS AFTERNOON, I text back with a heart emoji. I did not tell him that I was meeting Timor for lunch—a bistro he'd chosen, a short walk from campus in the leafy northern suburb not far from where Eyal had gone to high school.

Timor was there when I arrived, at a small round table by a window. Outside, trees.

"Cappuccino?" he asked me, as I sat down.

I nodded yes, and he signaled with his hand toward the waitress who stood by the bar. He must have told her something before, like, *I think she'll want a cappuccino, but let me check and let you know*, because she brought over a cappuccino almost immediately. Frothy in a white porcelain cup.

My menu was in English: sandwiches, salads, yogurt, and the grilled cheese that Israelis call "toast." I felt relaxed for the first time in days. Timor was taking care of me.

"You're ready to order?" the waitress asked in English, following the lead of my English menu, I assumed.

Timor glanced at me, and I nodded. To her he said, "Listen, we're here to practice her Hebrew, so no switching to English, *beseder*?" He winked. She blushed. A young girl with long, flat gold hair.

We both ordered sandwiches. Although when mine came, I worried I should have ordered a salad—more elegant. Then I second-guessed why I would worry about what I ordered. This wasn't a date, after all. It couldn't be a date. I had a boyfriend. Not a date because that would be cheating.

"I like that you eat," Timor said, cutting through my thoughts. "Some girls, they just eat salads."

I thought of Penelope, chastely hiding in her room while the shameless suitors feast in the absent Odysseus's home. But here I was, descending into the banquet hall, eating an avocado sandwich with someone who was not my lover. Or was I Odysseus? Way beyond my known world, while Eyal waited at home, sleeping deep into his sorrow.

Timor paid for the meal.

"Are you sure you don't want to split it?" I asked.

"Let me take care of it," he said. This could be the unofficial motto of our home. *Let me take care of it.* Steady, capable, consistent Timor— handling the logistics like a gardener weeding around a flower. That's me: I'm the flower.

Eyal tried to tell me one last time. After dinner with his parents, he and I sat on the swings near his apartment. Already, the extra week had passed. Tomorrow, he would go back to base in Hebron. Our feet dragged in the dirt as we swung, not looking at each other. Our shadows stretched long under the streetlights. Once, this spot had held magic.

"In Gaza," he said. Then he paused. He paused for so long I thought he had changed his mind. But eventually he went on. "In Gaza, there was someone." He took an audible breath. His eyes were closed tight.

Dread crept up my spine. What would he tell me? A friend died. Someone in his unit was killed. Right next to him. He watched it happen. Oh God. Or Gil was dead. He hadn't told anyone, but Gil was dead. *Be brave*, I said to myself. *He needs you. Be brave.*

He started again. "In Gaza, there was a man," he said. "There was a man who came almost every night to sift through the rubble. We watched him, night after night. He was looking for his family. It was stupid. They were dead. The whole building had collapsed. Of course, they were dead. But he was looking, night after night. Sometimes, when he was in my scope, I pleaded with him to leave. Other times, I wanted him to stay. I wanted to be the one who killed him. In the end, I don't know who killed him, and I can't tell if I hope it was me or I hope it wasn't. After I wandered around in an apartment that could have been anyone's apartment. They had the same microwave as us. Same milk. The kid liked Spiderman. When we left, we smeared shit on their walls." It came out in a single breath. "What are we doing?" he asked.

I felt like I might throw up.

"What have I done and how——"

I cut him off. "You survived."

He looked at me startled, like I'd woken him suddenly. "What?"

"Your job was to survive," I said. "And you survived."

He frowned down at his feet, his eyebrows contorted like he was trying to figure something out. "It was not good," he said. His voice was so soft. "What I did——"

I cut him off again. "You were guarding over us," I said.

He winced.

"You were guarding over us. And yourself." I looked at him and he looked away. "That was your only obligation: to survive."

We sat in silence for another minute. "I'm tired," he said eventually. We went home. The next day, he took a bus back to the West Bank.

For the rest of the time I knew him, Eyal cried out in his sleep every night. Every night, he cried out in the darkness.

Nineteen

We began to watch a lot of television, streaming American shows on his computer or mine. TV while we ate, TV after dinner. "What should we watch?" I asked. "The show with the werewolves?"

"Whatever you want," he said.

All the shows were set in high school. Immortals in high school, socialites in high school, murderers in high school. We watched these English-language shows with English subtitles; he said seeing the words in writing helped him follow better. I'd thought this was specific to Eyal, but actually Timor is the same way.

"Let's try the show with the vampires," I said, clicking around on my computer. I was in bed, he at my desk. He'd slept over the night before. We hadn't had sex in two days, and I was trying not to ask myself what that meant. When I went to close my email tab, I saw a new message from Erica. One sentence, no subject: *I'm ready to talk whenever you are.* A week before, she'd emailed the whole family to announce her engagement to Cee.

"Everything okay?" Eyal asked.

I don't know what expression was on my face. "Just an email from Erica," I said. "That she wants to talk."

"Maybe you should talk to her," he said. "She's family."

I groaned. "She's so critical of Israel."

He nodded.

I pressed on, "But does she criticize Saudi Arabia for not letting women drive?"

"Maybe she sees something we don't," he said, picking at a thread on his pants.

"What do you mean?" I asked, surprised.

"How much of the situation do I really see? Half? Less than half?"

Such a circumspect boy. For the first time, I wondered what he would think about my friendship with Aisha. Not that I'd seen her much since the invasion ended, but she was there—on reserve in my Facebook contacts. Would he find it impressive? Heartening? "I'll talk to Erica" was all I said.

The video call with Erica began awkwardly. "Hey! How have you been?" she asked with what felt like excess warmth to me. The way that a yoga teacher might talk, hand over her heart.

"Things have been pretty good," I said. Then, not wanting to be an asshole: "Congratulations on your engagement. That's really exciting."

She thanked me. We made what I suppose you'd call small talk for a few minutes. Then Erica said, "I was wondering if we could talk about what happened this summer." She waited until I nodded to continue, "I want to acknowledge my part in the conflict."

This was a relief for me to hear. "It did really hurt my feelings," I said. Then, not wanting to make her feel too bad, I added hurriedly, "But also I totally get that you were just repeating stuff Cee said!"

Even on the slightly pixelated video call, I could see Erica stiffen. "I don't know what you—"

I jumped in again. "I just mean, I understand that it wasn't you," I explained. "Like, all of that aggression against Israel."

"Wasn't me?"

I couldn't read her body language. Did I say something wrong? "Yeah, I—"

This time, she cut me off. "Allie, you don't know me." Pause. "Like, at all."

I opened and closed my mouth.

"You left when I was sixteen years old," Erica continued.

"That's not—"

"Don't treat me like some pawn." She laughed in that sad, derisive way when someone is disappointed but not surprised. "My therapist told me this, and I didn't believe her. She said you don't see me as a whole person."

This hurt enough that I said the meanest thing I could think of in the moment. "Maybe you don't see *yourself* as a whole person." I didn't even know what that meant.

She was almost yelling. "If I see you as radicalizing toward fascism— and by the way, I absolutely do—it has nothing to do with my partner and . . ." She caught herself. Shook her head. Took a deep breath. "Oh, Allie," she said sadly.

Wait, I wanted to say, *let's start again. Let's start over. We were children together. We were orphans; we played in snowbanks.* I said nothing.

"Allie, what happened to you?"

I became my own person, I thought. "I guess we both changed," I said stiffly.

She nodded. "I guess so." Pause. "You're still invited to the wedding."

"How did it go?" Eyal asked.

"Horrible," I said. "She's this totally self-hating Jew."

"Oh," he said.

I waited, but he didn't say more. Just "Oh."

We were at his parents' place, but I would be leaving soon. He had to leave for the army the next morning, and anyway, I had a lot of student quizzes to mark. If it was more than that, we were scared to admit it.

The next day, I found myself rehashing the Erica call with Timor at our regular coffee spot.

"And so she's like, 'You've been radicalized,' as if, what? Not hating yourself as a Jew is so radical?" I was speaking in English. Timor was, apparently, letting it slide. I repeated the point I'd made to Eyal: "Is she criticizing Saudi Arabia for oppressing women? No!" I took a not particularly dainty swig of my coffee, milky and, by now, cool.

Timor laughed. "You're becoming an Israeli," he said.

"What?" I asked, even though I'd heard him. I was trying not to smile.

He repeated himself. "You're becoming an Israeli." Shrug. "Everyone hates us."

That's what I'd wanted to hear, I understood. That's what I'd been hoping Eyal would say all along.

Everybody hates us, I thought, as Gaza flooded with untreated sewage and in Jerusalem a new trend emerged. Lone Wolf attacks, they were called—Palestinian teenagers without any Hamas affiliation coming after Israelis with whatever they found lying around the house. Screwdrivers, steak knives, once a nail file. Unplanned and unpredictable, spontaneous acts.

When it finally happened in Tel Aviv—a stabbing in the southern port where, many evenings, I jogged beside the ocean—I took to Facebook. *Can you imagine*, I wrote in a post to accompany the article I was sharing, *living with that much hate in your heart?* A Palestinian teenager from the West Bank had wielded a kitchen knife, stabbing three civilians—one of them Arab-Israeli, the article noted—killing none, before he himself was taken down. *That terrorist died with hate in his heart.*

I closed the post with perhaps the most nationalistic words I'd ever used, but why not? *Am Yisrael Chai.* The people of Israel live.

According to the theories of Sigmund Freud, an error may be seen as a telltale slip that reveals an unconscious wish, which is why I suppose if you show up late to therapy you spend the whole session speaking about what it *means* that you made yourself late to therapy.

A Freudian might contend, therefore, that part of me wanted to get caught by Aisha when I made the post public instead of, as I usually did, blocking her from viewing it.

I didn't realize she had seen the post about the attack until she messaged me on Facebook. No words, just a line of question marks: *?????*

Fuck, fuck, fuck, I thought. Erase it? But it was too late. It was too late. A door closed in me. *You know what?* I thought. *Fuck it.* I couldn't lead a double life forever. I thought of Timor: *Everybody hates us.* I didn't reply, just waited for her to unfriend me. *That's that*, I thought.

When, a week later, I caught sight of Aisha across a campus cafe, I assumed we would ignore each other. I was wrong. She made a beeline right for the table where I was studying alone.

"Hey," she called out, as she weaved through tables. She looked hip as always, in her Docs and tight jeans, a T-shirt with the sleeves slightly rolled. "Allison, hey, is everything okay?"

"What do you mean?" I asked. I must have looked uncomfortable.

"Your Facebook posts," she said. "They don't sound like you."

"I mean, I just think it's bad for anyone to hate," I said.

"But, I mean, you and I have talked about, like, larger systems of oppression," she said. "I mean, I'm just"—she was floundering—"I'm just a little surprised at what you posted."

In my Facebook post, I had written, *That terrorist died with hate in his heart.* I nodded. "Right, right," I said. I was smiling with my lips hidden, a kind of grimace.

"Did you see the video?" She looked concerned. "The police executed that boy." Pause. "In the street, you know?"

I did know. The word I'd heard Israelis use for that kind of execution was "*lenatrel*"—a loan word directly from American policing: "neutralize," as in, *The soldier was able to* lenatrel *the terrorist.* "It's really sad," I said. "It's heartbreaking." Pause. "It's also sad that he chose violence."

"'Chose violence.'" She repeated my words quietly. "I feel like I'm missing something," she said. "It just, um, it seems not like you? To post Zionist stuff, I mean."

"Well, maybe you don't know me," I said, my mouth feeling tight.

She looked shocked. "What?"

I pushed on. "What's so bad about being a Zionist anyway?" I asked. My lower jaw was set defiantly. I would not apologize.

"Wait, you identify as a Zionist?" she asked, openly bewildered.

I felt a swell of defensiveness. "If believing Israel has the right to exist," I said, "if that makes me a Zionist, then I guess so, yes."

"But you were in my home." She took a step toward me.

I took a step back. She wouldn't. Would she? All I had to do was yell one word. One word, and they'd stop her. Someone would stop her: an armed guard or soldier or Timor himself. They'd neutralize her. If she came for me, I'd do it. One word. My breath was choppy. You can't hurt me, I thought.

As if I'd uttered the thought aloud, she recoiled. "Oh my God," she said in English. Then again, more quietly, "Oh my God." She sounded exhausted as she wrapped her arms around herself. "I'm thinking of you in our home, eating my mother's food," she said. She closed her eyes, bagged with shadows. "I'm thinking of my grandmother reciting her trauma for you." Shook her head. "Nothing is ever enough for you." She was talking to me, but she was also talking to Israel. "That's the terrifying thing: nothing will ever be enough." When she opened her eyes, it was like she was waking up. "You will live in a prison of your own fear," she said. A kind of prophecy. When she walked away, she did not look back.

That weekend, Eyal came over. I'd spent the rest of the week having arguments with Aisha in my head—justifying myself to her, then annoyed at the very notion that I had to justify myself to her at all. None of this I said to Eyal. "What should we watch?" I asked.

He was in a chair, on his phone. "Who's Aisha?"

I may have actually gasped. "What?" I asked. Then, correcting, "I mean, why?"

"I saw her on your list of Facebook friends a while ago," he said. "Just curious." He looked at me through lovely eyelashes. "She's Arab?"

"Yes," I said, watching his face carefully. I had no idea how any of this would land with him. "She studies at the university."

There was relief in his smile. "You have an Arab friend."

Had, I thought, but he seemed so interested. "It was funny, we met in a skin-care shop," I said.

He came and sat on the bed. "You love your creams," he said.

I took his hands. I'd missed his hands. "I love my creams," I echoed. "After we exchanged numbers, we sometimes met for coffee on campus."

"What do you talk about?"

"At first, we stuck to safe topics. Like, school, skin creams, shopping in New York."

"New York?"

"Yeah, she wants to live there," I said. "She's very Lower East Side." Realizing he wouldn't get the reference, I gave the Tel Aviv equivalent. "Very Florentine."

"You're really friends with an Arab," he said, wonder in his voice.

"Really, really," I said. "I even went to her home in Nazareth."

"*Wallah*, and met her parents?"

"Her mom, yes. Hold on." I took out my phone. "I'll show you her photo." I scrolled down until I found Aisha's mother in her kitchen, smiling shyly. I tried not to remember Aisha's admonishments. *I'm thinking of you in our home, eating my mother's food.*

"She doesn't wear hijab," he said.

"No, not in this family."

He touched my knee, more engaged than in all the weeks (or was it months?) since the invasion.

"I was nervous," I said. "To go there."

"But they loved you." His eyes were shining.

"In a way."

He lay down on the bed, his head in my lap. My beautiful boy.

He asked me about how I got there (bus); what I ate (chicken served on gummy greens with a name I could no longer remember); what I did (listened to family stories, then we watched TV).

"That's beautiful," he said. "It's so beautiful that you have this friend."

"Well, I'm not sure"—I sighed, ran my hand over his buzzed hair— "I'm not sure we're friends anymore."

"What happened?" He looked up to me, and asked sadly, "Do they know about me?"

"They do now," I said.

He waited.

"I didn't tell Aisha about you at first. I was guarding myself."

"Yes." He understood. Any Israeli would.

"I didn't speak Hebrew, didn't mention you," I went on. "Actually, it was a little funny"—I could hear myself trying to control his reaction. *It was a little funny*—"when politics came up, I used Erica's opinions more than my own."

"What do you mean, you used her opinions?"

"Like, things Erica says to me about the Occupation and fascism or whatever." I kept my tone light. "It was a little funny," I said again. "Like, instead of what I think, I repeated Erica."

His head was still in my lap.

I kept talking. "Sometimes I said that I had a sister who was a Zionist.

Shook my head about it, the way that Erica must talk about me. It began to feel almost that I was Erica—that I was my own sister, or maybe, I mean, a version of myself I could have been if I didn't love you and love Israel. I told Aisha that my sister had this boyfriend who was radicalizing her. I said my sister dehumanized Palestinians. The more I told Aisha these things, the more she liked me, until she invited me to her home in Nazareth. But wow, when I was there I felt so far away. Really, I've never felt so far away in my whole life. On their TV, we were watching the invasion of Gaza. We were watching the soldiers go in, and Aisha's family were all clutching their hands, thinking of the Palestinians, but I was thinking of you. I wanted to come back. I wanted to come home." I was talking quickly. I recalled what Timor had told me once, early on: that I'd be easy to interrogate. I kept rambling. "Honestly, it was almost a relief when she found out. Oh, I didn't mention this—she found out. I posted something on Facebook about a terrorist, and she came up to me at school all like, 'How can you say he's a terrorist? He's living under occupation.' Like, I'm pretty sure a terrorist is a terrorist, but anyway, it was almost a relief to not have to pretend anymore. It's all a little funny."

Eyal had been quiet with his head in my lap the whole time I was talking. Slowly, he got up. I thought to hug me. I really thought that.

"It is not a little funny," he said, his face so grave.

"Well, I mean, not funny-funny, but—"

"You lied to her." He looked almost plaintive. "You lied to her," he said again. "You were in their home. She invited you into her home."

"I was guarding myself." Reproach swelled in me.

"You ate at their table," he said. He closed his eyes. "You met her grandmother. You were in their home." His face in his hands now. "Oh my God," he said in English. "We were in their homes. We were in their homes."

When I tried to touch him, he recoiled.

"Why?" he pleaded. "Why? Why didn't you leave her alone?" He looked up at the ceiling. "Just leave them alone."

"You're scaring me," I said softly.

"No, *you're* scaring *me*," he whispered. "Who are you?" And I saw he was crying. "I loved you. I loved you so much." He stood up.

"Whoa, Eyal."

"To me you were so . . . so good, so different from everyone here, I—" He felt his pocket for his wallet. There was nothing else. "I have to go," he said.

I did not stop him.

"Why is he so freaked out?" I asked Timor. I'd told him about lying to Aisha, meeting her family, Eyal's reaction—the whole thing. Timor had nodded along. "It's good that you guarded yourself," he'd said, to my relief.

"It sounds like he's torturing himself," Timor said.

"I don't get it."

"He wants there to be consequences." Timor was checking something on his phone, but in a way that told me his attention was still on me.

"For what?"

He glanced up at me. "For all we've done," Timor said. "He wants there to be consequences."

"Will there be?"

"No." He said it with the unadorned confidence I love him for. "That's not how this works."

"How what works?"

"Power."

After days of not hearing from Eyal, I was at Talia's when he texted me.

I AM SO, SO SORRY.

IT'S OKAY, I wrote. I KNOW YOU'RE HAVING A HARD TIME. Around me, Talia's family was bustling around their house. It was Friday afternoon.

The TV was on in the living room—another Lone Wolf attack, this time on a settlement nearby.

NO, I'M SORRY BECAUSE I KNOW I'M A COWARD TO DO IT THIS WAY.

Oh my God. My heart picked up. It was actually happening. DO WHAT? Talia's siblings were talking about the stabbing, but I didn't lift up my head to engage. I was locked into my phone, waiting for the dots on my screen to resolve into a message from Eyal.

I FEEL LIKE I DON'T KNOW YOU, he wrote. YOU'RE A STRANGER. AND I . . .

I waited. Someone was turning off the TV—enough terrorism for one day—and turning on the radio.

. . . I DON'T LOVE YOU ANYMORE.

Despair, shame, anger. He was a child, breaking up with his long-term girlfriend over text. What a dick. YOU REALLY ARE A COWARD, I wrote.

He called, and I rejected the call. Instead, I texted, I WANT MY STUFF BACK. Then I shut off my phone. It was over.

"I don't know, do you think he's cute?"

I looked up from my phone. I didn't know how long Talia had been talking. On the radio it was that song about Friday, how it came just in time.

"Sorry," I said. "What?"

Talia looked a little annoyed, but she repeated herself. "I asked if you think he's cute," she said. "The guy who drove us that time, the one with the sunburn." As she spoke, she took ingredients out from the pantry. We were going to make challah with her mom after she finished putting one of her grandbabies down for a nap.

"Super cute," I said, not remembering. My thoughts were all over.

For maybe one second, I sensed how alone Eyal was. Even when he was with me, he was alone. He wanted to be a whole person, but I needed him to be a soldier. Once, I'd been different from everyone around him, and in that way, I'd helped him feel different. Now I was the same. Now I was Israeli.

I must have missed another question because Talia nudged my foot with her foot. "Allie, what's going on?"

"Sorry," I said.

"Are you okay? Is it the stabbing? It's crazy, that Lone Wolf stuff."

"No," I said. "Eyal and I just broke up. Like, on WhatsApp."

"Oh, fuck," she said. "Do you want to talk about it?"

"No," I said. "Let's make this bread."

"*Yalla*," she said. Then called out to her mom, elsewhere in the house, "*Ima*, we're ready!"

That night, I blessed the Shabbat candles with the women of her family. The whole house was filled with warmth and light.

Eventually, Talia and I came to laugh about that night: "I don't know, do you think he's cute? The sunburnt boy with the soft eyes?" She married him.

It was years later that I saw a Lone Wolf attack for myself. I was in Jerusalem with Timor—we had been dating for about a year by that point. We were spending Yom Kippur with his family. The Israeli tradition is to wear white during the fast. It's striking to see—a whole city dressed in white. White for our salvation, white like the robes worn by the priests of our destroyed temple. "You shall be to me a kingdom of priests, a holy nation," the Holy One promised us in the desert.

The whole family was walking to services for Kol Nidre, the evening prayers that usher in the day of repentance. Near the Old City, the Jewish stores were closed, but the Arab vegetable stall across the street was open, cardboard boxes of grapes stacked up in front of it. Timor's family absorbed me as easily as Eyal's had. Perhaps even easier, as he and I are the same age. I walked with his younger sister, a talkative gap-toothed girl. His father was already at shul; his mother walked with us. Contrary to Ashkenazi stereotype, I had found my future mother-in-law to be anything but overbearing; rather, she was soft-spoken, almost shy. The night air was warm. Timor's sister was telling me about enlisting to a cyber defense unit in the army. "It will lead to good job opportunities after," she said, clearly quoting one of her parents. The fast had only just begun. What we heard first were booms: three big booms. Timor's mom instinctively reached for her daughter in a protective gesture; Timor reached for me. "What was that?" I asked. "What is happening?"

He did not respond. He was watching across the street as uniformed police and soldiers ran toward the vegetable stand. Someone was on the ground. A crumpled body on the ground. Then it was obscured by the uniforms.

Passersby began to congregate on our side of the street and in the middle of the street itself. It's illegal to drive on Yom Kippur, except for the army vehicles that soon made a barricade. "Did we get him?" asked a middle-aged man all in white. He asked to no one in particular, looking around excitedly. "Did we get the son of a whore?"

"What happened?" I asked Timor again.

"Probably an attack," Timor said.

"*Oy va voy*," his sister said worriedly.

The middle-aged man called out to a soldier in the middle of the street. I could see the shoes of the person on the ground still. Most of the body was obscured, but I could see shoes. One on, one off. "Did we get him?" the man in white asked loudly again. "Did we get the son of a whore?"

The soldier approached the man. I thought he was going to tell him to show some decorum, but instead he shook his hand. "We got him," the soldier said.

The middle-aged man patted the soldier on the shoulder.

"Stay here," Timor said. He approached them in the middle of the street.

I stood close to Timor's mom and sister—three women in white, watching as the men conferred.

The foot moved. The body on the ground. I could have sworn I saw the foot move. Another family was asking Timor's mom about what happened. A terrorist? "I think so," she said quietly, holding her daughter close.

The Arab fruit seller was standing on the corner, hand over his eyes.

Timor came back. "A terrorist," he told us. "He went after a soldier." He made a stabbing motion. "Neutralized."

"And the soldier?" his mom asked. She was in a long white caftan over wide pants. She looked angelic.

"He's fine," Timor said.

"*Baruch hashem*," his mom said. *Thank God.*

Everyone echoed, "*Baruch hashem.*"

None of us had our phones, in keeping with the customs of fasting. Later, when we looked online, we learned that a fifteen-year-old boy had attempted to stab a soldier with a screwdriver. He was shot down in the street, where he slowly bled out. He was dying as we all stood there. We stood there in white as he was dying. *Thank God*, we said. *Thank God no one was hurt.* Those might have been the last words the dying boy ever heard.

You think that's hate? I can feel you objecting. You think that's hate, my little one. But listen—my little Erica, little Eyal, little baby I'm growing in me—listen to me when I tell you, that's not hate. It's love.

I'm telling you. It is not hate that makes us value Palestinian lives less (because I do; I know I do)—it's love. You ask yourself, *Whose death would have meaning to me?* You ask yourself, *Whose names do I know? The soldiers going into Gaza or the Gazans buried under buildings?* I do not say this lightly. I know that I have walls inside my heart. I know that loving in a violent place has changed me, yes, in ways that are lamentable, sure. But I also know that I do not want to change back. I know that the night of Yom Kippur, as I stood with a family on a Jerusalem sidewalk—all of us fasting for our atonement, wearing white to awaken God's mercy— thanking God while a Palestinian teenager died, I was part of something. I belonged. And in this way I was happy.

The Talmud teaches us that after death, each soul is questioned by the heavenly tribunal: "Did you anticipate redemption?" We will all have to answer this question.

I am happy with my life. I have seen the cost of my happiness—the power we wield, the losses to protect that power—and I accept these costs. But I do not know, I truly do not know, if we can be redeemed.

A few months later, Timor proposed.

"Build your life with me," he said. It wasn't a question, and he didn't kneel.

"Yes," I whispered. We were at a desolate stretch of sea I love. More moody than romantic. He knows me so well.

Over the years, I have sometimes probed Timor for hints about when he began to want me. "Were you ever envious of Eyal?" I may tease.

"No," he'll say, his thumb rubbing over the back of my neck.

"Not even a little?"

"No." Easy, assured.

"Why?"

"Because I knew you were for me."

In all things, Timor is so certain. His stability and consistency allow me to blossom. He is the trellis; I am the vine. Divine masculine, divine feminine—we are at home in these eternal roles. He is the anchor; I am the scarf undulating in the wind. Erica would surely laugh at this. I'm sure she does. I'm sure she and Cee sit around and make fun of us, "the straights." But what a relief it is. They can't even imagine what a relief it is to let Timor be strong for me, to let myself be rooted by his strength. What a relief it is to fall into my place.

Smadar came to our wedding. Timor stood and toasted her. "To Smadar," he said, "who gave me the best conversation partner in this life or the next." Everyone cheered. I looked beautiful.

My parents were there, but Erica was not. I had to translate all the toasts for them.

Now, we live in a high-ceilinged apartment by the sea. Timor cooks dinner while I mark student papers. When our baby is born, I'll teach him the names of all the birds in English, and Timor will teach him in Hebrew.

On evening strolls on the boardwalks of Tel Aviv's Old North, Timor and I are the image of the Jewish future. Young and beautiful. He is strong, and I am pregnant. We are blessing the land with another generation of Jews. There are big Friday-night dinners with his family. We aren't as religious as Talia's family, but we sing songs to Shabbat and make blessings over candles. There are kids running all over his parents' house. Cousins and neighbors. Our life is full. My parents and Erica and Cee watch from afar. They see a beautiful life unfolding in a language they do not speak.

What can I say? There are worse things than living on the so-called wrong side of history.

I saw Aisha one last time. Not in person, but in a news article that popped up on my feed. It was May 15. Timor had warned me to stay home: "Nakba Day," he said. A day when Palestinians mourn their expulsion. "There might be trouble." So I did. I stayed home and looked at the coverage on my phone, scrolling through images of Arab-Israelis in Sakneen and Nazareth, West Bank Palestinians in Ramallah and Bethlehem—all draped in checkered keffiyeh scarves, carrying homemade posters with the names of erased villages.

And here is Aisha, here she is, in a photo taken a few moments before the police descend to make arrests on the crowd. She's wearing a T-shirt with Arabic writing I cannot read. Her hand is joined with another girl's—a girl that could have been me—and together they raise a single entwined fist to the sky. On her face, an immutable joy.

Twenty

After the breakup, Koral and I continued to follow each other on socials. Through her feed, I saw photos of Eyal finishing his service. A classic pose: wielding scissors and a smile as he cut his army ID in half.

It was Koral who dropped off my things and picked up his, although he had not left much with me. I handed her a plastic bag with a phone charger, his flipflops, and—after hesitating—his death letter, unopened. The only letter of his I would never read.

Out of her car, she hefted a jumbo shopping bag from H&M, her favorite store, piled high with my clothes. I put it on the ground so we could hug.

"He's young," Koral began.

She would have said more, but I said, "It's okay, it's really okay."

We hugged again. And then she left.

⤫ ⤬

Eyal goes by himself to the cabin he rented for the two of them. This weekend, Koral will bring back the bag of Allie's things. I WANT MY STUFF BACK, she wrote. Nothing else.

He'd wanted to be the one to take her to the Dead Sea. Smear mud on her cheeks and float. The whole thing. Now he's here alone. Why did he come? Mourning, maybe.

He borrowed the car to get here. Drove south down Highway 90. Descending lower and lower, hundreds of meters below sea level. He drove with the windows open, the air dry and hot. Pale, crumbling rocks lined the sides of the highway. Sometimes Gaza came back to him in a deep shudder. Fear and stench.

When he slowed for the checkpoint at the northern tip of the Dead Sea, it felt weird to be a civilian without an army ID. He wanted someone to ask him—the girl soldier who leaned toward his open window, or her commander, spread lazily in a plastic chair—if he had been in Gaza, but no one did. "Where to?" the girl asked, bending stiffly in her combat vest. Her voice was friendly.

"The Dead Sea," he said. "A little cabin."

"Alone?" she asked. More out of curiosity, he sensed.

"No," he lied, "I'm meeting friends there."

"Nice," she said, and that was it.

He kept driving south, on his left the Dead Sea was a smudged band of blue in the blurry heat.

Now he's in a cabin dominated by a huge bed overflowing with pillows. Rose petals in the bathtub. He doesn't know where to sit, so he sits on the floor.

∽ ∾

On the floor of my room I sat with the bag of my returned things. Sweaters and dresses on top. Carefully folded, probably by Eyal's mom. Underneath the clothes were more delicate items. Swimsuits, underwear, bras. A stray bottle of sunscreen. Some face wash I'd left in their bathroom. A moisturizer. Old tube of mascara.

At the bottom of the bag was that pine box. Wooden with a brass latch, it was cheap but made to look antique like a stage prop. I did not know what to expect when I opened it. Was I surprised to find all the letters I had written to Eyal? Yes and no. There they were, delicate and creased, pale pinks and translucent creams. Doodled hearts and, ah, here, a vine drawn around the letters of his name. All of them piled under all the seashells I had collected along his windowsill. Such is the fate of all our tenderness.

I could not bear to revisit the letters. I shoved the small box under my bed, where it remained for the full year I spent single, not dating anyone but allowing myself to be sad.

༄ ༄

He asks himself, *Where is she?* The version of Allie who wrote to him—those letters overflowing with tenderness and curiosity. Where is she? Caring and openhearted. No lies. Innocent. The version of Allie he missed each time he left, the one whose name he whispered when he was in Gaza. Where is she?

Come back, he thinks, in this rented room where they were supposed to love each other. But she won't come back.

He invented her. He invented a version of her where he could store his heart. If that Allie ever existed, she's gone.

Or maybe she invented him. Maybe she wanted to date Eyal the soldier, Eyal who was tough and brave. When he offered her a version of himself that contradicted her fantasy, she rejected him.

Maybe he'll never know who invented whom. Maybe that's love.

∽ ∾

After Timor finished his degree, it was a while before I saw him—by chance, it turned out, at a cafe not far from my apartment.

By then, my one year was extending into two, would soon extend into three . . .

"And how is your soldier?" Timor asked as we sat down with our coffees.

"Oh, that's long over," I said, embarrassed. "He dumped me."

"He's an idiot," Timor said in his uninflected way.

I looked up. "He is?"

"Of course he is," Timor said. "If you were mine, you'd stay mine."

My heart was beating too fast.

"How long has it been?" he asked.

"Since the breakup? A year."

He nodded, like checking a box. "Come out with me," he said. His voice was irresistible, soft and sure.

Wasn't this all I ever wanted? The force and certainty of a man? "Okay." I nodded.

∽ ∾

What Eyal can't stop picturing is Allie in the Arab girl's home. Allie eating their food, smiling. Allie pretending to be her own sister, lying. So much lying. And more than that, her lack of guilt. She said it so simply: "I said that I had a sister who was a Zionist. Shook my head about it." He had lain with his head in her lap, listening as her voice became more and more foreign to him. He was in a stranger's bedroom. *I repeated stuff Erica says to me.* She laughed. Allie laughed when she said it. Almost as if she expected him to find it amusing, what she'd done.

Who are you? he thinks. *Who am I?* Still on the floor, he rests his forehead on his bent knees, curled up like a baby.

⌘ ⌘

The box of letters was under my bed the first time Timor slept over. I was pleased to find he was a tender lover. He went down on me until I came—twice—before he'd even get undressed.

Talia got engaged to the boy with soft eyes. When they moved in together, I moved into my first studio apartment—by then, I had secured a work visa and was applying for jobs at various universities and, for good measure, at various religious programs where they taught Talmud. The box of letters must have come with me when I moved, although I don't remember packing it.

The box came to the apartment that Timor and I rented together. One of us must have shoved it under the bed. Maybe him. Maybe he read the letters. It's possible. There is so much he keeps to himself.

⌘ ⌘

Eyal does not want to be in this room. He cannot stay in this room with its rose petals and oversized bed. He stands. He'll drive to the shore of the Dead Sea.

Before he leaves, he tucks his own death letter—unopened, returned from Allie—in his back pocket.

⌘ ⌘

At some point, I must have fallen asleep, because I wake up. The light is a soft, muffled gray, tending toward evening. I am in a bed surrounded by letters unfolded and spread out, journals cracked open and overflowing with ephemera. Timor will be home from work soon.

When I push aside the soft white covers to rise unsteadily from the bed, pastel pink pages fall to the floor. I leave them.

After peeing, I go to the kitchen for another glass of water. Hand on my belly, I lean against the sink to eat a yogurt. On the fridge, there are photos of me and Timor at our wedding, joyful up on those chairs. We did not marry in Israel. Here, only those considered Jews by the Orthodox rabbis may have weddings. I will admit, that was painful for me. "I'm afraid I can't give you what you want," I cried one night into Timor's shoulder.

He held up my chin to look me in the eye. "You're exactly what I want," he said.

We were married in Cyprus, where all the wrong-half Jews and gay couples wed. It was joyous. The resort where we had our wedding is used to this kind of thing. The staff all spoke Hebrew.

In the years since, I've come to understand that he takes pride in landing an exotic wife. Jewish but not Jewish. When I took citizenship, he used his family's connections—that old Ashkenazi *protectsiah* again—to have me listed as a Jew on the paperwork. Not by the religious authorities (that would be impossible) but by the state apparatus that keeps track of who is who. He did it so that our children will be able to enlist smoothly when they turn eighteen.

Why does our life feel, at this moment, so faint to me? As if it is all hinging on a decision I have not yet made? Could still unmake? *This is real*, I say to myself. My hand on my belly; this is real. Over a year of fertility treatments to be standing in this kitchen with my hand on my belly. The Israeli government paid for it all. *This is real*, I say to myself. But part of me is still inside those letters, inside that summer.

It will grow dark soon. All day I have spent reading our letters, drifting in and out of sleep and remembering. I think I dreamt of love. Love or something like it. I remember Eyal rolling on top of me in the grass, saying, "You are a sleepy cat," saying, "You are dreaming us, we are in your dream." Didn't he say something like that?

The neighborhood piano player is still practicing all these hours later. The notes drift through the walls. I feel the music in my heart. We loved, and we let go, but no, we didn't forget, no. Such emotionally manipulative chord progressions.

Timor will be home soon. He'll wonder where I am, but I do not leave a note before I grab my keys and a jacket. I leave, down the wide stairwell to the street. I will walk to the sea. Where else to bring such yearning?

The days are short now. What should be late afternoon is early evening. Soon, the sun will set. I walk on a damp sidewalk, avoiding piles of dog poo. Closer to the sea, the stores sell oversized beach towels and matkot paddles. Everyone is closing up for the day.

When I break free of the buildings and cross the street to reach the beach, the sky opens up to an expansive, moody gray.

∽ ∾

He passes great sinkholes that separate the highway from the sea. Each year, the sinkholes grow and the sea shrinks as the rivers that once fed her are diverted. He watched a YouTube lecture on the Dead Sea's ecology. A dead and dying sea, the scientist sadly called it.

He passes abandoned shacks covered with bullet holes from war with the Jordanians. He passes ugly hotels perched on the receding oblivion of the pale water. At a spot without sinkholes, he pulls over to the wide shoulder of the highway.

∽ ∾

I take off my shoes and walk across the cool sand. The wind blows from behind me, teasing my hair into my face. The baby must sense the waves of the Mediterranean, because he begins kicking. My little fish. The doctor said our heartbeats are aligned. Kick, kick, kick.

∽ ∾

He makes his way down the rocky incline to a sea too salty to support life. The air is spicy with minerals that make his eyes blurry. At the water's edge, the small pools are blue's dream of blue, shimmering and poisonous.

They fed her.

Aisha and her family fed her. Why hadn't she left them alone? That's what he doesn't understand. Why this whole performance just to enter their home? Why not just leave them alone? Wasn't it that way—he never lets himself think about this, but wasn't it that way with Saba? In the years before the war of independence, didn't his grandfather go to the Palestinian villages? Villages that would soon be massacred. Didn't Saba count the men in secret? The pregnant women too. And didn't the Arabs invite him in? They must have. Saba spoke Arabic. Didn't they invite him in? Didn't he eat their food? Jews and Arabs, eating rice and meat together.

∽ ∾

I remember his nose at my neck. I remember the urgent relief across his face when I helped him find the right word—when I made him feel understood. I remember the way he pinned me down as we play-wrestled, how delighted he was by his own strength.

I love him. More than I could love him when he was a whole person. Now that he is not asking me to hear what he saw in Gaza, now that he is not threatening me with knowledge I do not want, now that he is a stranger—I love him more than ever.

∽ ∾

He sees Allie in Aisha's home. Allie on her belly, positioned by a window. Allie with a red dot and optic, watching Aisha hold up a photograph of her murdered ancestors. Allie pissing on their walls. Allie, a soldier.

Night vision green.

The Arab falling, silent among the rubble. Dead. Eyal's was one of a dozen shots fired. He can't know. Dead. Was it him? Does it matter? The outcome was always going to be the same, wasn't it? The man was always going to die. So it's not really like Eyal—meaning, regardless of whether his bullet, you know—was the one. Dead. It doesn't matter. He did what soldiers do. It really doesn't matter. He just wanted to tell someone who cared.

∽ ∾

In the last minutes before setting, the sun emerges from her dark cover. Electric pinks reach across water that is hazardous from winter rain run-off. Yellow safety tape, ignored by the surfers, shudders in the wind.

∽ ∾

The wind is picking up. Warm on his face. Behind him, the sun is disappearing past the desert hills of Judah. Already, darkness is seeping across the eastern sky. His feet crunch the crystals of salt that line the briny pools.

∽ ∾

I can almost smell him on the wind. This is the evening breeze that the Bible refers to as the "wind of the day." There is a startlingly human moment in Genesis when God, we're told, goes out walking in the garden to enjoy these very breezes. It is the great commentator Rashi who posits that the "wind of the day" refers to wind traveling in the direction of the sun. In Hebrew, the word for "wind," "*ruach*," can also mean "spirit," creating a rich textual moment when God breathes "*ruach* of life" into the red clay of Adam.

All the light is slipping away across the surface of the Mediterranean.

My hair twists in the wind, wringing the last of the sunshine out. As the light fades, the wind picks up. It really is as Rashi wrote, as if it were the light itself rushing toward the horizon that created the wind.

∽ ∾

Trash flutters past him in a wind that is picking up just as darkness falls. He remembers that in the Talmud, the future is to our backs. Maybe she told him that.

The wind on his face tells him that he does not want to die, not exactly. But he wishes he could become part of this landscape. Disappear into the rocks, the sand, the poisonous water, the tomato plants he saw growing on the balcony in Gaza, the parsley planted in an old yogurt container, the cracked hands of an old man.

∽ ∾

In the Talmud, the future is behind us. We move through life walking backward, not so unlike the Angel of History that Walter Benjamin imagined, facing the wreckage of what we call progress, blown backward by a storm from heaven. "Turn around," God says to Moses on the mountain. *Turn around and see the future at your back.*

The surfers are coming in for the night. The light has all but disappeared, and with it a chill descends. I duck under the yellow hazard tape in order to get closer to the sea, to feel it on my feet.

∽ ∾

He bends down to touch the sea, the water slick with salt. He is the only person here.

Out of his back pocket, he takes the letter, still stapled shut. One word on the front: "you." A letter he'd written to Allison, in case he died in Gaza. He wrote it while she was sleeping. How hard it had been to find the words. He wrote and rewrote, until he came to the truth in a single sentence that she never read: *Loving you has been the greatest honor of my life, thank you.*

With two fingers, he holds the letter underwater. The paper becomes soggy. The "you" begins to bleed. But it's the Dead Sea, so when he lets go, the paper floats back up. No matter. Let someone else find it.

As he stands, he tastes the water from his fingertips. Sting on his tongue.

Tiny waves crest along the abandoned shoreline. He wonders if this sea has a tide. Is it possible? Once it was alive, once it supported life. But that was long before human memory.

The waters lap at his feet. *Nobody has told her*, he thinks. *Nobody has told her she's dead. She thinks she's a real live sea.*

∽ ∾

I touch my lips. Unto me there was a lover. Who was I before? Who am I now? I have no way to answer these questions. Or maybe I mean I have forfeited these questions in order to make a home in a place that does not reward too much questioning.

My right hand rests on my belly, my future growing inside me. Every day, I'm more and more whole.

Early in our relationship, Eyal received some basic first aid training: recognizing the signs of a concussion, performing the Heimlich, using a tourniquet to stop someone from bleeding out. He wanted to practice CPR on me. I lay in bed while he checked my spine for injuries, stabilized my neck with his knees, cleared my mouth of imaginary debris. The chest compressions he only pantomimed; if he actually pumped my heart he would break my ribs. But he really did give me the breaths, interspersed with little kisses. Breath, kiss, breath, kiss. I kept my eyes closed, pretending to be unconscious so he could fill me with his air, causing my chest to lift.

∽ ∾

You can breathe that way.

Acknowledgments

Thank you to my fierce agent, Joy Harris, whose love and counsel I rely on always. Thank to my brilliant editor at HarperCollins, Terry Karten, who saw what *The Lover* could be. Thank you, Chris Connolly and Tracy Locke, for supporting this book. I'm honored by the care that everyone at Harper has shown my work. Thank you, Milan Bozic, for another unforgettable cover.

My deepest gratitude to the readers and friends who coaxed this book through its various forms: Vu Tran (so much started with you!), Michelle Latiolais (who opened the door), Amy Gerstler (who helped me return to this work), Haley Morris (for helping me find Allie, for continued spiritual guidance, and for reading this book countless times—thank you), Daniel Levin (stay close), and Miles Parnegg (the last man).

Additional thanks to Clare Needham (my forever reader), Erica Wachs (my sister in love and art), Sarah Shun-lien Bynum, Becker Grumet (my heart), Jennifer Percy, Benjamin Balint, David Morris, Adrienne Gaffney, Honor Moore, Paul Lisicky, Dana Brown, David Stuart MacLean, Daniel Raeburn, Kit White, and Richard Stamelman.

Grants from the Elizabeth George Foundation and the Canada Council for the Arts allowed me much-needed time to work on *The Lover*. Thank you for the support when it mattered most.

My ability to write with any kind of political consciousness has benefited directly from the labor of people of color. I extend my wholehearted thanks to the readers who helped me keep characters outside my identity—i.e., Palestinians and Mizrachi Jewish Israelis—safe in my hands. Thank you, Daleen AbuNi'aj and Hadar Cohen, who graciously took on the project of sensitivity reading. Additional gratitude to Farouk Yaseen, Omar Hmidat (still my teacher), and, always, always, always, Hadeel Hisham, my sister. (Hadeel's natural beauty products can be found at facebook.com/HH.Out.of.Nature.) Thank you, Caesar Hisham. Once, on your patio in Bethlehem, you told me about the breeze blowing from the past—how your family fled the Zionist army, how you hid in caves. Thank you for teaching me. (Caesar, the finest tour guide in the Holy Land, is available for bookings via facebook.com/caesar.hisham or Ikhmayes22@gmail.com.)

I am indebted to the following sources of wisdom: the teachings of the Arab Jewish artist, healer, and educator Hadar Cohen (hadarcohen.me); the anti-racist community-building of Mira Stern (mirastern.com), especially her Undoing Zionism course, where I powerfully encountered anti-Zionism as an urgent matter for the Jewish soul; Karen Isaacs at Achvat Amim; the lived example of my dear Noa Levy; Professor Nadia Abu El-Haj's remarks at the June 1, 2021, panel "Said's Palestine," hosted on Zoom by Columbia University, moderated by Judith Butler; Amy Horowitz's contribution to *Palestine, Israel, and the Politics of Popular Culture* (Duke University Press, 2005): "Dueling Narratives: Zehava Ben Sings Umm Kulthum"; *Rifqa* by Mohammed El-Kurd (Haymarket Books, 2021); Stephen Mitchell's translations of Rainer Maria Rilke. Who could write about the Nakba and Nazareth without referring to the poems of Taha Muhammad Ali? I worked from *So What?: New and Selected Poems, 1971–2005*, by Taha Muhammad Ali, translated by Peter Cole, Yahya Hijazi, and Gabriel Levin (Copper Canyon Press, 2008).

Any errors or misrepresentations in this book are entirely my own.

Thank you to Inbal Oychon, Sarai Darmon, Rotem Kahalon, Elad and Naama Ariel, Debbie and Yair Amichi, and Idan Ariel for keeping my heart soft. Thank you to Tal Farber, though we are lost to each other.

My understanding of biblical philology and the academic study of rabbinics—limited and patchy as that understanding may be—was propped up by the following sources: *The Languages of Paradise: Race, Religion, and Philology in the Nineteenth Century*, by Maurice Olender, translated by Arthur Goldhammer (Harvard University Press, 1992); Edward W. Said's "The Return to Philology" in *Humanism and Democratic Criticism* (Columbia University Press, 2004)—thank you, Professor Radhakrishnan; Dr. Julia Lipton's 2013 class on "Freedom and Restraint in Rabbinic Use and Interpretation of the Bible," taught at Tel Aviv University; the Bible faculty at the University of Chicago Divinity School as well as Matthew Richey and Jessie DeGrado; the Bible and the Ancient Near East program at Hebrew University in Jerusalem, especially Dr. Tania Notarius's teachings on biblical poetry and Professor Ohad Cohen's discussion of the morphology of Genesis 1.

Since my first novel came out, I myself came out as a nonbinary dyke. Finding queer, Jewish spaces saved my life. Thank you to the trans family I have found at Svara: A Traditionally Radical Yeshiva. Thank you to everyone at Svara, especially Rashei Yeshiva R' Benay Lappe and Laynie Solomon, R' Becky Silverstein, and R' Bronwen Mullin, for creating a venue where I can encounter my full self: as a Jew, as a queer. The joy and exuberance I bring to Talmud has been shaped by the learning I endeavor each week with my brilliant chavruta, Ari Emet Monts, available for ritual consultations for anyone not lucky enough to be their learning partner: arilaraemonts.net.

The music of this book was inspired in part by the work of Sarai Darmon (saraidarmon.bandcamp.com). Thank you, Sarai and the entire Darmon family, for giving me a home at Kibbutz Regavim. The Homeric references in this book rested almost entirely on translations generously provided to me by my dad, David Sacks; I refer frequently to his brilliant *A Dictionary of the Ancient Greek World* (Oxford University Press, 1995).

It is a true blessing to be born into a family that continues to love and hold me in all my forms. Thank you to my parents, Joan and David, who support all my dreams. Thank you to my little bird, Katie, who is nurturing new life. May we all be brave for Louis.

About the Author

Rebecca Sacks (they/she) graduated from the Programs in Writing at the University of California, Irvine. In 2019 they received a Canada Council for the Arts grant and the Joseph F. McCrindle Foundation's Henfield Prize for fiction. After graduating from Dartmouth College, Sacks worked for several years at *Vanity Fair* and later moved to Israel, where they received a master's degree in Jewish studies. They are the author of the highly praised debut novel *City of a Thousand Gates*, which was awarded the prestigious Janet Heidinger Kafka Prize for fiction in 2023. They live in Los Angeles with their dog, Pupik.